STE
VENICE

STEALING VENICE

ANNA E. BENDEWALD

HUDSON-IVY PRESS

A wise woman once said, "It takes a village to raise a child," and the same has been true of bringing Stealing Venice before the public. Here are my villagers, in no particular order.

Kate Summers, who was the first to read my rough draft, and encouraged me. Stacey Aswad, Judi Bendewald, Cindy and John Lytle, Lana Stenerson, Rebecca Bush, Heather Church, Lyn Healy, Hollie Bendewald, Charlotte Tinker, Heather Ussery, and Pam Duncan for reading the next drafts and supporting my writing process. Thanks to Maureen Cutajar at GoPublishing, for making my book look like a novel. And I'm indebted to Francesco Sinatra, my dear Venetian friend who provides me with *affogatos,* and his Mama Paola who makes the best pasta!

Thank you to my husband, Mason Bendewald, who doesn't enjoy reading and yet made this book possible because he believes in me, and to my daughters, Jem and Julia, for being patient with me while we did our homework together.

The biggest thanks goes to Monique Huenergardt, because all of the patience and encouragement in the world wouldn't have been enough. For every good book, there is someone who knows how to polish the flow of the plot, and elicit even more intrigue from a tired writer. What's beyond me is how she stayed so cool, understanding, and correct through the whole process. I thank God for Mo Reads You. Mo took a chance on me, and I will be forever in her debt.

Finally, you, Dear Reader, I am honored to have you visit my village, too. I hope you stay.

And now, I offer you the first step down the dark path with these families.

—*Anna Erikssön Bendewald*

STEALING VENICE

1

Giselle's plans were about to spin out of her control. She'd just arrived at the Musée Maillol in Paris, excited to see their new modern sculpture exhibition. Brochure in hand, she stepped into the hushed gallery, blissfully unaware that in rapid succession she would be accosted, escape, and witness a robbery-turned-murder.

She was immediately drawn toward the largest sculpture in the room, an enormous gorilla constructed entirely of clothes hangers. A group of art students encircled the beast, they were holding their ground against eager patrons jostling to get a glimpse of it. With her tall stature and three-inch heels, Giselle had no trouble peeking over shoulders and impromptu easels. She was at home among other artists, each student intensely focused on their sketchpad, their charcoal pencils flying over pages to capture every facet of their subject. Leaning in closer to study one of the developing sketches, she caught a whiff of

Gauliose cigarettes and clothing in need of a good washing. Peeking over the shoulder of a lanky boy, she noted that he was sketching only the gorilla's powerful hind legs.

"You're drawn to his legs," she observed.

"I prefer yours," he replied without looking away from the sculpture.

She ignored his flirtation, and noticed a sculpted school of fish dangling near the ceiling to her left. Careful to avoid the jumble of book bags on the floor, she moved toward it, entranced. The slightest air currents caused the wire filigree fish to undulate as if it was a live school swimming in an invisible stream. The effect had a dreamy quality that was remarkable. She imagined what this piece might look like near an open window, catching the breeze and sunlight.

"Giselle!"

She startled and cringed inwardly at the sound of the booming voice. *Ah, merde! This was supposed to be a quiet evening alone!* Trying to appear oblivious, she casually looked around the room as if orienting herself. Out of the corner of her eye, she spotted a big man in a lilac-colored Izod shirt on the far side of the gallery waving a museum brochure over his head like a distress flag. Looming over him was an enormous bird of prey made of fuzzy white feathers and fragile bones.

Who on earth is that? Maybe if I move quickly enough, I can avoid him.

Ducking around a sculpture that appeared to represent the female reproductive system, it came to her. *I recognize that shirt! It's that American art collector!* She'd never met him, but last night at a charity dinner, she was seated next to his wife, "Candice-just-call-me-Candy" Taft. Candy spent the entire meal pushing her phone under Giselle's nose, tapping a sculpted nail on pictures of her husband posing in front of his latest art purchases. The photos made two things clear: he owned a lot of art, and he owned a lot of Izod sports shirts.

Giselle slipped into the next gallery, moving through its displays of various-sized pink, white and brown Neapolitan ice cream-inspired boxes and bright multi-colored birdcages, but heard his shoes slapping against the polished floor behind her. *Ugh! What was I thinking, telling Candy Taft that I was dying to see this exhibit? Why can't these collectors just leave me in peace? Maybe he'll be too embarrassed to keep following me.* She hustled into the next gallery, but her heart sank as she heard another distinct set of pounding shoes and realized Taft had been joined by another pursuer. She tried to hide behind a small tour group, but in her fiery-peach silk sheath and bronze heels, she stood out like a flamingo hiding in a flock of pelicans.

"Giselle!" He boomed, "It's me, Hank Taft! My wife was at a fundraiser with you last night!"

With a deep sigh, she turned to face Taft and saw that he was in a footrace with a fastidious little man in an impeccable puce-colored suit. The agile little whip-of-a-man zipped past the American and skidded to a stop before her, just a half step ahead of Taft. She coughed as she was enveloped by a vapor of strong aftershave, and could only guess which of them had been so liberal with their fragrance application.

"Giselle, I simply *must* have a word with you," the dapper little fellow huffed.

"*Oui, monsieur...*" she smiled. Although she recognized the Turkish collector who had been profiled in a recent art magazine, she was not inclined to acknowledge that.

"I am Atan." He pronounced it with obvious pride, and thrust his thin chest out like a rooster posing before a hen. "I believe your last sculpture should *never* have been banned by the British! *No!* But then, my tastes run to outrageous, even *dangerous* art." He arched an eyebrow lewdly as his eyes dropped to her décolletage.

Likes dangerous art, does he? My next sculpture will make him re-think that position.

Before she could comment, Taft waved a manicured and meaty paw of dismissal toward Atan. "Oh, cut the crap, Ant Man." She watched the smaller man bristle at the intentional mispronunciation. "The only thing outrageous about the art you collect are the price tags hanging from 'em." He leaned toward Giselle and squinted. "I gotta be frank with you, Giselle, your last sculpture makes me think you've got a screw loose in that pretty head of yours. But all the same, I want one of your pieces for my collection. What are you working on now? I want you to slap a 'Sold' sticker on it."

The diminutive Turk had risen onto the balls of his feet to get a better look at her earrings. "My dear, I know antique jewelry, and your earrings are superb. They perfectly compliment your emerald eyes. From Cyprus?" Giselle smoothed a stray lock of blonde hair behind her ear and forced a smile at the compliment.

Startled by the vibration of her phone, she reached into her little evening clutch, withdrew it, and peered at the screen.

"Oh, I have to take this. It's my agent, she's the person you'll be dealing with if you're going to buy any of my sculptures. Will you excuse me for a moment Atan, Mr. Taft?"

The men nodded, and she stepped out of the nearest exhibit hall door into an alcove for privacy.

"*Alo?*"

"*Alo,* Giselle?"

"Fiamina, how are you?" Glancing over her shoulder, she ducked down an employee service passage.

"Good. I just called to tell you the funds from your last show have been transferred to the Africa Outreach Project."

"Oh, that's great news." She hurried down a handicap access ramp with her phone pressed to her ear.

"Are you all right, *chérie*? You sound out of breath."

"Just trying to evade a couple of collectors, named Taft and Atan."

"Ooh! Good money there! Have them call me."

"You know I hate dealing with them."

"*Ah, oui.* Give them my number. I've got another line holding, so I'll leave you to your escape."

"*À bientôt.*"

Nodding to a security guard, Giselle popped the phone back into her purse, then moved fast down a long hallway, and slipped out a side exit. *What now?* Her driver was expecting her to be occupied for hours. If she called and waited for him, she'd be left standing on the sidewalk and risk being caught by Taft and Atan. They were probably already looking for her.

Making a snap decision, she walked across the street and down a flight of stairs to the Metro. High-heeled sandals wouldn't be her footwear of choice for the commuter train, but tired feet were preferable to being trapped alone with a couple of rabid collectors. Since she couldn't enjoy the exhibit, she would go to her husband's office and persuade him to take her some place fun.

Giselle groaned when she reached the crowded platform. The underground station felt hot, filled with a growing mass of listless commuters all vying for a bit of personal space. An overhead speaker announced that the train was delayed, and her fellow travelers grumbled in unison before returning to their phones. A man near Giselle opened a bag and produced a sandwich, causing her to pivot away from the aroma of pâté and onions on brioche. This was becoming an evening she'd like to forget.

As she stood fanning herself with her exhibit brochure, she felt a dampening patch of sweat at the small of her back that stuck her dress to her skin. It seemed that time was standing still, and she was beginning to regret her mode of escape. The forlorn sounds of a busker's saxophone floated from a nearby pedestrian tunnel, only to peter out after a few lazy notes. The roar of an approaching train caused everyone to crane their necks and look down the tunnel in expectation. No luck. It was on another track and blew straight through the station with a blast of heat that ruffled everyone's hair.

"Adele!" It was a screech. "*Oh la!* Look at this mess!"

Giselle turned, along with the crowd, to stare at an old woman in an outrageous rainbow caftan scolding a toddler. The pair stood in the center of a widening pool of red juice as it fanned across the tile floor. People shuffled backward, bumping one another to avoid the fruit-scented mess. The child held her hands up for assistance, and the woman led her out of the puddle. Taking mincing steps in her green jelly sandals, she lifted her hem and unwittingly gave everyone a peek of support hose rolled down below swollen knees.

A flash of movement to Giselle's left made her glance over just in time to see the evening go from bad to tragic. She saw a teenager wearing a headband wrench a briefcase out of an old man's grasp, then shove him hard and sprint away. A second man with ultra-short blonde hair made a lightning-fast swoop, caught the senior, and then lowered him to the floor. Sprinting up the stairs after the mugger, the agile blonde yelled, *"Zupynyty yoho!* Stop him!"

People glanced around trying to figure out what had just happened as Giselle hurried over to help the old man. Passing a woman standing at the edge of the crowd, she said, "Please, call the police." The woman nodded and made the call.

"He pushed the old grandpa!" the little girl garbled, pointing to the stairs where the men had just fled.

Giselle knelt next to the fallen man. The old man's eyes were squeezed shut, and the color was draining from his face. She unbuttoned his collar, loosened his tie, and fanned him with her brochure. She noticed his white shirt was ironed and starched, and his suit was tailored. But judging from the frayed cuffs and lapels of his suit jacket, he'd fallen on hard times.

"You're going to be okay. Do you have a heart condition?" She stroked his cheek with the backs of her fingers in an effort to get him to open his eyes.

"Ehhhh..." It came out a sigh.

"Do you take any medication?" She started to lift his head.

"I'm a doctor. Please leave his head on the ground." A man came down to his knees and opened the old man's jacket. He glanced at Giselle. "We want his airway open, and cradling his head can restrict that."

Giselle complied, but it felt cruel to leave the man's head on the floor. As she took his hand in hers, her eyes fell on a handcuff with a broken chain link dangling from his wrist. The doctor did a quick examination, then looked up at the crowd and yelled, "Someone call an ambulance!" before beginning CPR.

The sound of police sirens drifted from the street above, and Giselle saw a female police officer escorting the blonde Good Samaritan down the stairs. She was carrying the briefcase with the other half of the broken chain hanging from the handle. At the edge of the stairway, she set the case down, handcuffed the Good Samaritan to the handrail, and tried unsuccessfully to open the case. The hushed crowd stood fascinated as the officer questioned her suspect.

Next, a burly policeman hustled down the stairs, mopping his forehead with a handkerchief as he squeezed past the arriving commuters.

"Now, who got robbed?" Following everyone's pointed fingers, he ignored the cuffed blonde suspect and headed toward the victim, with the female officer following. Seeing the red pool on the floor, he stopped short and his hands fluttered for his handkerchief again. A bystander pointed to the fallen plastic cup. "That's fruit juice." Stepping around the mess, the officer whipped out a notebook as he approached the sprawled man.

"This is the victim of the robbery? He was assaulted?" The policeman addressed the doctor, but when he got a look at Giselle, his mouth dropped open and he blinked. The doctor was breathing into the fallen man's mouth, so Giselle answered for him.

"He was pushed."

The rainbow-clad grandmother charged toward Giselle and the officer, dragging the toddler by the arm and shouting, "You've got the mugger! My granddaughter saw the whole thing!" She pointed at the handcuffed suspect triumphantly. "That guy with the buzzed blonde hair robbed the old man! He yelled something Slavic!"

"No, officer." Giselle stood up. "You've handcuffed an innocent bystander who was helping. The mugger was a teenager."

Another voice called out, "*Oui*, I think two or three men ran from the station."

The conversation was interrupted as paramedics arrived. The medical team came down the stairs toting a gurney and equipment. They quickly assessed him, and after a word with the doctor who'd been performing CPR, they lifted the fallen man onto the stretcher. Just then the delayed train pulled into the station and the platform erupted into chaos. Trying to stay ahead of the wave of jostling bodies, the female police officer grabbed the briefcase, took Giselle's hand, and rushed her over to the stairway where the suspect was chained.

Disembarking passengers poured from the train's doors and shoved toward the exits. Impatient commuters bumped against one another, all trying to board the train at once. Even more people stampeded down the steps, jamming onto the already crowded platform in the hopes of just making this train. Frustrated voices raised and echoed off the tile walls, creating a confused roar over the conductor's announcements from the train's speakers.

As the melee pushed Giselle and the female officer into the suspect, Giselle felt panic surge through her at the very real possibility of being trampled. She saw that the force of being dragged by the streaming crowd was cutting the handcuff into the man's wrist, so she tried to shield him with her body. Together they leaned against the churning passers-by, but she was alternately pushed against him, and dragged away. She gasped as something hard slammed into her from the side, almost knocking her to her knees, and then suddenly felt a strong arm around her waist holding her upright. She peeked over her shoulder and caught sight of a tourist with a towering backpack crashing his way through the crowd. The female police officer had latched onto the railing with one hand, and was gripping the briefcase handle with the other as she fought to stay on her feet.

"Back up!" she yelled, but no one paid any attention.

The tide of bodies lessened as the train pulled out of the station, but the blonde man didn't immediately release her.

Meaning to thank him, she looked up into his face, and immediately forgot what she was going to say.

His eyes were a startling blue and crystal-clear as aquamarines, set in a classic Eastern European, chiseled face. He had even, white teeth, sculpted lips, and the barest twitch of a smile playing at the corners of his mouth. His blonde hair was incredibly short and impeccably cut. His features were so perfectly matched, he reminded her of an Italian sculpture. She was aware that his strong arm was still holding her tightly against him.

"Ummmm..." was all that came out of her mouth and she cursed her inability say anything else.

She felt his hand trail across her back as he withdrew it, and nodding toward her arm where she'd been hit by the backpack, he asked, "Are you hurt?"

"No. I'm fine." She shook her head and took a step back from him. "*Merci.*"

"Okay, *mademoiselle.*" The policeman had arrived at her elbow. "What's your name, and what did you see?" His pen was already jotting notes.

"It's *Madame* Giselle Verona, and I saw a teenager shove the old gentleman, grab his briefcase, and run away with it."

"Race?"

"What? Oh...sorry. White."

"What did he look like?"

"Medium height, wearing a camouflage bandana as a headband, and a grey tank top. And he had tattoos down both arms."

"Can you give me a description of any of the tattoos?"

"No. I'm sorry."

"Hair color?"

"Dark."

"Pants? Shoes?"

"Jeans and white high-tops."

"Anything else?"

"He ran up those stairs." She pointed to the stairs on the opposite end of the platform, then put her hand on the blonde suspect's shoulder. "This gentleman broke the old man's fall and then ran to stop the mugger. You have the wrong person."

"What's in the briefcase?" The cop was staring at her.

"Uh, what? I wouldn't know. I don't know the victim."

"My granddaughter saw the whole thing!" The colorful old woman had been watching the paramedics carry the old man from the station, and now she stomped over, bulldozing her way into the conversation. "That blonde skinhead Slav pushed the old man and stole his briefcase!"

Giselle snapped her head around. "No, he didn't."

"My granddaughter doesn't lie!" She drew in a dramatic breath, and yelled up at Giselle, "*Are you saying she's lying?*"

"No. I'm saying she's mistaken."

The female officer drew the irate woman off to the side. "*Oui, madame.* Let me take down your phone number."

The policeman flipped his notebook shut and studied her. "You're Countess Giselle Verona, the artist?"

"*Oui...*" She looked at his name badge, "...Officer Bretton, I am."

"Which is it? Countess or contessa? I see it both ways in the papers."

"Both are correct, they're just French or Italian for the same title."

"Your husband is Italian royalty, so why are you in *le Metro?*"

"I just came from the museum and was going to my husband's office at Pont Marie."

He furrowed his brows in apparent disbelief. "Hrmphf," he exhaled peevishly. "We'll need to get a signed statement from you. Let's take this to headquarters before the next train arrives."

Giselle nodded. The female officer had dismissed the old woman, unlocked the blonde suspect from the handrail, and was now guiding him up the stairs and out of the station. Giselle followed along with Bretton, who hauled himself upward with the aid of the railing while sneaking glances at her. "Have you ever modeled, Giselle?"

"No."

"You should."

He seemed to be expecting a response to this career advice, so she replied faintly, "Mmm, I should check into that." She stepped past him and moved quickly up the stairs to see what was happening to the Good Samaritan.

Two police cars were parked side-by-side on the sidewalk. The suspect was being put into one car by the female officer, who was speaking loudly into her radio. "Suspect is thirty years of age, last name is Shevchenko."

Bretton pointed to the other car. "We're over here." He opened the door for Giselle, and then glanced back over his shoulder at the suspect, his distaste apparent on his face. He turned back to her. "Sorry for the inconvenience, but a statement won't take long."

"Don't apologize. I'm happy to help. That man is to be thanked, not handcuffed." Sliding into the back seat, Giselle caught her breath in the confined space. *Bretton's last suspect must have been busted for marijuana.* She looked out her window and into the other car. The blonde was looking at her. Meeting his eyes, she mouthed, "It'll be okay." He gave her a little smile, but she could see that he was nervous.

Officer Bretton flopped into the driver's seat, causing the vehicle to sag. He started the engine and drove off the curb with a bump. Giselle made eye contact with Bretton in the rearview mirror.

"What's going to happen to him?"

———※◉※———

Salvio Scortini cruised at a stately pace along Venice's Rio Apostoli Canal enjoying the admiring looks that his new Riva Iseo speedboat received. The Pope had just stood him up, but he was still in a good mood. Supposedly the Pope's busy schedule prevented him from attending Salvio's presentation, but the Vatican advisors who had been present were impressed by his plans to rebuild and gentrify Venice's crumbling Verdu Mer neighborhood. He knew his vision for the Pope's pet project was ambitious, but the Vatican housed the world's richest treasury, so money wasn't going to be an issue.

Gliding up to the formal entrance of his home, Salvio throttled the engine back and disappeared into his palazzo's water garage just as a tour boat came by. The automatic gate of the garage swung closed behind him, and he killed the engine so the prow of his boat just kissed the foam buoys on the indoor dock. The sleek race boat bobbed violently as the wakes from the big tourist boat sloshed their way into the stone garage. Hidden from view of the gawking tourists and their cameras, Salvio ignored the shouting loudspeaker.

"And here is the mysterious Scortini Palazzo with its unique black stonework, the second-oldest palazzo in Venice...even older than the Doge's Palace. What you see here is the relatively new entrance to the palace, added as part of the 1902 renovation. It replaced the entrance around to the left at Il ponte Diamanti, the Diamond Bridge, which dates back to the sixteen hundreds. But farther along is the original entrance at Il ponte di Smeraldi, the Emerald Bridge. You can see that it's actually green from the moss covering every inch of it..."

As the tour moved down the canal, taking its turbulence and noise pollution with it, Salvio emerged from the garage and climbed the stone steps to his front door. He passed under the marble arches with their carved motifs of boats and horses, and hauled the great door open. His elderly butler met him in the foyer. He had always looked to Salvio as if he'd just stepped off one of the pedestals set along the palace's foyer—just another marble statue, rigid and lifeless.

"As instructed, I have put Signor Tosca in your office."

Salvio waved the servant off and marched down the wide corridor. Instead of going to greet his guest, he went to the music room at the far-west corner of the palace to watch the sunset. Standing at the floor-to-ceiling windows, he admired his city from the very spot his family had chosen to found Venice and establish their seat of power. The historic palace had been added onto and renovated every hundred years or so, and as a result had become a sprawling maze with secret areas no one, not even Salvio, had knowledge of.

Once twilight reduced his city to shadow, his mind returned to this afternoon's meeting. If it had been Salvio's father or grandfather giving the presentation, the Pope would have been there. They had always enjoyed a close relationship with the Holy See, but for some reason Salvio didn't enjoy the same access...yet. With the recent death of his father, Salvio was the only living Scortini, and he was ready to step forward to receive the Vatican's respect, as was his birthright.

Salvio ran his palms over the coarse material of his suit jacket. He'd always been disappointed that his body lacked the sturdy frame and strong edges that his mind possessed, but he'd devised a solution. He had his tailor construct all of his clothing from sturdy material that masked his rounded shoulders, sloped neck, thick hips, and flat backside, creating the illusion of an imposing physical structure. When he was wearing one of his suits, he was visually impressive.

He glanced down at his watch and decided it was time to see what his visitor wanted. Genero Tosca represented the Venetian Brotherhood of Ironworkers, and this was the first time he'd requested a meeting with Salvio. Tosca had been a frequent visitor of his father's, but this was a new era.

Salvio did an about-face, exited the music room, and turned down several dark hallways. Moving unseen, he grazed his fingertips along a heavy wall tapestry, lifted a section of it, and disappeared into a secret passageway. He slipped out from behind another panel in his office and silently approached his guest from behind. When he suddenly appeared, as if being revealed in a magic trick, Tosca startled out of his chair and dropped his hat onto the black rug. As Tosca stooped to retrieve it, Salvio was tickled to greet a man who was kneeling before him in his best suit. *An appropriate way to begin our working relationship.*

"*Bunoasera*, Tosca. Please sit down."

Looking embarrassed, Tosca jumped to his feet and moved back to the chair.

"I've just come from a Vatican meeting on Verdu Mer, but I'm never too busy for the Brotherhood."

"Forgive me for such short notice, *signore.*"

"Call me Salvio. Can I get you anything to drink?"

"No, *grazie.*"

"Well then, Genero... May I use your Christian name?"

"Oh, *sì.*"

"So Genero, what brings you here?" Salvio settled behind his desk. "How can I help the Brotherhood?"

Genero's brows knit in consternation. "I thought you knew...I came for our patents, *signore*...er, Salvio."

"Oh? Now that *is* disappointing Genero. I assumed you'd come to pledge your commitment to working with me on the Verdu Mer project, just as you and the building establishment have always worked with the House of Scortini."

"Well, no...you know which documents I'm referring to..."

"My iron casting patents? I inherited them from my father as part of my family's estate."

"No, that is a mistake...they belong to the Brotherhood of Ironworkers."

"No. They belong to me."

"Your father was our patron, and he—"

"He was entrusted with them for the benefit of all of the Venetian building associations, and that is how they are being used...by me."

"Ah, well, no. That's not the agreement we had with your father." Tosca started to worry the edge of his hat with a fingernail.

Who does this little man think he is? How did my father ever tolerate such an imbecile? Salvio took a breath, and attempted the paternal tone his father would have adopted under these circumstances.

"Don't give this matter another thought, Genero. I'm using every tool at my disposal to grow your businesses."

"We thank you for your family's continued patronage. But the Brotherhood assigned those patents to your father for the sole purpose of safeguarding them for the duration of the Mafia trial. To ensure that the new Mafia-owned building concerns couldn't get their hands on them."

"There's no danger of the patents being exploited by anyone now that they are my property, so your constituents can rest easy."

"But your father agreed to revert them back to us at the end of the trial, and that date has passed." Tosca was crushing his hat brim now. "My instructions are to not leave here without our patents. Your father was a man of honor. He gave his word to the Brotherhood in front of the entire membership, with every intention of giving them back..."

Salvio lost the paternal tone, but still fought to keep his voice calm. "I can't think what I've done to cause this mistrust. I don't have to remind you that my family founded Venice—"

"*Mi scusi—*"

"Stop interrupting me, Genero!" Salvio snapped. "You dare come into my home and intimate that the Brotherhood has been scheming behind my back to steal my patents from me? Me! Your *benefactor!* Patents that have been legally deeded to my family—"

"No, sorry, it isn't like that—"

Salvio sprang from his chair, slamming both palms on the desk. Leaning toward Tosca, he roared, "To be used by *ME* in concert with *THE POPE* for *VERDU MER!* The single biggest building project Venice has ever known!" He was shaking, the heat rising from his armpits, and he felt his face flush. "If you and the rest of the Venetian building community can't pull yourselves out of the last century and embrace the future that I'm trying to realize on your behalf, you will jeopardize this project and deeply regret your short-sightedness! Now, get out of my home!"

Tosca was out of his chair and out the door as fast as he could manage without breaking into a run.

Count Vincenzo Verona sat behind the medieval carved-oak desk in his Paris office suite, signing what seemed like an endless river of papers. The elegant space was silent except for the sound of papers shuffling and his fountain pen repeatedly scratching out his signature. His accountant, Leonardo, hovered over him, alternately pointing where to initial or sign, and then whisking documents away.

Vincenzo knew that many businessmen had little patience for the mountains of paperwork and documentation global banking required, but he had always felt a deep satisfaction personally completing the contracts and transfers for his charitable deals. He'd grasped his life's purpose before he was out of diapers. A born philanthropist, what started out as his penchant for sharing his cookies with those who had none was now the part of his character that drove him to donate on a global level.

The silence was unexpectedly broken by his wife's ringtone, George Harrison's "Here Comes the Sun." He smiled as he reached for his cell phone. "*Ciao,* Gigi. How was the museum?"

"*Ciao,* V. Would you mind coming to get me at the police station on Rue Pierre Lescot? I don't want to call for my driver, and I need to be with you after the evening I've just had."

"What? The police station?" He set his phone down on the desk and tapped the speaker output as he stood up and began putting files into his briefcase. "Of course. Are you all right? What happened?"

"I'm fine. I witnessed a crime and came down to sign a statement."

"I'm on my way."

"*Grazie.*"

"*Prego.*" Vincenzo glanced at Leonardo and saw the concern on his face.

"V, I'll finish here. You get going. But don't leave me in suspense. Call me on speaker when she tells you what happened so I can hear, too."

"The transfer's been initiated, so we don't have anything to do until the bank accepts the funds. Why don't you come along and hear her story for yourself?"

"I thought you'd never ask!"

Vincenzo called his driver to bring the car around, and within minutes they pulled up to the Commissariat de Police. Waiting for his bodyguard, Petro, to perform his customary visual sweep and open the door for him, Vincenzo saw Giselle stride out of the building with two men attempting to keep up with her. A man in a suit with an air of authority moved along at her elbow, and an officer in uniform hovered at her heels while undressing her with his eyes.

Leonardo scoffed, "Reactions to Giselle never cease to amaze me. It's actually getting worse as she gets older. These French are completely obsessed with her. It looks like that police officer is about to proposition her. Helpless *libertino.*"

"She does look spectacular in that dress. And if possible, she's even more beautiful with her hair coming undone than when it was perfectly coiffed at lunch this afternoon." Vincenzo felt a familiar protectiveness as he watched the uniformed officer leering at his wife.

"There's something so creepy about a policeman being a lecher." Leonardo's face showed his disgust.

"Okay, that's it. Now he's letting his tongue hang out."

As if on cue, Petro swung the rear door open. Vincenzo got out of the car and walked over to the cop.

"Leave something on my wife. She might catch cold."

The officer pretended he hadn't heard him and whipped out a handkerchief to hide behind as he mopped his face. The man in the suit reached out and gave Vincenzo's hand a firm shake.

"Count Verona, I'm Commissioner Laurent. Please excuse this imposition, but your wife has done a great civic service. She was eyewitness to a murder, and she has given us a statement."

"A murder? *Dio mio!*" He reached out to Giselle, who moved into his arms. He hugged her protectively as the commissioner continued to explain.

"Sadly, we've just learned that the victim of the robbery she witnessed has died." He cleared his throat. "So as I say, this is now a murder investigation and we're looking for the perpetrator."

"I hope you find the man responsible." Returning his attention to his wife, Vincenzo gently cupped her face with a palm. "Oh Gigi, I'm sorry this happened." He turned at the unexpected sound of a shutter clicking.

"Damn paparazzi," the commissioner growled, and pointed at the man taking pictures. "Bretton, get rid of that idiot." The officer began waving his handkerchief at the photographers as he ran at them.

Petro expertly blocked the paparazzi's line of sight as

Vincenzo helped Giselle into the car. Once everyone was inside, the driver neatly cut into traffic, barely missing an approaching photographer on a scooter. Thanks to the car's black windows, he wouldn't be getting a shot for his gossip rag.

Giselle kicked off her shoes and stretched her legs across Vincenzo's lap. Squeezing her leg reassuringly, he asked, "So, what happened?" and then both he and Leonardo listened intently as Giselle told them the events of the crime. She ended with a shake of her head.

"The police told me they've released the Good Samaritan. The way he moved was unreal! You wouldn't have believed how he closed the distance to catch the old man. Then he ran so fast up the station stairs, he even got the briefcase back."

"He's a good person to help that man. And lucky for him you saw the whole thing and spoke up on his behalf."

"That poor old man," Leonardo said. "May he rest in peace."

Vincenzo crossed himself earnestly as Leonardo did likewise. "I'm sure they'll catch the mugger soon," he soothed his wife.

"What could have been in that briefcase?" asked Leonardo.

"My guess would be jewelry," answered Giselle. "He was well-dressed, though his suit was worn. I can't image it was a random crime, since the mugger apparently had bolt cutters." Giselle smiled wanly and turned to Vincenzo. "I can use some good news. Were you able to save the rainforest today?"

"Actually, at this moment we're paying off a large portion of Caapiranga Brazil's debt to buy back part of the

Amazon's land rights, which we're handing over to their Nature Conservancy."

"Well done! That's so exciting!" She brightened. "Hey, while your mother is still here in Paris, let's ask her to make *taglietelle alle verdure* to celebrate your rainforest coup. *Please...*" She put her hands together as if praying.

Vincenzo tapped a button to call his mother, and she answered after the first ring.

"*Ciao,* Vincenzo."

"Are you busy, Mama?"

"Not at all. Just dictating some correspondence to Ippy. Where are you?"

"I'm done working for the night, and Giselle is in the car with me. Can you make us some pasta, and we'll tell you about our day?"

"*Sì,* you know I would love to. Come straight to my house."

Giselle mouthed, "*Taglietelle.*"

Vincenzo dutifully requested, "Mama, Gigi wants *taglietelle.*"

"*Sì, taglietelle alle verdure.* And invite Leonardo, unless he is flying back to Venice tonight."

"He's coming with us. *Grazie,* Mama."

"You know it is my pleasure."

———— ◉ ————

Markus Shevchenko walked out of the police station a free man. Deciding to walk home, he headed down unfamiliar avenues toward the outer edge of the Eleventh Arrondissement heading toward the neighborhood near the Cimetière du Père Lachaise. As he walked, he kept replaying the crime in his head, and wrestled with his fury at the mugger's escape. He'd been able to tackle the kid from behind and yank the briefcase out of his grasp, but the kid had gotten back to his feet and rounded the corner, just before the police arrived. He was incredibly lucky Giselle Verona had vouched for his innocence.

Arriving at the stout little factory his friends had renovated, he unlocked the old door and stepped inside calling out, "Ivar? Yvania? I am home." He closed and locked the door and inhaled deeply. *Ahhhhh, home cooking...* He smiled and headed straight down the back hall to the kitchen.

"Dinner is just ready." Yvania whisked a clay casserole dish from the oven. "I have made the most beautiful fish." She was the quintessential mother, with her apron wrapped around her stout body, her twinkling eyes, and an old-fashioned bun perched on the top of her head. He'd always imagined she was what his own mother might have been like.

"It smells wonderful. I must tell you about my day."

"Come. Sit," Ivar said as he set glasses on the table and poured each of them some of Yvania's fresh *uzvar*.

"Did you find a wife?" Yvania began serving as soon as they were all settled around the table. "You know I am needing a baby to bounce and to sing to."

"Always the matchmaker," Ivar sighed.

Markus was so used to her constant plea for him to find love, he ignored her question and took a bite of the whitefish and red peppers. He always appreciated Yvania's ability to raise old-fashioned meals to the level of gourmet.

"Mmmm, this tastes like when we vacationed at the Dnipro River. Do you remember that party on the shore?"

"Your father caught the biggest carp." Ivar smiled. "So, what of your day?"

As they ate, Markus told them what happened in the Metro and the police station, lingering over the description of his outspoken defender.

"Countess Giselle Verona made the police let you go?" Ivar asked.

"Oh!" Yvania became animated. "She is everywhere! She is in magazines for her art and her style and her charity! I cannot wait to tell the ladies at the market!"

"*Da*. She is a woman of strong convictions, and she does look like a magazine cover."

"I am glad that you are not in trouble with the police. Murder would have you in prison for life, I think," Ivar said while refilling their glasses. "Many people would not go to the trouble of speaking up for you."

"I am going to make her a gift of thanks."

"True, you must thank Giselle," Yvania agreed as she cleared the table.

Ivar's brows shot up. "You refer to a countess by her first name?"

"She is famous as 'Giselle.' Everyone in Paris calls her by her first name."

"I tell you, she is the most unforgettable woman." Markus' mind drifted back to the Metro.

"Yes, that is what all the magazines say," Yvania agreed. Her tone brought his attention back to the kitchen, and Markus ducked as she swatted at him. "Ach! Silly! She is not for you! She is married, and the Veronas are the golden couple. So much in love is what everyone says. Vincenzo, her Italian husband, he is tall and dark and handsome and...a count!"

"Markus, do not go and break your own heart." Ivar looked worried. "If she is so beautiful as you say, her looks have confused you. Made your brain fevered and you do not think right."

"The debt I owe her for my freedom is very large," he reasoned

Yvania tapped him on the top of his head as she took his empty plate. "You are infatuated."

"I will go into the workshop now and make her a small gift."

"You know, she is artist like you. She makes sculptures everyone is talking about. She will love your beautiful art!"

Markus got up, kissed Yvania on the cheek, and headed down the hall. He recalled the vision of Giselle walking so elegantly through the crowded station, and her enticing perfume that enveloped him when he had his arm around her waist.

Giselle moved down the upstairs hall of the mansion, just out of her husband's reach. Vincenzo was making sweeping motions behind her, herding her along so she wouldn't make him late. The morning sun dappled between the silk curtains, and the sound of their footsteps was swallowed by the lush carpet runners.

"Giselle, what happened to your clothes? You were dressed at breakfast."

"Oh, I changed my mind and ran back up to put this on."

"Where's Marcella?"

"She already dressed me once this morning. I can manage."

"It's what she does, darling."

"*Oui,* but she's already left for her appointment with the seamstress."

Hustling along partially dressed, she was too busy giggling at Vincenzo's little swats to pull herself into a presentable state. He pulled her to a stop, zipped up her sleek Versace dress, and then spun her around to face him for a quick kiss. She stroked his perfectly adjusted tie.

"You look ready to buy back the rest of the rain forest."

Her husband was easily the most beautiful man Giselle had ever seen, breaking hearts with just a smile since she'd first laid eyes on him in high school. His features were even, classical perfection, but the most magnetic thing about Vincenzo were his big brown eyes. They were ringed with such thick, dark lashes he reminded her of the romantic leading men from old movies.

"Gigi, come now, *andiamo*. I can't be late for my meeting."

He gave her bottom a little smack to encourage her forward, and then began delivering light smacks in time with their strides descending the staircase. Smack, step, smack, step. Giselle playfully defended herself with her purse and shoes. She stopped at the front door and set her shoes before her feet. Vincenzo deftly held her hand and steadied her as she stepped into her ruby satin pumps. Their butler, Dinofrio, held the door open for them.

"*Arrivederci*," he murmured.

"*Arrivederci*, Dino," they replied in unison.

Just as they stepped out into the sunshine, her cell phone rang from deep inside her tote, and she stopped to fish for it. Vincenzo stopped beside her, waiting.

Retrieving her phone, she saw it was her supply foreman. "*Alo*, can you hold on a moment?" She jutted her chin toward the waiting car. "You go on, it's Wilbur. I'm going to have to go back up to my desk to go over my sculpture materials with him."

"Okay. Are you seeing Mama before she goes back to Venice?"

"Later today I'm going to meet her to get some shoes made." Dinofrio was still holding the door for her as she blew Vincenzo a kiss. "See you at dinner."

"*Sì, ciao bella.*" He blew a kiss back.

Fifteen minutes later she stepped back outside and paused on her top step to enjoy the feel of the morning. The early fall sun was breaking through the morning haze, and a light breeze blew off La Seine with a mixture of wet river smell and boat fumes. Turning toward the street, she realized a man holding a gift-wrapped box had appeared at the bottom of her steps. It took her a second to recognize the Good Samaritan from the Metro.

"Oh! Uh...umm..." she tried to recall if she'd heard his name at the police station.

"Markus," he finished for her with a smile. "*Bonjour.*" He offered the box to her. "I did not mean to scare you, Countess. I made a gift for you."

"Oh, no one uses that title for me. Please call me Giselle." She was charmed by his heavy Eastern European accent and found herself admiring his startling blue eyes, then realized he was waiting for her to say something else. "How do you know where I live?"

"I learned that you are very famous, and I used Google. Is it true that you are a countess?"

She wrinkled her nose at the word "famous," and

brushing away her usual hesitancy around new people, she walked down the steps to join him on the sidewalk.

"Well, yes, I am a countess by marriage. But most people use the family title in reference to my mother-in-law."

"Ah, I see. I wanted to give you a gift of thanks... for...for my freedom. It is not much, but I made for you last night."

She didn't reach out for the gift. "Markus, this is so sweet. But, there's no need. Really." A bit uncertain at accepting a gift from a stranger, she rocked on the balls of her feet, her heels clicking on the concrete. "I'm just glad you aren't in trouble with the police."

He once again extended his arms, offering the box without crowding her.

"Well, you're very thoughtful." She paused a moment, then dismissed her reservations and took the box from him. "Thank you."

"I see you are going someplace, but maybe you have time for a coffee?" He lifted his brows and flashed her a beautiful white smile. She couldn't help but smile back.

"I was just going to an art exhibit, but a coffee would be nice." She looked over her shoulder into the courtyard where her car and driver were waiting and gave a wave of dismissal.

Markus offered her his arm, and she took it, happy that there were no photographers lurking around. Their pace was slow as they talked about yesterday's events, each filling in what the other had missed. She pointed to an orange-and-black awning as they approached it.

"This little bistro is good."

He opened the door for her, and she allowed him to guide her toward a booth. Sliding into a seat across from him, she took the opportunity to study Markus again. She wondered if he used an electric shaver on his hair each morning; it was so perfect. He wore the same style of clothes as the day before—a neatly pressed, grey button-down cotton work shirt, lightweight charcoal pants, and black work boots that had an old-fashioned practicality to them. She had the impression he gave as much thought to dressing for the day as he would putting on a uniform. He had an easy confidence that made her feel relaxed, too.

Their waiter approached and stopped mid-stride when he saw Giselle. He fumbled his order pad, almost dropping it.

"*B'jour,* ah, what, ah...what would you like?" he stammered, as if he was asking for her phone number.

"*Café crème.*"

"Heh, heh," the waiter giggled awkwardly. "*Café,* oh right, oh good. I...I really like it. You'll like it." He took a deep breath and did a forced half-turn toward Markus, who ordered the same.

As the waiter departed, Markus glanced after him and then back to Giselle. "Very nervous."

He placed his hand lightly on the box in front of her. "Thank you for helping me, Giselle. Without you, I could be in jail for murder."

"I was glad to speak up, Markus."

Giselle took the package, removed the bright blue ribbon and crisp white paper, and opened the box to reveal soft blue velvet swaddling. She slipped her fingers into the folds and found a delicate creation of metal and etched glass. Holding it up to the light, she was astonished.

"*You* made this?"

"I hope you like. You are a great artist, so if you like it, I am happy."

"Oh, I'm no great artist. I'm just *an* artist. But this is incredible! How do you create something like this?"

"I show you how I make anytime. I very much want to see *your* art. I have only seen little pictures on the Internet."

"Um, when can you show me?" She swept a piece of hair away from her eyes.

"If you want, we can go to where I make art now. It is also where I am living with some friends."

Their coffee arrived, and Giselle watched as Markus busied himself with his cup, adding a spoon of sugar and stirring with precise movements. She glanced from the exquisite piece to Markus' strong hands. Could hands like those make something like the object of sleek metal strands and etched glass she was holding? Giselle found herself grinning. This was a thrill! She held up his creation and looked at her talented new friend through the prisms of glass fragments.

"Okay. Now is good."

"What about your plans for the day?"

"I'll go to the museum another time. Seeing how you made this will be much more interesting than an art exhibit. Later today I'm meeting my mother-in-law, but that's not for a while yet." She set the little sculpture on the table between them and prepared her coffee. "So Markus, I haven't been able to place your accent. Where are you from?"

"Guess."

"Well, you sound a bit like someone I knew from Romania."

"No. Would you like to make a second guess?"

"Hmm...Latvia?"

"Latvia? Ha! What a guess. Latvia. No."

She bobbled her head, thinking. "Belarus?"

He sat back against the leather banquette. "Ukrayina. I am from some kilometers outside a village called Zalishchyky."

"Ah! You're Ukrainian. I don't think I've ever met anyone from there. What's it like?"

"Very beautiful. Endless pastures and forests."

"Sounds peaceful."

"Not all of the country, but where I come from, it is."

"How long have you been in Paris?"

"Two weeks."

"How long will you be here?"

"I have no plans to leave. I have a work visa to help restore the windows in some buildings on Boulevard de Ménilmontant. But the permits are delayed, so I have not started that work yet."

"Hmmm, did you always want to come here?"

"No, but I lost my father recently. We were very close. His friend, Ivar, invited me to come to Paris to live. So I live here now with Ivar and Yvania."

"I'm sorry for your loss, Markus."

"Thank you. Ivar was my father's teacher, and my teacher also. I lived with my father and worked with him in his stained glass business. But now he is gone, and I am here." He smiled and gestured around the hip café.

She picked up the fragile piece again. "Your father's business was making things like this?"

"No," he chuckled. "We made windows for churches and for castles with a technique we learned from Ivar. It is very special and very old. That was our business. Making things like this," he pointed at the piece in her hands, "is not a way to make money I think...but it makes me happy."

"Oh, I think you could make quite a lot of money selling pieces like this." She raised an eyebrow. "You may be surprised what people would pay for this piece. An *object d'art* like this could start a bidding war at auction."

"Oh, well, then I must get back to my workshop right away. I am late for making myself rich." Markus puffed up his chest and leaned forward with an eyebrow arched seriously. Then, unable to maintain the facade of self-importance, he gave up the pretense, leaned back, and laughed lightly.

"Are your friends artists?"

"Not artists, no. Ivar is retired. Yvania is retired also, but still does some work here for the Ukrainian Embassy. She says her new job is to find me a wife." He rolled his eyes. "You have matchmaking women in France too, right?"

"Doesn't every culture?"

They finished their coffee and Markus paid the bill, then he escorted Giselle out to the street and hailed a taxi.

"Now, we go to see my work."

Salvio awoke atop the unyielding surface of his bed within the solitude of his austere, putty-colored room. He was in a good mood until he began to move his legs, and his breath caught as crystal shards of pain shot through his feet and ankles. The fact that God had afflicted him with gout wounded him deeply. It went far beyond the physical discomfort, which he could overcome. But as God's chosen one, Salvio was bitter about being tested. He forced an exhale through gritted teeth, and then swung his legs over the side of the bed. Pushing himself to stand, he tottered painfully and then began grunting his way through deep knee bends, flexing forward on the balls of his feet. He would eradicate this corporeal weakness through pain.

Shutting out his physical discomfort, his mind turned with pleasant anticipation to this morning's visit from the Pope's messenger, and his good mood returned. At eight thirty he would receive the Vatican's response to his Verdu Mer proposal. It was a mere formality; there was no question he would be granted control over the demolition and reconstruction of that historic neighborhood. He would rebuild Verdu Mer from the bottom of the canals up, and not only revitalize that sector, but also revitalize Venice's construction industry. Every builder in il Veneto would forge a new relationship with the House of Scortini.

His knee bends complete, he turned to see his valet, Guiseppe, hovering just inside the bedroom door. Unlike the welcome silence of the stony butler, Salvio found Guiseppe's enervated and feeble ways infuriating. But in so many ways, he was more tolerable than the overbearing governess who had dressed him as a boy.

"When I'm showered, I'll get right into my black tufted twill suit," Salvio instructed.

"*Sì*, but it is already warm outside. Perhaps you would reconsider—"

"Get that suit!"

Guiseppe jumped into the closet as if goosed.

Salvio never allowed his valet in the bathroom, and didn't allow himself to be seen naked by anyone, including his wife. He felt that a man having a servant's assistance with grooming was disgusting and smacked of self-worship. Showering was a sacramental cleansing of one's divine temple, and should be done in solitary contemplation of the Almighty God.

He stepped under the forceful spray, doused a brush with castile soap, and began his scrubbing ritual. Deliberate not to miss any flesh that cried out for less punishment, he considered an area pure only when it was slightly swollen and pulsing. He turned off the water and dried himself with a rough towel before stepping out onto the marble floor.

Moving more nimbly now, and slightly inebriated from pain-blocking endorphins, he glided over to the sink to brush his teeth. Although not a vain man, he regarded himself in the mirror. He knew he wasn't handsome, but didn't waste time trying to fool others into thinking he was. He had pale skin, smallish eyes, inordinately red lips, and a bulbous nose with large nostrils that frequently flared without consulting him—when that happened, he pinched them back into place. While he took great care when cutting his own hair, it always had an uneven, chopped look, and his eyebrows were unruly. When his mother was alive, she used to humiliate him by smoothing wax over them. Now he simply ran his fingers over his brows in an effort to groom them.

After pulling on his cotton underwear, he allowed Guiseppe to assist him with the rest of his clothing. Then, leaving the effete little valet behind in his quarters, Salvio slipped silently down the hall toward his office, keeping to the shadowy side of the empty hallway. Once inside, he took a seat behind his desk and broke his fast with water, seed crackers, and a single pitted date. He had just finished when he heard a light rap on his door and felt a flood of adrenaline. He stood up as a show of respect and called, "Show Excelsior in."

The butler opened the door for the Pope's messenger, who offered a nod as a greeting to Salvio before moving to a chair. He sat down and folded his hands in his lap as Salvio retook his seat.

"Welcome, Excelsior. This is the first time you have come to my home since my father's passing."

"*Sì*. My condolences."

"*Grazie.* My father always liked you."

"*Sì*, Salvatore was a good man, as was your grandfather."

"You come with news of my Verdu Mer appointment?"

"I come with news that the Holy Father has given the project to Count Gabrieli Verona." Excelsior stated it with utter finality.

Mentally smashing his fist through glass, Salvio strove to remain outwardly calm. "Ah, of course I will work closely with Verona. But Verdu Mer falls within the build-ers' purview, and my family has always represented the Venetian building establishment. I assumed the Pope would naturally consider it *my* project." His mouth was dry, but he refused to lick his lips.

"Not at all. Verdu Mer is Verona's, one hundred per-cent." Excelsior stood and offered a minute bow.

Salvio rose from his seat and, putting his hands on his desk, he leaned forward. "Overseeing and leading the Venetian builders is my birthright. I assure you, I am more than fit to step into my father's role."

"I will convey your sentiments to the Holy Father. Now, I must depart. If you will excuse me."

Salvio curled his toes and clenched his sphincter in a desperate attempt to keep his rage in check. "Thank you for coming. I am, as ever, the Pope's humble servant. God be with you, Excelsior."

"And also with you." The messenger walked out.

———————

Glancing down at the schedule before him, Count Gabrieli Verona was encouraged by how this morning's business was progressing. The esteemed Verdu Mer consortium members had flown in from all over the world for this meeting in Venice, and many had to catch afternoon flights to other destinations. Every minute together counted, and every expert in the room had their sleeves rolled up tackling the tasks at hand. The enormous fifteenth-century table was covered with laptops, reports, and schematics of cutting-edge technology, while experts were clustered in front of a whiteboard passing sleek tablets back and forth.

Looking up, he was surprised to see Salvio Scortini push through the doors of his adjoining office suite. He'd never had an interaction with Salvio that was anything short of unsettling. His bodyguard, Tiberius, intercepted the uninvited visitor smoothly, while Gabrieli stood and addressed the group.

"Please excuse me a moment." Stepping away from the table, he nodded his intent to Tiberius, who allowed Salvio to enter.

"Verona! I made it as soon as I could." Salvio's voice was brittle, between a shout and a cry, his words tumbling out. "I know you agree that nothing should delay our work on Verdu Mer, so I'm here to work with you as our families always have."

Gabrieli approached him, but was careful not to shake his hand. The count had once seen Salvio misinterpret a handshake as an agreement, and he was not about to make that mistake.

"This is a surprise, Salvio."

"I have just been paid a personal visit from the Pope's emissary, and am here to set up our protocols for demolition of the old sector."

"You can't mean Verdu Mer," a voice at the table challenged. "You are mistaken, *signore*."

Hoping to avoid a conflict, Gabrieli stepped in. "Allow me to introduce Yani Chizzoli. He and his team will be rebuilding the foundations of the entire Verdu Mer neighborhood."

"Ah, certainly. I have heard of Chizzoli." Salvio reached up and pinched his nostrils like he smelled something offensive. "I am well aware that Venice is sinking."

Chizzoli blinked and offered Salvio a bland stare. "You joke of course, *signore*. It has been more than thirty years since measurements proved that Venice is *not* sinking."

"Perhaps he is not familiar with global warming and the practice of factoring future subsidence," another voice at the table suggested in an exaggerated stage whisper.

Salvio's whole body jerked as he turned back to Gabrieli. "I must get moving on my end with the demolition plans. You can just send me the blueprints and I can begin immediately."

"No." Gabrieli took care to speak clearly. "We do not require your efforts."

"Oh, it's no imposition. The builders of Venice are standing by, waiting for word from me."

Gabrieli remained impassive. In an effort to end the conversation, he refrained from repeating himself.

Salvio's lips stretched and his voice lowered. "Building is my business, so I'm offering my assistance. I won't take 'no' for an answer."

"I'm afraid this is not open for discussion, Salvio. The Verdu Mer consortium will not include you."

Salvio's lips stretched farther into a smile, but his eyes were dead. "I will work through papal channels as always."

"I would expect nothing less. Now excuse us, we are on a tight schedule." He gestured toward the exit.

Tiberius opened the conference room door, and Gabrieli returned to his seat at the table, but Salvio showed no sign of leaving. At a nod from Gabrieli, Tiberius moved forward to usher him out. At first Salvio took awkward steps toward the door as if struggling against a strong wind, and then he spoke up.

"May God guide you all. I must be off to my own meetings."

A silent security guard joined Salvio as he left the now-hushed conference room.

Giselle looked out the taxi window and noticed that the leaves of the trees in Square de la Roquette were just beginning to turn gold. "It's been unseasonably hot recently, but you've arrived just in time for autumn, Markus. I think it's the best time to be in Paris." She turned to meet his eyes. "So, you've told me about your father. Tell me about your mother."

"I never knew her. She died of the flu when I was a baby."

"Oh...I'm sorry she died, Markus." She reached out and squeezed his hand.

"Thank you. But now, living with the Czerneys, I am not alone."

"You said Yvania works for the embassy. What does she do there?"

Markus paused and looked down, as if deciding how to answer.

"I'm sorry. I didn't mean to pry."

He gave a small shrug as if it were nothing. "It is not something we talk about."

"You're a good friend."

Their cab pulled up to a red brick building with all the earmarks of a small factory from a bygone era: the faded remains of signage, a large, solid entry door, and a flat roof. Markus paid the driver and stepped out of the taxi. Reaching back to assist her, he walked Giselle to the door.

"This is where I am living."

"You live in a factory?" She liked the look of it. "Perfect place for an artist."

Markus produced a skeleton key and inserted it into one of the door's iron locks. When it released with a satisfying *click*, he gave the big door a light push, and it swung open on well-oiled hinges. A bell tinkled softly overhead, obviously a holdover from when customers had used this door. She stepped into an entryway bathed in amber light that filtered through antique windows set high up on the walls and through skylights overhead. The furnishings for this former place of business had been removed, and it was empty now. But looking at the well-worn floor, she could see the outlines where a counter and file cabinets once stood. Every surface was scrupulously clean, yet tiny dust motes danced in the light. There were polished wood stairs with well-worn steps and railings off to the left, a hallway straight ahead, and doors off to the left and right. Giselle inhaled a complex aroma of stew that made her mouth water.

"*Tse ty?*" called a man's voice.

"*Da*, I am back," Markus responded.

"How did it go?" Giselle heard the purposeful clicking sounds of a metal walker approaching. "Did you find her?"

A stout, white-haired man appeared in the doorway to her right. She guessed he was in his seventies, and he was dressed like Markus, in soft grey work clothes. His face was wizened with age, but he looked to be in good health and his silver hair was worn in a tight military brush-cut. When he caught sight of Giselle, the walker pitched forward out of his grasp and clattered to the floor.

"Ivar!" Markus was at the old man's side in an instant.

"What you *do*, Markus?" His voice was forceful, but not angry. "You bring a royal goddess to our hovel? What is your sense, boy?" He shuffled past his forgotten walker and stretched his hands out to Giselle, his eyes twinkling with good humor.

She heard heavy wooden shoes approaching fast from down the hallway, and a little fireplug-of-a-woman in a white blouse, grey skirt, and faded flower-print apron skidded into view.

"What now?" She looked past Markus to her husband, and then saw Giselle. Peering over the most improbable rhinestone-studded cat's-eye glasses Giselle had ever seen, the matronly woman's mouth fell open. "Oh! Such a beauty! No wonder Paris is in love with you!" She had a heavy accent but her pronunciation was succinct. Grasping her hands in front of her, she gave a tiny bow. "*Bonjour*, Countess Verona. It is *you* who makes my husband have the surprise. He is lucky you do not stop his heart!" Her eyes traveled up and down Giselle in admiration, paying special attention to her red heels. She swiveled on her clogs and smacked Markus' shoulder.

"I would have make *nice* food for Countess Verona! You will have me serve midday goulash to a great woman? How will I find you the wife if you are not sensitive to making the preparation?"

Markus held up his hands against his tiny aggressor. "I am sorry, Yvania." He kept his defense up as she rapped him on the bicep. "Giselle asked to see how I work so..." He gestured vaguely toward the back hall.

Yvania tapped her upper lip with an index finger. "Well! This is true, then. Not to be rude. Of course, then. You bring." She spun back to Giselle and fanned her face. "Countess, you must be making the cars to crash when you are walking!"

Markus made the introductions. "Giselle, meet Ivar and Yvania Czerney."

"Please excuse how we are acting, Countess," Ivar said. "Welcome to our home. Will you honor us by sharing our lunch?"

"Hello, Yvania and Ivar. Please call me Giselle." She reached out to shake Ivar's hand, and then turned and took Yvania's. "I would love to join you for lunch. *Merci*."

"Hoh-kay young ones, you will go to the workshop." Ivar gestured farther down the hall.

Giselle followed Markus and stopped just inside the door of the big workshop, thrilled by the space. "Now *this* is a workshop!" It smelled of old wood, iron, oils, and solvents. The light poured down from more skylights and high windows, and each bench had a long fixture of halogen lights suspended above it. Cabinets filled with tools and supplies stood on wheeled casters here and there, able to be repositioned anywhere in the gymnasium-sized room with an easy push. Glancing up, she admired the turn-of-the-century ceiling track with chains that could move large objects about with the press of a button. Beautiful, practical, professional, and exciting.

"Mmm, now I'm in my element."

"Ah, you like it. Good." He pointed to a nearby work area. "Here is where I am working now." He led her over to a crowded workbench that held part of a small glass-and-metal sculpture. "What do you want to know about my process?"

Giselle admired the sculpture before her. "Can you work while you answer questions? I really want to watch your process instead of just hearing you explain. Is that all right?"

They sat side by side on wheeled chairs, and she watched as Markus selected a tiny etched pane of glass, placed it into a frame made from a tiny ribbon of copper, and secured it.

"It is the same idea as Ivar and my father's glass craft. But I like to make art, not just windows for buildings. Making windows is good money, but not interesting for me."

She was impressed as she watched him deftly attach the tiny piece to his sculpture. "Well, this art of yours is something special...like attaching glass flower petals to twisted metal."

As he worked, his leg rested against hers in a comfortably friendly way. He fashioned a new copper ribbon, slipped another tiny glass pane into it, and then used a rubber-coated flat-edged screwdriver to crimp the copper around the glass. She studied his movements as he attached the piece to the sculpture and began the process again, and noticed he stole a glance at her legs now and then while working.

"I hope I'm not distracting you too much."

"Not too distracting. No."

"I don't like anyone around when I work. My husband complains that talking to me while I'm working is like talking to a fork. He even gave me a little fork pendant as a joke." She fell silent and studied everything Markus' hands were doing. After a while she said, "You possess a rare economy of movement."

He reached for a small tool and snipped a notch into a malleable ribbon with a soft *click*. He performed the task smoothly and without adjustment. Giselle studied his profile. He appeared to be relaxed—clearly not a tortured artist.

"You're not like artists who can't help second-guessing themselves."

He pivoted to look her in the eye, one of her knees now nestled between both of his. "I see clearly and do not hesitate to act. Ever. It has always been so with me." He licked his lips and then bit his bottom lip as though expecting a response.

"Nooo...you're certainly not one to hesitate."

A corner of his mouth drew up and he quirked an eyebrow. He released her knee from between his and turned back to his sculpture.

"I have never understood the artist who does a bit of work and then throws down their tools and then paces and runs hands through their hair in frustration and then goes away and drinks too much wine." He rubbed his hand over his head to mimic the angst. "I am not like that."

She laughed. He'd completed one side of his sculpture, and he started on the other side. Giselle glanced at the next workbench.

"What are those bottles and brushes over there?"

"My etching solutions. I will show you how I etch the glass."

After a few hours of work, Giselle heard Yvania's clogs approaching. The bun on the top of her head bobbed as she bustled into the workroom. Drying her hands on her apron, she beckoned.

"Come. We eat."

Giselle followed Yvania to the back of the building, with Markus close behind. The kitchen was well equipped with pots, pans, and knives of all sizes. Lunch was arranged on a wooden trestle table with bench seating. Steam rose from freshly baked bread, and a little crock of home-churned butter sat on the cutting board next to it. Ivar was ladling four bowls of deep-red paprika stew. The fragrant mix of spices was heady, and Giselle couldn't recall smelling anything quite like it before. Markus helped her get situated on the low bench, and she appreciated that he was gentleman enough to avert his eyes as her hem rode up in the process. She smoothed it down quickly, and feeling the rumble of hunger she breathed, "I can't tell you how excited I am to taste this."

She reached for the bowl Ivar offered her, and Yvania spooned something that looked like *crème fraiche* into the center of Giselle's bowl.

"You must to try with homemade *smetana*, my sour cream. I made best in my village. I am told it is best of *any* place."

Together the four went about the business of eating.

The bread was a feathery-soft revelation with a moist interior and an addictive cracker crust. It was by far the best bread Giselle had ever tasted, but her hosts ate it without comment. The butter was whipped from fresh cream, with light flakes of sea salt added that melted on her tongue. The goulash was a symphony of rich peppers, sweet onions, and deep, rich spices simmered together. Finishing her bowl, she smacked her lips discretely.

"This was an incredible lunch," she continued in an impulsive gush. "I absolutely love your cooking, Yvania."

Ivar ladled more goulash into their bowls, and Markus sliced more bread to pass around. The proud hostess puffed out her chest and then flipped a pudgy hand casually.

"Just goulash. I am glad you like. I am not being mad at Markus, but if I knew I was making lunch for company, I would have make something else." Then she abruptly dropped her palm onto the table with a thump. "Tell me. You were always so beautiful? I mean since baby?" She looked across the table at Giselle with eyes comically magnified by her thick cat's-eye glasses.

Ivar barked a laugh, while Markus chuckled and ducked his head. Clearly the two men were used to being embarrassed by her directness.

"*Wot?*" Yvania reproved her men with a glance. "The swan can start as ugly leetle bird. Giselle, here, is not minding this question. Ach! Such beauty cannot be ignored!"

Giselle laughed, and the men joined her. "I don't know. I think all babies are beautiful. Right?" Changing the subject she said, "So, Ivar, you teach the art of window making?"

"I do. The old Crimean glass process that I teach makes the most beautiful light inside the home."

Markus pointed toward the front of the building. "You must have noticed the quality of light in the entryway?"

"I did actually. Did you make the skylights and those unusual windows?"

"*Da*, those are my work."

"They're wonderful!"

"I am glad you like them. So you are seeing how Markus makes his sculptures?"

"Uh-huh. I've never seen anything like them...or him."

"Is he maybe influencing your next artistic creation?"

"He's influencing me, but I couldn't work like him."

"Can his method be so different from other artists?"

"Absolutely! I'm also studying the way he moves." She tried to mimic his minimalistic movements with her hands and body. "He has the precision of a surgeon, but his hands...he has...*refinement*, I guess is the word."

Ivar seemed to be considering her comments, and Markus was obviously pleased as he wiped his mouth with his napkin.

She looked over at him. "Markus, you join components as if you've assembled them many times before. Like you move from memory."

"I have never given it thought." He tilted his head thinking. "It is the only way I know."

"Now we have leetle cup of chocolate." Yvania got up from the table and turned the low flame off from under a pot of cream and chocolate on the stove. She then gave it a couple of brisk beats with an old-fashioned wooden frother. While pouring their drinks into cups, she gushed, "The wonderful Countess Giselle Verona, here in our home! You know, everyone loves you! Loves your art! Loves your husband! So handsome he is!"

After relaxing over the chocolate, Giselle looked down at her watch and announced, "Oh, I'm afraid I'm going to have to leave soon. I'm meeting my mother-in-law. Would you excuse me while I call my driver?" While Giselle stepped into the hall to use her phone, Markus returned to the workshop to retrieve her gift, and then rejoined her as she said her goodbyes.

"Ivar, what a pleasure it's been to meet you. I hope I never startle you again. I'd like to be a frequent guest in your home." She turned to her hostess. "Yvania, thank you for sharing your lunch with me. I'd like to introduce you to my mother-in-law, Juliette. She's a great Italian cook, but what you do with spices and peppers would knock her out."

"Sure! I could do the knocking out! You tell the countess to come!"

Markus escorted Giselle outside to her car. After trading phone numbers, she blurted impulsively, "Markus, what are you doing tomorrow? Can I come watch you work again?"

"I will be here."

"*Bon! Au revoir.*" She kissed him lightly on both cheeks and got into her car. Giselle gave instructions to her driver, and then laid her head back to think about Markus. It was good to have a discreet new friend that she could trust. This gave her an idea of something she'd like to do with him, and she felt a secret thrill.

3

Markus looked out the window at the gray morning rain. Giselle had called before breakfast asking if she could come over within the hour, and now here she was. She dismissed her driver with a wave and made her way to the factory door, thigh-high black boots flashing from the front slit of her bottle-green trench coat. Despite the dismal weather, she looked happy and energetic.

He opened the door and drew her inside. Taking her umbrella, he pointed it out the open door, flicked the water off, retracted it, and set it over a drain in the corner. Closing the big door, he noticed she was watching his movements again, and it made him happy.

"Good morning, Giselle." He pulled her into his arms for a hug.

"Oh, no," she sputtered, "I'm getting you all wet."

He held her against him. "I do not mind." After a slow

squeeze, he released her and stepped back as she untied the belt of her trench.

"Let me take that for you." He slid his fingertips beneath her coat collar, eased the raincoat off, and hung it on a peg. He admired her deep-green dress. It formed to her body like a wetsuit from her neck to her hipbones, where it flared away creating an extreme version of the feminine form. "I am glad you are here." He opened his hands as if heat was radiating off her. "And I have never seen anything like this dress...beautiful!"

"Isn't it? I didn't wear designer clothes growing up, but now that I'm a Verona it's expected of me..." She shrugged casually and then picked up where they'd left off yesterday. "Can I ask you some questions about copper alloy?"

He took her hand and led her back to the workshop. When they were seated at the workbench, Ivar shuffled in and kissed her cheek.

"Wonderful to see you, my angel."

Yvania bustled in and set mugs of coffee in front of them. She bent close and exchanged little cheek *busses* with Giselle.

"I am so happy you are coming back to us!" Chuckling, she straightened up and swatted her hands in front of her own face as if waving off a desire to prattle on. "I will be in kitchen with making the lunch. Please, you will stay to have *varenyky* with filling of fried onions, and my home-made farm cheese." Chugging out of the room, she scooted past Ivar as he closed the door.

Markus had dressed in his usual grey work shirt and pants, but he'd chosen heavier material for the chilly morning. He looked at Giselle with concern.

"It is cold in the workshop. I will bring you something warm. Although I do not think it will go with your dress." He disappeared through a side door and returned with a soft, grey cardigan, which he draped around her shoulders in a courtly gesture.

"*Merci.*"

He smiled and picked up his coffee cup. "Last night I began a new piece, so you will want to watch me work on it while we talk about copper?"

"Please. I'm glad you don't mind having me watch you." She lifted her cup to her lips and blew across the hot foamed milk. "I told Vincenzo that watching you is like good theatre."

"Theatre? Ha!" He twirled a spool of copper wire and looked at her. "I have shown you my process. What about you? When can I see *you* work?"

Giselle swallowed a mouthful of coffee, and then said in a confidential tone, "Well...I'm about to begin assembly on a really big piece. The materials have been shipped out to the country where I'll be working on it." Her eyes watched his hands as he twirled a segment of wire with his pliers.

"Oh? When will you go?"

"Next week."

"That *is* soon." He tried not to let his disappointment show. "How long will you be away?"

"I don't know, a few months maybe. I've never attempted a piece this massive."

"You do this *massive* piece alone?"

"Well, you see, it's a secret." She leaned over, touching

her shoulder against his conspiratorially and whispered, "I haven't told anyone what it is."

"Your husband knows this secret, does he not?"

"No, he doesn't." She squared her shoulders and pivoted in her seat to face him. "He only knows that I'm going to the country to work. I haven't told a single soul what it is."

Markus set his pliers aside and he faced her. She looked like a cat that had eaten the family goldfish. He narrowed his eyes and tried to discern what she was trying to tell him.

"Your husband will know when you both arrive in the country, will he not?"

"When I go to work, I go alone. He stays here in Paris to work, or goes to Italy to be with family and his best friend Leonardo. He visits me for a day or two once in a while, but he leaves me to my process." Markus didn't try to hide his surprise as she continued. "Vincenzo doesn't like to be stuck out there when I'm working. He used to come with me, but he'd just spend days driving around the countryside or riding his horse to neighboring farms looking for company while I worked."

"You know, to hold a secret is to carry a weight." Markus picked up his coffee and took a drink. "Would you consider sharing your burden with me?" He could see that she wanted to tell him, but she was hesitating. He set down his cup and took both of her hands. "You can trust me."

"Well, one of the elements that I'm going to use in the creation is not..."

He raised one eyebrow slowly, requesting her to continue.

"...legal."

"Ah. Not a confession I would expect from a woman like you. You are not worried about the authorities?"

"I'm going to build this sculpture," she shrugged, "and then the authorities will do what they must."

Markus tipped his head to the side, regarding her. He could see that she was excited at the prospect of her forbidden art. *What a fascinating woman.* "You have great conviction, or are very stubborn."

Giselle clapped her hands and rocked back in her chair. "Both!" she grinned.

———◦◦◦———

It was late in the day when Ivar came into the workshop and told Markus he had a phone call. Markus left the workshop to talk on the old landline down the hall, and Ivar sat down to keep her company.

"You do not need a nap after eating our big lunch?"

"Ah, no," she grinned. "Yvania's cooking is really special."

"*Da.*" Ivar tapped a fingertip on the worktop and said matter-of-factly, "Giselle, I want to pay you the compliment of being frank with you."

"Okay." She felt a pang, because that preface was usually followed by something hard to take. Bracing herself she said, "Of course."

"You have a special quality that makes people lose their heads." That didn't seem to need any response, but she nodded her understanding. "Now, I would like for you to ask yourself if you have any intention of toying with

Markus' heart—as hidden as that intention might be—or if you are only here to learn his craft."

"I would never toy with his heart. I'm only... I assure you, I'm only interested in his techniques."

"All right. Then perhaps you could think of your affect on him and wear something less..." He gestured to the sprayed-on effect of her dress. "...distracting."

"You're right, this was thoughtless. I won't wear things like this around him anymore."

Ivar chuckled in spite of his attempt to counsel her. "This dark mermaid dress sparks the imagination even of an old man like me."

They were both chuckling when Markus returned. "My employer called with news of more delays on his project. But he says my work visa is safe."

She stayed at the factory four more hours, engrossed in watching Markus, and was surprised when she glanced at her watch that the day had slipped past her.

"Oh, Markus, I've got to go now." Retrieving her phone, she sent a quick text to her driver.

"You could stay for dinner. I am sure Yvania is already cooking something memorable."

"No doubt." Her eyes involuntarily grew big for an instant at the prospect of going back to Yvania's table. "But no, I've got a ball to get dressed for." She stood up and eased out of the cardigan.

His eyes swept over her as he took it from her, and she thought of Ivar's plea.

"A ball? That sounds like fun."

"It will be, and Vincenzo hates to be late, so I've got to run."

Vincenzo had just arrived home when Giselle rushed through the front door and over to him, offering reassurances.

"We won't be late. I'll be ready before you know it." She put a hand on his shoulder, raised her left leg, and offered her foot to him. "Here, help me off with my boots." She took hold of both his shoulders as he crouched down to help.

"You know, Marcella would do this for you, darling."

"I always feel guilty when I have to manhandle her as she wrestles my boots off. You're my husband. We're supposed to wrestle." She leaned down and nipped his ear with her teeth, and he laughed while they did, indeed, end up wrestling the black boots off her feet. He handed them to her, and watched as she trotted up the stairs toward her dressing room and waiting maid.

He and Giselle were attending a charity gala for human rights at the Louvre's Pavillon de Flore, where he would accept an award on behalf of his family for the three million euros they'd donated to the cause. The celebrity attendees liked to wear the most outrageous formal wear, but that kind of fashion had never appealed to Vincenzo. He was a man of simple style, and after showering he donned a classic Armani tuxedo. As he peeked into Giselle's dressing room, his breath caught at the sight of her in a fiery coral couture gown.

"My God, Gigi..."

"You like?" She looked pleased and raised her hands up in a "ta-da" gesture.

"You look exquisite."

"You look exquisite yourself," she said as she picked up her crystal-encrusted evening bag and came to take his arm.

They chatted in the car, and he heard more about the Ukrainian artist Giselle was currently studying—something to do with glass and copper. She was even more preoccupied than usual. Tonight he'd have to work harder to lure her out of her art bubble.

Dinner was prepared by a celebrated Parisian chef who had a flair for sauces and an affinity for shallots, but gossip was on the attendee's lips far more frequently than their forks. When the dinner portion of the evening gave way to dancing, their enjoyment of one other was apparent to everyone, and the society photographers couldn't get enough of their embraces on the dance floor. Vincenzo loved dancing with Giselle. She was a perfect partner, with the grace to follow his lead and the athletic ability to make any dance step look effortless. As was expected of them, they both danced with other partners, and meeting their social obligations while traveling around the polished floor song after song was harder work than it looked.

It was after two a.m. when Vincenzo escorted Giselle to their front door and entered the security code. The staff wasn't required to wait up for them, and even Dinofrio had gone to bed at his regular time. Acting like naughty teenagers returning past their curfew, they didn't wait to shed their formal wear. Kicking off their shoes in the foyer, they undressed as they climbed the main staircase. Vincenzo dutifully unhooked Giselle's buttons and zipper as she offered them to him, and she unhooked his cuff links and removed collar stays for him in return. Ready to be rid of her couture confection, Giselle stopped mid-flight and raised her arms lazily over her head. Vincenzo climbed up another stair and bent to whisk her gown up over her head. She leaned against the balustrade for balance as she stripped off her silk stockings, while he continued upward shedding his tuxedo. Arriving at the top of the stairs, they piled their clothing on the side table outside his dressing room, and he followed Giselle into her bedroom. She freed her breasts from her corset, tossing it aside, and collapsed onto the bed dramatically, wearing nothing but a skimpy half-slip that made clear she wasn't wearing panties.

"Oh! I don't know how many times my feet were stepped on."

She flung herself back onto the bed, lifted her legs in the air, and bent her knees to inspect her smarting toes. Vincenzo was down to boxers as he regarded his wife holding her feet with her sex exposed, like a baby waiting to be diapered.

"Gigi, for the most feminine creature I've ever known, that is one unladylike pose."

"What? You don't like my frog-holding-feet-pose?" She dropped her legs demurely and yawned.

He collapsed next to her, picked up one of her feet, gently massaged it, and echoed her yawn.

She yawned again, gave a satisfied "mmm" at his ministrations, and smiled as she stuffed a pillow under her head.

After another long yawn, he set her foot down and laid

his head back. "Let's have breakfast together before I leave for the airport."

She murmured, "Yum," as she began to fall asleep.

He pulled the cover over them and was snoring softly beside her within moments.

———◦◉◦———

Raphielli Scortini had been married to Salvio for over a year, and it was a constant strain on her good humor. She'd lived in an abbey until she was eighteen, and had thoroughly enjoyed her life there—studying theology and languages, and even perfecting the painstaking art of hand-copying church scrolls with a quill and ink. But now her life had no purpose, and Salvio refused to let her out of this cold dark palazzo unless she was attending Mass with her mother and grandmother who she secretly thought of as the Dour Doublet. She didn't spend any other time with them because Salvio didn't like them, and so they served only as chaperones for church trips. She'd been six-years-old when her father had died, and the very next morning the Dour Doublet had taken her to live at the abbey. Now that she was married, Salvio wanted her to spend her days reading the Bible, but he generally avoided her at all cost.

Yesterday she'd learned that he was throwing a luncheon party today to announce his management of the new Verdu Mer construction project. They'd never thrown a party before, but when Raphielli asked what she could do to help, Salvio's only instruction had been to not embarrass him. The prospect of hosting a fancy lunch was exciting, and today instead of wearing her usual black skirt and white blouse, her maid, Rosa, had laid out both of her church dresses so Raphielli could choose which to wear. They'd been given to her by the Dour Doublet, and were both black with round necks, long sleeves, and mid-calf hemlines. She selected the one with the dark green inset panels, thinking it would be nice for the party. Slipping on her black dress shoes, she looked to Rosa for approval.

"Very nice."

About an hour later, Rosa came and found her.

"*Signora,* the party planner has asked that you please come up to the roof."

"They asked for me? Did they say what they want?"

"No." Rosa shrugged. "Perhaps just to meet the lady of the house."

"Oh, that makes sense." Then she felt uneasy. "You don't suppose Salvio will be angry with me for speaking to the party planner, do you?"

"Perhaps if you don't take long with her—just greet her— I think that should be acceptable to him. Her name is Marilynn Bergoni."

Moving through the palazzo, Raphielli saw hired staff rushing in every direction. Big crates were being rolled on carts toward the kitchen at the back of the building, and a piano disappeared into the service elevator. She stood aside, breathing in the perfume as lush topiaries and flower arrangements sailed past, followed closely by racks of crystal stemware making gentle tinkling sounds. Raphielli made her way to the front of the palazzo, where Dante called the formal elevator for her.

When the doors opened on the rooftop deck, she was shocked by the transformation that had taken place. Signora Bergoni had performed magic and made the neglected roof come alive. It looked like a movie set. Now *this* was efficiency! The withered gardens had been replanted with bright flowers, and trees with impossibly green leaves. The gritty marble floors had been polished and now glistened in the sun. Raphielli stepped out into a cheerful hive of activity, and stopped a passing woman in a white smock.

"*Per favore,* where can I find Marilynn Bergoni?"

She pointed to a woman in an exquisite suit with soft caramel hair twisted at the nape of her neck. Raphielli could see the woman was busy directing people, so she approached tentatively.

"Um...Signora Bergoni?" The staff hovering around the party planner stopped, their pens poised above their clipboards.

"*Sì?*" The voice was relaxed and warm, with no hint of irritation at the interruption.

"I understand you wanted to see me. I'm Raphielli Scortini."

The surrounding army of staff paused for a beat to look her over. Marilynn waved her hand, a maestro cueing her players to continue, and stepped forward on beautiful shoes that Raphielli looked down at in admiration.

"Ah, Signora Scortini. It's lovely to meet you." She offered her hand. "Please call me Marilynn."

"Your shoes are..."

"Bruno Magli. You like them?"

"Oh, *sì*."

"They're my favorites! I've admired this shoe ever since seeing them on Christina Onassis."

"Oh, Christina Onassis. My! It's lovely to meet you as well, Marilynn. Please call me Raphielli."

"*Grazie*. I believe you're going to love your party, Raphielli."

"I'm sure I will."

"Is there anything special you require?"

"Require?"

"*Sì*. Your husband didn't give me any specifics. Very unusual. He hired me over the phone, provided invitee names, specifics for the invitations, square footage of the rooftop, and told me to make an impressive party."

"That's unusual?"

"*Sì*. He provided a generous budget and asked that I not call him again."

"Oh, *sì*, that sounds like him." She was relieved that someone else found his behavior odd.

"And it *will* be impressive. But without any direction, I'm throwing a luncheon that pleases *my* tastes. I've selected my favorite foods, flowers, and musicians...but I was wondering if there's anything I can do to make it special for *you*."

"Well, I...no...nothing I can think of."

"Come, I'll show you what we're creating." She slipped her arm around Raphielli's shoulder and walked her across the rooftop to the far side of the space. "Over here we're finishing the dance floor installation, and assembling the bandstand. It will be an outdoor ballroom."

More crates were being rolled past as Marilynn walked her over to where a dining area had been created. They approached the long table set with twenty-four places, covered with layers of white and teal fabric, glossy china, and crystal glassware that made prisms with the sunlight. A team of florists were assembling cheerful arrangements and placing them along the center of the table. Each centerpiece had a small glass candle lantern nested within flowers growing out of a smooth moss disk.

"Raphielli, let's look at the seating chart while I have you here."

Marilynn drew an electronic tablet from under her arm, flicked a fingertip over the surface, and a drawing of the table appeared with names at each place.

"I have your guests arranged alternating the ladies and gentleman, and separating spouses as is customary to promote lively conversation. Is there anyone that you'd like to sit next to?"

Raphielli scanned the names. "No."

Marilynn looked surprised. "You can tell me. I want you to enjoy your meal."

"I don't actually know these people."

"None of them?"

"Well, they attended my wedding, and I've been at some parties at their homes, but I haven't had a chance to get to know them..." Feeling lame, she finished, "Salvio thinks of social events more as business obligations, so he prefers that I not talk much."

Marilynn gave her a conspiratorial wink. "Well, you'll have time today to relax and get to know everyone. Let's go take a look at the party's seating area. Everyone can gather there before luncheon is served, and later when they're not dancing." They walked toward the center of the roof. "Although, trust me, with this band, everyone will be dancing. I promise you."

"I can't believe how you've turned this dusty old roof into a showplace."

"It's what I do." Marilynn looked nonchalant, but Raphielli could tell she was pleased. "We started work at dawn. Landscapers replanted your gardens, carpenters built the bandstand risers, electricians installed a sound system, and your kitchen has been taken over by the chef of Osteria Da Fiore, who is personally creating your meal with his own staff. Your lunch will be incredible." The cool businesswoman pressed a hand to her heart, and she looked transported. "I've selected the most delicious foods you will ever put in your mouth." Then back into business mode, she stated seriously, "Everyone will be talking about your lunch, and anyone who was not invited today will be eager to receive your next invitation." Raphielli felt a moment of concern when Marilynn said, "May I ask where the rest of your household staff are today? Your butler's explanation was so vague."

"Oh, well, when Salvio's parents died, he got rid of the all but three of the staff."

"With a house this size?" Marilynn's jaw dropped. "I can't imagine how that would be possible!"

"He believes that having servants is vulgar."

"I see."

"We have a houseman, too. I've only seen him a handful of times. He keeps the repairs up and reports to Dante."

Marilynn seemed stymied, and abandoned the topic as she pointed. "As you can see, I have a decorator creating a temporary living room for you." Raphielli watched as a beautiful woman wearing high heels and an ultra-tight skirt directed the placement of furniture.

"That's Domina, an interior decorator I've just discovered. She's beyond talented. Soon I'm afraid she'll be so fought-over that I won't be able to book her."

Domina had wild, jet-black curls just like Raphielli's. But instead of being coiled up under a clip, her curls tossed about in the breeze. She paced gracefully back and forth like she was dancing to mambo music only she could hear. Her arms directed the men like a traffic cop, and bangles shimmied along her wrists. Domina was enjoying her work.

It all seemed so unreal. Raphielli tried to picture sitting up here on that white upholstery with guests, everyone enjoying the rooftop view of the lagoon. The space had been made cozy with partitions here and there which were hung with colorful silk curtains that billowed in the warm breezes.

Suddenly Salvio appeared and walked straight over to the dining table. Marilynn beckoned Raphielli to follow as she trailed him.

"Signor Scortini, I'm Marilynn Bergoni. I'm so pleased to..."

Salvio ignored her as he began snatching up place cards and dropping them onto different plates.

The two women drew near, and Marilynn said, "If you had a seating order in mind, we would have been happy to take care of that."

He walked around her to the other end of the table, dropped cards onto plates, and was about to depart when Raphielli commented on his changes.

"You don't want to sit with the Falconettis and the Mayor?"

Salvio spun toward her. "This isn't a party, it's a strategic event. I need to sit with the men who own the demolition and infrastructure businesses to plan the first stages of Verdu Mer. I have no need of the mayor's ear when I work with the Pope, and I won't need Falconetti's marble finishes for at least a year from now. Falconetti's only invited today because he's got a big mouth and will talk about my appointment to anyone who'll listen."

"What about alternating the men and women?" Raphielli blinked at the odd grouping of women he'd placed in the middle of the table by themselves. She didn't want to abandon what Marilynn had just taught her.

He snapped, "I don't care what you do at your end of the table." With that, he hurried away without a single comment on the renovations.

Marilynn's face was a mask of professionalism as she turned to Raphielli.

"Let's see, what else do we need to discuss? Oh, *sì*. We have a mixologist who makes the best drinks. I thought you'd find *limoncello* refreshing on this warm day."

"I don't know. I don't drink."

"Not at all?"

"No. Just water."

"Well, I don't want to give you something that would make you tipsy. That would be embarrassing. I'll have him make you a delicious lemon drink...maybe shaken with a bit of verbena and mixed with sweetened seltzer. How does that sound?"

Raphielli stared in awe at this woman who could concoct something like that on the spot, like some sort of fairy godmother creating a dream for her.

"I'd like a glass of that, I'm sure."

They walked back to where they'd started. The staff was eyeing their boss, hoping for her attention. By way of wrapping up their meeting, Marilynn said, "I'll be here. If you think of anything, just ask one of my staff and we'll try to make it happen. Now, I mustn't keep you. I'm sure you'll want to go get ready."

Looking down at her dress and slightly scuffed shoes, Raphielli replied, "I *am* ready." She sensed she'd said something wrong when she saw Marilynn stiffen, and rushed to explain. "I really only have dresses for church."

"Oh, well, what's good enough for God is more than good enough for your guests." She smiled reassuringly. "But you know, with these rooftop breezes you really should have something soft to float around you, to add a bit of drama. Perhaps a pop of color, don't you think?"

She was already unwinding a sumptuous silk scarf from around her own neck and stepped close to tie it softly around Raphielli's. The silk was a weightless flow of the entire green color palette that drifted out behind her.

"Please, if I can't do anything special for you, then accept this as my gift."

Raphielli had been cloistered without glamorous possessions, but she wasn't dumb. She was aware that

Marilynn was dressing her up, and she was grateful for the generosity.

"You're very kind. *Grazie.*"

"It's my pleasure."

Turning, Marilynn broke the spell as she spoke up, "On the double now, everyone! We're racing the clock until the first guests arrive!"

Less than two hours later the luncheon was under way, and Raphielli was in heaven. She was flanked on her right by Venice's Mayor Massimo Buonocore and his wife, Elene. On Raphielli's left were Venice's marble magnate, Marco Falconetti, and his wife, Agata. It was exciting to have people in the palazzo. This afternoon it felt like a grand home rather than the dreary mausoleum it usually was. And so Raphielli found herself having the time of her life. Everyone at her end of the table sat enjoying themselves in the early fall air, and Raphielli was able to hear about the latest plays, books, and gossip. Up at the head of the table, Salvio looked intense and he never stopped talking.

It was a rare chance to enjoy the foods she always craved; rich pastas with exotic sauces, succulent seafood, and colorful salads. Her daily meals were so limited, based on Salvio's interpretation of what Jesus and his disciples would have eaten. Therefore, she and Salvio subsisted on plain food with absolutely no seasoning; just grains, watery vegetables, and small oily fish. At times Raphielli wondered if Salvio had any taste for food at all. She took a bite of the baked spider crab, and tried to imprint its flavor on her memory.

Marco looked at her as if he was impressed. "Raphielli, what a pleasure to get to know you. I love your sense of humor."

"*Grazi*, Marco. But I'm enjoying this party more than a hostess should, I believe." She laughed lightly.

"You're positively beaming, my dear." Elene reached out and patted her hand. "Such a shame we never see you. Salvio keeps you too closeted. When we arrived I asked him why we never see you, and he said he's not a man who likes his young bride to be on display. In February you didn't attend carnival's masquerade season, and there were twenty big parties for you to choose from."

"Well, Salvio doesn't care for parties..." *What am I saying? My own wedding reception left me sitting with the Dour Doublet accepting congratulations from strangers, while Salvio complained that he'd been expecting the Pope and pestered Cardinal Negrali. Some party.*

Elene addressed her husband. "Massimo, can't you demand that Salvio let Raphielli accept our dinner invitations when we send them? She's a Scortini, it's expected of her."

The mayor gave her a doubtful look, but nodded. "I'll mention it."

Elene turned back to her. "Speaking of staying in, I have a portrait artist who could rival Titian! You *must* sit for a painting to add some warmth to this palazzo. None of the Scortini women on these walls have your classic beauty."

The mayor glanced down to the other end of the table, apparently concerned that Salvio may have heard his wife slighting Salvio's late mother and all the women in the Scortini family tree.

Marco added, "I understand your husband's plight, but I'd get a certain thrill having a woman like you represent my manhood in society." He patted his wife's sleek shoulder. "Agata is my greatest pride and joy."

"Ah, I'm a close second to our son, Reynaldo." She nodded indulgently. "Your husband will eventually loosen his grip and allow you a social life. Young love settles down, you'll see."

If they only knew. He doesn't love me. Bringing herself back from that dark thought, she realized she'd missed an announcement that Marco had just made. He held his glass up for a toast.

"Let's drink to Reynaldo."

"To Reynaldo!" The people at her end of the table raised their glasses. "Much success!"

Catching Salvio's look of irritation from the head of the table, Raphielli felt her heart lurch, and her smile disappeared. She knew he didn't like her to talk, but what was she supposed to do? It wasn't as if the guests at this end of the table were going to sit silently and try to eavesdrop on him at the other end of the table. Was he angry the mayor was drinking a toast to someone else?

She was relieved when Salvio's attention abruptly turned to Guiseppe, who was approaching the dining area with an envelope. Salvio motioned for him to go instead to the greenhouse over beyond the gardens. He pushed back from the table, hurried to the greenhouse, and entered it with Guiseppe. The guests paid no attention to his departure, and carried on talking. Raphielli listened to Marco's news of Reynaldo's marble artistry, but she watched what was happening in the greenhouse as casually as she could manage. She saw Salvio rip open the envelope, read the message, and then go rigid with fury. He clutched the paper and raised it over his head.

Oh, no! Not a scene! This isn't happening! She thought miserably.

With lightning speed he heaved forward, slamming his fists down on a table of potted plants. A tin of soil went flying, and from Guiseppe's attempts to brush at his face, apparently a spray of dirt had hit him. With his arms outstretched like a blind man, Salvio spun around in an arc, sweeping pots and watering cans off the work surface. At the luncheon table a few heads turned, but no one paid much attention. The music, animated conversation, and laughter obscured his remote hysterics. Terrified, Raphielli took a deep breath and held it as she watched Salvio stalk to the far side of the greenhouse and disappear toward the service elevator.

Guiseppe made his way over to her and murmured next to her ear, "*Signore* has asked me to tell you he has been called away on behalf of the Pope."

"Oh, my goodness. Was that a letter from the Pope?" she whispered.

"No, *signora*."

⚜

Salvio speed-walked through the stone lanes of the *sestiere*, heading for the Chiesa d'Oro. Verona was trying to steal Venice from him, but he was in for a rude awakening if he thought Salvio was going to allow it—to simply put his hands up like some little old lady handing over her pearls. If he hurried, the College of Cardinals would still be in session. His rushed arrival would lend urgency to his request, and the cardinals would have to take what he said more seriously. But it wouldn't do for him to simply insist that they pressure the Pope on his behalf; he had to give them some probable cause. His mind spun wildly, trying to come up with a strategy that would make them choose him over Verona.

But first he'd have to get past the two ancient administrators who'd been sitting at their post outside the inner sanctum doors since he was a young boy. Salvio attempted to breeze through the entryway, but he was blocked so adroitly they seemed like secret service rather than just two old codgers. He now had two obstacles between himself and the assembled cardinals.

"Signor Scortini, there is no audience with the College of Cardinals today." One of the administrators advanced, causing Salvio to retreat on the stone floor like a piece in a chess game. "They are in private session."

Salvio tried to arrange his expression into an appropriately pious composition. "I know! I have just received a message from the College, and I must see them immediately!" He held up the filthy letter. Seeing the distaste on the old men's faces, he tried to smooth the paper and wipe off the potting soil to show its legitimacy. They remained unimpressed. Unable to contain himself, he broke past them and grabbed hold of the chamber's door latch. It was locked. He turned around and bluffed, "The College and I are in the midst of critical business on behalf of the Pope! You must open this door!"

"Wait here. I will inform them."

Still expressionless, the smaller of the two old priests produced a key from the folds of his robe, and in an eerily evasive move, slipped around Salvio, through the door, and locked it again behind him. The maneuver was so fluid that Salvio would have had to tackle the old fool to get through the door. *I've got to calm down. Injuring one of their administrators—no matter how senile the old codger might be—is no way to get the cardinals on my side.*

Gritting his teeth, Salvio stretched his mouth into a smile even though it was the last thing that felt natural. He was furious and desperate, but the heads of the Catholic Church would find those emotions repellant. He looked at the remaining administrator, who stood staring at him with no expression whatsoever. This made him even more uncomfortable, and his lips stretched a bit wider, revealing his teeth in a way Salvio hoped looked friendly.

The first administrator reappeared and opened the door wide. "Signor Scortini, the College of Cardinals will hear you now."

Salvio pushed past the administrators and strode up the nave. The chairs had been removed, and the cathedral was transformed for the convening of the venerable College. Top cardinals from the most influential dioceses in the world sat stiffly in formal wooden chairs forming a ring around the space. The holy men sat erect, resplendent in their finest cassocks and jewelry, in a timeless theological display worthy of a painting. Salvio refused to be intimidated by the looks of frank annoyance on their faces.

"*Grazie* for seeing me on such short notice, your most gracious Eminences—"

"*Senza preavviso*. No notice, Scortini!" a strong voice cut him off. It was Cardinal Negrali, the most powerful cardinal in the world. He was seated on an impressive throne in line with the altar. "You have interrupted sacred business with no notice. We have just sent you our written conclusion." The usually gentle man raised his voice in a formal decree that filled the chamber. "We are in unanimous support of the Pope's decision to award Verdu Mer to Count Verona. The College of Cardinals is unwilling to revive this matter."

Salvio bowed his head and held up both hands. "Wait! What I have to tell you...well...I couldn't put it in writing or trust it to a messenger! I couldn't go through the formal channels of requesting an audience with the College, for fear of Gabrieli Verona's spies catching wind of it. I, myself, I'm reeling from the discovery!"

The entire assembly of cardinals leaned forward in their seats. He'd gotten their full attention when he uttered the name Verona.

"I've always been a champion of Verona's. Gabrieli and I couldn't be closer...we're like brothers."

Negrali's expression was doubtful. "I had no idea you two were close."

"Oh, *sì*! We're...like brothers! Our families have grown together through the ages, forming the very roots of our great Venice. But now...I've uncovered...the awful truth."

Salvio looked at the inquisitive eyes and rapt attention on each holy man's face, but he couldn't think of a single action, or even a rumor, he could exploit against Verona.

"What on earth are you talking about, Scortini?" Cardinal Negrali's voice was choked.

"I'm here to tell you that I'm the only man fit to bear the solemn responsibility of Verdu Mer, as...Verona...he..." Salvio stalled. Unable to meet their eyes, he looked up at the painted ceiling and blinked back tears of frustration at his ineffectiveness. "Oh...all I can say is that Verona is *unfit.*"

"Count Verona, unfit?" Negrali gasped. "Is his health not sound? What is the affliction?" Color drained from each cardinal's face, and there was a flutter of hands as they crossed themselves.

Salvio wrung his hands to keep them from shaking. "Oh no, your Eminence, it's his *character* that's unfit. His repugnant sins...they've morally corrupted him and affected his mind as well. So thoroughly has Verona demonstrated to me that he is unfit, I suspect that his claimed faith in God is nothing but a mask he wears to gain your protection. He's exploiting the Catholic Church!"

"*Basta!* Enough!" Negrali held up his hand. "You are incorrect, Scortini. What has he done?"

"Now isn't the time...I can't tell you quite yet. But when I bring you proof—that Verona is unfit and his family is no longer even remotely devout to the Catholic faith—I want your promise to ask our Holy Father to give *me* the Verdu Mer commission."

Around the chamber, stunned looks were exchanged, and every single eyebrow was elevated. Negrali placed his fingertips together and looked soberly at Salvio.

"Before we consider revisiting your request for stewardship of the project, you must bring us proof of what you find distressing with regard to Count Verona."

Warming to the distant glimmer of hope, he nodded. "I will bring you the horrible truth. I beg that you carefully guard my secret visit to you. I'm afraid Verona has become dangerous."

Salvio turned and hurried out of the church, leaving behind a very disturbed group of holy men.

How has Verona managed to blind them all? Venice belongs in the hands of a Scortini! I'm going to knock that perceived halo off Verona's head and right onto the Pope's foot! I'll find someone to unearth that family's secrets. They pretend to be so perfect, but inside there is rot!

He didn't want to return home to a crowd of luncheon guests, but he wasn't sure where to go. Unlike the Veronas with their pretentious office building, the Scortinis had always run Venice from their palazzo. So he headed to la Biblioteca Nazionale Marciana to think, and on the way, it came to him. Of course! He'd hire a private investigator! He'd get that man who was always bringing down corrupt politicians. What was his name? Alphonso Vitali! It would be easy for Vitali to discover the nasty weakness Verona was hiding, and the Pope would see that he's not someone to be trusted with a sacred commission like Verdu Mer. Salvio was sick to the point of retching at the way the Pope favored Verona. It was as if the two of them were on first name terms or something. He chuckled at the ridiculous idea of someone being a regular friend of His Holiness. Ha! A good laugh.

———••)•———

Pope Leopold XIV was enjoying tea with his best friend, Gabrieli, in one of the sitting rooms of the Verona palazzo. Casimir was wearing tailored shirt vestments over soft cotton chino pants. He was completely devoted to the Church—body, mind, and spirit—yet in private he saw no need to abandon the pants that had been his favorites since his boyhood in Lublin, Poland.

Casimir secretly stayed with the Veronas whenever his papal schedule allowed, and he was spending quite a bit of time in Venice now that the College of Cardinals was in session here, and the Verdu Mer project was finally under way. Living with the Veronas was incredibly grounding, and his personal security team loved the time they spent here. The palace was a veritable fortress, and no one but the Verona family and their loyal staff knew he was in residence. Popes had been secret guests of the Veronas as far back as he had been able to trace.

Casimir's relationship with this special family began just as all the other popes' had. The late Count Fabrizo Verona had been like a second father to him, and his son, Gabrieli, was like a brother. He relied on their excellent judgment, strong character, and unshakable faith in the Church. They were a fountain of love and strength that replenished him without fail.

No one knew the exact time in history when the Verona family first began supporting popes, but Casimir had seen a holy relic in a secret chamber below the Vatican that depicted images of Pope Callixtus the First and a Verona. It bore an etched description: "*Saint Callixtus traveling with the Verona from the Iberian Peninsula to Rome for his inauguration.*" So he knew his best friend's family had assisted the papacy since at least the third century. With no concrete proof, Casimir personally believed there must have been a Verona at the time of Jesus the Christ. It just made sense to him that when the Messiah made St. Peter "the Rock" upon which His church was built, He gave Peter a Verona to support him. The idea was comforting.

Traditionally upon the death of a pope, the College of Cardinals undertakes the election process of a new pope. And while Veronas never hold an office of the Church, they are always secretly consulted during the evaluation process. The cardinals universally respect the Veronas, and each new pope naturally gravitates to them as his adopted family. As he undertakes his awesome responsibility, he allows the Veronas to know, support, and nurture him, as everyone else on earth—even his biological family—falls back to a degree. Each pope forms a natural dependence upon the Veronas, who have intimate knowledge of the papal duties and pressures, and who are literally born to understand him.

When Casimir became Pope Leopold XIV, he spent two weeks with the Veronas in their household in Rome. Deep in contemplation and reflection, they'd spent days discussing all of his emotions and hopes. As often as he sought advice from Gabrieli, Casimir also sought support from Gabrieli's stalwart wife, Contessa Juliette, and their brilliant son, Vincenzo. Vincenzo's gift for making inspired financial investments was only matched by his philanthropy, which was positively awe-inspiring.

Casimir looked across the table at his best friend and mused, "Last night I saw the new homes of Verdu Mer in a dream, and they had the most graceful arching design." He traced the shape in the air with his hand. "It was so vivid."

Gabrieli put down his teacup. "Sounds nice. Can you sketch it for me, Casimir?"

"Sì. Good idea." He tapped the table and nodded happily. "Before it fades from my mind, I will get paper and pencil."

"I'll call for some." Gabrieli reached to pull a corded bell for an assistant.

"Oh, no. You know I like to write in my notebook with special paper." He hopped up from the table and waved excitely. "Be right back! Oh! I have a clear picture still in my head." He moved off down the splendidly carpeted corridor to his private suite, a haven of green and gold silk furnished with antiques made of burnished alder wood. He crossed the room and leaned over his desk, scooped up his personal notebook, and then returned to Gabrieli.

"Now, let me see if I can put the design onto paper..." As he bent over the book and began sketching, Gabrieli came around to Casimir's side of the table and watched the sketch began to take shape.

"In my dream, Verdu Mer was really so beautiful. These houses were so...*inviting*...and I had the awareness that they were energy efficient."

"Well, the consortium's architectural team has rejected all the housing designs they've received so far. Apparently each design had flaws, so we've extended a new submission deadline to architects." Glancing at his watch, he said, "Oh! And now I must be off. I have a meeting with Chizzoli and his underwater trench team."

Casimir looked up from his sketch. "You do know I am elated that Verdu Mer is finally underway..."

"*Sì*..." Gabrieli paused. "Of course."

"I have been weighed down recently...but it has nothing to do with how the consortium is performing..."

"What is it, Casimir?"

"This disquiet that has sapped my enthusiasm these past days...it is Salvio Scortini's recent demand to be given the project."

"*Sì*, but we both know Salvio's never been involved in any business of any sort. Even Salvatore never worked with him. You've made the right choice."

"But more than that, I am ashamed to say that on the few occasions when he has been in my presence...even though I have not been able to put my finger on any word or action...I have felt disturbed by him. This feeling of unease has been persistent, making it impossible for me to remain true to the established Vatican relationship with the Scortini family."

"I share your opinion. But unlike you, I have had several distinctly...bizarre... interactions with him, going back from the time he was young and our fathers worked closely together. I don't think Salvio even respects the Venetian building establishment. So there's no way you could consider him to helm Verdu Mer. It would be a disaster. The residents of that decrepit neighborhood have endured enough hardship living in ruins for decades. They shouldn't have to endure mismanagement during reconstruction."

Casimir bent over his sketchbook again and came to the heart of the matter. "I do not like to be challenged in this way. It requires me to set aside theological matters on behalf of political efforts."

"It's wise to set aside things that take you away from your holy duties." He gave Casimir's shoulder a gentle squeeze. "Now I really must be going. I'll see you at dinner tonight."

Moments after Gabrieli left, Juliette and Vincenzo came into the sitting room. Casimir always appreciated their natural blend of calm-yet-vibrant energy. And despite the fact that he'd known him from birth, he was continually startled by Vincenzo's physical beauty; he was unlike anyone he'd ever seen. Except for Vincenzo's wife, Giselle—now *that* girl was positively angelic. Casimir couldn't wait for them to have a baby and make him the happiest godfather in history.

Vincenzo approached, waving his phone. "Oh, Papa! You won't believe the design for Verdu Mer's new water system!"

Looking at Vincenzo's phone, he kidded, "You want me to make a call?"

"No, just tap here. Chizzoli just sent us an animation of his 3D model."

Casimir poked the screen and watched as a deceptively simple-looking system of locks and channels moved water in great volumes. While he was engrossed in the video, Juliette and Vincenzo perused his drawings.

"Papa, these are beautiful." Vincenzo gestured to them. "What are they?"

"I had a dream of the houses at Verdu Mer." He stepped between mother and son, and the three of them studied the sketches. "And this is what came to me."

"What are these halos?"

"I saw soft glowing lights on the houses."

"Rather more graceful than the typical Venetian-style home," Juliette remarked.

Vincenzo added, "And a vast improvement over the current hovels that lean so dangerously in that *sestiere.* Growing up, that was the only area of Venice I was never allowed to go."

Juliette shuddered. "That was for your safety. One afternoon when I was pregnant with you, I was walking past the neighborhood when a building collapsed, crushing six people." She crossed herself. "Not to mention what happened to poor Leonardo. I'll never be so relieved as when it is all rebuilt. No more threat of a piece of rooftop cracking a passerby on the head, or someone falling from inside their home into the canal." Pointing at Casimir's drawings, she nodded decisively. "Gabrieli's consortium is looking for new housing designs. You should send this to them right away."

Vincenzo agreed. "At least to test the viability of your concept for general housing."

"Not *my* concept. It came in a dream, so I will have to offer it to them as divine inspiration."

Juliette gave that a moment's thought and nodded. "That may not be fair to the other architects. How can the consortium do anything but accept God's Dream House as the winner?" She turned away from the drawing. "Now, I shall prepare my squid ink *linguine* for lunch. Casimir, are you coming to the kitchen to assist me?"

He loved cooking, and he'd learned some of his favorite recipes at Juliette's side. "There is nothing I would rather do right now. Let me change my shirt."

"I will go and get started with the preparation."

"Can we make the *calamari fritti,* too?"

"*Sì,* I have just gotten beautiful squid from the Rialto market."

———⊕———

Raphielli was relieved when the luncheon continued in an even lighter mood after Salvio's departure. No one seemed to miss her volatile husband. She thoroughly enjoyed the day, and especially the dancing when Mayor Buonocore decided to serve as bandleader. The musicians played song after song that had everyone on the dance floor, which was set between shimmering topiaries. She'd never danced before—it had never been allowed in the abbey, and Salvio had forbidden it at their wedding—but she learned quickly and danced to every song. No one considered leaving the party until after they'd savored the last bites of sweets, and the sun was setting. They were all lightly bronzed by the afternoon sun, and faintly tired from dancing in the rooftop breezes.

After accompanying her guests downstairs and saying her final goodbyes, Raphielli pressed her back to the elaborately carved wood door of her home, and relished all the warm kisses that had been pressed onto her cheeks. What she wouldn't give to have married a man who kissed her. The vitality draining from her body, she felt older than her twenty years as she walked down the hall to her suite.

She sat in her dark bedroom, the wrought iron lamps high up on the stone walls providing only small pools of light. Her windows didn't have much of a view, but she watched the buildings across the water change color in the final glow of sunset. She found herself wishing she wasn't ensconced in her late mother-in-law's suite. The shadowy room was exactly as Salvio's mother had left it. It even smelled of her; Gelsonima she had worn heavy musk perfume. Raphielli concentrated on recalling the delightful afternoon and the companionship of her guests.

When Rosa entered the room carrying rubbing alcohol, metal scrapers, cotton pads, and a red ribbon to prepare Raphielli for her wifely duty, her spirits sank. Rosa carried everything into the bathroom and began to run a bath that would be almost too hot to bear. So, Salvio had returned home and sent her maid to begin all the strange ministrations he required before he would visit her. *Tonight while he does his worst to me, my mind will be dancing on the roof with my friends. And no matter what happens, I won't make the mistake of looking him in the eye.*

Alphonso Vitali wanted to get the meeting over with. As soon as he'd gotten off the phone with Salvio, he'd started digging into Count Gabrieli Verona's activities. He had emailed his initial report to Scortini, who now sat in silence at his enormous desk, leaving Alphonso to study his peeved profile. So Alphonso took the opportunity to do just that. He was used to all manner of client requiring his investigative services, and was adept at uncovering their motives for hiring him. This old-world tycoon was trying to appear as if he was studying the report, but his eyes weren't tracking appropriately; they were just scanning around the computer screen. So this was a ploy to make him wait, an effort to intimidate him. And why would a client want to intimidate someone he'd hired? Because he was insecure. Alphonso wished he was sitting almost anywhere else than in this big, spooky mansion across from a client who disliked him. Alphonso's instincts about people made him an extremely effective private investigator, but he didn't need any great powers of perception to see that this titan of Venice was on the verge of a tantrum. *Ah. He finally turned his head.*

"Signor Vitali, I hired you because of your reputation for uncovering the hidden vices of powerful men. But your initial findings are unacceptable. Only an imbecile would expect me to believe that you've found no evidence of illicit activities during your investigation of Verona. Are you being bribed by him?"

Alphonso became hyper-alert when he saw the look in Scortini's eyes. They were flat, but also a bit unhinged. He'd never gotten into an altercation with a client and didn't want to risk provoking this one, so he let the "imbecile" comment slide.

"I'm not taking any money from Verona, and as I said, these are my initial findings. An investigation like this takes time and finesse."

Scortini leaned forward and came out of his chair slowly, then advanced around the corner of the desk toward Alphonso. He was small compared to Alphonso's height and mass, but he had a certain creepy menace.

"Have I heard you correctly? You came here to inform me that you have yet to earn any of the money I generously advanced you? And did you just claim you need more time to *finesse?*" His voice shifted into a rude tone. "I have abandoned my assumption that you would know a moral transgression if it hit you in the middle of your oversized forehead. Verona has a wife and a son whose illicit activities could be exposed, and by extension, Verona himself would be accountable."

Alphonso kept his expression respectful. "Understood."

Scortini pointed at the door by way of dismissal and shouted, "Find the dirt that I know they're hiding, and be quick about it! The Pope himself is relying on me to prevent a monumental scandal, *you mongoloid!*"

Alphonso got up and left, hoping to make it out of the building before he lost his temper. A trembling valet joined him in the hall and showed him to the front door. The little man needed a prescription for his nerves, and Scortini needed a punch in the face. Alphonso was a patient man who prided himself on his cool head, but *damn,* he wanted to grab Scortini by his rigid-looking lapels and demand an apology. How did he expect Alphonso to believe he'd been hired to do anything other than find a way to blackmail Count Verona? Surely Scortini didn't expect him to be that stupid. Verona was the royal son of Venice, but it wasn't Alphonso's responsibility to preserve that reputation. If there was dirt to be found, he'd find it and hand it over to Scortini—and the sooner the better. He needed to bring on some help, and his cousin Zelph might be just the man.

Zelph had always been shrewd in a street-savvy sort of way, and he was making a real effort to outgrow his hotheaded ways. Alphonso decided to feel him out, so he walked in the direction of his uncle's apartment over in the Castello *sestiere.* The walk had the effect of calming his temper, so he felt cool-headed when he buzzed his uncle's bell.

Zelph opened the door. "Hey, Cuz. *Come va?*"

"I've got a big job, and I could use your help." Alphonso squeezed past him and headed straight to the kitchen to talk business. The cousins were both built like bulls, and the slim hallway barely accommodated their broad shoulders.

Closing the door and following, Zelph was clearly excited. "That's really good news, because this afternoon Pim sent that scar-faced lieutenant over to make sure I hadn't skipped town without paying. Did you get a visit, too?"

"I haven't been home. I've been busy all over the islands since yesterday with this new job."

"I tried to talk to this guy, to get him to see he was working for a dirty cheat, but he said that poker game was fair and square."

"Don't talk to any of Pim's people. If we'd known he rigged games, we'd never have been in that tournament. Now we just need to pay him off so he'll forget about us."

Alphonso sat in one of the old cane kitchen chairs and regarded his cousin sitting across from him. It was like looking in a mirror. They both had long, dark hair, dark eyes, strong jaws, the same shade of olive skin, and both tall enough to have to duck under doors in Venice where they were born. Their personalities were where they differed. Alphonso was more of a kind-hearted homebody, while Zelph was always prowling the *calles* looking for action. Zelph was shrewd, energetic, and alert, skills he'd honed over years of being more than a bit shady.

"So, what's the job?" Zelph leaned forward on his elbows. "Tell me it's something big enough to pay off Pim."

"It's big enough to pay him, including his outrageous interest."

"I'm in! What's the split?"

"We'll do the work fifty-fifty, and that's how we'll split the pay."

"Deal!"

"Let me bring you up to speed." Alphonso told him how he'd been hired by Scortini to find dirt on Count Gabrieli Verona.

"Hmm...the two big families of Venice? So you've been hired by the big builder to spy on Venice's favorite son?"

"Well... *sì.*"

"The builder wants to blackmail the count?"

He was gratified at his cousin's immediate grasp of the situation. "Looks like it, and we've got a fat expense allowance that I insisted on getting up front."

"Cash?"

"Of course, cash. But after following Gabrieli, digging through business affairs, financial records, and the rumor mill, I've got *nada* on him."

"What if there's nothing to find?"

Alphonso rapped his knuckles gently on the scarred wooden tabletop. "We've got to get something on the Veronas to get our money."

"Yeah, okay. So he wants blackmail ammunition. Does he care if it's the younger count or the older count? It shouldn't matter to him, right?"

"Right. Gabrieli or Vincenzo, who spends a lot of time in Paris. I can tell Scortini's ultimate goal is to humiliate the father, but exposing his son, or even his wife, would be useful. So let's outline our surveillance plan and get to work."

"Thanks for giving me this chance, Alphonso. I can do this. I'll find any dirty laundry there is. I know I haven't always been reliable in the past, but you gotta believe I've changed. I've put gambling behind me, and I'm starting a new life."

Alphonso reached across the table and gripped Zelph's forearm. "Hey, Cuz, you gotta be straight up on this job. This is all mixed up with powers we don't mess with. You hear me? I've already done some very thorough online sleuthing. I went through a ton of records on the Veronas and the Scortinis, and these old families go way back...like to the beginning of record keeping. But there are references to, like, the beginning of time if I interpreted correctly. And while I can't put my finger on it, I can feel something's wrong here. Scortini made it sound like secret characters in the Vatican, and even the Pope, are involved."

"I'll focus on making our client happy." Zelph raised his hands in emphasis. "I won't fuck up this job. I promise you."

Alphonso sighed heavily and hunched forward, putting his elbows on the table. "I wouldn't have taken this job if I had any idea this Scortini was off his beam. But how could I have known? I don't investigate the *client*."

Zelph sighed, too. "Look, we'll find whatever dirt there is on the Veronas, and Scortini can do whatever he wants with it. When we're done with this job, we're straight with Pim, and then we can have a fresh start without lieutenants threatening to kill us."

They got down to business and formed their game plan. Alphonso would familiarize himself with the son, Vincenzo, and the count's wife, Contessa Juliette, while Zelph would take over spying on Count Gabrieli.

Alphonso got into the particulars. "Having you tail Gabrieli is like giving you a babysitting job. There doesn't appear to be anything illegal or exciting in the count's life. You won't even have the temptation of fast driving because he mostly stays in Venice. He typically travels on foot or at a leisurely boating pace through the canals. He mixes with people during walks to his appointments, and after following him for a day, he doesn't seem to make any effort to move secretly or evade anyone, even on his nightly walks near his palace. He has a bodyguard, a guy named Tiberius, who takes his job seriously. He's in his mid-thirties, has all the credentials of elite training, and he walks around with the smug satisfaction of knowing he's guarding a man who has nothing to fear."

Zelph was taking notes as Alphonso continued to bring him up to speed.

"The Veronas' lives are transparent if you care to look—and we're gonna be looking. But unlike the criminals I've tailed in the past, the Verona family does their business out in the open. Gabrieli moves among people who apparently love him, and they act like awestruck fans. It's a strange lifestyle to witness, and you're gonna find it even stranger when you go to ask questions. People are so eager with their answers."

Zelph stopped writing and looked up. "Explain."

"In my experience, if I ask a barber what a Mafioso was doing in his barbershop, the barber goes hopelessly deaf and dumb, even if the soldier was just getting an innocent haircut. But when I ask anyone what a Verona is up to, people offer up everything they know, and in great detail."

"How nice of them. That's very convenient for us."

"Just remember what kind of powerful people we're investigating so you don't ask the wrong person the wrong question."

"I'll be careful."

"I don't need you tripping Scortini's hair trigger." Alphonso found it hard not to lecture his previously wayward cousin.

"Don't worry about me."

———◦◉◦———

A week after meeting her new Ukrainian friends, Giselle was alone with Ivar in the brick-walled garden behind his old building. She really liked the charming old man, so when he called and asked her to visit, she came immediately. He sat on an old stool, dressed in grey work clothes, tying vines onto a trellis. Comfortably warmed by the fall sun, Giselle moved around the garden. Heeding Ivar's advice about not wearing form-fitting couture outfits around Markus, and just on the off chance she would see him during this visit, she wore crisp, mandarin-orange capris with an Aztec-blue silk blouse and matching blue suede sandals. Her ropes of eighteenth-century gold trinkets made soft clattering sounds occasionally as she hovered over Ivar, holding twine and assisting him with his chore.

"I know you have preparations to make before your trip, so thank you for coming to see me." He waved his hand around the garden. "Giselle, you know I do not ask you here to help with picking vegetables." He seemed pleased when she nodded solemnly. "I arranged for Markus to go on an errand so I could talk to you. He has never been so happy since you have come here to watch him work and talk with him. And we have enjoyed having you in our home to share meals with us. But having you so close to Markus has been an unfortunate distraction for him. He should be dating and meeting eligible women. Last night as I watched him say goodbye to you, it made me feel that something more needed to be said."

She waited patiently.

"I know you could see he was not himself yesterday, and I do not believe you were fooled by his hearty well-wishes for your trip." Ivar let down the vines, and motioned for her to pull up a chair and sit beside him. He looked at her seriously and sighed. "You leave tomorrow, and this has made him very sad."

"I've been thinking that I'll miss him, too. I haven't known how to ask, but I'd like Markus to come to the country and help me."

"Go away with you to work?" He looked shocked.

"It's the largest sculpture I've ever attempted, and I had planned to do it on my own. But it would be so much easier if Markus could come along and help me." She plucked a grape from a nearby vine and nibbled it. "I want him to come work with me, but I don't know if I should invite him. Will *you* think it over? And if you decide you approve, would you tell him I'd like him to join me? I depart tomorrow from Gare du Nord on the four o'clock northeasterly train in car number three."

Ivar sat in silence for a moment before he shook his head and sighed. "I must think of what is best for *him*. At this moment, I am thinking I will *not* tell him of your invitation...to give him some time away from you. But I promise you that I will think on it."

"That's all I ask. *Merci*. And now, I hate to rush off, but I really must go." She leaned over and pecked a little kiss on each of Ivar's cheeks before going to the kitchen to say goodbye to Yvania.

Giselle needed to double-check all of her final sculpture preparations before heading back out to meet Vincenzo for dinner. So when she arrived home, she headed straight to her first-floor office. Moving past the antique drafting table and her neat library of sketches, she sat down at the elaborate seventeenth-century desk. It had belonged to the painter, Simon Vouet, and the chubby cherubs crouching on pedestals holding up the corners of the desk always made her smile. Getting down to the task at hand, she consulted her work plan and telephoned Selma, her childhood friend and the caretaker of her home in the country, to check which supplies had been delivered. Next, she called her best friend, Fauve, to tell her what train she'd be taking to Aiglemont tomorrow. When all her preparations were confirmed, she tidied her desk and headed upstairs to get ready for dinner.

After showering, she massaged her favorite Nyakio moisturizing cream onto her face and neck. Then she padded into the dressing room wearing her favorite robe, an opulent gift out of the Verona estate. Originally made for the archduke of Venice, its balanced weight was the ultimate luxury. She was about to shrug it off when she felt it lifted from her shoulders by Marcella, her ever-discreet maid. With her assistance, Giselle slipped into a strapless dress of deep navy blue. It looked quite demure, providing full coverage down to her knees...until she took a step, and then the slits on both sides flashed a daring amount of leg.

Marcella clipped her hair into a twist, then fastened her pearl necklace before laying out her earrings and pumps. Next Marcella slipped a wrap and the dainty strap of her evening purse over Giselle's outstretched arm. Finally, she dispensed the perfect amount of perfume into the air for her to walk through, and Giselle strode out the door. Not fussing with cosmetic or hairstyling rituals allowed Giselle to be ready in no time with only a dab of Bunny Balm on her lips. Thankfully, Vincenzo agreed that she didn't need makeup. She left the house excited to spend a leisurely dinner with him before leaving for the country.

When her car pulled up in front of Le Meurice restaurant, Vincenzo came out to the curb for her. He offered his hand as she stepped out into the glare of photographer's flashes. He slipped his arm around her waist and kissed her.

"Gigi. How was your day?"

They entered the dining room hand in hand. People stopped to look at them and fantasize about love, beauty, and celebrity. Tomorrow's social media would pour over Giselle's clothing and accessories.

5

Markus climbed aboard the moderately crowded four o'clock train, stashed his duffle bag in the luggage rack next to the door, and scanned the first-class car for Giselle. He spotted her sitting with her back to him, and started down the aisle toward her. He paused mid-stride when he caught sight of her face reflected in the train window. Her expression was ecstatic, and he allowed himself a moment to daydream that she was thinking of him. Shaking off the fantasy, he moved forward and swung into the seat across from her.

"I accept your invitation. Now what laws do we break?" He tried to sound casual.

"Markus! I'm so glad you're here!" She rushed forward and gave each of his cheeks a little kiss before bouncing back into her seat.

"I am glad, too. You and I will work very well together."

She looked so polished, wearing a demure cream-and-blue eyelet dress with impeccable cream-colored high-heeled sandals. He couldn't help but notice that while others in the first-class car seemed drab and vaguely disheveled by comparison, this golden goddess sat coolly composed, her tailored dress effortlessly skimming her firm body here and there. He was on an illicit adventure, and he made no effort to hide the enthusiasm he was feeling.

"I have shown you mine." He said seriously. "Now you will show me yours. It is your turn to tell me everything."

"I'm so excited to get started...I feel like I'm vibrating." She released the clip from her hair and tousled the strands with her fingers. "I've been sitting here with my design swirling through my head."

"Tell me about this massive art piece."

"It's called *Star Fall.* I've already made a prototype, but this will be big. It's an arching web made of hollow steel arms, inset with copper curlicues and inter-joined glass spindles." Making delicate movements with her fingers, she outlined the general shapes and patterns in the air for him.

"Glass spindles?"

"*Oui.* Each spindle has two compartments." She glanced around the car, then slipped into the seat next to him and put her lips against his ear. "One compartment contains hydrogen, and the other contains irrodium." It was a whisper that enveloped him in her lovely perfume and made the hairs on his neck tingle. She pulled back and her eyes searched his for a reaction.

He maneuvered to place his mouth to her ear. "This irrodium...it is what is illegal?"

She nodded and her hair stroked against his cheek. "Uh-huh, and when we mix the two chemicals, the vials glow."

"Green like in mad scientist movies?"

"No, a kind of a blush-rose color."

"It sounds beautiful. Is it dangerous?"

She pulled back and waved her hand dismissively. "We can't get any on us."

"Then we will be careful. So, we are going to your real home?"

She relaxed against him and took his hand, which made him feel more excited than he cared to admit. Intertwining her fingers naturally with his, she looked contentedly out the window.

"Uh-huh, I was born there. It's been in my family for generations. But everyone else is gone now, so it's mine."

"To pass down to your children."

"Uh-huh."

"What happened to your family?"

"If it's all right with you, I'd prefer not to talk about it."

"Let us talk about something else, then. I have never seen your hair down before."

"Mmm...right, I normally wear it up. Do you like it?"

"Very much."

"You're really good at changing the subject." She smiled and ran a hand through her hair.

"So I still have a hope of finding a wife?" He knew he was being self-deprecating, but he couldn't resist.

"With skills like changing the subject smoothly? Absolutely." She laughed and nodded.

The train picked up speed as it left the city behind, and Markus felt like a schoolboy, giddy to be holding a girl's hand. He recalled the last woman he'd taken to bed, and realized he was more excited at this moment than he had been while actually having sex. He had better keep his wits about him, and remember Giselle was only friend material.

He enjoyed passing the time on the train talking about art. The subject could have gotten tiresome for any other two people, but he found that she was endlessly engrossed in all manner of artistic style and expression. When he tried to change the subject she became monosyllabic and then maneuvered the conversation back to art. He barely glanced over to register the splendor of the Champagne region's landscape racing by just outside the windows.

It was early evening when they arrived in Aiglemont. The old station was nestled amidst a handful of quaint eighteenth-century buildings connected by stone lanes. Markus retrieved his bag and discovered that Giselle was only traveling with a little purse. Stepping onto the platform, he found a porter and claimed the wooden chest he had checked, before he and Giselle left the station together. Her happiness was contagious, and he found himself feeling buoyant and free as he walked alongside her.

"So, what's in the wooden box?" She arched a brow at him.

"My glass cutters, lead wire...you know...art supplies."

"A man after my own heart."

"*Da.* Like you, I am always working on something. Where is your irrodium? You did not have it shipped with the rest of your supplies, did you?"

"No, the spindles are in an insulated case that was delivered to my home by a courier company that specializes in transporting dangerous live specimens."

"Live specimens?"

"Oh, you know…viruses, vipers…dangerous things."

"I cannot even think of how much insurance one of those couriers would need to have."

"Probably a lot."

Just steps from the station, they ducked into a building that functioned as a hotel and restaurant. Staff members called out, "*Bienvenue,* Giselle," as they went about their business. A man who looked to be in his thirties and a dark-haired woman in her twenties were behind the counter, working and chatting. They looked up as Markus and Giselle entered, and Giselle called out, "*Salut!* Henri! Fauve!"

"Ah! Giselle! Let me get your keys!" Henri cried as he simultaneously blushed, sucked in his gut, and tried to look taller. Fauve darted around the counter, grabbed Giselle, and spun her around in a hug.

"*B'jour, chérie!* I told the gang you've invited us over for cards tomorrow. Oh! And you've got to hear the latest news! I swear marriages are ending left, right, and center around here!"

Henri approached. "Not all marriages can be as solid as Giselle and Vinny's." He planted a friendly kiss on Giselle's lips. "Now, you two are a couple for the ages."

Fauve stopped her verbal barrage when she noticed Markus. "Well, hello there. Are you with Giselle?" When he nodded, she looked him over from head to toe and glanced back to Giselle, silently communicating her appreciation. "I'm Fauve," she reached for his hand, "Giselle's best friend. And you are...?"

"Markus. *Enchanté,* Fauve."

Holding his hand, she reached for his bicep and pretended she wasn't checking him out as she appraised him with her hands. Giselle took the keys from Henri and stepped over to make introductions.

"Fauve, Henri, this is Markus. He's an artist I've been studying. He's going to help me with my sculpture."

Markus smiled. "*Bonjour,* Henri."

"Judging from the sheer number of crates and the stacks of metal Giselle's had delivered up at her château, it's going to be enormous." Henri stepped forward to shake his hand. "Call me, I'll help if you need me. And don't let her get hurt. Her property's a long way from a doctor."

Markus nodded.

"We're going to go get settled." Giselle started toward the door and waved the keys. "See you tomorrow night."

"*Oui, bonsoir!*" they called back.

Markus followed Giselle back out into the warm evening and watched as she paused on the sidewalk just outside the hotel to kick off her heels. She picked them up and walked barefoot, swinging her shoes by her side in a loose-limbed way that was touchingly childlike. He followed her around the back of the building and into a garage where she unlocked a huge, old Renault truck that seemed vaguely military. This was turning into his kind of adventure.

She had seemed happier on the train than she'd been since Markus had met her. Then, another layer of reserve had fallen away when they arrived at the station. And now, at the door of this antique truck, she was a woman he didn't know. She handed him her Prada sandals, hiked up the hem of her dress, climbed into the cab, and bounced lightly on the worn leather seat.

Carrying her shoes he moved around the back of the truck and as he dropped his luggage into a cargo slot in the truck's flatbed, she turned the key and revved the big engine. He walked around to the passenger side and climbed in. Giselle backed the monster truck out of the cramped stone garage and into the alley with one masterful movement, then fluidly shifted from reverse into drive. The powerful old beast ran smoothly, and she drove it with total command, as though it was an extension of her body. Occasionally returning waves from local pedestrians, she cruised straight out of town and onto deserted country roads.

"It'll take us a little while to drive out to the property. When we get there, I'd like to take a quick shower, and then we'll have dinner. Does that sound good?"

"*Da*, me too." He had to make himself stop staring at her.

"Markus, I can't tell you how glad I am that you're here." She reached over and smacked his thigh affectionately. "Over dinner I'll show you the *Star Fall* prototype, my sketches, and the sculpture schematics. I hope you can teach me how to move with more confidence in my assembly."

"Hmmm, *da*. With your dangerous chemical, that would be helpful. You drive with confidence, so I think it is natural to you in art as well."

"This was my grandfather's truck, and I've been driving it as long as I can remember. He taught me how to drive when I was too small to work the pedals, so he'd hold me on his lap and let me shift and steer." She caressed the steering wheel before gripping it with both hands to take a bend in the road at full speed. "I call it the Tank!" She let out a whoop.

"It looks to be from the late nineteen forties."

"Nineteen forty-three. My grandfather helped out in World War Two, and you can't imagine the adventures he had with this Tank, here." She waved her hand, gesturing fondly about the truck.

He nodded and looked around the truck's cab with more appreciation.

Turning on the radio, Giselle sang quietly to a medley of songs by France Gall, and Markus sat back to enjoy the ride. He turned, looking at the quiet farms and fields as they sailed past his window, and watched the countryside shift from the groomed fields of the Champagne region toward the primordial wildness of the Ardennes Forest.

Finally with a spray of white gravel, they turned off the rural road and started down a driveway that disappeared into a long tunnel of arching tree limbs. Wafting through the open windows, the mixed smells of mossy forest, green fields, and night-blooming jasmine filled the truck. Markus looked over at Giselle's hair blowing around her shoulders, and she tossed her head to flick it out of her eyes. Not that he didn't adore the buttoned-up, chic city woman who was his friend, but this natural girl beside him was even more to his taste. His attention was captured then as the trees finally retreated from the driveway to reveal an imposing three-story building made of white stone.

"Your family home is a castle?"

"It's not a castle, it's a *château*."

"Those round parts on the sides are turrets. Why is it not a castle?"

"In 1647 when my family built it, King Louis visited for a hunting party and called it a château."

"What is the difference between a château of this size and a castle?"

"I don't know. Maybe if a king didn't live in it, or it wasn't a seat of power, it wasn't called a castle."

"No king has ever lived here?"

"Only my ancestors have lived here, and they weren't royal."

"Well, now you are a countess through marriage."

She rolled her eyes. "It's well established as a château at this point. I don't think I can go around referring to it as a castle without sounding pretty silly."

As they swung into a grand flagstone courtyard, other buildings on the property came into view. The door of the great house opened, and an energetic tomboy-of-a-woman wearing a t-shirt and faded jeans came trotting down the steps and jogged toward them.

Giselle called out the window as she pulled the truck to a stop. "Selma! *Comment ça va?*"

Selma jumped onto the running board. "So glad you're...*two?*" She was staring at Markus. "Hell-*oh*." She looked back at Giselle and raised her eyebrows in question.

"I've brought an artist to help me with my sculpture.

This is Markus. Markus, meet Selma. She and her mother, Veronique, take care of my home while I'm away. Selma, he'll be using the workshop for his own art, so please put him in the stable house."

Markus smiled. "*Bonsoir*, Selma." He handed Giselle her shoes and stepped down onto the flagstone drive.

Selma nodded her greeting and jumped down from Giselle's side of the truck.

"Sure. I've got to run, but I'll open the stable house and workshop for...er...Markus."

"Let me guess. You're off to see Fabrice."

"*Oui*, we're watching a retrospective of Dustin Hoffman films." Selma sounded pleased.

"Fun! Is tonight *Marathon Man?*" Giselle asked while putting on her shoes. "Now that's an intense film."

"No, *Tootsie.*"

"Isn't Bill Murray in that one?"

"*Oui*, and Jessica Lange."

Arriving around the other side of the Tank, Selma clapped Markus on the arms with both hands, feeling his muscles unapologetically.

"Well Markus, you're going to need all of your strength. I can't imagine how big this sculpture is going to be, but I'm guessing very large based on everything she's had delivered."

She turned and called back to Giselle, "By the way, a crane was delivered this morning, and I just took delivery of your armored briefcase. It's locked in the cabinet just as you asked. I've shopped for you, and your favorite dinner goodies are already set up in the kitchen."

Giselle climbed down from the truck. "*Ah, merci.* And tell your mother that because of our guest, the guard dogs need to be kept off the main property."

"*Oui.* I'll see you for cards tomorrow night, *chérie.*"

"Can't wait."

Selma turned back to Markus. "Come with me, and I'll show you your place."

Giselle was moving away toward the sweeping steps of the château, then stopped mid-stride, calling, "Markus, after you're showered, come find me in the kitchen and we'll eat dinner."

"*Da,*" he called as he collected his things from the bed of the truck.

Selma moved at a brisk pace, and he had to catch up to her as she sped across the drive, then behind the *château* and down the lane to the stable house. Apparently "his place" was nowhere near where the young countess slept, even though that château must have enough rooms to accommodate the entire population of Gernelle.

After unlocking the heavy oak door, Selma led him inside a house with an open floor plan, clicked the light on, and then turned abruptly to face him.

"So, are you a friend of Vincenzo's, too?"

"No, I have not met her husband," Markus replied blandly.

Selma gave no response as she turned away from him and went to the armoire to retrieve sheets. Together they set about preparing the bed.

"So, has Giselle had other artists come out here with her?" he couldn't help asking.

"*Oui.*"

Ah, apparently I am not special, if she has asked other artists to stay here.

Selma gestured to a large door on the other side of the room.

"The workshop is just through there. There's a smaller studio beyond it, but those spaces are way too small for whatever she plans to build this time. So she's got her work area set up out in the courtyard, over by the greenhouse."

Markus liked Selma's no-nonsense manner. They made the bed in silence, and then she handed him a key and walked out the door with a cheerful, "*Bonsoir,* Markus." No idle small talk or inquisitiveness.

He took his wooden chest to the adjoining workshop. It was a perfect place for him to work, well maintained with basic tools and good lighting. It was a happy discovery to be given a place to work on his art, rather than having to improvise his own work space. On one side of the workshop was an antique loom, which someone was still taking care to dust and maintain. He wondered whose it was.

Returning to the living quarters, he turned his interest to the beautiful little stable house as he hung his clothes in the armoire. There were no interior walls, except for a brightly painted partition shielding what must be the bathroom, and the areas of the house were delineated by the furniture groupings. The main area was a living room decorated by someone who must have loved to lounge around. There was a worn velvet sofa, a settee the size of a small bed, in addition to a giant easy chair and matching ottoman that were made for a much larger room. He could

picture people sprawled about, relaxing away lazy afternoons. It was rounded out with tables here and there, and
a desk over by one of the windows.

The sleeping area had large slanting windows hung with
heavy brown velvet curtains, shelves stacked with an array
of old books, a collection of antique canes displayed on a
wall, and mismatched pewter lamps were set here and
there. A big bed took up most of the bedroom space, and
Markus guessed its polished wood frame was probably
hewn from nearby trees. He tested the mattress; it was
yielding and topped with a featherbed added by someone
determined to sink up to their ears in comfort. The small
kitchen was outfitted with an old soapstone sink, butcher-
block counters, and a worn stone floor.

He undressed, leaving his clothes on a chair, and walked
behind the brightly painted partition into the sizable
bathroom. Dominating the space was an over-sized Mo-
roccan-tiled showpiece. It was almost a swimming pool,
and could easily bathe six people at once. An elaborate
swan head fixture overhead aimed its open beak at the
center of the tub, which had no curtains surrounding it.
The whole affair was completely open and looked like
something designed for a bathhouse.

He opened the faucet and water came into the basin with
considerable force. When he pulled a chain, he laughed in
surprise as the swan began pouring great streams of hot water
from its mouth overhead. Spectacular! He stepped beneath the
shower and let it invigorate him.

Alphonso had been staked out in front of one of the ritziest apartment buildings in Venice for two hours now. Vincenzo and his bodyguard, Petro, had arrived in Venice that morning via private jet, and gone straight to this residential building with expensive views of the lagoon. Alphonso's phone rang. Recognizing the ringtone, he kept his eyes on the front of the building as he answered.

"Hey, Zelph. I'm on Vincenzo right now. He just flew in from Paris. What have you got?"

"*Nada.* Just checking in to tell you that I've been tracking Gabrieli as he casually goes to meetings and presses the flesh with everyone who wants to shake his hand."

"Yep, that's all I saw him do. Stay on him."

"Will do. But if it's all the same to you, I'd like to make some subtle inquiries as well."

"Just make sure you keep them subtle, Cuz."

"Absolutely."

"Vincenzo's on the move. Gotta go."

Alphonso pocketed his phone as he watched Vincenzo and Petro exit the building and walk down the *calle.* He needed to find out what Vincenzo had been doing there, and if possible, the number of the apartment he'd been visiting. So instead of following him, Alphonso walked inside and approached the *portiere.*

"*Ciao,*" he said casually. "I swear Vincenzo Verona just walked past me. I have an appointment with him later today at his office. I wonder what he was doing here."

The concierge's face lit up. "Oh! Signor Vincenzo! *Sì!* He was upstairs working with Signor Leonardo."

"Oh, right." Alphonso nodded as if this made perfect sense to him.

The *portiere* continued proudly, "Of course, Vincenzo and Leonardo are old friends. Leonardo has the largest suite in the building, number three oh seven, where he lives and has his private accounting office."

A man sitting on a lobby sofa nearby folded his paper and chimed in, "My nephew went to primary school with Vincenzo and Leonardo. He was on their sculling team."

"Leonardo Trentori is the best tax man in all of Italy," the *portiere* continued, as if he were bragging about his own son. "Who does your taxes?"

Alphonso deflected. "My father."

"Well, you can't fire your father," the seated man *tut-tutted*. "That wouldn't do."

"I wonder where Vincenzo's going," Alphonso fished.

"We heard him on his phone saying he was going to the Hotel Valmarri for a meeting in the Chalsasoni banquet rooms."

"Ah, nice hotel. Okay, have a good day."

"You, too." The *portiere* nodded. "We just love Count Verona..."

"...like a son," the other man added as he disappeared behind his paper.

Alphonso walked out of the building and headed for the Hotel Valmarri, chuckling at how easy it was to get information about the Veronas. He didn't even have to use his cover story. This was an easy job in some respects, but none of this information would be helpful if he couldn't uncover anything to report to Scortini.

Arriving outside the Chalsasoni banquet rooms, Alphonso walked past some people milling about and peeked inside. The men at the accountant's building were correct. There sat Vincenzo, deep in conversation with someone. Alphonso took advantage of the opportunity to really observe Vincenzo. He seemed to be enjoying himself—not just pouring on charm—and he was extremely good looking. Some men had all the luck.

A helpful hotel employee identified the man Vincenzo was sitting with as a spokesperson for a confederation of tribes in Somalia. Alphonso also learned that Petro was called an "aide," but he knew Petro's primary purpose was to make sure no one harmed or snatched the Verona heir. Nothing queer about honest people having guards; it only made good sense if you thought about the ransom that could be asked for a Verona. He wondered if the rumors were true that the Vatican protected them; Scortini had professed to be spying on behalf of the Pope. He then wondered what the Vatican's policy was on paying hush money or ransoms. Had anyone ever kidnapped a big Catholic muckety-muck? He'd never heard of such a thing.

As Alphonso left the hotel to acquaint himself with Contessa Verona, he thought about what he'd learned from his background check on her. She was from one of the world's oldest lineages, dating back to Richard II of Normandy, one of the forces behind the Norman conquest of Italy beginning in 999. Juliette was now forty-five years old, but as a young woman from royal blood, she had done what everyone expected of her when she married a dashing count from the oldest and richest family in Venice.

She'd admitted in a magazine interview that, as a devout Catholic, her one disappointment in life was that only one of her babies had survived after birth.

Fifteen minutes later, Alphonso was standing outside of her home, the first palazzo built in Venice, and by far the most magnificent. It had always been his personal favorite— so romantic and timeless that tourists took photos in front of it at all times of the day and night. He wondered how he was going to find out if Contessa Juliette was at home. Figuring he'd stick with what had worked so far, he headed over a bridge to an exclusive flower boutique on the corner. He walked past the flowers displayed on the sidewalk and into the tasteful little shop. The drift of fragrance was heady, even though most of the floral treasures were sealed in refrigerators. He smiled at the shop girl.

"*Buongiorno.* Do you happen to know what Contessa Verona's favorite flower is?"

The young lady at the counter came to life at the name. "Certainly." She was the very essence of youthful business chic, and with the pride of a museum curator, she walked him over to a refrigerator. "Hibiscus. They're one of the oldest flowers of Venice, and she loves them in white and red. But it's hard to make arrangements with just hibiscus, as you can imagine, so she lets us combine them with other local flowers. I have some pictures of the ones we did for Giselle's birthday. Would you care to see them?"

"I'd love to." Alphonso quirked his head at the name of Vincenzo's wife. "Giselle had her birthday here in Venice?"

The clerk actually flushed and looked lovelorn for a moment. Then she laughed at herself. "*Sì,* the count and contessa persuaded her to leave France for a whole month this past spring, and she had her birthday here. She's only celebrated one other birthday here since she and Vincenzo were married."

Scortini hadn't mentioned tracking the Verona's in-laws, but he was striking out in Venice, so he'd snoop into this lady's affairs, too. The background check he'd done revealed her to be a hotshot artist from France, and Alphonso tossed his hook back to see if this knowledgeable girl would bite.

"What's that funny name of where she lives again?"

"Gernelle, originally. I just heard this morning that she's there working on a new sculpture right now. But she and Vincenzo spend most of their time in Paris, of course."

Alphonso was really starting to enjoy this job. He propped an elbow on the counter. "Of course. Hey, I almost forgot...um, what did you say your name was?"

The proper little clerk wiped imaginary dust from her impeccably clean hand and offered it. "Gina."

"Well, Gina, Giselle loaned me an art book when she was here, and I would love to mail it to her in Gernelle. You've got that address, right?"

Gina was writing down the address before he could move on to his next question. "And you wouldn't happen to know if Contessa Juliette is home at the moment, would you?"

Without looking up from her careful printing, Gina shook her shining head of perfectly bobbed hair. "No, she's at Rifugia della Dignità cooking dinner for the residents. When the homeless live there they get the best meals of their lives, I'm certain." Apparently a fan of the contessa's cooking, she rolled her eyes in quiet ecstasy.

"Wow. I knew the Veronas owned the homeless shelter, but I didn't know she cooked for the residents personally." Alphonso was impressed. "That's very nice of her."

"Oh, *sì*! The Veronas pay for the entire homeless shelter, one hundred percent. And la contessa says a big part of treating people with dignity is feeding them food that you make with love. Vincenzo teaches some of the classes. And do you know they provide job placement and medical, too?"

Alphonso tried to estimate what all that must cost, and it tallied with the public financial records he'd pulled on the family. "Those Veronas are something else."

"*Sì*, they're incredibly generous, and they care about everybody. Contessa Juliette comes in here every morning when she's in town to say '*buongiorno*.' And she even got me a scholarship to Università Ca' Foscari." She handed over Giselle's address in France, and he made it disappear into his jacket pocket.

Alphonso paid cash for a small bouquet of hibiscus. Then he thanked Gina, took the flower shop's card, since she was a rich source of intimate Verona information, and wished her a good day. He set off for Rifugia della Dignità, which was just a five minute walk toward Piazza San Marco. Perhaps Scortini was right. No one could be this squeaky clean. These Veronas sounded too good to be true.

Upon his arrival at the homeless shelter, Alphonso charmed the lady at the front desk by handing over his bouquet and presenting himself as a volunteer for the kitchen. He was escorted to the dining hall and pointed to a door helpfully labeled *cucina*. When he stepped into the kitchen, he heard a woman's voice cheering on the kitchen staff.

"*Andiamo!* Come on, let us make this a delicious dinner!" The woman clapped her hands in a catchy little rhythm. "Now we begin the preparations like I showed you."

She was slim, stylish, and a powerhouse of enthusiasm. A man called to her, "Juliette," and she turned to inspect the mushrooms he was holding. So, this was the matriarch of the Verona family. Fantastic! She looked up from the *funghi* and smiled at Alphonso.

"Come! Roll up your sleeves! Today we make *la pasta degli amanti*. You will be good at this. I can see you have an abundance of love in your heart."

Alphonso normally didn't interact directly with people he was investigating, but he couldn't retreat from this charismatic woman. And, what the heck, he could learn something about the lady herself for his report. Stepping forward and rolling up his sleeves, he found himself walking up to Contessa Juliette Verona.

"Ah, you smell of hibiscus! So nice! You and I will make good pasta together." She produced an apron from a shelf, slipped it over his head, spun him around, and tied it neatly at his waist. Then she spun him back around and pinched one of his cheeks with the gentlest tug. "Wash your hands, and then we begin."

"*Sì*, Contessa." He was nervous about trying to cook, since he tended to buy ready-made pasta and rely on jarred sauces. Could he get away with pretending?

"You will not call me by my title." She pivoted on her stylish pumps to look him in the eye. "No. You will call me Juliette. Eh? Always. Got it?" She smiled so charmingly, he found himself grinning at her like a fool.

"*Sì*. Got it, Juliette." While he washed his hands, everyone in the kitchen began chopping vegetables, grating cheese, and heating pans. While they prepared dinner for the city's homeless, Juliette positioned Alphonso at a long wooden table and worked beside him, showing him how to make pasta dough and then roll it into smooth sheets. Her instructions were mixed with gentle encouragement and the occasional song that he hadn't heard since he was a boy.

One hour later, after having his hand smacked repeatedly, he was making perfectly uniform *tortelloni* with just the right amount of mushroom filling plumping out the dough in the most pleasing way. When Alphonso and Juliette placed the final *tortelloni* on a tray, he was surprised to be spun toward her. She rose up onto her toes to bestow a little kiss on each of his cheeks. As the shelter residents assembled in the dining hall, Alphonso and most of the volunteers were shooed out of the kitchen. The last thing he saw was Juliette hovering with the serving ladies over simmering soup pots that were about to receive his *tortelloni*.

———◉———

That evening, Alphonso braced for a confrontation as he arrived at Scortini's palazzo to give Salvio an update. The continued lack of dirt would not make him happy. Gabrieli spent his days talking to the citizens of Venice and working to repair a slum, Vincenzo was busy being a philanthropist, and after meeting Juliette, Alphonso knew she was a good woman, through and through.

The staid old butler ushered him into Scortini's office, and Alphonso settled into a chair. While waiting for Scortini, he thought about his own mother. His grandmother had raised him with the help of various family members, because his mother had run off shortly after he was born, and his father was in prison. He'd always fantasized that his mother was a good Catholic woman who loved him more than anything. He was just realizing that Contessa Juliette Verona had all the qualities he would've wished for in his own mother.

Suddenly Scortini popped up at his elbow, causing Alphonso to startle and fall off the edge of his chair. Catching himself hard on his knee, he yelped, "Shit! I didn't see you!"

"Don't you ever curse in my home!" Salvio flushed red. "*Do you hear me?*"

"I'm sorry, it slipped out." Alphonso lifted himself back onto the chair and rubbed his smarting kneecap.

"What do you have on Verona?" Salvio harrumphed.

"Nothing new today."

"Still *finessing?*" He made the word a sneer. "What did you find out about his son and wife?"

Alphonso let out an involuntary laugh at the thought of Juliette having a dark side.

"You find this funny?" Salvio turned purple. "When His Holiness, the Pope himself is relying on full disclosure of their sins?" Spittle flew from his mouth.

"No. I don't know why that came out. I take my job very seriously. But I haven't found anything yet on either the wife or the son. I have a good man on the count, and tomorrow while I head to France to check out Giselle, Zelph will expand his surveillance to Vincenzo and Juliette. Anything this family does, we'll find out about." Then he made a dangerous mistake. "As far as I can tell, the Veronas are good people."

Salvio sprung like a coiled snake and screamed, "Get out and find me evidence to the contrary, you colossal-headed charlatan!"

Caught off guard by the lightning-quick change from anger to hysteria, Alphonso got the hell out of there and headed straight to see Zelph. *Holy fuck! Scortini is bat-shit crazy!*

Half an hour later, they were sitting in his uncle's kitchen having a drink. After he'd brought Zelph up to speed on what he knew, Zelph was cautious.

"I gotta tell you, if the Veronas are doing anything illegal or dirty, they've got a really good cover. The count appears to be totally credible. Acts like he doesn't have a secret to hide."

"Okay, while I'm in France, do your best to tail Gabrieli and Vincenzo. Without calling any attention to yourself, ask people for an explanation for everything they do, and see if you can find any hidden motives. Or, like, any place they shouldn't be that they are."

"So we're taking la contessa off the list?"

"Absolutely. I'll eat this glass if that woman has anything to hide."

"How much money are you taking to France?"

Alphonso took a swallow of his drink and thought about it. "We haven't had to pay any bribes for information here in Venice, but it may be a different story in France. I'd better take half of it. I have no idea what I'll find there, but if the daughter-in-law has anything to hide, maybe she'll be as careless with her movements as her in-laws."

"Well, I'm not gonna need any bribe money here in Venice, so I'll give Pim the other half as a down payment on our debt." Zelph jotted some notes in his ever-present notebook. "You're flying to Paris?"

"No, I land in Reims. I'll rent a car and drive to Aiglemont to find out what I can about Giselle. Aiglemont is the closest town to where she lives in a place called Gernelle. I Googled her, and she's really photogenic. Like a supermodel."

Zelph set down his pen and got up to make himself another drink. "Well, a guy as good looking as Vincenzo wouldn't marry an ugly *ragazza,* now would he?"

"I dunno about these Veronas." Alphonso sucked his teeth and mused. "I got no feeling about these guys. And unless I was some sort of accounting investigator, I wouldn't know if they give as much money to charities as everyone seems to think. But I really like Juliette."

Zelph tasted his drink and sat back down. "So you call Contessa Verona 'Juliette' now, do you?"

"*Sì, Juliette* asked me to call her by her Christian name."

"Oh yeah?" Zelph made a haughty face.

"Yeah. She's the kind of mother I wish I'd had."

"Nice lady, eh?"

"She taught me how to make *tortelloni.*"

"Says you," Zelph mocked. "What did they look like? Could anyone else tell they were supposed to be *tortelloni?*"

Alphonso started making the same delicate movements with his big hands that Juliette had taught him. "Shut up, ya jerk. Juliette insists on perfection in the kitchen. She did every step of making the pasta dough with me. And with our fingers—no forks for her!"

"Oh, so you'll be changing professions to work in a kitchen with the *nonnas* now?"

"Hey, it's a real skill. And sure, she slapped my hand a lot when I was doing it wrong. But then I relaxed my fingers and stopped trying to kill the pasta."

"Right, I've heard that," Zelph teased. "Everybody knows you gotta relax your fingers."

"'*Non li strangolare, Romeo,*' she kept saying."

"She calls you *Romeo?*" Zelph laughed and then became serious. "Listen Loverboy, we gotta come up with something on these Veronas, or it's not pasta that's gonna get strangled."

After his meeting with the detective, Salvio slipped back into his secret passageway and popped out inside his wife's darkened chamber. He was a man on a mission: to make an heir. He removed all of his clothes except for his shirt, and folded them carefully. Raphielli lay motionless and prepared beneath a white cotton sheet. He whisked the sheet off her with enough momentum that it hung in the air like a ghost in the dim pools of light before falling to the floor. Raphielli lay naked with her eyes on the ceiling. He'd seen the vague trembling beneath the sheet. She was too stupid to understand that she was the luckiest fat cow in the world. She didn't deserve to have such a powerful man be true to her. His wife was a huge disappointment. But did he hold that against her? No, he gave her the world. And now he was going to give her his seed until she was full, whether or not she deserved it. She was withholding a son from him, but he was going to spear his essence right into her womb.

He grabbed her under her thighs and hauled her hips down to the edge of the table. Her eyes didn't leave the ceiling because she knew if they did, he would pluck them out. He would not tolerate being looked at while he was undressed. Yanking her legs apart, he thrust inside her, then held her in place with his hands clamped on her breasts. He stabbed himself into her repeatedly, and as he finished, he yanked the ribbon from her hair so her curls tumbled down. Then he shoved her off the table onto the floor where she landed on her elbow and hip. She didn't react or make a sound. She lay perfectly still as he got dressed, and then he disappeared behind the heavy tapestry into the secret passage.

———◦《◦》◦———

The night was cool, and the stately grounds on the edge of the forest were silent except for the wind in the trees as Markus walked up to the château door. He remembered that Giselle had asked for the guard dogs be locked up, and was glad she'd thought of that detail. He wouldn't want to be attacked out here alone in the dark. Giselle had left the door unlocked for him, and he entered the foyer of the grand house, which was dimly lit from wall sconces. He looked around a moment, admiring the statues and the ornate chandelier suspended in the shadows above, before walking to the back of the home to find her. The sound of his footsteps echoed hollowly back to him as he crossed the large rooms. Giselle's home was furnished with expensive antiques that were well maintained, but clearly used by their owners. There were magnificent paintings on the walls, but it didn't feel like a museum. The floors and walls were cold stone surfaces, so even though it had been warm outside today, the heat never made it far enough inside to warm the sprawling rooms.

As he neared the back of the mansion, he heard the distinctive clink and clatter of dishes and silverware being handled, and he followed the sound to the end of the main hall. He stopped outside the kitchen and watched Giselle as she moved back and forth in front of an open hearth, pulling a meal together. Her hair was damp and hung down past her shoulders in pale blonde waves. She was wearing a brief silk housedress that buttoned down the front, and a cardigan sweater hung unbuttoned from her shoulders. Illuminated by the dim firelight, the glow of her skin was arresting. He moved into the room toward her.

"You have a beautiful home."

"I do." She gave him a contented smile and walked toward him in white scuff slippers.

"I feel under-dressed." He gestured to her attire. "You are wearing silk."

"Mmmm, my whole closet here is nothing but my friend, Ava's, dresses. Her designs are so comfortable. They're the best dresses to live in." She pointed at the cutting board laden with cheeses, bread, vegetables, champagne, and jars of homemade pate. "Let's have dinner. Aren't you starving?"

"Looking at this now, I am as you say, *starving.*"

They assembled an array of small tastes and tempting bites on a tray. He followed her into an adjacent room that was decorated in the Moroccan style, with a low, tiled fireplace that was crackling from within. She kneeled down at a low table surrounded by padded ottomans, and he bent to set their tray on it.

"This is an unusual decorating style for the French countryside."

"My great-great-uncle married a woman from Morocco, and she decorated this room. I like eating in here. I avoid the dining room unless we're having a party...you know, less formal."

"Then that is your aunt's shower in the stable house bathroom...or should I call it a swimming pool?"

"*Oui,* she lived there in her later years. Her knees got bad, and she couldn't climb the stairs here in the big house, so she lived out there for a while. Even after the family had the elevator installed here, she preferred the stable house at the end of her life. My grandparents used to tell stories about how happy she was making her Moroccan-style blankets with her friends in the workshop."

"I noticed her loom is still in good condition."

"Uh-huh. I believe she made the bedding that you'll be sleeping in."

"Sleeping under a family heirloom. I am honored."

Giselle sat on the rug and leaned back against one of the ottomans. She poured each of them a glass of champagne, and lifted hers.

"Now that we're here, let's drink a toast to art."

He sat near her on the rug, accepted the glass and raised it. "To art."

She touched her glass to his. After he took a sip, he said what was on his mind.

"I asked Selma, and she told me you have had other artists come here to work with you." He didn't want to pry, but he had to ask. "I thought you said you always work alone."

"I should've said I *prefer* to work alone. But there've been two people who've helped me in the past."

"Ah."

"I had a metallurgy instructor here from Paris for a summer. She lived in the stable house during the week and went home to her family on weekends."

"Ah."

"I also had this crazy kid who makes gyroscopes come help me with my sculpture that had spinning crowns on it. He was here for two weeks."

"Now you have me to help you with *Star Fall.*" He set a small plate before her. "So, how will we begin?"

"Here are my prototype and sketches with the dimensions." She gestured to a wire model and a stack of rolled papers nearby. "Tomorrow we'll set the beams inside the base pattern. I've been thinking that if you pour the cement bases for the structural beams while I organize the materials, we could move quickly to the main framework assembly."

"That will save time." He nodded. "When will I see these glowing spindles?"

She popped a piece of cheese into her mouth and smiled. "They won't be glowing until I make them glow, but we should be ready for them before too long."

After dinner, they moved the ottomans aside and Giselle spread her paperwork on the floor in front of the fire. She stretched out on her stomach and traced the drawings with her finger.

"I've developed a design that will suspend the spindles together in a simple star pattern. When we get the glass tubes to fuse, I make a tiny fissure in the main spindle connection, allowing the fluid and gas to mix. It's the same concept as combining carbon dioxide and water. The irrodium-hydrogen mixture inside the spindles will cause the glass stars on my sculpture to glow for a hundred years."

Markus lay beside her and followed her explanation. He was surprised at how good her drawings were. He hadn't heard that her talents extended to pencil on paper, but her sketches were rendered in rich charcoal and would have been impressive in frames. Studying the schematic, he focused on the assembly.

"I see all of your measurements for holes in the steel girders. Did you have the factory drill them already?"

"*Oui.*" She shimmied closer to him and pointed out the junctions. "These holes here are where the girders join, and these here are where we'll insert the copper curls, and then the spindles go here."

He looked at the copper curlicues in her design, and then at an inset sketch that illustrated some sort of a tool.

"You have custom made something to form your copper curls?"

"Mm-hmm. I worked with different lengths of copper for months in Paris, bending them around everything from bottles to chair legs. But I finally built a wooden form that works like magic, and now they come out perfectly. It'll be fun...you'll see. And we have lots of copper curls to make."

"I see your *Star Fall* has the strong industrial elements of the beams, and then these clouds of copper curls that house the one-hundred-year-glow of your dangerous stars."

"My first concept was a steel sculpture that looked like a burst of fireworks. It was covered with blades, with actual fireworks at the base that I planned to detonate at my first exhibit, leaving burn marks all over the metal frame..."

He shook his head in disbelief. Her art had certainly earned its dangerous reputation.

"But as I played with that concept, I found it wasn't the explosion of the fireworks that I loved. I wanted to capture the weightlessness of the falling stars after the violence."

The embers of the fire had died down when Giselle rolled onto her back.

"I can't believe I was foolish enough to think I could do this alone. Without you, I would've come up here and had to hire workers. They would have thought I'd lost my mind." She looked at him happily. "Thank you for coming with me, Markus."

He stretched out on his side and gave her a long look. "When Ivar told me that you wanted me, I did not hesitate."

She yawned. "I've got to call Vincenzo. Let's get some sleep, and have an early breakfast tomorrow."

Markus watched with appreciation as she rolled with fluid ease onto her stomach, lifted her hips to stretch like a cat, and then stood to stretch again.

"Okay, Giselle, go make your call. I will clean up."

"Sleep well."

Carrying the tray toward the kitchen, he admired the way her hips undulated as she disappeared down the hall. After cleaning up and dampening the fires, he clicked the lock on the front door and let himself out. He made his way to the stable house, and headed into the bathroom to brush his teeth and plug in his shaver. Then he stripped off his clothes before clicking off the lights and climbing into the big bed. He drifted to sleep thinking of Giselle's body stretched before him in the firelight.

He woke in the middle of the night restless, so he dragged on a pair of pants, went to the workshop, and started a new sculpture from the wealth of scrap materials on hand. Working with his hands was like meditation for him and quieted his mind. But even after busying himself in the process of creation, he couldn't stop thinking of Giselle. So he headed back to the bathroom to take a cold shower under the swan head.

6

Alphonso arrived in the quiet town of Aiglemont early in the morning and found a tiny hotel with a restaurant near the train station. He parked his rental car and went in to see if he could get a room. If not, at least he could get something to eat. From the front door, he could see into the café where locals were relaxing over coffee and omelets, and his nose told him they employed a talented cook. As he approached the front desk, a man peeked out from a back office and eyed Alphonso's suitcase.

"Ah, *bonjour.* Looking for a room?"

"*Oui.*"

"Just you?"

"Just me."

"How many nights?"

"It depends on how long it takes to do some local business. I'm not sure, but let's start with three nights."

"You sound Italian." Alphonso was aware he was being

felt out. This must be the proprietor, to take such an interest in him. "Where are you visiting from?"

"Venice." Alphonso learned early in his career to lie as little as possible; it helped him keep his story straight.

"Ah, welcome." The man placed a form on the counter and took a key from a cubbyhole. "I have a good room for you. Just fill this out, please."

While jotting down his information, Alphonso fished, "I hear there's a famous Italian family in this area..."

The Frenchman ignored the bait and eyed Alphonso suspiciously. "So, what business brings you here?"

"I'm consulting on a champagne purchase for my cousin's restaurant." He pushed the completed form across the counter. "I've heard the Verona family has a home here."

"A restaurant? What's the name? Perhaps I know it."

"Il Gusto di Mama. But it hasn't opened yet."

"Well, that's what everyone wants from a meal—mama's cooking, right? Running a restaurant isn't easy. I wish your cousin luck..." He paused and glanced down at the form, "...Alphonso."

Ah, he's smart, and not touching the subject of the Veronas. "*Merci*..."

"Henri."

"*Merci*, Henri. Do you mind if I leave my suitcase behind your counter while I have breakfast?"

"Not at all. I'll just need your room deposit."

Alphonso counted over the cash.

"I can run a tab in the restaurant and put it on your hotel bill if you'd like."

"That would be good. *Merci.*"

"*Prego.*" Henri smiled, took the small suitcase, and put it in a closet behind the desk.

Spotting an empty table, Alphonso made his way into the café and sat down. He didn't have to wait long before a young brunette in a cotton dress, worn Mary Janes, and a red apron appeared and took his order. In only a matter of minutes, she had delivered his meal and left him to enjoy it in peace. He watched the goings on and decided that his waitress must be Henri's wife, judging from their matching wedding rings and her command of the place as she whisked about signing for deliveries.

Unlike the Venetians, the French didn't seem to be forthcoming about the Veronas. Going for broke, he waited until the brunette came to check on him. He tried a casual tone.

"So, do you know Giselle Verona?"

She looked at him with a distinctly cool French attitude, and let his question hang in the air.

He tried again. "I mean, she's just the most famous resident here, isn't she?"

She put her hands on her hips and looked him over. "She is from here. Everyone in Aiglemont knows her."

He could see her suspicion mounting. "I guess that's true. I didn't think of it that way. It's just that it's a coincidence I'm here in her hometown, and just the other day Contessa Juliette was teaching me how to make *tortelloni*..."

The woman's demeanor changed completely. "Ah, Juliette's *tortelloni!* The ricotta and ramp, or the three mushroom?" She smiled.

Alphonso smiled, too. "*Tre funghi*. But the foraged porcini weren't up to her standards."

She relaxed visibly and sat down across from him. "Ah, certainly not. But then, she's so particular about her porcini. You know, she refuses to even look at the cultivated ones."

Alphonso nodded animatedly. "That's what she told me. She said cultivated porcini are..."

"...*too watery,*" they said in unison, and both laughed.

"Right, that's just what she says!" Her hands flew up in surprise.

Unable to help himself, he continued proudly, "She taught me this trick with a cheese cloth."

She held her hands up. "*Oh la la la la la!* Please! I've even seen her do it with a coffee filter!"

"*Sì!* I can picture her doing that!" he laughed.

She clapped her hands over her mouth and giggled through her fingers. "Juliette told me that one time while they were visiting friends on an island, her husband's *nonna* used a silk stocking to strain the porcini she had brought with her, because it was all that was on hand!"

He nodded in admiration. "The Verona women are so practical, and I think maybe...unstoppable."

"Sorry I was rude. I'm Fauve. Giselle and I are old friends from when we were toddlers. Why do you ask about her?"

"Oh, no reason." Then he thought of a strategy. "It's just that I've seen articles about Giselle, and she looks completely unlike someone who would be close to Juliette. You know...the Paris tabloid cover girl, the dangerous artist. Does she get along with her mother-in-law?"

"*Oh, mais oui!* Juliette loves her like she was her own daughter. And Giselle's not at all like what the papers and magazines say about her or Vincenzo."

"They must love being out here in the country together."

"Since they graduated high school, they spend most of their time in Paris. But Vincenzo hops all over the world saving the planet, and Giselle comes up here to work on her art projects."

"Alone?"

"Well, without Vincenzo. But she has me, and all the friends she grew up with. The truth is, she's totally focused on her art, and doesn't give herself much time for anything else. She never has. Vincenzo is exactly the same about his charity work. They're both really driven. Perfect for each other."

Alphonso figured it was time to get moving. "Well, I should start my day. I'll be back here for dinner tonight. Even after my breakfast, thinking about Juliette's pasta has made me hungry again."

"You won't find any pasta here in Aiglemont that's as good as Juliette's, I'm sorry to say." Fauve smacked the table in mock frustration, and then had a thought that made her grin. "But I'm making a white bean *cassoulet* to die for. It'll be on the menu tonight." She hopped up and went to check on her other diners.

"I can't wait," he called. Then he went to the front desk, claimed his suitcase, and headed up to his room.

——⊗——

Markus was already dressed as the sun rose over the forest. He found Giselle in the château's kitchen, wearing a briefer version of the housedress he'd seen the night before. This one was made of faded blue silk, with buttons down the front, and the hem was three inches above her knees. She had on soft, off-white suede oxford shoes, with no socks. *She is working in that? How am I supposed to focus on building if she is not wearing work clothes?*

She looked up at him and smiled.

"Good morning, Giselle. How did you sleep?"

"I didn't sleep much. I just laid there willing the hours to pass so we could get started." She poured him coffee. "How did you find Moroccan dreamland?"

"I also did not sleep much, so I began working on a new sculpture in the workshop."

"I would've done the same thing, but I figured working with a crane in the dark was too crazy even for even me to attempt."

As they prepared a breakfast tray to share, Giselle mixed grated orange peel into softened butter and flicked in bits of pulp. She tasted the citrus butter and nodded approval. Then she dipped her finger into it and held it up to Markus' lips for him to taste. Startled by the intimate gesture that she offered so naturally, he took her finger into his mouth and sucked on it as she slowly withdrew it. The butter was creamy and bright with orange on his tongue. It was delightful. She didn't wait for a response, but moved over to the hearth where she rescued their bread from a blackened fate. He poured milk into their coffee, slightly flustered by what had just happened.

After breakfast they walked out behind the house and past the stable house to a large courtyard bordered by two impressive buildings.

"Here's where we're going to work. Last month I had the ground measured by a surveyor, and then graded perfectly level so it's ready for us to begin." She gestured to industrial brackets on the ground. "Be careful not to move any of those mold bases." Then she headed toward a glass building. "We'll use the greenhouse as our workshop."

Following her toward the greenhouse, he pointed to the structure on the far side of the large courtyard. "What is that other building?"

"That was used for an entertainment called 'follies' back in the seventeen hundreds. In the old days when my family entertained, it was on a really grand scale."

"I can imagine. My father and I worked on a property in Ukrayina that had a zoo with exotic pets."

"Hmm, we didn't have a zoo that I know of." She continued pointing around the property. "Well, the stable house you already know, and over there is the garage."

"Any cars?"

"You mean besides my Tank?"

"Your Tank is not a car. It is more like a military transport."

"Ha! We also have a Jeep, and Vincenzo's Exagon Furtive-eGT. It's battery powered. Very eco."

"Also very expensive."

"That too. He really believes in the company and the environment."

"Clearly. But it is not made for these roads."

"You'd be surprised. And over there are the barn, pad-dock, and stables."

"Any horses?"

"I have five, Vincenzo has one, and Selma has two. When I'm away, our groom boards Vincenzo's and mine at his farm nearby, and brings them back when we're here."

"Where does Selma live?"

Giselle turned to face the back of the property, pointing past the courtyard and into the distance. "See down that road that runs along the forest? You can barely see them, but we have some nice guesthouses, and Selma lives in one of them with her mother, Veronique. When I'm in Paris, Veronique moves into the main house and lives in an apartment behind that Moroccan breakfast room."

"I have not seen them around the property since we arrived."

"When they come and go from the property, they use an access road that's all the way down by their garage. It's more direct than coming back this way if they're going into town."

"So you are very solitary when you are here."

"Just the way I like it."

"Not like your life in Paris."

"I need to be alone to work. That's why I can't create in Paris. Collectors always find me and just 'happen to' stop by any studio I use."

"Hmmm. I see. It is a good thing I do not bother you, Giselle."

She squinched her face up at his humor and then tilted her head. "You'd better not." Then she slipped her arm in his and walked him inside the greenhouse.

"These crates contain the materials that will become *Star Fall.* I had the delivery company open them to make everything accessible."

He eyed the wooden packing crates with waybills hanging from them. "Convenient."

"And there's our crane."

"I see it is a Bobcat. Lots of fun to use!"

He knew she could see how excited he was to have this machine at his disposal, but not wanting to look too immature, he recovered himself quickly.

"Sadly, it is not battery powered," he commented.

"Sadly, no."

"Not eco."

"No."

Giselle fastened a small tool belt around her waist, felt for her pencils and measuring tape, and walked past the crates to a table where she unfolded a surveying chart. She opened her blueprint and walked out to the courtyard. She paced out the design on the ground, tracing her trajectory on the drawing with her finger so Markus could see where each part of the sculpture would stand.

"You'll use the Bobcat to set the base girders upright inside the molds, then we'll pour the cement in. Once that's set, you'll use the Bobcat again to lift the arches in place and affix them here, here, and here."

"Your art is so big, while mine is so small."

"I hadn't thought of that."

"We are lucky I do not get intimidated. Your big sculpture might put another man in a bad mood."

She wrapped an arm around his shoulders, giving him a

condolence squeeze. "Enough *small* talk. Get up into that crane, will you?"

Markus climbed aboard the Bobcat and thoroughly enjoyed himself as he lifted the girders from their crates and drove around the courtyard, placing them neatly upright into their molds. He'd used this type of machinery before to move everything from church windows to boulders, but using one to assemble art materials was new to him. After double-checking measurements, he joined Giselle in the greenhouse and got to work measuring the cement mix from sacks and water into buckets. They spent the rest of the morning mixing cement and pouring it into the molds from a small mixer on wheels. He was used to working hard, and was impressed that Giselle hadn't uttered a word of complaint even though she was sheened with sweat. Working alongside her, he felt a mixture of desire and respect. She was an efficient manager, and precise when giving directions.

Once the last support strut was cemented in place, they took a break. Markus rinsed out the cement mixer while Giselle went to the kitchen and brought some food out to a table by the greenhouse where they sat down to a late lunch. Giselle kicked her shoes off and poured them each a big glass of water as he prepared plates for them.

"Which side of the sculpture do you think we should begin our assembly on?" she asked.

"I would begin on the right side...there," he pointed.

"I agree."

Markus noticed that, just like her friend Selma, there was no small talk in Giselle. She never talked about herself, and she hadn't asked him anything personal since their first cab ride together. She seemed to be all art, all the time.

It was evening before she called an end to their work, and they headed to their respective rooms to clean up before Fauve and Giselle's other friends arrived. Stripping off his clothes and walking toward the Moroccan shower, he thought for the umpteenth time, *What am I doing out here embarking on some illegal-substance-covered art piece? There is something here I am not understanding. I do not know what it is, but I think it could be trouble.*

——⟫•⟪——

Alphonso stashed his suitcase on the luggage stand in the corner of his room and went over to the window. Drawing the dark blue curtain aside, he looked out on a nice view of the quaint towns rooftops, and directly below was a spacious yard with a vegetable garden and a big section that had been left wild. Judging from the floor plan downstairs, he figured the goat munching on weeds below his window probably belonged to Henri and Fauve, as well as the chickens and rabbits that occupied the neat coops and hutch on the far edge.

Turning back to the room, it was just what you'd expect in an eighteenth-century hotel. He eyed the brass bedframe suspiciously, but when he sat down on the bed and bounced, he was pleased to find the frame sturdy. And when he pulled back the cornflower-blue bedding, he was happy to see that the mattress appeared to be new. The walls held collages of photos of the countryside in antique off-white frames that had chipping paint on their worn surfaces. Nice pictures, whoever took them had an eye for composition. Listening, he didn't hear any conversations or music from nearby rooms, so he felt hopeful it would be a quiet place to relax after long days of spying on Vincenzo's wife.

He went to investigate the bathroom. While it was obvious it had been added on some time in the last hundred years, he was relieved to see it was outfitted adequately. A fresh plastic curtain surrounded the shower basin, although the overhead rain attachment was a holdover from another time. The sink was tiny, but mercifully the toilet was a standard size. The towels were clean, and fluffy. He accidentally turned on the bathroom exhaust fan when he turned on the light, and it sounded like an airplane engine. There was no window, but the overhead light was bright enough to shave without cutting himself. Being tall and broad shouldered, he'd have preferred a larger bathroom. But it was about the size of the one in the apartment he'd grown up in, so he was fine with his accommodations.

He called Zelph and gave him the hotel information, before heading out into the countryside to locate Giselle's home in Gernelle. He arrived near her property almost an hour later after repeatedly taking wrong turns, and even ended up in Belgium at one point. Anxious not to raise suspicion, he avoided asking directions from the locals and from the old women he occasionally saw chatting near mailboxes at the end of quiet lanes.

He eased his rented Renault up to a wide-open gate that offered access to a white gravel driveway, and spotted an iron postal locker with the address Gina, the florist, had given him. Success! He drove a few hundred meters past the estate drive, and turned onto a rutted lane that bordered the property. He drove until he arrived at a stand of trees that would shield his car from view of the main road. Leaving it parked on the edge of the forest, he approached Giselle's property on foot, keeping himself sheltered in the first line of trees. It was quite a hike, and he had to keep crouching and watching to be sure no one saw him. He needed to observe Giselle's activities, and he wouldn't get the chance if he got caught trespassing.

As he skirted past a small fruit orchard, the back of a beautiful castle and estate compound finally came into view. Her property was what he expected of a Verona home; it could have been an exclusive boarding school or a destination hotel. Even from the back, he could tell it was classy, the sort of place he would never get invited to. *Why is it the super-rich only associate with themselves?* Well, in fairness, that didn't seem true about this particular family. The Veronas appeared to reach out to everyone. So what could they be hiding?

While being cautious to stay out of view from the château and the other buildings on the estate grounds, Alphonso made his way as close to the rear of the château as he dared. What he glimpsed in the back courtyard was the most beautiful young woman he'd ever seen. Wow! Vincenzo certainly hadn't married an ugly *ragazza!* Giselle and some Icelandic-looking athlete were working with long struts of metal, wheeling them around with a little crane. Alphonso hunkered down in the tall grass of a field and made himself comfortable for his stakeout.

After several hours of work, they put their tools away, and then the man walked alone to a small house attached to a stable on the edge of the courtyard. Giselle walked past the stable house and was continuing around the back of the castle when he heard the whine of a small engine approaching. He dropped into the top of a push-up and watched a woman on a motorcycle approaching on a road from deeper on the property. She zipped past him on the other side of the field and banked around the front of the castle and out of sight, just as Giselle disappeared around the same corner. *She has a visitor.* He perked up and came onto his hands and knees when he saw vehicles approaching from the driveway at the front of the property. Here came a Range Rover, and a Fiat, and some mid-sized minivan model he didn't recognize. *Well now, what's going on here?* He crept forward to find out.

⎯⎯◦⟨◉⟩◦⎯⎯

Salvio still had nothing to leverage against Verona. In an effort to buy himself more time, he sat down at his desk and wrote a note to the College of Cardinals, who were still convened in Venice.

> *I am writing to assure you that, although the iniquity I must bring before you breaks my heart, I am only days away from providing you with the proof as promised. Please join me in a request to the pope that he grant me absolution for sullying my soul with the proving of these sins, and*

immediately appoint me as head of Verdu Mer, for the sake
of its vulnerable residents and their future comfort.
    Salvio Davide Scortini

After handing the sealed note to Guiseppe with instructions
to deliver it to the College, Salvio hurried off to the emergency meeting of builders he had called. The key builders of
Venice were assembled in a warehouse, the only building
large enough to hold such a gathering. Each of the attendees
expected him to award them lucrative contracts for the
Verdu Mer project, and he was certain that, without exception, they all understood that this would put them in his debt.

He strode into the warehouse, and voices hushed as he
approached the podium. He tapped the microphone to test
it before beginning.

"Because we are all busy men, I've come with a very
short message. The Verdu Mer project is far more complicated than any of you could possibly imagine. I'm working
closely with the Vatican and global experts to set a plan for
demolition and building to begin."

No one moved. They all seemed to be waiting for him
to provide specific information on their contracts. He saw
one of the titans of demolition looking at him speculative-
ly; no doubt he was already working with Verona. Perhaps
he even had an inkling that Verona was currently the head
of the project, but the man wouldn't dare risk challenging
Salvio outright.

"Of course, behind closed doors I am working tirelessly
on the logistics with Verona, a close advisor. But at this
time, I cannot give you more information."

A voice called out, "Signor Scortini, can you at least give us a start date and an estimated budget? We need to schedule our upcoming contracts accordingly, so we'll be ready to begin work on Verdu Mer."

Salvio made a brushing gesture with his hand at this non-issue. "You'll have it soon. And once I give you the sums we're talking about—which I am receiving directly from the Vatican treasury—you'll be able to return any moneys from current jobs if needed."

Another voice called out, "Signor Scortini, it's bad business to take a job, then hand the client's money back and leave for another job."

Salvio fought to reign in his flaring temper and appear calm. He raked his fingernails as quietly as he could against the underside of the podium to relieve his cresting anger.

"If your current clients are more important to you than the Vatican, and you don't wish to be a part of this God-given opportunity, then you don't need to give it another thought!" He was at his limit with being nitpicked and challenged. He was losing control of himself. "But at this moment, I'm urgently expected back at my Verdu Mer consortium. I only called this brief meeting to personally tell you how much I appreciate your patience. Now if you will excuse me..."

He stalked off toward the side exit, ignoring the attendees who were gathering together in small groups, no doubt to discuss the upcoming opportunity like women gossiping over a laundry line. Once outside, Salvio slipped around a corner and hurried alone down a tiny, dark alley. He heard running steps behind him, and turned to see who was trotting to catch him.

"Who are you?" Salvio demanded.

"I'm Reynaldo Falconetti."

Salvio offered him a blank look.

"We're in marble."

"Ah *sì*, Marco's boy. Your parents were just at my home."

"*Per favore,* Signor Scortini, I hope you'll clear something up for me."

"I have no secrets. What I have to say, I say to the whole building establishment."

"Signor Scortini, my father couldn't be here today because he was at a meeting of the Verdu Mer consortium."

"*Sì,*" he murmured in a bored tone, "I'm working with a global consortium, and am on my way there now."

"Well, *signore*, what you say doesn't make sense, because the consortium members say...uh..." His courage appeared to desert him.

Salvio slapped a smile on his face and purred, "*They say what?*"

Reynaldo choked out, "That the Pope already chose Verona over you—"

Before he realized what he was doing, Salvio grabbed Reynaldo's face and slammed his head straight back into the stone wall. He'd thrown all of his force behind the pistoning momentum of his arm, and there was a muffled crunch as Reynaldo's skull fractured. He appeared to be trying to say something as blood slipped over his bottom teeth and out the corners of his mouth. His brown eyes fluttered shut, and his limp body dropped onto the stones in the darkest shadow of the alley's gutter.

Stunned by the explosive force of his own violence, Salvio reflexively jumped back into the shadows. *My God! What just happened? I've got to get away from here. Move, Salvio!* He looked in both directions and then hurried unseen from the alley.

Moving quickly down the *calle*, Salvio tried to reassure himself. That young man had paid for bearing false witness. Salvio was an instrument of the Almighty God, and while he bore no personal ill feelings toward that lowly marble artisan, it wasn't in Salvio's nature to question God's will. As an instrument of divine will, his conscience was clear. When that sinner's body was found, no one would think to question Salvio. He'd never had any business with the young man. He didn't even know him.

Salvio walked directly home and went straight to his office, dismissing Guiseppe's attempt to inquire about the evening's plans. Slamming the office door, he moved behind his desk to plan his next move. He snatched up a golden drapery cord that he kept on his desk, and began to reflexively wind it around his hand as he pondered his future. He had taken the cord from the Vatican while he'd been left waiting in a hallway next to some curtains. True, the cord didn't belong to him, but unlike his forefathers, he'd never been given gifts from the Pope. So he'd helped himself to this little trifle as a symbol of gifts yet to come. He had faith he would soon earn the Pope's affection and gifts.

Giselle threw open the front door for two of her oldest friends, who moved past her carrying a painting between them.

"What on earth?" She hadn't expected them to bring anything other than, maybe, a wheel of cheese.

Laetitia moved awkwardly into the grand foyer, clutching the gilded frame as her long legs backpedaled, and her fine brown hair hung in her eyes. She flicked her head in an effort to see, and blew an air kiss at Giselle.

"It's your Caillebotte, Gigi. Thanks for loaning it to Pierre. Wait till you see his copy."

"Right. I forgot." Giselle reached out to scoop a bit of hair behind her friend's ear.

Solange strutted past holding the other end of the painting, pretending she was dancing in a conga line. She was shaking her ample derriere to music only she could hear from her ear buds. She blew an air kiss and called out loudly as she passed, "Bah! Gigi! You're all sweaty and dirty! Fuck, you look good enough to turn me on!"

"I've been working...and you're not a lesbian."

Solange winked, but Giselle was pretty sure she couldn't hear her over her private concert. She plucked the buds from her friend's ears, and reached to help with the painting. Together they set it against the far wall of the foyer, then Giselle leaned close to Solange's shoulder and put a bud in her own ear.

"Ah! Now I get the conga moves!"

Solange clipped her little device onto Giselle's dress.

"It's Queen's "I Want to Break Free," my new favorite song." She conga-ed over to greet Fauve and Henri, who were coming in the door.

Henri gaped at Giselle and pretended to be horrified.

"Tell me what kind of art theft was just averted? Why were those two crazies carrying a painting that should have been hanging safely here in your château?"

"Don't play dumb. Pierre was copying it." Fauve walked past him to greet Laetitia. "Did he get accepted to L'École des Beaux-Arts?"

"We don't know yet." The lanky brunette pushed out her lower lip. "But he's positively obsessed with Caillebotte now. When we were in Paris for the student exhibition, we went to visit his grave in Père Lachaise Cemetery." Then suddenly looking pleased, she beamed. "It turned out to be a very romantic afternoon, and we even found some privacy in the mausoleum across from Caillebotte's."

"Wow, gettin' it on in a mausoleum. How Goth," Solange smirked.

Giselle walked over to examine Solange's hair. "I brought an artist here to help me, and he lives over near Père Lachaise." Taking a handful of the newly bleached locks she asked, "When did you bleach your hair?"

"Um, two days ago. I think I look like Debbie Harry, *non?*" Solange ruffled her fingers through her hair to muss it up. "So, you brought an artist here to help?"

"*Oui.* He's getting cleaned up now. You'll meet him soon."

Fauve looked around and asked Laetitia, "Where are your brothers?"

"They're coming with Pierre. They'll be here any time now."

As Giselle swooped over to offer Henri and Fauve little kisses of greeting, Carolette came bursting dramatically through the door wearing her typical skin-tight dress with as much cleavage as she could manage spilling from her scooped neckline, her stilettos clacking on the marble floor.

"My spin instructor is married!" she wailed.

The group shared a quick, "Oh no, not again" look, and Laetitia said, "Oh, Carolette, I told you he was no good." She looked at her lovelorn buddy. "He's a dog."

Proving how upset she was, Carolette walked right past the hall mirror without so much as a glance at her hair, which was in a fetching low beehive up-do with a spray that made her blonde hair shine. "Right! That's what he is! A cur!" Carolette looked crushed.

"Did you just use the word 'cur'?" Henri asked

"What? *Oui*, you know a mongrel dog."

"I didn't know we were throwing out old fashioned words." Clearly uncomfortable on the man-bashing subject, he tried to lighten the mood.

"I can use old-fashioned words. And what kind of man spends that much time caressing a single woman's behind while she's spinning...when he's *married?*"

"A dog," Giselle and Laetitia replied in unison.

Giselle moved over to give Carolette's cheek a quick peck and then headed for the stairs.

"Forgive me. I've only just now stopped working. I've got to run upstairs and rinse this sweat and cement dust off me. You all go back to the kitchen and get yourselves something to drink. I'll be right down."

As the group headed toward the kitchen, Giselle heard a shout.

"Fuck!"

"What?" Giselle yelled down the stairs.

Solange yelled back, "Oh nothing. Selma just scared the shit out of us! She was sneaking around here in the dark dining room and then lit candle."

Selma raised her voice, "I'm not sneaking, I'm creating ambiance, Blondie."

"Well, try to create some noise while you're doing it. We didn't know you were here," Solange griped loudly.

"Really? My bike's parked right by the front steps."

Giselle went to her bedroom suite where she showered, pulled a fresh dress over her head, and drew a comb through her damp hair. As she entered the dining room, she saw that everyone had arrived except for Markus. She sighed happily. This was going to be just the sort of night at home with her friends that she longed for when she was away. They'd carried food in from the kitchen, and arranged trays of sandwiches, fruits, and snacks on the sideboard so they could make plates as they liked.

Solange, who was tending the fire, stopped poking the glowing wood and called, "Gigi, what was that dance you did in the talent contest that one time?"

"Which one?"

"The seductive one, that went like this..." Solange raised her arms and swiveled her hips.

"You look like you're struggling into a pair of Spanx," Laetitia guffawed.

Solange stuck her tongue out at her detractor. "Don't mock me." But she caught sight of herself in a wall mirror and nodded while still swiveling. "Oh, God! You're right! I look like my aunt Germaine getting into her girdle!"

Giselle popped a pear slice into her mouth and wiped her hands on a napkin. "It wasn't for the talent contest. It was for that adaptation we did of Oscar Wilde's *Salomé* for drama class."

She walked over to Solange and became serious, getting into character. She slowly shifted her weight onto her right leg, then lifted her left foot and stepped it in front of her, just resting on the toe. Snaking her arms seductively upward and then moving them just so, as if she was caressing a column of smoke, she began to undulate her hips and perform a very slow belly dance.

Auguste commented, "Now why can't women still dance like that?"

Pierre offered, "So much lovelier than all the krunkin' girls do nowadays."

Robert agreed. "Right. How did that ever go out of style? Solange, slower, you're doing more of a bump and grind."

Just then Fauve called out, "Markus!"

Heads turned, and Giselle followed their eyes to the door where Markus stood watching her. Henri walked across the room to welcome him as Fauve turned to Carolette. "You'll have to try to restrain yourself."

Carolette was staring at Markus with hungry eyes and whispered to Giselle, "You brought me a hot man!"

"Don't get too excited." Fauve held up a hand. "I'm sure it's hands off until they're done building the sculpture. You know how Giselle works. She won't be taking any time off, so there's no way Markus will be free to take you on any dates."

"There's no need to go out," Carolette murmured, staring

at him. "He's got those Eastern Bloc steel-blue eyes and he's gorgeous. I'd be happy to come to him." She glanced at Giselle. "You know—when you say it's okay."

Selma said, "He's not my type, but he's striking."

Fauve walked over and took hold of Markus' arm. "There you are! Were your ears burning? We were just talking about you." Giselle watched Fauve lead him around the room, gripping his arm and petting him as she made introductions.

"This is Carolette."

Carolette smiled and took a deep breath, which caused her breasts to practically fall the rest of the way out of her daring neckline. Giselle felt embarrassed at how shameless she acted around men. Apparently her recent romantic disappointment was making her extra forward.

Carolette giggled, "Don't believe anything they say about me, Markus." She offered her hand as if she expected him to kiss it.

He took it and gave it a gentle squeeze. "Carolette."

Fauve rolled her eyes. "We don't make things up about you, Carolette. The things that happen to you are stranger than fiction."

Carolette licked her glossy lips. "I'd be happy to show you around when you have a night free."

"*Merci.*"

"That's Selma over there," Fauve continued.

"We've met. *Bonsoir,* Markus."

"*Bonsoir,* Selma."

Fauve walked him over to Solange, who had stopped dancing. "And this is Solange."

"*Bonsoir,*" he said.

Solange looked star struck. "*Alo.*"

"And that tall drink of water over there is Laetitia."

"*Alo,*" she called and gave a little wave.

"*Alo.*"

The men looked on and rolled their eyes at how the women were reacting to this new acquaintance. Fauve pointed to each of them.

"So you know Henri. And the tall twins are Auguste and Robert, they're Laetitia's brothers. And that's Pierre, and this is Fabrice. We all went to school together, but Fabrice is from Switzerland—he studied here as an exchange student. Just like Vincenzo who came here from Venice to study."

Henri cleared his throat. "Okay ladies, we're taking Blue Eyes to shoot pool with the boys. You're free to do your matchmaking and catch Giselle up on the latest news without us." He picked up a tray of sandwiches and led the men's retreat to the game room.

Giselle and her girlfriends carried their food and drinks to the salon, and broke out six decks of cards. Falling into shorthand communication, they chatted and giggled like schoolgirls. Assembled around the table, they played Mort des Rois, a card game they'd made up when they were little. The game required three hundred and twelve cards, which took a long time to shuffle, and was incomprehensible to anyone but them.

"You must tell me, where did you find my future husband?" Carolette shuffled her cards and tossed a king onto the table.

Laetitia nodded enthusiastically. "*Oui!* And if Carolette gets him, does he have a brother?" She snatched the king, and dropped two aces in its place.

Giselle gave Laetitia a disapproving look. "What about Pierre?"

"He hasn't put a ring on my finger, and Marcus is drool-worthy."

Selma chided her, "You Jezebel."

Laetitia raised her brows with mock indignation, "*Moi?*"

Selma waved her left ring finger and started play-acting. "Oh Pierre, hurry up and put a ring on it, or I'll let some hot artist have his sexy way with me." She giggled when Laetitia stuck her tongue out at her.

Solange sighed, "Yeah, are there more like him back home? He has a nice package." She laid an eight on top of the aces.

"Solange!" Giselle let out a shocked guffaw. "*What?*"

"That was what we could see in those work pants." Carolette was matter-of-fact. "Which are nicely cut, I might add."

Fauve was eyeing her cards as she murmured, "His butt looks like it would be fun to spank. And I agree, his pants must be tailored."

Giselle shook her head as she discarded a jack and a king. "No wonder the men left! You're such slutty sex fiends!"

"Oh honey, we wish!" Solange took a sip of her champagne. "And evaluating a man coming and going does not qualify us as sluts." She picked up all the cards and laid down a two.

"Thank you, Solange!" Fauve crowed and grabbed the two. She turned to Giselle. "We all wish we were getting enough action to make us sex fiends."

The topic of conversation meandered on to the divorces, affairs, disagreements, and pregnancies of local residents. Late that night as the card game wound down, the men returned and together they carried everything into the kitchen, washing dishes like a big family. Giselle noticed that Carolette found more than one reason to brush up against Markus.

"Oh, excuse me, Markus. Oh, your body is so hard. Do you work out?"

"I do."

"Have you tried spinning?"

"No, I have not."

"What do you do to get muscles like these?"

"I do calisthenics every morning when I wake up."

Solange asked what Laetitia was too shy to ask. "So, do you have a brother?"

"No," he replied. "No family now."

"Oh, how sad. Just like Giselle," Fauve said and rubbed Giselle's back.

As her guests departed, Giselle watched with amusement as Carolette and Solange tried to outdo each other with lingering goodnight kisses on Markus' cheeks, and she saw Carolette press her number into his palm. When all the guests had gone, Giselle bid Markus goodnight and climbed the great staircase to her room alone.

<hr/>

From the shadows, Alphonso watched the breakup of what he guessed was a dinner party. Henri and Fauve, who he recognized from the hotel, got into their Range Rover as the rest of the guests got into various cars and headed off down the driveway. The woman in jeans hopped back on her motorcycle and zoomed down the back road to deeper parts of the estate. And he saw "Iceman," as he had nicknamed Giselle's art assistant, walk around the back of the château heading for the stable house.

Well, he'd seen everything there was to see here. It was time to call it a night and get back to his hotel room. Alphonso moved stealthily across the property toward his car, without a flashlight he was grateful for the light of the moon. Other than learning that Giselle was working with Iceman, he hadn't learned much. While the party was underway, Alphonso had found the stable house unlocked, and he went through every square inch of the place. In an adjoining workshop, he found some sort of really cool-looking sculpture in progress that was about the size of a large orange. But nothing else of interest, and no passport or license or anything he could use to aid his investigation. Who doesn't have ID on hand? He drove back to Aiglemont without seeing another car on the road.

Cardinal Americo Negrali had been praying for guidance on how to handle Scortini's visit to the College, but when he received Scortini's note to the cardinals, he knew exactly what to do. He would tell Gabrieli everything. Once he arrived at that decision, he was ashamed he'd let Scortini's plea for secrecy prevent him from going immediately to his best friend. Now as he picked up the phone, his skin tingled with fear and he prayed that Gabrieli would answer. Verona invited him to come to his office at once, but Americo sensed it would be unwise to be seen going there. Instead, they arranged to meet in the last confession booth at the Little Church. Sitting inside the confessional fifteen minutes later, Americo heard someone enter the booth. He swiped the screen aside and was relieved to see his friend.

"Gabrieli, I need to ask your forgiveness, and let me tell you why."

He looked surprised, but remained silent as Americo continued.

"You see, I didn't believe a recent assertion to be true, and I wrestled with the thought that because it wasn't true, nothing would come of it."

"I understand." Gabrielli put his hand up in a calming gesture. "Together we'll know what to do, Americo. How can I help?"

"Salvio Scortini barged into a College session and told all the cardinals present that you are unfit to head the Verdu Mer project."

"*He what?*" The count practically choked on the words, he was so shocked.

"He told us he knows of some evilness that will strip you of papal trust, and this morning we received a note saying that he plans to deliver proof of your iniquity any day now. He again urged us to ask the Pope to remove you as head of Verdu Mer and award authority to him."

"I don't need to forgive you, Americo." His look of shock was replaced by empathy and understanding, as if he was the priest hearing his friend's confession. And in a very real way, he was performing a sort of absolution. "Hesitation and indecision are human nature, Americo. But I'm extremely disappointed in Salvio—though I can't say I'm surprised. Did he say what this evilness was?"

"No. But he was so dire, I believe he hoped that the gravity of his assertion alone would darken your family's reputation...just by sounding the alarm."

"Where there's smoke there's fire, eh? Was this evil supposedly being done now, or something in the past?"

"He refused to be specific, but said your family was no longer devout."

"My family?" He jerked backward, looking appalled.

"*Sì*, something so evil the Church would have to distance itself from both the sin, and from you. He called it 'a repugnance' that could not be permitted to tarnish the Verdu Mer project."

"Well, then he's going to try to frame us with something."

"How can I help you, Gabrieli? Because while Scortini *acted* pained at the prospect, I have a sneaking suspicion that he's the orchestrator of this evil. How can I help protect your family from such a campaign?"

Gabrieli put his hand up to the delicate metalwork of the lattice screen. "You've already done my family a great service by telling me this."

"Now that I've reflected on it, I saw something in Scortini's eyes that tells me he'll stop at nothing to obtain control of Verdu Mer. Gabrieli, I'm afraid for you and for your family."

"I'm relieved that Salvatore and Gelsonima Scortini didn't live to see their only son become so twisted."

Americo put his hand up to the screen that separated them in a symbolic handshake. "I'm sorry I failed to warn you sooner. I'll keep my eyes open and help you in any way I can."

The two old friends left the church separately, Tiberius joined Gabrieli, and Zelph trailed from the shadows on the opposite side of the canal.

———— ◉ ————

Markus and Giselle stood side by side making graceful curls by bending lengths of copper over the mold she'd made in Paris, and then polished them on a buffing wheel. It was a hot Indian summer day with clouds passing overhead frequently enough to keep the sun from beating upon them. As they worked, Markus was aware of Giselle's eyes on him and her efforts to mimic his precise movements, almost like a dance. It was incredibly flattering to be the object of her attention, and it made him hyper-aware of their delicate interactions. It was energizing in a way that made it difficult for him to relax into contemplation of the work at hand. She was extremely distracting.

When they'd fashioned the last curl, Markus was ready for a break, but Giselle ticked her pencil along her list of tasks and went straight back to work. The next step of assembly was inserting the copper curls into the girders, and Giselle set about carefully inspecting each of the pre-drilled holes. Markus stood in the shadow of the greenhouse and watched as she climbed around the metal beams in bare feet, like a child on playground monkey bars. He gave himself over to his longing for her—the ache was constant now.

Once satisfied with her inspection, Giselle swung down off a beam in an athletic move made incongruous by her soft dress, and walked over to the shaded table for a break. He joined her and poured glasses of lemonade as she put her bare feet up on a chair and stretched her legs. She was concentrating on the sculpture, which now looked like three-quarters of a fanciful igloo.

"I'd planned on making a simple scaffold to hold me while I welded the curls to the beams, then I'd use it again to affix the glass spindles. But…" She trailed off, deep in thought, and looked discouraged as she pointed to all the different heights of the steel. He picked up one of her feet and began massaging it as his eyes followed hers to the sculpture. He could see what she was just now considering.

"But to make a scaffold, and then have to change the height of that scaffold at every junction for every height, and move it to each position… That would be more work than making the sculpture, no?"

"I could order a pneumatic elevator platform from Paris, or maybe Brussels…" She sighed as he moved his hand up to knead her calf. Moving her other foot onto his thigh, she pointed to the ground, and then to the top of the sculpture. "It might make more sense for me to just stand on a ladder."

"No, too unstable. And do not forget that after the phase of the copper curls, we will next be holding glass spindles filled with irrodium. We want your neck and those spindles to be unbroken when you finish this sculpture. We build one small scaffold with different levels that we can move easily with the Bobcat, and I will hold you."

Giselle dropped her gaze to meet his eyes. "You'll hold me? You mean like in a circus act?"

"I will not drop you." He picked up her other foot, and gently pressed his thumbs into her arch and heel.

She closed her eyes and let her head drop back. "I'll rub your feet on our next break, Markus. I promise."

"*Da.*" And while trying to give nothing away in his expression, he poured all of his sexual frustration into giving her pleasure through her feet. His eyes swept up her thighs as far as her little dress allowed. Giselle's eyes returned to the sculpture, and when she twisted sideways to grab her blueprint, he was rewarded with the briefest view of her white panties. He was also rewarded with two sighs and a compliment.

"*Mon Dieu...*that feels so good."

After their break, they fashioned a small, lightweight scaffold with a ladder built right through the center of it. Then while Markus used the Bobcat and pulled it into place under their first junction, Giselle donned her work glasses and gloves, and prepared her tiny welding torch. After selecting a copper curl and a piece of flux core wire, she stood at the ready.

"Come now, we begin." Markus took off his work boots and socks, climbed onto the scaffold, and then beckoned to her. She climbed to the base platform of the scaffold, then ascended three rungs of the ladder and hooked one leg around Markus. He held her waist with both hands while she neatly welded the first copper flourish into place.

She unhooked her leg and he lowered her slowly. She gripped his hips with her thighs and her face was an inch from his.

"You're so convenient to have around! Now we can really get to work!"

Grinning, she let him lower her a bit more until her feet were back on the scaffold, then she pushed her protective glasses up and raised her hand for a high-five.

"*Da*, we are here to make art, not rebuild a scaffold eight hundred times." He patted her hand in victory.

They made quick work of welding copper curls to an entire section of one span, and Markus enjoyed every second of holding Giselle.

When Selma and a team of maids arrived at the château to clean, Giselle declared it was time for a break, and they drove the Tank into Aiglemont to buy supplies. Walking along the medieval streets, Giselle stopped frequently to receive little kisses on the cheek from local residents, and to answer questions about Markus. Entering a charming little grocery shop, Markus heard a familiar voice call out.

"Hey, you two! How's the piece coming?"

"Fauve! It's still in pieces." Giselle hurried over to chat while he stopped at a display of apples. He didn't want to intrude on their conversation, so he inspected the shelves nearby. But they didn't drop their voices, and he could hear them clearly.

"Can I see it when Vincenzo comes?" Fauve sounded excited, apparently gearing up for a ramble. "He just called Henri. He arrives this Saturday, right? *Mon Dieu*, if I had a husband like yours I wouldn't be out here in the country getting callouses with a bunch of boring tools. Let's all just forget work and have fun this weekend. Please say you will."

"Okay." Giselle nodded, and then arched an eyebrow. "But Markus and I still need to find time to work, so just be flexible when scheduling the fun."

Fauve turned in his direction and called out, "That tool remark wasn't aimed at you. Pardon my rudeness." She showed no embarrassment whatsoever.

Markus smiled, and accepting her acknowledgement as an invitation, he walked back over to join them.

"I am not insulted."

Tapping him on the arm, Fauve turned to Giselle in a conspiratorial tone. "Don't tell Carolette, but Markus here would be perfect for Simone."

"Your cousin?"

"It's time she moved on from Oscar."

"But she lives in Spain."

"You're right, geographically that won't work. But he's her type."

"You're such a matchmaker. His friend, Yvania, would approve of your efforts."

"Hey, when I see a man I want and I can't have, I try to pass on the gift."

"The gift can hear you. He's not deaf." Giselle scowled and pinched her.

"Ow! I'm sure he doesn't mind." She flicked her eyes back and forth between them. "What is it about you gorgeous people? You don't seem to care that you're making the rest of us drool. Seriously, can you honestly not want to mount him and ride him like a stallion?"

Giselle looked flustered, and he could have sworn he saw a guilty expression. She swatted Fauve away, and with her face flushing bright red, she moved off to claim the groceries the store had set aside for her.

Fauve pivoted to face him. "You're not married, right?"

"No."

She sidelined him with her body, making it clear she didn't want him wandering around the shop while she was trying to interrogate him.

"Never been married?"

"No." He kept his tone soft because he could see her pushiness was not mean spirited.

"So, what's your story? Are you dating anyone special?"

"No."

"Really? Why is that?"

"Ah, the same question always. Such a personal inquiry, and I believe this is the one area where women allow themselves license to pry."

"You're right. How are women supposed to learn the playing field if we don't ask questions? And, well, look at you." She vaguely gestured from is face to his body. "Of course every woman wants to know your situation so she can act accordingly."

He could see her interest was building, so he offered, "The women I have met since moving to Paris have been either too pushy, or they pretend to be hard-to-get and play silly games. I have not found 'the one,' and it is not right to use a woman as a place-holder, so I am alone."

"That sounds lonely. What about back home?"

"I lived in a very small area that did not have any women I desired."

"Let me see if I can fix you up with 'the one.'" She made air quotes with her fingers. "There are too many desirable women around here to have lonely men."

Giselle arrived at his side and handed over some packages for him to carry. Turning to Fauve, she broke in.

"We have to get back to work. But sure, come Saturday when Vincenzo arrives."

After returning to the château, they deposited the groceries in the kitchen and walked back to the greenhouse.

Giselle produced a set of keys and unlocked a cabinet. When she opened the door, Markus saw a heavily reinforced case sitting on a shelf. She took it over to the worktable and set it down with care.

"I bet you can guess what's in here."

"Now we break the law?" he whispered.

"*Oui.* Just possessing this irrodium is illegal. We have to make absolutely certain the spindles stay intact until we fuse them into their star patterns. Then I'll fracture the junction to join the chemical compartments."

"Not a big fracture, right?"

"No, the fuse point will be about the size of a pea, and the fracture will be no larger than an eyelash."

He helped her lay out a thick cotton pad, and a non-skid sheet of anti-static rubber on top of that. "Which side of the glass tube has the poison?"

She picked up a spindle and gave it to him.

"This compartment contains the hydrogen," she pointed, "and here's the irrodium. I had each spindle filled by two different chemists. The first chemist received all the spindles with two empty compartments. He filled one compartment in each spindle with hydrogen, and then sealed those halves. I picked them up and took them to the second chemist, along with a canister of irrodium. He used that to fill the remaining compartments."

"It was *your* irrodium?"

"It had been my late father's. I found it here in the basement in his personal laboratory."

"You trust these chemists?"

"I do. But the truth is, I never told them what I was going

to do. I simply engaged them to do their specific task, and that was all they knew. The first chemist specializes in hydrogen, so he had no questions. And the second is a very old friend of my father's who works in the safest laboratory environment possible. I personally delivered the irrodium to him in a container that still had my father's handwritten notes on it. He never directly asked me what it was."

He quirked an eyebrow and gave her a questioning look. "Hmmm."

"Oh, *he knew* what it was. He did it out of loyalty because I asked him to. There was nothing in writing, no papers. No one will ever know how I did it."

"When the authorities see *Star Fall,* they will ask questions."

"My father's lab still has the equipment to do what the chemists did for me, and I know how to use it. I used to fill spindles with all sorts of things when I was little."

"Sure, children do things like filling vials with glitter, but filling hundreds of vials with a deadly chemical is not the same thing."

"I won't ever admit to it happening any other way."

"There are times when I do not know what to think of you."

"Can you pick a new subject?"

Clearly he had pushed her as far as he could.

"Okay, new subject." Markus handed her back the spindle. "How long have you been married?"

Accepting the glass tube, she laid it down on the prepared surface. "Five years. We got married right out of high school."

He handed her another tube. "You were in a hurry?"

"*Oui*." She kept her eyes on the spindles.

"Will you tell me why?"

"My family's business was chemical manufacturing—industrial explosives. We made our fortune in munitions manufacturing, fireworks, and things like that. By my father's time we owned the biggest chemical company in the world."

"Ah, now your estate makes sense."

"I was seventeen when everything came to an end." Her voice dropped to a whisper. "Every last member of my family was at the unveiling of a new plant. But one static charge in a mixing room caused an explosion that was felt as far away as Brussels." Her voice broke and her shoulders sagged.

He took the spindle out of her hand, set it gently on the table, and pulled Giselle onto his lap. She rested her head on his shoulder and let him comfort her. He felt her hot tears slip onto his neck.

"I don't talk about it. I wasn't at the unveiling because I had a very bad cold. I was at home with a nurse. After the tragedy, our family business was ruined. The estate was sued for the wrongful death of everyone who died. After paying out everything our company had in the bank, the company was sold off to cover lost income lawsuits in six countries. I would have lost my home without Vincenzo and his family. In this region of France, anything in the bride's name legally becomes the property of the husband upon marriage. We were racing to save my home from all of the lawsuits that kept pouring in. So we married quickly.

My family really liked Vincenzo and they would have loved our wedding."

"I see." He wrapped his arms around her as she buried her face in his neck. He nuzzled his cheek into her hair, and melted into her for as long as she would stay in his arms.

Finally she sat up, wiped her eyes, and moved away. Returning to the work before them, she cleared her throat.

"Anyway, about the irrodium. When I was about fourteen years old, I started sneaking into my father's private laboratory here in the château's basement to experiment with his chemicals, and I came upon some vials of irrodium. They had clear warnings on them, so I was careful never to break one. But I found by accident that if I touched irrodium vials to vials filled with hydrogen and held them together, the irrodium would have a momentary reaction through the glass and cause the glass to fuse. I thought I would get in trouble because I had ruined the vials, so I tried a light tap on the fusion point to separate them. But I created a tiny fracture in the fused joint and the irrodium flowed between the two vials. Well, the glass stayed stable, and the most beautiful glow appeared. I snuck the glowing vials out of his lab and kept them hidden in the back of my closet so no one would find them and realize what I'd done. One night at dinner, I asked my father how long irrodium would glow if it was mixed with hydrogen, and he told me one hundred years." A sad laugh hiccupped out. "He believed me when I told him that I'd read about the reaction in one of his notebooks. I guess he never dreamed that I would experiment on my own."

"Where are those glowing vials from your childhood now?"

"Still in my closet upstairs."

"Ah. Most parents are only worried that their child will smoke cigarettes, I see that yours had something else to protect you from."

She stood up and stretched, arching her back in her profoundly sexy fashion.

"True, well, let's get one of the spindle stars set into the structure and begin lighting up *Star Fall*, shall we?"

"Giselle." He put his hand on her arm. "What if it spills on us?"

"Oh!" Fear flashed across her face, and then he saw her grim resolve. "We have to make sure that never happens. Irrodium quickly eats through skin, and when it get into the bloodstream, it rapidly kills off blood cells like wildfire. Death is almost instant. We can't get any on us." She was already kicking off her shoes.

Markus shuddered and took both of her hands in his. "You will show me one, and if I think it is too dangerous, I will ask you to quit this plan. I will not help you further."

"I can accept that." She nodded and selected four spindles, which she separated between her fingers, and then she led the way out to the sculpture.

Markus climbed the scaffold barefoot and stood balanced under the drilled holes. Giselle reached up and handed him the four spindles, which he kept separated between his fingers to prevent them from touching. She climbed the scaffold, and once in position she wound her legs around him to steady herself. Resting her body against the front of him she asked, "Do you feel solid?"

"*Da*, I am good."

"Okay, I'm going to take two of the vials now, so we'll each have two."

Her mouth was so close to his, he could smell the faint watermelon scent of her lip balm. Her body was warm and firm through the thin layer of dress material. He nodded and watched what she was doing. She carefully took two of the vials from him and exhaled to calm herself.

"Now, together we'll slip the four spindles into the four adjoining holes, and hold them completely still for one minute to ensure their tips fuse together."

She aimed her two spindles at the two holes on her side of the metal arm, and he did the same from his side. Together they inserted the spindles into the four holes and froze. Markus settled into sixty seconds of savoring Giselle against his body, feeling her supple feminine strength. Her breath became shallow and fast, and her eyes were gleaming. The smell of her made him both happy and miserable. He kept his eyes fixed on the deadly spindles in their hands, and sniffed the air for any odor that might warn him of leaking chemicals. But there was nothing except this beautiful creature braced against him, whose excitement was driving him mad.

"Now let's both lean back a bit, Markus. I'm going to flick one of them, and it should be just enough to cause a hairline fracture at the joint."

He gave her a meaningful look as he withdrew his hands and leaned backward. "Then the glow appears?"

"*Oui.*"

There wasn't a trace of fear on her face as she gently flicked a spindle. He heard the click of her nail against glass, and there in the early evening light he saw all four spindles blush with iridescent light that was as bright white as it was peach as it was rose. His mouth dropped open and he admired its glimmer across Giselle's enraptured face. The glow was extraordinary, and so was her response. She was transfixed. She wrapped her legs tighter around him, her hands floated away from her glowing star, and then she ducked under it to hug him tightly.

"*Voila,*" she whispered into his ear.

"Incredible."

He wrapped his arms around her and stared up at the star, feeling transfixed as well, and then realized he was about to go over a line she'd never given him permission to cross. He had to set her down. The urge to kiss her was now unbearable, and in another second he would be unable to resist. Lowering her to her feet, he knew his self-control was at its limit.

"Now that the test is a success, we put your chemicals away for the night. Okay?"

She nodded and followed him over to the greenhouse tables to lock the spindles away and clean up. They worked in silence, stealing looks at the glowing star mounted in the sculpture.

That evening in the cold stone château, they ate dinner in front of the fire and talked. Both felt satisfied that the glowing stars were being realized, and he was beginning to understand the potential of such a remarkable piece of art on the world. After their meal, Giselle lay stretched along Markus' body on the floor as they shared their personal reactions to the great art they'd seen. Markus was conscious that he was hovering just on the edge of heaven. He was relaxed and warm, but the heat of longing was a dull ache that drained him. When he returned to the stable house, he went straight for a cold shower before he fell headfirst into the feather mattress and lost consciousness.

———

Alphonso packed up his meager stakeout supplies and started slinking back behind the trees to his car. This had to be the strangest job imaginable. He knew better than to believe his eyes. As a private detective, he knew better than anybody that often things were not what they appeared to be. But he also had to be honest that he'd fallen in lust with Giselle the moment he'd set eyes on her, so his judgment was slightly impaired. He'd been sneaking out to her property every chance he got, and he'd tried to get some intel on this mystery man from Fauve one morning as she served him breakfast in the café.

"So is Giselle working on any new art?"

"Uh-huh, a really big sculpture."

"Big, huh? She must have assistants."

"*Mais non*, she likes to work alone. But this time she's brought the sexy Russian with her."

"Sexy Russian? Really? Does her husband mind?"

She'd simply waved her hand in a bored fashion. "*Non.*"

So he sat for hours hiding in that field in Gernelle trying to understand this piece of the Verona puzzle—trying to make sense of what he was watching. Ruskie, as he now called her shaved blonde assistant, had a body of steel, and focus to match if he could stay unaffected as he held Giselle. Other men would have risked getting slapped or scolded with a "Not now! We're working!" just for the thrill of running their hand up her thigh. Alphonso was a red-blooded man, and the sight of her body was driving him mad. He wondered what her wardrobe was made of, because each dress seemed to be made of water that shimmered over her curves. She moved with gymnastic grace, and watching them climb up into the sculpture, and hold positions wound around each other—they crackled with sexuality. He was watching the most smoldering flirtation, and yet neither of them was acknowledging it. He could feel their chemistry from across the field. And he had to bite his thumb to try to remain present when his mind wanted to take off in flights of fantasy about what the two of them did together inside the château after a day's work. What he wouldn't give for Zelph's lock-picking talent! Now that his stakeout was coming to a close, he'd arrived at his conclusion: unless Ruskie was a eunuch, they were lovers. He would bet on it, if he hadn't given up gambling.

He was disappointed he hadn't caught them actually having sex, but he had to get back to Venice. He was leaving France in the morning, certain of what was going on between Giselle and her Russian stud. True, he had no solid proof...yet. He just prayed to God that Zelph had something on the Verona men. They were going to have to make a detailed report of their findings to Scortini. If worse came to worse, Alphonso could tell him that Giselle had a lover. Would that be "evil" enough for his taste?

He touched down in Venice's Marco Polo Airport the next day and went straight to his uncle's to find Zelph. They sat down to lunch and volleyed bits of information back and forth.

"So Giselle has a Russian lover that she keeps at her château in France?"

"That's right."

"And you didn't get any photos?"

"No. There was no way to get close enough to get anything with the camera on my phone. I had to stay way out in the field or behind trees. It's a risky stakeout, what with all the other buildings on that property. I had to constantly keep on the lookout, couldn't take for granted that they were all empty. I couldn't be exposed in case someone came popping out of a stable door or opened a curtain on the back of the château."

"It didn't look like anyone else lives out there?"

"No, not in the big main castle. I checked out some guesthouses on the property, way down the lane on the back of one part of the estate. I think two women live in one of the houses, but they have guard dogs in a kennel that went crazy when I pulled into the driveway. I pretended to be lost and turned right around when an old woman came out onto the porch to check me out. Then a young woman came outside, too. She rides a motorcycle, and was in and out of the château a number of times. I saw her around town too, but she never spotted me."

"That's it? Just two women on the estate?"

"Yeah."

"Okay, well, here's what I've got. Count Gabrieli has been doing his usual rounds of meetings."

"Uh-huh."

"He goes to the Verdu Mer neighborhood, which is completely vacant now, to meet the demolition teams who have started tearing the buildings down section by section. Plus he has regular meetings all around the canals on the deserted *calles* with some famous underwater expert named Chizzoli and his team of guys in scuba gear."

"Uh-huh."

"And every night the count walks around his *sestieri* talking to his neighbors and anybody else who walks up to him."

"Yeah, I saw that. Everybody comes out of their homes to greet him."

"Right. A man of the people."

"Anything unusual?"

"Yeah. So the other day he had what appeared to be an impromptu confession over at a church that's known as the Little Church."

"Oh? It doesn't ring a bell."

"It's small and non-descript, located between the count's office and Scortini's palazzo."

"Oh, yeah. Really old? Sort of white stone?"

"That's it."

"So the count went for a confession?"

"Yeah, hurried out of his office and made a beeline for the Little Church with Tiberious moving fast at his side. And instead of confessing to a priest, Gabrieli was having a private conversation with Cardinal Americo Negrali. I'm sure my instincts are right on this. I did some checking on Negrali, and he's the most powerful cardinal in the world.

Top honcho in the Church, considered next in line to be pope if something were to happen to Pope Leopold."

"Uh-huh. Well, not a stretch since Gabrieli has such strong ties to the Church."

"Yeah well, the count has a reputation as sort of a super Catholic."

"Who've you been asking?"

"Every priest I could find."

"Oh."

"They all consider him to be their best friend."

"All of them said that?"

"Yeah, and that was the term they used. 'Oh, Count Verona is my best friend.'"

"Hmmm. Friendly guy."

"Yeah. There's no way he's not getting into heaven." Zelph laughed at own his joke. "Anyway, I'm going to tail Vincenzo when I leave here, and let you have the pleasure of watching Gabrieli."

"Do me a favor, and pray we find something before we meet with Scortini."

———— ⚙ ————

It was just past nine p.m. and Zelph had been standing in the shadows outside the Verona office building for hours when he saw Vincenzo and Petro come out the front door. He tailed them to Leonardo's building, and while Vincenzo disappeared inside, Petro fell into his usual routine of doing sweeps around the property and sitting in the lobby. Zelph got tired of standing outside in the shadows. He consulted the surveillance notes Alphonso had given him, slipped around the back of the building, and climbed a fire escape to the third floor. He had no problem eluding Petro, because he'd been spying on him, too. From the fire escape, Zelph eased the hallway window open and dropped silently inside. Then he made his way down the hall to Leonardo's apartment door and listened. He could hear male voices, but couldn't hear anything of use.

He eyed the adjacent apartment, walked over to the door, pressed his ear to it, and listened. Silence. He hadn't seen any lights in this apartment from outside the building during his recent stakeouts. If he could get inside, he could open the window next to Leonardo's apartment, and hear what they were saying. Perhaps he would hear a third voice.

Making up a cover story in case someone was inside, Zelph knocked lightly on the door. When there was no answer, he took out his lock-picking kit and was inside in less than nine seconds. He closed the door quietly behind him, and with the lights off, he swept the apartment. No one was currently living in this partially furnished unit. He eased the lock on the window and silently pulled the French-door style windows inward. Then he made himself comfortable with his head resting in the shadows just outside of the accountant's apartment. He heard Leonardo and Vincenzo talking.

"We've always known that Salvio's emotionally off-kilter."

"Well, my father feels that for all his social faults, he's still a good Catholic."

"There's no innocent explanation for him to say what he said to the College."

"No. Maybe the death of his parents was too much for him."

"A mental breakdown doesn't cause you to slander a person to the Holy Council for getting a job you wanted. No, there's no way Scortini actually believes your father is evil. It's a plan to cut him off from the Vatican as a power play for Verdu Mer."

"We've agreed that our best strategy is to proceed with care—not to reject or inflame him. If Salvio forces a confrontation, we'll calmly respond to his accusations."

"Should he ever become desperate enough to make any."

Zelph didn't hear a third voice, and he had no problem hearing the conversation between Vincenzo and Leonardo as they went on to discuss business deals, Verdu Mer, charity, opera, clothes shopping, rowing, and wine. They were very relaxed, so this was no business marathon, just two old friends making dinner together and relaxing.

"I have a meeting at nine tomorrow morning, then I'll be off to Gernelle for the weekend."

"We have the meeting with the lawyers tomorrow late afternoon."

"Let's have that meeting by phone. I'll call when I get settled at the château."

"I think their attorneys are close to agreeing to our terms."

"Me too. Can you set up the call?"

"Sure. How's Giselle?"

"Oh, you know. Now that she's working, it's hard to get her to put two sentences together."

"What's she working on?"

"Some very secret piece that's really big."

"Really big? Selma's keeping an eye out to make sure she's safe?"

"Uh-hun, and she took that artist whose process she's been studying. He's helping with the assembly."

"Do I know him?"

"No, we haven't met him. It's Markus, the Good Samaritan from the Metro."

"Oh, yeah. He made that cool little glass sculpture on your mantle in Paris."

"That's him."

They took their dinner farther into the apartment and it became difficult to hear what they said. The conversation slowed during dinner around muffled dining sounds and laughter. Something was apparently hilarious over there. Then the two moved off into a room still farther away, and he could no longer hear them. Odd. Where had they gone? He glanced around at the floor plan of the apartment he was in. Looking down the hall of this empty unit, he judged they'd headed to a bedroom. But his notes said Leonardo had the biggest place in the building, and that he also kept his office here, so Zelph was just guessing at what type of room they'd gone into. He poked his head out the French door, and looking into the glass reflection from Leonardo's open windows he could see Vincenzo's briefcase, confirming that he hadn't left. There was nothing definitive Zelph could point to, but he was forming a strange impression that he was eager to discuss with Alphonso.

Vincenzo finally left the apartment at two a.m. After following him to the Verona palazzo, Zelph called it a night and went home to bed.

W hile Giselle seemed to have a level of comfort with the hideous vials, Markus found it nerve-wracking as they went about creating the illicit stars. They would work together for hours within the sculpture performing their intimate dance. Giselle wound around Markus for support, and each silent sixty-second pause culminated in the tiny flick of her fingernail, and a beautiful glow. They assembled Giselle's vision with total focus, thighs encircled, arms laid against arms, holding perfectly still.

When taking breaks, they stretched out on cushions in the greenhouse massaging each other's necks, backs, and feet. They grew more engrossed in the sculpture as it materialized. Once after hours of work, Giselle lost her focus for a split second, and tapped a spindle a bit too forcefully. Alerted by the irregular-sounding *crack*, Markus reacted faster than a muscle twitch. He rocked to the side swinging Giselle feet-first off the scaffold as irrodium fluid trickled out of a hairline crack. The smoking liquid evaporated immediately in the wind and blew away from them as he landed beside her on the ground, scooped her up, and carried her over to the greenhouse. He set her down and ran his hands all over her checking for signs that she'd been splattered. Finding none, he took her face in his hands.

"Giselle, there is no place for any mistake in this."

She nodded, shaken, and he pulled her into an embrace, hugging her protectively.

"I am not mad at you. But from now on, I will tell you when you need a break. You push yourself too hard."

"That's what everybody tells me," Giselle said into his chest. "Let's take a break."

"*Da.*"

When they got back to work, Markus balanced on the scaffold, and Giselle balanced on Markus. They had just touched the spindles together for the glass to begin fusing when she got an urgent itch on her nose. Panicked, she gritted her teeth and whimpered, "*Ah merde!* Shit! Markus! My nose! I have an itch!" Her eyes began to tear in frustration as she tried to stay focused on the spindles above.

"No!" he warned, as if he could command the itch to disappear.

"Oh! Iee-eh!" She gritted her teeth in fear.

"Do not move. I will get it."

He eased his head forward a few inches and rubbed her nose with his own to satisfy her itch. It felt like the initiation of the most seductive kiss. She kept her eyes on the fragile glass above them, but she could feel their breath mingling, and couldn't be certain that she wouldn't lean in a fraction closer and press her lips to his. *What am I thinking? Focus, girl!*

The sound of car tires crunching gravel broke the spell, and Markus eased his head away from her. She tapped the glass tube, and the glow blushed over their faces, already rosy with the intensity of their almost-kiss. She looked beyond the stable house toward the driveway, and felt weakened with longing. Markus wrapped his arms around her waist, and pressed his face against her neck. Unthinkingly she responded, grinding herself against him. Then she heard a hearty shout from the front of the château.

"Gigi? Where's my gorgeous wife?" Vincenzo's voice grew louder as he came in their direction. "Are you in the greenhouse?" She climbed off Markus, and they both jumped down from the scaffold. She ran toward her husband's voice, banked around the greenhouse, and spotted him.

"There she is!" His face broke into a grin.

She jogged toward him waving her shoes, and then stopped to put them on.

"I thought you were working with metal and glass." Vincenzo looked skeptical as he took in her shoe situation. "Please tell me why you're not wearing proper footwear."

Giselle had just gotten back to her feet as he trotted over and tackled her, then swung her around, making her clutch at her dress hem as one of her shoes fell back off. He was peppering her face with little pecks as Markus walked around the greenhouse and stared at them.

"We have to climb the sculpture to affix the glass spindles..." She swatted away his playful assault, embarrassed that he would do this in front of Markus.

Vincenzo grabbed her around the waist again, and this time he bent down, and in one fluid movement put her over his shoulder. Turning around to face Markus, he was presenting her rear-end and bare legs to him.

"Markus! I'm her other half. Please come inside, and we can relax. If I know Gigi, she's been working you from sunup to sundown, but now the weekend has begun!"

"*Bonjour*, Vincenzo. I must go clean up now. I will come later." Markus nodded and turned in the direction of the stable house.

"Of course, I understand," Vincenzo called as he turned and carried Giselle toward the château. "We'll see you at the dinner party tonight. We've got all weekend to get acquainted."

Speaking in a mixture of French and Italian, Giselle scolded her happy husband. "Stop! You're crazy, V! Seriously, knock it off! My shoe! You do this in front of someone you haven't met? I'm telling your mother on you."

Giselle looked up in time to see Markus stalk into the stable house. Vincenzo swung her back down to her feet and waited while she put her shoe back on.

"Where's Henri?"

"He just dropped me off. He had to get back to the hotel." Vincenzo draped his arm around her shoulders. Together they walked around to the front of the château and retrieved his small suitcase and briefcase from the front steps before climbing the stairs.

From her bedroom suite, Giselle could hear Vincenzo rustling around in his own suite of rooms across the hall, unpacking his briefcase and setting his work out on his desk. Talking loudly so she could hear him, he updated her on their weekend plans and his work schedule, while she hid away from him to conceal her confusion. *My God! I almost kissed Markus! Am I turning into one of my slutty bunny friends? With my thighs wrapped around him, so help me God, I wanted to...*

She was snapped back to the present as Vincenzo called out to her, "I have a couple of business calls to get out of the way. But the most exciting deals are about to be signed. Mama will be here any time now, but please don't worry. She's coming with enough food for an army, by the sound of it, and she's called Selma to help her. Apparently the whole gang has invited themselves to get a peek at what you've been creating."

"I should get my work area cleaned up so no one breaks anything..."

"Right, can't have anyone getting hurt." He sounded distracted.

"I'll go do that now."

"Need any help?"

"No, you know I don't like anyone touching my supplies." She headed into the hall.

"Okay, I'll get on these calls. I promise I'll be done in time for dinner and we can enjoy our weekend. Sound good?"

"*Sì, sì,*" she acknowledged on her way past his room. She hurried out of the great house, feeling a languid warmth in her lower belly. Once in the greenhouse, she secured the irrodium case, then locked it in the cabinet.

She'd just packed up the rest of her supplies when she heard the sound of a crash coming from the direction of the stable house. She heard a quick succession of bangs that sounded like violent smashing of metal and glass, and ran to investigate. She twisted the doorknob of the stable house, let herself in and closed the door behind her, before following the sound toward the workshop. Markus was standing shirtless in front of an art piece he'd made, holding a cane. The sculpture was ruined, and he was shaking.

She winced. "Oh Markus, no."

He dropped the cane, turned away from his trashed sculpture, and walked past her into the stable house.

"I am going crazy," he choked. "I have no right...he is your husband...Ivar was right...I cannot be near you."

"No. Please. I..." She hunted for something to say.

Markus looked at her. His face was streaked with tears, his mixed emotions exposed, revealing anguished conflict. "I want you so...completely. *I am in Hell!*"

She walked over and tentatively stroked the tears from his face. She didn't know how to tell him she felt the same way. Feeling as if words had deserted her, she moaned, "Oh, Markus please don't cry."

Surprising her, he pulled her to him until their foreheads touched.

"I cannot stay here any longer." He breathed softly and closed his eyes.

"Don't go." She kissed him softly on the lips.

He grasped her to him fiercely, but returned her kiss with tenderness. He half sighed, half growled with frustration as she allowed his tongue to softly lick the inner pillows of her lips and then caress her tongue. Shocked that she would allow such a sexual kiss, but unable to stop himself, he kissed and licked her mouth with infinite gentleness. His hand slipped under the soft film of her dress and slowly followed the shape of her body. Conflicted, he stopped kissing her, dropped onto a cane-backed chair and pressed his face into her stomach.

"I want you so…" He stroked his fingers along her waist and made a stark confession. "I am completely in love with you, Giselle."

The delicious kiss had made the warm pool in her belly spread, and now feeling his hot breath on her stomach pushed her over the edge. Giselle placed a fingertip under his chin and gently tipped his face up to look at her. With her other hand she flicked the snaps of her dress open revealing her bare breasts, and he gasped as she offered them to him. She kicked off her shoes and he groaned, but was too immersed in his longing to question her motives. Looking up at her, his hands cupped her breasts and he began to stroke them with his agile fingers. Her breath caught in her throat, and she looked into his blue eyes as he leaned forward and sucked one of her nipples until she felt an electric *zzzing* between her legs. His teeth grazed so lightly, she wasn't sure what she was feeling at first. And then he swirled his tongue around her nipple again and sucked as he slipped his hand under her dress and squeezed her rounded cheek.

Giselle unfastened his pants, freeing him. And then pulling her panties to one side, she sat down on his lap, straddling him with a raw gasp.

All of her snaps gave way with one pull as he whisked her dress off. He held her slowly undulating hips and kissed every part of her that she offered him. Markus watched as Giselle gave herself over to pleasure with complete abandon. He ached with desire to move with her as she ground onto him, riding him, but he was afraid to break the spell.

He held on to her until she came completely undone, her breathing ragged, and she shuddered to a stop. Markus felt no shame and allowed himself to finish with her. He felt right and glorious. After kicking off his shoes and pants, he stood up and carried her across the room to the bed. There he laid her down and pressed his body against her, not wanting this experience to end. They were kissing and nuzzling each other when Markus looked down and noticed the blood.

"This is your monthly time?"

She wrapped her arms around him and buried her face in his chest.

"No. It's my first time."

It took his breath away, and he stayed completely still for a moment. "What do you mean?" He ducked his head down to look into her eyes. "I do not understand."

She shook her head and made as if to say something, but then just puffed her cheeks out and shrugged.

At that moment, the sound of tires crunching gravel came from outside not far from the stable house, and then car doors slammed, interrupting her chance to explain. A woman's voice called in a cultured Italian accent, "Giselle! Come give me a hug! Put down your tools for the night!"

In a lower tone the voice began issuing orders.

Giselle raised herself magnificently up onto her hands and knees. "Oh, *mon Dieu!* My mother-in-law!" Like a lioness, she leapt, stripped off her askew panties, and skirting the multicolored partition wall, she ran to the oversized Moroccan tub. She began rinsing between her legs, water splashing across her stomach and pinkish water running down her thighs before running clear. "I've got to get up to the main house or Juliette will walk in here at any moment!"

The contessa's happy voice was growing closer. "Giselle! Do not make me wait!"

Giselle hopped out of the tub, dried quickly with a towel, ran across the room, shrugged into her dress, and started fastening her snaps.

She looked at Markus, and smoothed her hair. "Do I look different? Do I look like I'm not a virgin?"

"What?" Markus stared at her in disbelief. "I...I never thought you looked like a virgin." Smiling, he ignored her activities and said slowly, "You look...like a woman...who is in love...with me."

She pulled on her shoes, fanned her face with her hands, and called as she ducked out the door, "Dinner is at eight!"

Markus lay on the Moroccan blankets and closed his eyes. Did that just happen, or had he fallen asleep and had another of his wild dreams about her? He opened his eyes and smelled his hands. They smelled of her, but he'd been holding her all day. He got up, retrieved her towel from the chair where she'd tossed it, and went to take a shower as he gathered his thoughts. She was kidding about being a virgin. She had to just be embarrassed about having her time of the month. Right?

When he turned off the gushing swan he heard more cars arrive outside and went to the window in time to see Henri and Fauve parking their Range Rover in the courtyard. Carolette was hanging on to her parked car while putting on a pair of dangerously high heels. She righted herself, swung her car door shut, and while rushing to catch up with someone out of sight, she reached down into her blouse and adjusted her boobs. This was going to be an interesting evening.

———— ·◉· ————

Markus took his time dressing before making his way to the main house for dinner. He had a lot to think about, but in his gut he felt Giselle was his. Stepping into the grand dining room, he saw flickering candles on every available surface, and food and champagne arrayed on the formally set table. Lively conversation echoed in the regal stone and marble chamber, made comfortable by a roaring fire in the stately hearth. Apparently he'd arrived just in time for dinner, and his eyes sought out Giselle, who was being seated next to her mother-in-law at the table. She looked refreshed and had found time to change into a softly falling dress of Chinese red and smoky grey panels. She noticed his entrance and gave him a happy smile and a little nod. His heart raced just looking at her, and he returned her nod as he approached the table.

"Ah! There he is." Vincenzo came over to shake his hand and then walked him to Giselle's end of the table. "Markus, this is Juliette, my mother. She tells me that she, too, has been hearing about you for weeks now. It would appear my wife has become obsessed with you."

Markus presented himself to Juliette and bowed. "Contessa, I am honored to meet you."

She made a minute gesture, and a servant responded by adjusting her chair, allowing her to stand gracefully and embrace him.

"Please, you must not call me by that title—only Juliette. I have never heard Giselle so enthusiastic—positively enraptured by your talent since the day she first saw your work."

Vincenzo headed to the other side of the table and beckoned. "Markus, please come sit near me."

Feeling awkward, he followed the man whose wife he had just had sex with, and told himself to stay calm.

Servants wearing crisp black-and-white uniforms attended to the dinner. They placed food before each guest and then retreated, leaving only two staff. One seemed to be for the general party, and one hovered discretely near the contessa.

Fauve called down the table. "So nice of you to join us, Markus. I thought you were standing us up."

Markus smiled at her and raised his eyebrows in greeting.

"Ah, there's that lady-killer smile of his!" Solange prodded Carolette.

"Juliette," Fauve queried, "don't you think Markus should have a wife?"

"Of course." The contessa looked at him appraisingly. "And a good catch for a young lady. Talented and handsome."

"Since I'm taken," Fauve smiled, "I think that Giselle—"

Giselle's fork clattered to the polished stone floor, and all heads turned to look at her. She seemed unperturbed as she accepted another fork from the servant, coolly used it to spear a mushroom, and took a bite.

Fauve continued, "Giselle should give Markus a night off so he can take Carolette out for dinner."

"*Merci*, Fauve." Carolette grinned. "A girl could starve waiting for a man to become available." She favored Markus with a flirty expression.

Juliette nodded. "Gigi, you work too hard."

Henri, who was seated at Juliette's left, asked, "What do you think of the mushrooms? They're chanterelle in truffle crème, I believe. "

The server offered more of the dish. Accepting another helping with an aristocratic nod, the countess seemed utterly comfortable in her role as nobility.

"*Sì*, this dish is superb, Henri. You must have more yourself." She smiled warmly at him, and he blushed as another helping was spooned onto his plate. She turned to the table and raised her glass. "A toast to Markus. We thank you for keeping our Giselle safe while she works, and for helping her so much."

"*Santé!*" everyone echoed.

Uncomfortable with the kind words and attention, Markus looked over his glass at Giselle. "This is my pleasure."

"She's the most incredible woman," Vincenzo commented. "Don't you agree, Markus?"

"She has no equal." Markus saw the love in Vincenzo's eyes and felt a stab of guilt.

"No. No equal." Vincenzo nodded in agreement and gazed at his radiant wife.

After dinner, the party gathered in the salon to relax with coffee, sweets, fruits, and cheeses. Markus stood near the windows, bookended between Carolette and Henri. He could only feign interest in what they were saying as he watched Giselle's graceful movements across the room. She was demonstrating something with her arms and hands that made her dress shimmer over her curves. He was reliving her determined pleasure as she straddled him on that chair, the taste of her mouth, her thighs wrapped around his hips as she rode him. It was all he could do not to cross the room, and throw her onto the couch that her husband was sitting on.

Oh God! The image of Vincenzo sweeping Giselle into his arms and over his shoulder slammed into his mind, and he almost clamped his hands against his temples. No wonder Vincenzo did that to her. How could a man help it if he was allowed to take possession of Giselle like that?

Carolette was giggling and hanging on his arm, while shaking her finger at Henri. He could see Henri was embarrassed for her, by how desperately she was seeking attention. When Laetitia called Carolette away, Henri remarked, "She's a bit of a wild child, but she's a really good person. The right husband could tame her."

Markus nodded distractedly.

Fauve was lounging in front of Markus and Henri on a velvet sofa, and Juliette came to sit next to her. Fauve turned to Juliette and gushed, "We can't thank you enough for allowing my parents to stay with you in Venice last month. I can't imagine what you had to do to arrange their audience with the Pope!"

Juliette nodded. "I was happy to do it. The Vatican and our family are the oldest of friends, since...well... *forever.*"

"It was the highlight of their lives."

"They came back calling him *Sua Santità.*"

"*Sì,* that is what Italians call the pope."

Vincenzo clinked his glass with a spoon and asked, "Now, who would like to see what Gigi is working on?" He beamed at her. "I know it's late, but from what you just told me, the thing *glows.* We can see something tonight, can't we?"

Giselle nodded and stood up. "*Oui,* it's in the early stages of assembly, but you'll get the idea."

Juliette walked over to her daughter-in-law and gestured for her to lead the way. The group claimed sweaters at the front door as they streamed out into the chill evening air and across the courtyard. As they cleared the far side of the stable house, they saw the small pinkish stars glowing steadily in the dark. Everyone's step quickened toward what looked like floating clusters of embers.

"Oh, Gigi. It's wonderful!" Vincenzo said.

"Holy shit! Is that pink lava in glass?" burst Carolette.

Giselle walked over to one of the metal struts and stroked it appreciatively. "This is *Star Fall.*"

Markus watched Giselle with her family and friends

drifting around the unfinished sculpture. She cautioned, "Don't come too close. It isn't safe to touch the stars."

Vincenzo and Juliette came together under the sculpture.

"This looks like the pope's drawings." Juliette was staring in wonder. "Even the glowing halos."

"*Sì*, exactly like the dream."

Markus found their comments puzzling. What dream were they talking about?

"Gigi, this is the size of a house!" came Juliette's awed voice. "How did you construct it?"

Giselle walked over to Markus, and put her hand on his shoulder. "We used a crane for the big materials, and for the rest, I climb Markus."

"Did you hear that, Carolette?" Solange gestured toward Markus with her drink. "He's slim, but he's sturdy."

"Not to interfere with your art process darling, but we can afford scaffolds." Vincenzo gave an indulgent shake of his head.

Intensely aroused by the scent of Giselle and the warmth of her hand on him, Markus enjoyed watching the shadows play across her face in the rosy light of the sculpture.

After giving everyone a few more minutes to appreciate the beginnings of the sculpture, Giselle announced that she was getting cold and asked that they all return to the house to finish dessert. Still uttering "oohs" and "ahs," the group returned to the house. Markus noticed that Vincenzo and Juliette stayed behind, and that Vincenzo was taking photos of *Star Fall* with his phone.

T he ultimate Italian mother, Juliette was already
working in the kitchen as everyone in the château was
waking up. It had been a fun party last night with everyone
joining in a marathon of board games and charades that
lasted until the wee hours of the morning before everyone
found a bed to fall into. Even her secretary had joined in
the activities after she'd completed her duties. As Juliette
assembled ingredients for breakfast, she heard the boys on
the stairs. She had just poured some fresh stovetop espresso into her cup as Auguste, Robert, and Fabrice entered
the kitchen.

"Ah, and here are my early birds..." She looked at them
fondly, wishing she'd had more sons. She poured glossy
frothed milk into her first cup of cappuccino of the day.

Fabrice came to stand next to her. "Juliette, you like
chocolate..."

"Of course."

"May I show you something beautiful?"

"With my cappuccino?"

With a proud flourish he squirted two fine circles of chocolate sauce onto the milk froth and then grabbed a toothpick and made a few quick movements. He placed the cup in front of her, and she was delighted to see a picture of a gondola in the foam.

"Oh! Pierre is not the only one of you boys with artistic talent! It is almost too beautiful to drink!"

Fabrice looked pleased. Vincenzo arrived in the kitchen, looking well rested, and happy to join his friends. She offered him her cheek and he kissed it.

"*Buongiorno,* Mama. Did you sleep well?"

She took a satisfying sip of cappuccino and nodded, smiling. *"Sì, sì."*

Having already cut holes out of thick slices of fresh country bread, she took them to an over-sized cast iron pan she'd been preheating. "Go on, sit boys." She pointed to the breakfast bar on the other side of the kitchen fireplace. "Start your day with strength and happy stomachs."

She drizzled a bit of olive oil in the pan, arranged the bread slices as the oil began to sizzle, and then neatly cracked an egg into each hole.

Fabrice stayed close and leaned over the pan. "What are you making?"

"Nido d'uovo."

"Egg's nest?"

"Sì." Juliette used a fork to add a bit of roasted red pepper on top of each bubbling egg, and then sprinkled sea salt across the whole pan from up high, looking just like a chef.

"It smells incredible!" Robert said as he carried espressos for each of them to the table.

Auguste came close to her holding a plate, and she pinched his cheek lightly. "You will like it because it is fried."

"We'll like it because you made it," Fabrice countered sweetly.

"I'll have two," Robert called.

"Oh, then you would just want to nap." She waved her audience away from the stove.

"What are you baking?" Fabrice asked.

"Nothing for you boys. Those are scones for the girls."

"Good morning all," Henri said, appearing in the doorway. "Got any espresso for me?" The twins guarded their cups and pointed to the pot on the stove.

"Do not worry. There is another pot ready to brew."

Auguste asked, "Now why is this espresso so amazing? What did you do to it?"

"It is Passero's...the best. I import it from Philadelphia in America. I take it everywhere with me."

"It's incredible!"

"So, what have you boys planned for today?" Juliette asked.

"We're going fishing," they all replied in unison.

"On the lake at the far end of the property?" She expertly flipped the frying toasts.

"*Sì*. We're going to catch some bass for dinner," Vincenzo said.

"And if they aren't biting, we'll go for a swim." Henri attempted to get espresso from the empty pot.

"Just be careful. That old rope swing and diving platform should be taken down."

"Don't worry, Mama," Vincenzo assured her while he set the fresh pot of espresso to percolate on the stove.

"We will build new swimming features for the lake when you start giving me grandchildren to play there." She raised her spatula and declared, "Okay, *mangiare.*"

They all grabbed plates and formed a line at the stove where she served them.

"Do you want a bit of grated Parmesan?"

When they nodded enthusiastically, she topped each egg with a snow shower of rich cheese.

The boys had finished eating by the time the women came sauntering down dressed in riding clothes. Juliette served them their usual egg whites with basil, and freshly baked scones with jam. They'd been eating the same thing on weekends since they were in high school.

Juliette was dictating letters to her secretary, Ippy, when Markus arrived.

Taking a quick pause to get him some breakfast, she got up and gestured for him to sit.

"Markus, come sit by me, dear. Do you like coffee and eggs?"

"I do, thank you." He sat and turned to Ippy. "*Bonjour.*" Ippy smiled. "*Bonjour.*"

"So, have you been Juliette's secretary long?"

"I've been with her for almost ten years, since just out of school."

"You have an unusual name."

"Short for Ipanema. My father always wanted to live there." She handed a napkin and fork to him.

Everyone was in the spirit of carefree childhood holidays.

The boys were packing lunches to take on their fishing trip, and the girls were finishing their breakfast. Juliette could tell from his eyes that Markus hadn't slept. She placed a cappuccino in front of him and moved back to the stove to whip up a quick meal for him. While continuing to give rapid dictation in Italian to Ippy, she brought him eggs, a scone, butter, jam, juice, and water. Smiling down at him, she pinched his cheek.

"There now, Markus, eat, my dear."

Having accomplished a successful breakfast, she removed her apron and sat down to enjoy a second cappuccino before setting off for her own plans for the day. She was excited to be visiting her friend Daniel and his fellow monks about an hour away at Abbaye d'Orval. Each time she came to the château, she loved to spend a day at the Abbaye because they had the most delicate preserves she'd ever tasted. If she hurried, she could be in their cellars before noon, and she liked to take her time finding just the right treats to ship back to Venice.

"Mama, you are going to see the monks today?" Vincenzo asked as he packed a final sandwich in the picnic basket.

"*Sì.*"

As the two groups headed out for their activities, Vincenzo swooped in among the girls and hugged Giselle.

"Have fun riding." He kissed the corner of her mouth and chuckled, "Mmm! Strawberry!"

Giselle laughed and wiped at the jam on her mouth. "Try to bring us enough fish for dinner."

Juliette watched as Vincenzo swung Giselle into a dramatic dip, and then quickly glanced over at Markus.

She didn't miss the look Vincenzo shot him, or that Markus seemed pained. Vincenzo's brows were knit as he looked from Markus to Giselle, who was laughing in his arms.

"Markus," Vincenzo said, "are you coming fishing with the boys?" Giselle pried herself from his arms and followed Fauve out the door. Markus swallowed a mouthful of eggs and looked at his plate.

"No. Today I will write to friends back home, and work to repair a sculpture that was broken."

Vincenzo gave him a long look. "You don't need to avoid us."

"I know."

Vincenzo nodded and headed outside to join the others.

Juliette took the opportunity to satisfy her curiosity. "So Markus, how long will you be here helping Giselle?"

"I do not know."

"You seem free with your time. You have no commitments elsewhere?"

"No, no other commitments right now."

"You live in Paris?"

"I do."

"And where are you from? Where is your homeland?"

"I come from Ukraine."

"You speak excellent French. Did you study it in school there?"

"*Oui*, it was important to learn because my father and I worked alongside so many French artisans when we restored churches and castles. It has been an important language for me."

"Especially now that you live in Paris. How long have you been living there?"

"I moved to Paris not long before I met Giselle. She asked me to come to Gernelle, and I was available while I am waiting for my job to start. There have been some delays."

"Giselle is lucky you were available. She says she wants to learn to be more like you in her art."

"I do not know about being like me, but she is a great artist."

"Just what she says about you."

"Did I hear you are going to visit some monks today?"

"*Sì*, out in the Ardennes forest there is an order of Trappist Cistercian monks who make some of the best preserved foods in the world."

"Well I hope you have a good day." Markus stood up and took his dish over to the sink. "Thank you for breakfast, Juliette. Now, if you will excuse me."

"Of course." Juliette nodded and turned to Ippy. "Let us get ready to leave as well."

⸻ ❈ ⸻

Markus spent the morning working in the stable house workshop on a new sculpture. The one he'd taken a cane to was a total loss and he'd had to sweep it all into the trash bin. When working with his hands wasn't enough to distract him, he exercised and then showered. It was late afternoon when he saw Giselle ride alone past his window. He peeked out the curtain and watched her dismount, and then she disappeared with her horse into the stables. He willed her to come see him, and his heart stopped when she opened the stable house door. She came inside, pulled the door closed, and leaned back against it to catch her breath. Keeping her eyes on his, she reached behind her back and turned the lock with a firm *click*. He approached her very slowly, nervous that she might turn and disappear. He couldn't take another sleepless night; he'd had too many lately.

"Markus..." She was on the verge of continuing, but when he reached her she felt overwhelmed with nervous excitement. He stopped so close that she could feel his chest touching her breasts every-so-slightly, and his thighs grazing her thighs. He tipped his head, brought his lips to her ear, and inhaled her scent.

"*Oui*, Giselle?" It was a whisper.

Now that she had daringly escaped her friends and brazenly rushed to be with him in secret, she was losing her nerve. Here she was, melting and inflamed and confused. What she'd prepared to say had flown out of her head.

"I..."

He exhaled, and she felt his breath on the tender skin behind her ear.

"I...I want your hands on me," she stammered.

His quick intake of breath caused a thrilling thump between her legs. Trying to cover her awkwardness, she moved around him into the room, and cringed inwardly at her own lack of cool. But it was the truth. She wanted his hands on every part of her. She wanted him to do the same things he'd done yesterday without being asked. Markus moved behind her, and his lips brushed the delicate hairs on the back of her neck.

"Mmm. You want my hands on you like this?" He placed his hands on her shoulders and pulled her back to lean against his chest. He trailed his left hand down from her ear, fingertips moving down the front of her neck and across her collarbone, while his right hand slid across her stomach. She leaned back against his hard body, feeling his breath in her ear.

"*Oui.*" It was a plea.

He smoothed his palm down over her left breast and cupped his hand underneath. With his other hand he unbuttoned her blouse, unfastened her bra, and began stroking the bare skin beneath. His fingertips grazed her nipples and they responded by hardening.

"You want my hands on you here?" He was caressing her bare stomach. She felt as if there was a direct current from there to her sex. The sensation was a liquid rush as heat pooled low in her belly.

"*Oui.*" She arched her back to let her shirt and bra drop to the floor.

Markus was lost in tides of emotion, his mind furiously capturing every sensation, every smell, and the image of every part of her in case this never happened again. He could feel the pull of animal hunger urging him to pour everything that he was as a man into her until he had nothing left.

He slowly exhaled. "Is there anything else you want, Giselle?" He unfastened her pants, slipped the fingertips of both hands into the waistband of her jodhpurs, and eased them down as he stroked her hips and thighs.

"I..." She couldn't think of a word to say.

"You?" She heard the smile in his voice, but she also heard something deep and almost pleading in his tone.

"I want your mouth on me."

"Ahhh, you want my mouth on you." He kissed her neck. "Will here do?"

He moved around in front of her, drew her over to the oversized chaise lounge, and sat her down. He knelt in front of her and pulled off her boots and pants before sitting next to her. He took her naked onto his lap for a full, deep kiss, licking her tongue slowly. His deep kisses made her head spin.

He stopped kissing to ask, "Or here?" He laid her back on the plush upholstery and trailed his lips and tongue slowly over her breasts. "Tell me where my mouth is needed." He took his time kissing and nibbling his way down her stomach while he parted her legs.

Giselle felt such freedom as she surrendered to the fantasies she'd pushed out of her mind while working with Markus, and she opened herself to him.

Just as he had fantasized during their long hours of work with her legs wound around him, he now made love to her with his mouth and his hands.

Giselle loved every moment until she had to draw her legs together and saw spots in front of her eyes. She lay panting and dazed as he contented himself with kissing her inner thighs. After a few moments she raised herself onto an elbow and smiled.

"*Merci.*"

"You are most welcome." He continued kissing her tenderly.

She felt relaxed and more confident now. "I would also like to see you naked. Will you take your clothes off please, Markus?"

He stood up without taking his eyes off her, removed his work shirt, and stepped out of his pants and slim knit boxers. Then he picked her up and carried her to the bed where he gently pushed her down onto the soft feather bed and murmured, "Now would you like to know what *I* want?"

"Of course. How rude of me. Can I offer you something?" she asked as he climbed on top of her. Thrilling as his hard body molded to hers, she squealed with delight as he raised his hips preparing to enter her.

Alarmed, he stopped. "Did I hurt you yesterday?"

"No! I want you inside me. It only hurt for a moment and then, well, it was..." she parted her thighs, inviting him, "soooo good."

He leaned down and brushed his lips over hers. "I want you to love having me inside you." He stroked his fingertips enticingly between her legs, opening her and testing her wetness. "I want you to feel the same pleasure that I feel." And then he was filling her. Even with her reassurances, he was gentle as he made love to her. Together they were united in their need to stimulate each other, and abandoned themselves to the primal rhythm of their bodies. As the pace picked up, she felt herself surrounded by his hard body, filled by him, and she raced him to the edge of ultimate satisfaction, rocking her hips and concentrating on the friction between them. Their arousal built until they strained against one another and came in a rush.

Just as she began to lose control, he allowed himself to come.

She was his. He'd known it the moment she accepted his gift on the sidewalk in front of her house. He caught his breath as he trailed his forehead along her jawline and planted kisses along her neck. He didn't want to break the spell, but he had to know the answers to the questions that plagued him.

"You tell me you have given me your virginity. Does Vincenzo prefer the alternative?" He reached down to stroke her thigh and trailed his fingers down to the curve of her buttocks.

She shook her head, blonde hair shimmering in long waves. "No. I'm still a virgin there, too."

"I do not understand. What is the nature of your relationship with Vincenzo? Is there something wrong with him? What am I missing?"

They heard whooping laughter as the ladies came racing into the courtyard on horseback.

Solange hollered, "Here comes the Jeep! We've beaten the men!"

Carolette yelled back, "Where's Giselle? Maybe I'll have time to pay Markus a quick visit."

He rose up on his hands to peek out the window and glimpsed the riders disappearing down the road toward the orchard.

"Oh!" Giselle reached her face up to quickly nibble his stomach. "I've got to go!"

She dashed over to the bathroom and climbed into the tub to rinse off. Markus followed her and sat at her feet as the water splashed over him. Looking up at her, he searched for answers.

"You must tell me what is going on. I feel that you are mine. I feel that you love me the way that I love you. What lie are you living with Vincenzo?"

Loud whoops now came from the men just outside as horses galloped past the stable house again. It sounded like the men were running after the women's horses.

Giselle sank down onto his lap, straddling him on the colorful tile. "What? He's my husband. Really. I'll tell you what I can. But some secrets I can't share."

"What are you afraid of?" He kissed her fingertips.

"Gigi?" Vincenzo was calling from near the greenhouse.

"I have to go!" She swooped down to kiss him, then rushed out of the bath, toweled with brisk efficiency, yanked her clothes and boots on, and disappeared out the door into the sunshine.

<hr />

Vincenzo was looking for Giselle in the greenhouse when he saw her come out of the stable house and start across the courtyard toward the château. He paused in the shadow of the door awning and was about to call out again, but something about her manner left him uncomfortably mute. He'd seen Giselle obsessed when working on her sculptures before, but she was acting differently this time. Just as he was about to step out of the shadows, he saw Carolette come around from the stables and approach the same door Gigi had just exited.

"Markus?" Carolette called. Then she leaned against the outside wall furtively applying lipstick.

Markus was dressed only in a pair of pants as he opened the door. "*Alo,* Carolette."

"I wanted to come get you. We're making dinner up at the house." She used the tip of a finger to wipe the edge of her lip.

"Oh, it looked like you came to offer me lipstick." He eyed the cosmetic tube in her hand.

She capped the tube and slipped it between her breasts into her bra. "No, but you can have a taste of mine if you like." She licked her lips and puckered them.

"You have a very safe storage place for your cosmetics." He laughed and made no move to accept her offered kiss.

She eyed his washboard abs. "You must do a lot of sit ups, Markus."

Auguste approach the outbuildings toting a bucket of cleaned fish, and Vincenzo fell into step with him. As they got to the stable house, Auguste said, "Hey you two, dinner isn't going to make itself, and I'm hungry. Come on up to the kitchen and let's get this party started."

Markus answered, "I will be up after I put my shirt and shoes on," and disappeared inside.

Carolette joined them in the walk to the château, chatting away as she always did. But Vincenzo's mind was on what Giselle had been doing in the stable house with Markus. She was probably talking to him about the sculpture; after all it was her favorite subject.

Soon everyone was in the kitchen having a good time, and Giselle seemed to be her normal self, enjoying her friends.

They all got busy making salads and dips, and his mother was in her glory working the grill on the patio just beyond the back door. Juliette had every early-fall vegetable imaginable on skewers and was brushing marinade on them, the roasted smoke acting as the ultimate appetizer. Fabrice stepped beside Juliette to place the fish on the grill, and Laetitia helpfully squeezed lemons and sprinkled salt over them.

Fauve stood next to Vincenzo, making neat little disks of goat cheese. He took each disk and rolled it in a bowl of chopped hazelnuts before setting them on a tray of salad toppings. He kept an eye on Markus, who was working with Carolette scraping cooked eggplants from their blackened skins. She was in full flirt mode trying to seduce him.

Giselle turned from the stove and announced, "I've got the onions sautéed. Who needs onion?"

"Over here for the baba ghanoush," Carolette answered.

Giselle picked up her sauté pan and carried it over to the baba ghanoush, while Carolette headed to the compost bin with her eggplant skins. As Giselle spooned her onions into the bowl, Markus stirred them into the eggplant.

"Careful, this is hot," Giselle cautioned. The way she said it made Vincenzo's ears perk up.

"I am not afraid of hot," Markus answered in a husky tone.

Vincenzo watched his wife blush and stare into her pan as if the onions had become fascinating.

"Eh, Gigi, are you feeling all right?" Carolette had returned to her spot and was looking at her with concern. "If it's too hot in here for you, I'll work at the stove. You step outside."

"What?" Giselle almost bumped Carolette with the pan. "Why?"

"Your face is beet red."

Giselle's gaze skittered over to Vincenzo, and they locked eyes for a moment before she dropped her stare back into her pan.

Wanting to break the tension he said, "Be careful not to over-salt that dip, Carolette. Remember last time?"

"Let him taste some before I add anything."

Giselle set her pan aside, scooped a bit of the dip with her spoon and brought it over to Vincenzo. Carolette waited with her seasonings while he tasted it. He nodded, then bending next to Giselle's ear he whispered, "Remember when that waiter got hit with the flying onion tart in Monaco?" She began to laugh at their inside joke, and Vincenzo licked the spoon, then handed it back to her. "Your onions are *soo-pair.*" She broke into giggles as he continued, "But which one of us is the baba ghanoush boss? You or me?"

He pretended he was about to wrestle her and she cried out amidst her giggles, "Okay, okay, you're the boss of the baba ghanoush!" As he took her into his arms and dipped her deeply, he could feel her relax. Swinging her back to her feet, he glanced up and saw a dark expression on Markus' face that startled him. It was only there for an instant before he turned away, shoulders tense. Vincenzo released Giselle and walked over to Markus.

"What's the matter? Are you all right?"

"*Oui.*" Markus replied calmly, but his nostrils flared minutely.

"You look...upset."

"No." He shook his head.

Vincenzo was inclined to push the issue, but just then his mother called out happily, "Everybody, *abbondanza!*" Juliette and Selma moved through the kitchen bearing trays piled high with antipasti, followed closely by the fish-bearing trio of Auguste, Fabrice, and Laetitia. Vincenzo noticed that Markus avoided him for the rest of the evening, but he didn't want to make a big deal out of something as tenuous as a look or a mood.

The next morning the whole property was busy. Maids arrived, the friends said their goodbyes, and Vincenzo and Petro drove his mother and Ippy to the airstrip for their return to Venice. Returning to the château, he drove around back and parked his car in the garage. He stopped briefly to greet the groom, who was packing up the horses, and then proceeded to the back door of the kitchen. He paused when he saw Markus sitting at the breakfast bar with his back to him. Giselle went over to pour him coffee, and then sat next to him.

"Now that everyone is clearing out, we can get back to work." She sounded relieved.

"When does Vincenzo leave?" Markus reached for her hand.

"I leave this afternoon," he called from the door, and he saw Giselle pull her hand away abruptly.

Markus turned around startled. "Oh, I did not see you there." Abandoning his cup, he got up from his seat. He looked toward Giselle, but she didn't meet his eyes. She pretended to be engrossed in the task of adding sugar to her coffee. "I will be ready when you are, Giselle." With that he walked out of the kitchen.

Vincenzo sat down across from her. "What's up with him?"

She shrugged.

"What's going on, Gigi?"

"What do you mean?" She took a sip of her coffee and then went back to stirring it.

"You haven't been yourself, and Markus seems very tense."

"I don't know. I can't say about him, but I'm dying to get back to work."

"Nothing else you want to tell me?"

She shrugged again. "No."

"He just tried to hold your hand."

"Oh, that was nothing." She sounded calm, but looked pained, and almost scared.

He pressed his lips together but didn't push her. The effect she had on men wasn't her fault. It was always the same story with men desiring her and her nonchalant attitude in return. She wandered off, and he headed up to his room to pack.

He made up his mind; leaving Giselle alone here with Markus was a bad idea. His instincts told him she wasn't safe with this Ukrainian stranger. He carried his briefcase and bag to the car before heading to the stable house. He let himself in and heard the shower in the bathroom turn off. Moments later Markus appeared from behind the multi-colored wall, towel in hand. He was naked and didn't appear surprised to see Vincenzo.

He looked at the artist's rippling musculature and felt envious. "Go ahead and get dressed. Don't let me interrupt you. I don't feel it's a good idea for you to be here alone with my wife. I want you to leave with me. I can drop you at the train station."

"Excuse me?"

"You heard me. I don't like the way you look at her, and I'm asking you nicely to leave here before something regrettable happens."

Markus scrubbed the towel over his body and then draped it over the bedpost. "That does not sound like a request. It sounds like a threat."

Vincenzo was no snob, but he'd never had anyone act aggressively toward him or his loved ones. He took a step forward. "You can take it as a threat."

"Then I want it to be clear. Are you threatening me or her?"

"My wife is very innocent. I don't know what you think you're doing with her, but I can spot manipulation when I see it, and I can see you trying to toy with her."

"I would never toy with her. What kind of toy is she to you?" He slipped into his pants.

"What did you just say?" Vincenzo felt his adrenaline surge at the audacity.

Barefoot, Markus came forward, warily approaching him like an opponent. "It is not as though you married her for money."

"Are you *deranged?*" Vincenzo raised his voice. "Get out of our home! And you'd better never see my wife again!"

"No marriage is legal without consummation! You never took her for your wife!"

Stunned, Vincenzo grappled with what Markus could possibly know about his marriage. "*She told you that?*"

Markus stood perfectly still, looking at Vincenzo as if waiting for him figure to it out.

"What? No." Vincenzo staggered back toward the window. All intensity draining from him, he dropped into a chair at the side table. "No. No. What did she tell you?"

Markus took the seat across from him. "You love her."

"She's my wife." It came out as a groan.

"Is something wrong with you?"

Vincenzo shook his head and choked out, "No."

"I have to know. Giselle is your wife legally, but she is *mine*. What is the lie?"

Giselle's voice startled them both. "Stop it. Both of you."

Vincenzo turned and gaped at her standing just inside the open door. "Gigi! Have you been unfaithful to our marriage vows?"

"Don't ask me that, V." She put her hands up. "We both know that you can't…"

"Can't what?" Markus begged her to finish. "*Can't what?*"

"Markus, stop."

"Gigi!" Vincenzo blurted painfully. "Are you in love with this man?"

She looked him in the eye. "*Oui.*" There was no hesitation. She looked between the two of them. "Markus, I want you to drop it. Vincenzo, please go back to Venice."

Vincenzo shook his head, ignoring Markus. "Gigi…we're happy…"

"We were."

Her words stung him. "You know I would never stand in the way of your happiness, but we know nothing of his motives. And the timing of your..." He fought to hide his displeasure. "...*seduction* is alarming."

Bristling, Markus leaned forward. "I did not seduce her."

Vincenzo ignored him. "Gigi, I love you *so* much. You know that."

She nodded.

"I only want what you want." His voice choked. "And I have to ask you if...oh this is so crazy...can you possibly know what you're doing?"

"Go home, V." She shook her head. "I've had enough distraction for one weekend, and all I want is to get back to work..."

"Now you're starting to sound like yourself." Vincenzo brightened.

"...with Markus."

Vincenzo took a deep breath to steady himself. He felt as if he'd been punched. Nodding slowly, he stood up and walked unsteadily from the stable house. He called Petro to bring the car, and then walked back to the open door.

"Giselle, I have to tell you something, and I need you to listen. It's important. Right now Salvio Scortini is waging a dangerous campaign to distance our family from the Vatican. He's trying to discredit us and take control of Verdu Mer. I personally suspect Scortini is going to try to hurt us. I think he's mentally unbalanced, but father doesn't agree."

"You should go to the police. Why are you telling me this?" Giselle's eyes narrowed.

"He's looking for a way to blackmail us."

"You think I can be used by Scortini?" Giselle gave Vincenzo a strange look and countered, "I'm not the first wife to take a secret lover."

"You're damn-well the first Verona wife who has, and this has to remain a secret until you get a hold of yourself."

"Please go home, V." Her voice was tender and almost sad.

"All right, I'll go." He walked away without their usual parting kiss. Petro pulled up in the car, and as Vincenzo climbed in he was already texting Leonardo.

———⊷◈⊷———

Giselle quietly pushed the stable house door closed and rested her forehead against it. "I can't believe this is happening. He must have noticed the way I looked at you." She rubbed her face with her hands and turned around to look at Markus. "He asked me what was going on, but I froze up. I wasn't ready to tell him about us."

"What was he talking about just before he left?"

"Vincenzo's father is heading up a very important environmental project, rebuilding the oldest neighborhood in Venice."

"That is Verdu Mer?"

"*Oui.*"

"Who is Scortini?"

"I don't know him personally, but his family has always been in charge of building in Venice."

"Vincenzo thinks he is dangerous, so I will take that to

heart." He walked over to her. "I will not let anyone hurt you. And what is it you are not telling me about—"

She made a tired gesture. "I don't want to talk about my marriage, or someone who may be trying to discredit my in-laws."

"All right, my beautiful one. I understand."

Sweeping his eyes over her, taking in her glowing skin and carelessly elegant stance, he felt the rush of longing to possess her and give her pleasure.

She leaned back against the door, kicked off one shoe and wiggled her toes.

Markus kneeled down at her feet and slipped off her other shoe. He squeezed her foot for a moment.

"Let us think of something to make you feel better."

He caressed her bare foot and the inside of her ankle. Then he stroked both hands up the backs of her legs to her rear end and squeezed the round firmness. Pressing his face into her belly, murmuring against her, "I liked hearing you say that you love me." He gently nibbled her through her dress. "But I am afraid that you will always make me crazy." He groaned into the material draped across her stomach.

She tipped her hips provocatively.

"Me? Make *you* crazy? What about you with your steel-blue eyes and your perfectly muscled body, *mon amour?*"

"That is the opinion of your friends, I believe. What do *you* think, my goddess?"

"Oh, I thought you were sexy the first time I saw you. I almost asked the police to give me a few minutes alone with you in your handcuffs, but a lady doesn't say things like that about a complete stranger."

"And, what type of lady are you, Giselle?" He swept his fingertips to her inner thighs. "Hmmm? I am learning that you are the kind of lady who sometimes does not wear underwear."

He stood, pulled her to him, and breathed in her ear, "I believe you are the type of lady that gives no thought to her virginity until she climbs on top of a Ukrainian artist who is in love with her, and rides him for her own pleasure."

Feeling waves of heat from his touch, she tried to sound chagrinned. "When you put it that way, I owe you an apology. But I'm new to sex, so I didn't know better." She pressed her body against him.

Markus' hands explored her, and he planted kisses along her neck. "You should have a good teacher, then."

"I agree. Do you recommend anyone in particular?" She was panting lightly now, but attempting to sound casual.

"No. I am sorry. But until we find you a good teacher, I can show you what little I know." He began to work on her buttons.

"You're very kind. Does any particular lesson come to mind?" She licked her lips and looked at him coolly, which drove him mad.

"*Many* things have come to my mind since I have known you." He freed the last button and let her dress fall to the floor. Looking at her magnificent naked form made his pulse quicken, and he began easing out of his pants.

Giselle watched him strip, and then they tumbled to the couch where they lost themselves in mutual exploration. Markus took his time following her body's cues and when he couldn't take it any longer he said, "Now I take you to bed to continue your education, okay?"

Her legs felt wobbly as she followed him. They climbed onto the big bed, and when she lay back, he began making love to her.

Looking into her eyes, a lazy smile playing at his lips, he declared in his sexy accent, "A good term to know, this is called the missionary position."

"I've heard of it." She tried to keep her voice cool despite what he was doing to her.

"You have?" He sighed and continued his slow undulations.

"My friends say that it's how a man has you if he likes you." His rhythms were making it difficult to breathe normally, and she found herself holding her breath.

He laughed—which did incredible things to his abs—and smiled down at her, flashing white teeth. "Oh, and what other positions did they tell you of?"

"They're quite sure that if a man doesn't like you but still wants to have sex with you, he'll want something called 'doggy style,'" she panted.

He shook his head, "I will want to have you that way, and it is not because I do not like you."

They spent the rest of the afternoon and evening lost in their quest for pleasure, and it was late when they took a long, hot bath in the pool-sized tub.

"You're a very good teacher, and it's about time that I learned these lessons." She poured soap onto a washcloth.

"I agree, it is time you learned about pleasure." He let her massage him with the washcloth.

"Markus, what has your sex life been like?" She poured water from cupped hands onto his skin to rinse the soap off.

"Well, where I grew up there were no girls around…at least no *desirable* girls." He leaned back into the water and the soap disappeared from his chest in a rush. "I lost my virginity when I accompanied my father on one of his business trips. I was fourteen. We were delivering windows to a castle, and a fifteen-year-old girl took me down into the dungeon."

"A dungeon?"

"Well, it was just a storeroom when we visited it. And then there was the woman near my hometown. She was a widow, and she took me as her lover for years in secret."

"An older woman. Did anyone find out?"

"No." He took the washcloth and started running it between her toes.

"Was she beautiful?" She wiggled her toes and giggled. "I'm ticklish."

"She was demanding. And I can see that."

"Demanding?"

"She had many sexual requirements, and insisted on having repeated satisfaction before allowing me release. We continued to meet until I was twenty-four, when she moved away to Kiev."

"That sounds difficult. Is that why you don't come too quickly?"

"How do you know about premature men?"

"My friends complain about that…happening."

"I had to have a lot of control with her."

"Did you love her?"

"No. But we both needed the sex."

She bit his shoulder. "With her demanding sexual appetite, maybe she was a widow because her husband died from all the physical effort."

"That could be true. At times it was very hard work with her. After that, I have only had short encounters with women who have not interested me."

"Did you break their hearts?"

"No. They were women who made it clear they only wanted to have sex with me, and I was honest that I only wanted sex from them."

"And you didn't see them again?"

"No. I never called any of them again. That would have been unfair."

Giselle bent over to playfully lick clean water off his chest, and then stood up. "I don't know why I feel jealous that those women got to have you, but also sorry for them."

They climbed out of the tub and Markus remarked, "Let us find a new subject other than jealousy. It is a quality I find unattractive, I must tell you."

She pulled him inside the towel with her and hugged him. "You're right. It isn't a good feeling at all."

With his natural agility, he slipped back out of the towel and swept her off her feet. He carried her out to the main room, and as they climbed back into bed he asked in a dubious tone, "If you have not had sex before me, who taught you that trick you did with your hand? What you did when you first had your way with me."

Embarrassed she hid her face under the covers. "Oh, no! Well, I'd never felt a man's, um, *parts* before. And I was feeling what you had...down there."

"And did you like what you discovered?"

She growled, "I sure did."

He burrowed under the covers and spooned her. "I would like you to do that trick again to me for many years, please." It was a contented murmur.

"You won't break my heart, will you?" Her voice was small.

"No. I am yours forever, Giselle."

Nestled together, they fell into a deep sleep.

10

O n the short drive to the airstrip, Vincenzo was in turmoil. Since marrying Giselle, he'd told himself that making her happy was the most important thing in his life, but now he was confronted with the ugly truth. He was a hypocrite. As he and Petro climbed aboard the waiting plane, his mind was playing a repetitive loop of awful thoughts, and he was beginning to feel sick over Giselle. His new feelings of jealousy and betrayal were like a poison that made him nauseous, and he'd never experienced anything as personally humiliating as that confrontation with Markus. Now that she'd found fulfillment in a sexual relationship—something he couldn't give her—how could he justify keeping her bound to him by marriage?

Upon landing in Venice, Vincenzo went straight home to share the news that Giselle and the Pope had apparently experienced a shared vision. He was walking through the main entry hall of the palazzo when his mother approached.

"Ah, I am glad you are home, dear."

"Me too, Mama. Are father and Papa home?"

"They are in the library."

"I'm going to show them the pictures I took of *Star Fall*. Would you like to come with me?"

"No, I am off to visit Rifugia della Dignità. One our residents just returned from the hospital."

"Oh? Who?"

"Signor Cumulo. He had an emergency appendectomy while we were in France."

"I'm sorry for that. Please give him my best."

"I will. I am going to see Gina. She is making a small flower arrangement to lift his spirits."

Juliette gave him a hug and a squeeze, leaving a fragrant trail of her hibiscus perfume. Vincenzo found his father and the Pope in the library and pulled up the photos on his phone. The Pope nodded in satisfaction.

"*Sì*, Juliette told us about Giselle's sculpture. It is hard to see here in your photos, but that is the basic design that I dreamed." As he traced his finger across the phone's screen, he became more excited. "This part here was the door, and over here were windows that looked out over the canal. She even has the beautiful lights I saw in the dream."

"Eh...well...Giselle has kept it a secret," Vincenzo hedged, "but this weekend she told me the light source is the result of a chemical reaction. It's caused by a rare element. I'd never heard of it, and it's illegal to possess because...well, it's lethal. She fuses glass vials containing hydrogen and this element, and then causes a tiny fracture in the fuse point, and when the contents mix it causes a glowing reaction."

The men stared at him not comprehending.

"I know I'm not explaining this properly. I'm a banker, not a chemist."

Gabrieli frowned. "What is this illegal element?"

"Something called irrodium. Apparently exposure to even a tiny amount leads to a quick and painful death."

"How does she create the fracture?" The Pope's jaw was tensing.

"I'm sorry to say...she taps it with her fingernail." Vincenzo wrung his hands and felt as if he should be apologizing for her audacious behavior.

"For the love of God!" Gabrieli slapped his forehead. "We have to get a better handle on our girl! She has to stop using that irrodium."

"She is the most stubborn girl I have met, but she will see to reason. We will put a stop to this illegal and dangerous work," Papa agreed.

"Of course. But, the idea of a long-term clean energy source is so attractive." Vincenzo turned to his father. "Can you get the consortium to look into coming up with a safe way to do that?"

"You have a good point. *Sì*, we'll look into it."

Vincenzo stretched and took a deep breath. "Now, I've got a ton of work to do, so please excuse me."

"You work too much." Papa sounded resigned. "I grow tired of lecturing you. You advise Giselle to get more rest, but then you work night and day yourself."

"I'm sorry, Papa. But, I've got a video conference with a group in San Francisco, and there's a nine hour time difference." He took his phone off the table and headed to his bedroom suite.

After a quick shower he headed straight to the Verona offices, arriving only two minutes late for his meeting with the International Water Federation. That was followed by a long conference call with a Brazilian Nature Conservancy, and then another with the Somalia Water Coalition. With little sleep the night before, the stress of Giselle's revelation, and working non-stop all day, he was exhausted when he finally left the office after midnight.

Vincenzo and Petro took one of the family's private boats to Leonardo's. After accompanying Vincenzo to the apartment door, Petro disappeared on his invisible routine of circling the property, monitoring the lobby, and inspecting the hallways. Vincenzo walked inside and into the living room. Looking into the open kitchen, he saw Leonardo standing by the stove wearing cotton pajama pants, sipping a cup of tea. He looked relieved.

"It's about time you got here. What's with all the cryptic messages?"

Vincenzo dropped his briefcase, loosened his tie, and took off his jacket.

"Giselle's fallen in love with that Ukrainian artist."

"Really?" Leonardo came over to him, handed him the cup of tea, and took his jacket. "The one from the Metro?" He went to hang it in the hall closet.

"*Sì.*" Dropping onto the sofa, Vincenzo croaked, "Him."

"Seriously? Hey, we always knew this would happen one day."

"Come sit with me." Vincenzo dropped his head into his hands.

Leonardo hurried over. "So our little Gigi has finally become a woman?"

He looked up from between his fingers, and his anguish started to dissolve. "Well, when you say it like that, it sounds natural." He let out a sigh that was part laugh.

"Well, it is. The fact that she'd never shown any carnal inclination before always made me uneasy."

"Well," Vincenzo quirked an eyebrow, "she's *carnal* now."

"Is he handsome?"

"Like you wouldn't believe." Vincenzo widened his eyes. "He's solid lean perfection."

"Really?" Leonardo's eyes widened, too. "Good for her. Do tell?"

"Ultra-short blonde hair, piercing blue eyes, twelve pack abs. He looks like a martial artist, and moves like one, too."

"I can't wait to meet the lucky artist who deflowered our girl."

"He was naked when I confronted him."

"Wait. A naked confrontation?" Leonardo sat up straighter, grinning. "Sorry I missed it. Back up and tell me everything."

After a full recitation of the events, Leonardo was shaking his head. "So everyone at the party thought Carolette was going to land Markus?"

"Correct." Vincenzo nodded. "But Gigi secretly got him first."

"I remember back when Carolette still thought my penis worked, she was very inventive in her romantic approaches."

"*Sì,* thank heavens everyone still thinks your dick is a loss, or you wouldn't be able to fight the ladies off." He pulled off his shoes and lay back on the couch.

"You're too tired to talk business tonight." Rolling on top of him, Leo nuzzled his nose against Vincenzo's ear and kissed it. "How about we go straight to bed, and I can show you how glad I am that you're home?"

Vincenzo felt himself becoming aroused and looked up at Leo. "I'm too tired to leave this couch."

Getting to his feet, Leo stood shirtless and beckoned, his eyes dark with interest. "Come to bed," he said, and then headed to the bedroom, his pajama pants hanging low on his athletic hips. Watching those back muscles undulating smoothly as Leo walked, his beautiful lats and traps sculpted from endless hours of rowing, got Vincenzo up off the couch. He stripped off his clothes while following his lover down the hall.

In the bedroom, Leo grabbed a decorative pillow off their bed, tossed it onto the floor at Vincenzo's feet, and dropped to his knees. Vincenzo naturally slid his hands onto his Leo's shoulders and began to knead his muscles.

"I may be too tired to stand up, babe."

Leo looked up, desire flashing in his eyes. "No, I don't think you're too tired."

They stopped talking and eventually ended up in bed. After years of intimacy, they each knew exactly what the other needed, and how to give each other pleasure.

Woozy from their quick foreplay and powerful orgasms, they lay catching their breath. Vincenzo moaned, "Oh God, how I needed that! I've been so emotional, I've been on the verge of screaming or crying for hours now. Whew!"

"We're always better after sex."

"True, I certainly think more clearly."

"What do you think now?"

"I think I just used up the last of my second wind. I'm going to sleep."

"Well, after a quick rinse we'll come straight back to bed." Leo got up and headed to the bathroom.

Vincenzo loved showering with Leo and the simple comfort of standing under the warm spray washing each other. Holding Leo's wet body in secret as the world outside hurried on, those were his most treasured moments.

Back in bed, they lay on their sides facing each other, warmed by the shower, their legs comfortably entwined. Vincenzo's body edged toward sleep, but his mind still tried to spin in an anxious whirl.

"I'm scared, Leo. You know I want the best for her."

"We both do."

"I remember my first day of school in France, I knew she was special."

"I remember I was jealous because you spent almost every waking minute with her while I was stuck here attending classes in Venice."

"You know, I did wonder if I would develop a sexual taste for her and become hetero."

"I know you two never had sex, but you never fooled around back then?"

"No. She treated me just like a brother, and I never developed any urge to engage in hetero-play...so...no... nothing."

"I wonder if perhaps she had some sort of delayed feminine maturation...you know...hormonally."

"You mean, why she didn't try to get frisky with me?"

"Right. She never had any romantic inkling that I ever saw. I still remember that spring when we all took that weekend trip down to Cap d'Ail. When Giselle woke up and walked in on us undressed and kissing, I'd never been so terrified. But she was so understanding and it was such a relief to have her protect our secret."

"Leo, we're so guilty. We're bad people to use her as our beard."

"Hey, that's not fair. We love her like a sister, and as our sister we've protected her, too."

"I shouldn't have married her."

"It was her idea, and it saved her family home."

"Agh, when we mentioned it to Mama the whole thing took on a life of its own with our lawyers charging in."

"Let's not talk anymore tonight. Get some rest." Leo leaned over and gave him a long kiss. "I love you, and together we'll figure out what Giselle's sexual awakening means for us."

With that, Vincenzo drifted off to sleep.

⚬⚬⚬

Alphonso sat in his tiny walk-up apartment with his cousin, preparing for their meeting at the Scortini palazzo. Zelph paid close attention as Alphonso recounted all of his discoveries in France.

"So, that's what I've found." Alphonso leaned back and

spread his hands wide. "Bring me up-to-date on what you've been doing here."

"I've been on this job one hundred percent while you were in France, Alphonso."

"Thanks for working hard on this. What do you have on Vincenzo?"

"He spends a lot of time with his accountant."

"Mmm-hmm. Leonardo Trentori's also his best friend."

"Yeah, well...more than that...I'm gonna go out on a limb and say they're lovers."

"*What?*"

"Yeah."

"What the..."

"Hear me out. They spent the night together a few times while you were in France. And while everyone chalks it up to all-night banking marathons, that doesn't sound like what they're doing alone in apartment 307."

"How could they have gotten away with it if Count Gabrieli is super Catholic? He'd have disowned Vincenzo."

"Well that's just the thing. I've spent a lot of time checking on the boys, and they're both super Catholic, too."

"Whoa, that's a stretch, Zelph. You're telling me they love the Church, and you think they're gay?"

"Yeah, they're real devout. But as far as the Catholic Church is concerned, they're real deviant."

"Nah, you've got to be off the mark. Vincenzo is the heart-throb husband..." He paused and thought a moment. "Well, that would explain why Giselle has a man on the side. She's a beard for her closeted husband. But, how has nobody noticed his relationship with Leonardo?"

"A few reasons. One, I found out that Leonardo had an accident at Verdu Mer when he was a teenager. Fell through a floor onto some broken rebar, and fucked up his junk for a while. To this day it's assumed he's impotent, but it would be a convenient cover for the two of them if Leonardo healed completely. Two, nobody's been trying to keep track of this family before. They own planes. They have houses all over the world. The boys go wherever they want to meet each other. They work together on huge financial bail out packages for charity that would legitimately keep them working at all hours. I've talked to people who say they're in Paris a lot, and here in Venice Vincenzo uses Leonardo's place about as often as he's at the family palazzo. I think the apartment that everyone thinks is Leonardo's is actually *their* apartment. Three, Vincenzo always puts his hands or his lips on Giselle in photos to reinforce the illusion of romance. And four, no one knows what goes on behind closed doors."

"What about his bodyguard? Does Petro know?"

"Probably not. As devout Catholics, they'd be very good at keeping their activities a secret. And Petro typically stays around the perimeter of wherever Vincenzo is, not in the same room. He never goes into the apartment. Not that he would ever tell. He appears to be a total pro."

"Well, we have a job to do, and I'm not gonna let anything stand in the way of handing all this over to Scortini and getting our money."

"Yeah, well, while you were away checking out Giselle, I've been able to get a vibe from the locals on Salvio Scortini. Old respected family or not, he's a nasty piece of work, as you've discovered. I talked to a foreman in the

Brotherhood of Iron Workers who told me Scortini is a patent thief. And there's a rumor that he personally killed that big marble magnate's kid. You know, the one who was attacked in an alley? Reynaldo Falconetti."

"What? *Scortini did?*"

"Yeah. No one is saying much, but they found Reynaldo's body immediately after a meeting Scortini had called."

"Was Reynaldo at that meeting?"

"Yep. He practically ran out of the meeting after it ended, and that was the last time anyone saw him alive. They found him in an alley behind the warehouse where the meeting was held, so he didn't make it far."

"Why do they suspect Scortini?"

"Reynaldo had no enemies, and he told other people at the meeting that Scortini may not have the clout he's pretending to have."

"Oh, no."

"Uh-huh. Then Reynaldo disappears, only to be found with his head bashed in."

"Maybe he was mugged."

"Nope. Reynaldo was found wearing an expensive watch and had a wad of cash on him."

"Why should I be surprised? I felt like Scortini wanted to kill *me* the other day."

"Let's get this job over with and never see Scortini again."

"What do you think I'm trying to do?" Alphonso stood up.

"Okay, let's get over to the haunted mansion and give Scortini the dirt."

"Ah, *Santa Maria*," he sighed. "Here we go."

———— ⋙⟨◉⟩⋘ ————

Salvio was in his secret passage listening to the conversation that was taking place in his office. He'd installed listening devices in strategic areas around his palazzo to monitor his staff, his wife, and his visitors. The mongoloid private detective and his associate were waiting to deliver their findings, and he hoped his eavesdropping would help him ascertain whether they were hiding anything from him. Oddly, their conversation seemed to be about how much pressure to apply to pasta with the tip of your index finger when making tortelloni. Salvio was growing impatient, but he willed himself to remain attentive to their rambling. Could it be some sort of code? How could they be thinking of anything but the sins of the Veronas? As the two operatives segued into whether or not a coffee filter could effectively be used to strain grit from porcini mushrooms, Salvio impatiently snapped the control panel switch to the "off" position.

When he performed his usual trick of popping into the room from behind the tapestry, he was irritated that his appearance didn't frighten the two detectives. The disappointment was not complete however, because the associate did utter a startled sound. What sounded like an expletive, ended up just being unintelligible. Salvio saw their eyes flicker to one another in a sly, knowing exchange. Obviously the fathead detective had warned his look-alike associate about his surprising entrances, and the look was "I told you so." Moving silently around his desk he sat down and stared at the two longhaired bulls seated before him.

"You're twins?"

"We're cousins."

"Let's not get sidetracked from the grave matter at hand. Tell me what you've found."

The detective leaned forward and cleared his throat. "The family allows Giselle Verona to have a lover that she spends time with alone at her château in France."

Salvio didn't react. It was an impossibility, and therefore incomprehensible to him. He looked from one man to the other, and then back.

"Speak man! Make sense! What do you report?"

"I've seen Vincenzo's wife in the arms of her Russian lover, and the Verona family is allowing the affair."

Salvio stared blankly. "A wife taking a lover? A wife of a Verona giving her body to a man who is not her husband?" The concept hit him with a noxious punch, and he bit his tongue in an attempt to avert a wave of vomit from rising into his gorge.

"*Sì*. And *signore*, we believe Vincenzo is homosexual, and that he has a male lover here in Venice."

Salvio flung himself up from his chair and raced to the window. He yanked it open and launched a sluice of vomit out into the canal below. Then he took in gulps of air, his body heaving involuntarily. Spinning around, he turned to face the detective.

"*Cuckolding, whoring, and sodomy?*"

The fatheads nodded. Salvio's slack jaw was replaced by a genuine smile. He wiped his mouth with a handkerchief and gurgled, "Well, well, well, gentleman. You have indeed earned your money. Now, I need proof of these repugnant sins."

"*Sì*, and to continue digging into their activities, we'll need substantially more money, *signore.*"

"You'll have it." Salvio sashayed over to his safe, reached inside, and produced a shoebox-sized packet of euros. He cleared his throat, then pulled out his handkerchief and spit into it. "Get me everything on these unpardonable sins." He shoved the money across the desk.

The detective and his partner rose to their feet. The fathead took the packet. "How much do we have here? We'll need to pay some pretty big bribes or, um, personal donations, of course..."

Salvio was fairly hugging himself in ecstasy. "Oh, that's a hundred thousand euros. Go put it to good use, you fathead!"

———— ⦿ ————

Alphonso stood, nodded to Scortini, and left the office with Zelph close on his heels. The butler intercepted them and moved along at a stately pace until he had ushered them out the front door of the palazzo. Once they were walking down the *calle,* Alphonso muttered, "We don't have a single person to pay off in this case. I say we take this money over to Pim. No one who knows anything about the Veronas would ever take a bribe, no matter how much we offered. And Giselle's countrymen would sooner drag me to a guillotine than betray her. I tell you, that family is loved by everybody except Scortini."

Zelph looked uneasy after his first meeting with their client. "If I'm right, Scortini isn't going to pay us our final fee. I get a strong feeling that when we give him the final report, he plans to kill us so we can't tell tales."

"Yeah, I don't know if he's scarier when he's enraged, or when he's pleased. What a scumbag."

"What have you gotten us into, Cuz? Seriously, I'm not meeting that Scortini again without leaving a note in case I don't make it out alive. And I'm bringing a weapon next time."

"Why does he say I have a big head? I've never heard anything like that before. I don't have a big head. And *mongoloid?* Who says that?"

"Alphonso, we don't have oversized heads. I think he sees what he wants to see, and it's ugly." Zelph chucked him on the shoulder. "You know we're both good looking guys. Women throw themselves at us all the time. You'd be getting laid every night if you didn't have such impossibly high standards."

"Don't start on my taste in women. Okay, so I'll head back to France to get the proof on Giselle. You get what proof you can on Vincenzo."

"I'm gonna keep digging on Scortini, too. Knowledge is power, and in the interest of self-preservation I'd feel safer if we had something to blackmail him with to ensure our long, healthy lives."

"Before we go to dinner, let's go buy a camera with a really powerful telephoto lens. I'll need it for getting proof on Giselle. Wait till you see what she and Ruskie do when they're working together. You're not going to believe your eyes."

"How can it be that hot if they're not having sex?"

"It's the stuff of fantasies."

"When are you going back to Gernelle?"

"As soon as I can."

11

The next day, Alphonso flew back to France, rented a car, and drove straight to Henri and Fauve's hotel in Aiglemont. The whole time, his mind struggled with the Scortini/Verona situation. As a private investigator he'd made a good living finding out where the bodies were buried—sometimes literally—and who was fucking whom—sometimes figuratively. But now he was struggling to find a way to extricate himself from his dangerous client and put an end to spying on these good people.

He was also struggling to keep some proper perspective where the Verona women were concerned. Giselle was his fantasy woman, and Juliette was the mother he'd always longed for. The notion of being responsible for humiliating either woman made him uncomfortable, at the very least.

But how bad could it really be if Scortini divulged some marital indiscretions to the Pope? Wasn't the Pope in the business of hearing confessions and forgiving people? How powerful was this Verona blackmail ammunition? Wasn't it just personal sexual matters that didn't hurt anyone? So Vincenzo was allowing his wife to have a discrete dalliance when she was away in the country. So what? And what of Zelph's impression that Vincenzo and Leonardo were doing more than accounting together? Whose business was it to care?

Alphonso entered the hotel lobby and headed straight for the check-in desk with his cover story already on his lips. Rolling his little suitcase behind him, he waved to Henri, who looked up from his work.

"*Bonjour,* Alphonso! This is a surprise. What are you doing back so soon?"

"*Bonjour,* Henri. I've made my recommendations for the restaurant's champagne order, and now I have some time for a vacation, so I'm back to relax. I think maybe I'll see if there are any homes for sale around here." He placed his hands flat on the old wooden counter and looked squarely at the proud Frenchman. "This is my kind of place."

"*Mais bien, sur.* There are some good houses for sale nearby." Henri nodded. "Everyone who visits wants to move here."

"Maybe I'll get a few of my relatives together and buy a big place. I hear the Veronas have a home out in Gernelle. We could be neighbors."

"Ha! There's nothing for sale out by that property."

"I imagine it's a nice place if it's anything like their palazzo in Venice."

"*Oui*, very beautiful. They don't make estates like that anymore. The château was built by Giselle Verona's ancestors before this town was even here—just rolling hills and forest."

"Ah well, I'm looking forward to a nice, relaxing vacation. It's good to be back." Alphonso grinned. "Do you have my same room available by chance?"

"Oh, *mais non.*" Henri clucked his tongue and reached into a cubbyhole for a key. "You'll have the blue room in back this time. It's a nice room with its own entrance. More private. You'll like it."

"Okay then." Alphonso bent to sign the form that Henry slid toward him with the key. The room sounded perfect. With his own entrance, he wouldn't have to sneak as much as last time. If he hurried, he could get back to Giselle's property by late afternoon and get some photos of them in their smoldering embraces.

In less than fifteen minutes, Alphonso was speeding toward the isolated château, armed with a new Nikon camera and a telephoto lens. Assuming Giselle and her Russian were keeping the same schedule, he had every expectation of seeing them at work. It was so quiet, he hadn't encountered any cars on the roads by the time he swung onto the deserted lane. He rolled to a quiet stop behind the bank of bushes, grabbed his spy gear, and got out of the car. He skirted along the forest, taking care to stay in a low crouch, and then trotted across the field, dodging from shrub to shrub on his way toward the back of the château.

He was running to a break in the little orchard when he caught sight of something so incredible, he tripped and went flying face-first into the uneven soil. Stupefied, he lay in the fragrantly loamy dirt as if he'd had a stroke. He'd taken a hard fall chest-first onto the Nikon, which hurt like hell and knocked the wind out of him. Trembling, he rolled onto his side and tentatively sipped some air into his lungs. God that hurt! He pushed himself up onto his hands and knees, and took another look at the spectacle that had stunned him.

There in the courtyard, Giselle Verona was wound around her Russian consort. Her dress was open, and her magnificent naked body was on display. She was gripping the sculpture above her with both hands as she rode her lucky assistant. Ruskie was naked to the waist, and his pants were pulled down to mid-thigh, revealing perfect abdominals and a sculpted butt. *Christ!* The sight of Giselle's spectacular body and erotic pleasure was so much more than he'd expected. He wondered if he'd hit his head and was unconsciously having another fantasy about her. He actually pinched himself. Now, afraid of being seen, he got down a bit lower to peer at the two making love in the open air. Well, there was certainly no conjecture now. Giselle really was cuckolding her husband with her Russian assistant, who was currently trapped within her luscious thighs.

Alphonso reached for his camera and raised it to his eye, but the settings were blinking in an erratic jitter across the screen. He turned the power off and on, only to receive an error signal. *Shit!* He fiddled with the buttons, then took the battery pack out and put it back in. No luck. *Damn it!* Giving up on the camera, he snatched his phone out of his pocket and quickly took several photos and a short video of the lovers. But the photos only registered a blurry smudge in the foreground of some shadowy buildings. The video looked like a blurry piece of playground equipment. He was too far away to get a decent shot with his phone. He'd have to get his camera repaired in town, or buy a new one, and return to photograph them tomorrow. If they weren't having sex outside again, he'd see about pushing his luck to get photos through a window under cover of darkness.

He watched them finish, then wantonly kiss each other with such passion he wondered what on earth he'd been doing with women his whole life. He'd certainly never shared kisses like these. Then, in various states of undress, the two climbed off the sculpture, walked over to the stable house, went in, and closed the door. Giselle and Ruskie were apparently taking their fun to that big wooden bed he's seen inside. *Okay, time to call Scortini.*

The moment Scortini answered, Alphonso blurted, "I've just seen it with my own eyes. I'm here at the French estate where Vincenzo's wife is having sex with her Russian lover *right now*. They're in a stable house that they use as a love nest. It's situated right behind her château."

Scortini made a gagging sound and the phone line went dead.

Alphonso suddenly felt ashamed. *I hope no one ever finds out what I've just done.*

———◉———

Salvio hung up on his detective and doubled over. The rush of relief was so powerful it made him light-headed. "I knew it! I knew it!" He looked upward, raising his hands to the heavens. "*Grazie Dio!*"

He snatched his father's address book off the desk and found the number for the Pope's private Vatican residence. After a few short rings, it was picked up.

"*Ciao, residenza...*"

Salvio cut in, fighting to sound calm. "This is Salvio Scortini. I must speak to Sua Santità immediately. I have urgent news regarding a tragedy in the Verona family."

"Tragedy?" The secretary gasped. "What has happened?"

"*Is happening!* I can only tell this to our Holy Father personally."

"But Signor Scortini, the Holy Father is not in residence at this time. Will you allow me to connect you to his personal security's cell phone?"

"Do it! Hurry!" Salvio listened to clicks on the line as he was transferred. He was ready to play his winning hand, and the excitement was too much. He got up from his chair and paced behind his desk.

"Your name is Scortini? What's the problem?" a curt voice demanded.

"Who is this?" Salvio's lips curled inward and he began nibbling them.

"You don't ask me questions, you answer mine."

Pushed beyond agitation, he felt on the verge of a tantrum. "I have the most urgent news for Sua Santità! Who are you? Are you connecting me?"

"I'm head of security, and you haven't answered my question."

"This is a private tragedy I can only tell the Holy Father!"

"Are you in your right mind? You sound…"

"*Upset? Sì!* If you don't put me through to Pope Leopold, it will be too late!"

After a brief, muffled exchange on the other end, the unmistakable voice of Sua Santità came on the line.

"Scortini?"

The effect of being personally spoken to by Pope Leopold himself sent a thrum through his entire body and galvanized him. He stood ramrod straight and blurted into the phone, "Holy Father? *Sì* it's me, Salvio Scortini. Forgive me, but I'm calling with grave news. The Veronas are wretched debauchers who mock God's law! I have proof!"

"*What?*" He sounded angry. "*How can you say such a thing?*"

"They pervert the sanctity of marriage by allowing Giselle Verona to have an extra-marital affair with a Russian. He is at this very moment using her body for his gratification at the Verona château in France."

"Say that again?" The Pope coughed. "How can you know this? Have you ever even met Giselle Verona?"

"I know what everyone knows, that she is a blonde French woman. But no, I haven't met her. My man there in France has just informed me that she and the Russian are *in flagrante delicto*—in a state of forbidden sin as I am speaking to you. She is having unholy, filthy, wicked sexual congress in a stable house behind her château at this very moment." He sputtered, and then caught hold of his tongue between his teeth to wait for a response.

"Your concern is noted. I will pray on the matter. And may God be with you."

The line went dead, and when Salvio hung up he was too excited to sit down, so he paced his office. He forced himself to take deep breaths. It wasn't the regular time, but he went over to the servant's bell cord and gave it a long pull. Within moments, pounding feet approached and Guiseppe appeared at the office door.

"*Signore?*"

"Have my wife's maid begin preparing her for her marital duties."

His valet closed the door and rushed off down the hall.

Finally Salvio sat behind his desk, enjoying the deep satisfaction of knowing that his plan was working perfectly.

<hr/>

Alphonso was caught by surprise as three vehicles zoomed up Giselle's normally deserted driveway. Coming to a hasty stop were a Jaguar, a Lexus, Henri's Range Rover, and a delivery truck. He ducked low and zipped from tree to tree trying to make it to the outbuildings to get a better look. Skidding to a stop in the shadow of the horse stables, he saw the woman who lived on the property heading toward him on her motorcycle. He jammed his body behind a grain bin to hide, and within moments she flew past him, drove through the courtyard, and disappeared around the corner to the front of the château. A fully dressed Giselle exited the stable house alone and crossed the courtyard to one of the château's back doors. Keeping to the shadows, but still exposed to anyone looking from an upper window, he made his way along the outbuildings until he could see the front of the château. People were exiting the vehicles and carrying boxes of supplies up the front steps. It looked like flowers and groceries. A woman in a pinstriped pantsuit was directing at a team of people. *Not the same vibe as the casual dinner party the other night.*

Motion in his periphery caught his attention, and he turned toward the main road. Approaching the property was a specially outfitted SUV that looked as if it was armored, followed by an official-looking stretched black sedan. *Okay, this doesn't look like a friends—this is something big.* There was too much activity; he had to get off the property before he was spotted. Sprinting back through the field from tree to overgrown bush, he cursed being so tall. He only felt less vulnerable after he'd made it to the forest where he could run to his car unseen. He dove inside his rental car and started the engine. He'd get back to his hotel room through his private entrance and pretend he'd been there the whole time.

On the main road, Alphonso drove at a conservative pace and thought fast. Either Henri or Fauve were on that property now, so next time he saw them he'd fish to see if they'd divulge what was happening out there today. As he approached Aiglemont, he tried to shake off the ridiculous notion that his call to Scortini had resulted in the sudden swarm onto the estate. There was no way that could be the case.

Carolette was in a deliciously naughty mood. The moment Ippy called with her invitation to this evening's dinner party, she hatched a plan to get Markus. Immediately after accepting, she went to her favorite salon, where she splurged on her hair and makeup. As she rode with Henri and Fauve to the château, she made final touch-ups in the visor mirror.

Fauve glanced at her, looking uneasy as they bounced along in the Range Rover. "Go easy with that iridescent stick."

"It's just a little highlighter."

"You're having dinner with Vincenzo's parents, Coco. You don't need to glow in the dark," Henri cautioned. "You look pretty without all that paint."

Carolette stroked her fingertips over her cheeks and brow bones to blend the application. "How do I look?"

"Like you should be hung up on *Star Fall*," Fauve declared.

As they arrived at the estate, she stuffed her cosmetics back into her purse and arched a brow. "I'll take that as a compliment."

They followed the caterer's truck and the florist's Lexus up the driveway and parked in the courtyard. Henri climbed out from behind the wheel and jogged up the château steps. Hurrying behind him, Fauve called over her shoulder, "Come on Glamour Puss, we should help set up."

Carolette hopped down from the passenger seat and took a moment to adjust her body-hugging knit dress. "I'll be there in a bit. I'm going to visit Markus first. We have time."

The couple disappeared inside as Carolette walked to the stable house to present Markus with an invitation he couldn't refuse. Boldly entering, she heard the shower running on the other side of the pastel partition. The thought of Markus' wet body gave her an audacious idea. She heard the crunch of gravel as more vehicles arrived, and hesitated for just a moment. *The Veronas are arriving, but they won't be looking for me.*

Feeling irresistible, she stepped out of her shoes, quickly stripped off her clothes, and hopped naked onto Markus' bed. Hearing the shower turn off, a thrill of anticipation made her pulse quicken, and she got up onto her knees at a flattering angle. She busied herself pinching her nipples to make them perky and smoothing her hair. Moments later, Markus walked naked into the bedroom, and she did her best burlesque pose. Reaching her arms out to him, she arched her back.

"Do you think we have time for sex before dinner, Markus?"

But, inexplicably, he was staring past her to the door. Carolette followed his eyes over her shoulder, and turned to see the head of the Roman Catholic Church and some bodyguards standing less than ten feet behind her. She shrieked and snatched at the bed covers to hide her body. The Pope made a minute head movement, and his security team ducked back out the door.

The Pope's eyes took in Markus' naked form before he turned to her. "My child, what is your name?"

"Carolette, Holy Father. Carolette," she stammered.

"Carolette, have you seen Giselle today?"

"No, Holy Father. I believe she's in the château, but no...I haven't seen her today...no."

The Pope turned to Markus. "Markus, forgive my intrusion." With that, he let himself out.

Rolling off the bed in a panic, Carolette began dragging on her clothes. "What the fuck was the Pope doing in your bedroom?"

Markus walked to the window and peered around the curtain as the leader of the most powerful church in the world walked down the lane toward Giselle's château. He shrugged.

"I do not know. Looking for sinners maybe?"

"The Pope knows you?" she croaked.

"No, of course not." He seemed unperturbed.

"He knew your name!" She was all thumbs trying to fasten her bra.

"He heard you say it."

"Oh, *mon Dieu!* Help me with this!" She backed over to him, and he hooked her bra for her. "*Un-fucking-believable!*" She pulled her dress over her head and tripped toward the door trying to slide her feet into her high-heeled sandals. "I have to call everybody I know, and tell them I just met the Pope! No! Wait, he saw me naked! I have to take this to my grave! No one can ever know!"

"As you say." Markus walked over to the armoire to retrieve a pair of pants.

Carolette yanked the door open, and then spun back to look at him. "You really are unbelievably hot. Can you see us getting together?"

"I think that there is no bigger warning sign from God than being interrupted by the Pope."

Cringing in shame she shrieked, "Too right!" and slammed out the door.

———=((•))=———

As Casimir climbed the château steps, he joined Gabrieli who asked, "What are you up to?"

"I just received a phone call from Scortini. He claimed that Giselle was having intercourse with a Russian man in that stable house. He is watching this property."

"*He what?*" Gabrieli ushered him into the foyer. "That's it. He's gone too far."

"I agree. Tell Petro and Tiberius to come in here at once." Casimir swept his eyes across the art-filled hall of the sumptuous home and was gratified to see Giselle safely in her husband's arms. Everything here was happily normal. He put his hand on Gabrieli's arm and they paused. "We have to make the family aware of the situation. But I am afraid I must cut this visit short and attend to this matter in Rome."

Gabrieli nodded his agreement as Giselle headed in their direction.

"Papa, I'm so happy to finally welcome you to my childhood home." She dropped into a graceful curtsey, then stood and offered her cheek.

"It is a splendid home, my child, most splendid." He gave her cheek a kiss. "And another time I will ask you to give me a tour. But right now, I have come to see your sculpture and to speak to you about your inspiration."

"Of course, Papa." He could see her surprise.

"You and I have shared a vision from God."

Her eyes widened, but he would have to explain later. He kept focused on the matter at hand.

"Right now I must speak to my team. I will join you shortly."

Giselle and her in-laws retreated to a receiving room to wait for him.

Casimir beckoned the Verona bodyguards and his security team to follow him to a cloakroom near the front door.

"Search this property for a spy. Question all the staff setting up for dinner tonight. I don't have a description other than Scortini called him, 'my man.' I have no idea if he is dangerous, but I want him found."

Turning on his heel, Casimir left the security team to their tactical logistics and walked back to the expectant faces awaiting him in the receiving room. He adjusted his vestments as he sat down on a velvet chair.

"My family, you are all so precious to me. I am sad to tell you that...well...it is perhaps through my actions that you are now in harm's way. I believe that by passing Salvio Scortini over for Verdu Mer, he has gotten certain ideas into his head. Ideas that have made him dangerous." When no one appeared surprised, he continued. "Just minutes ago he persuaded my Vatican staff to connect him to my mobile phone, and he tried to convince me that you, my dear," he opened his hand to Giselle, "were being untrue to your marital vows." Her face registered shock and her hands flew up to her face. Vincenzo put his arm around her protectively. Casimir sought to reassure her. "I know you are innocent, my child."

Juliette reached over and patted Giselle's knee. "If Salvio

thinks he can take over the project by humiliating us, he will be looking for bad conduct. But we are not afraid of him."

Gabrieli looked tense. "We have nothing to fear. Now that we are aware of his obsession with Verdu Mer—and by extension with us—we need to stay alert and keep ourselves safe. I've known him to be impetuous..."

"And erratic..." Vincenzo added.

Gabrieli nodded, but held his hand up. "Salvio has personality flaws, but he is devoutly Christian."

Juliette's expression was tense. "Well, I certainly do not have to give him the benefit of the doubt. It is un-Christian to prey on us like this." She grumbled, "Thank God his mother did not live to see this behavior." She made the sign of the cross and closed her fingers around the crucifix at her throat.

Casimir clasped his hands together. "Once back at the Vatican, I will begin an inquiry into Scortini's behavior and slanderous assertions. Then I will call him before an inquest to answer for himself."

Standing up, Casimir reached out again for Giselle's hand. "Because my visit has been cut short, I must ask you to take me to see your sculpture now, my dear."

Giselle led him to the construction area in the courtyard, with the family following behind them. Markus appeared, but stayed at a distance.

Standing in front of the huge metal structure, pride was evident on her face. "Papa, this is my newest sculpture. I call it *Star Fall.*"

"Extraordinary! I saw *Star Fall* in a dream, but it served as homes in Verdu Mer."

"*Sì*, it's just as you sketched." Gabrieli moved closer and gazed up at a glass star. "What you saw as halos, she's interpreted as glowing stars."

"We have been given the same vision from God, my child." He tore his eyes away from the sculpture just long enough to give his goddaughter a knowing look. "But from what I hear, your interpretation is far too dangerous for you to continue building."

Giselle threw a look of betrayal at Vincenzo, who explained, "I told them about the irrodium." She cocked her head and furrowed her brows. "I had to," he pled.

"Take me to your blueprints, my dear." Casimir put his arm around her as she walked him to the greenhouse. Gabrieli and Juliette followed close behind, listening intently to the genesis of this dream project.

"Tell me how your vision for *Star Fall* came to you."

———⧫———

Vincenzo watched as his family followed Giselle and the Pope inside the greenhouse to discuss miracles. He tilted his head toward the stable house for her boyfriend to follow him there. Once they were inside, Markus closed the door and turned on him.

"You are playing a dangerous game." Markus growled.

"I am?" He was caught off guard. "Me? What about you and Gigi!"

"Do not try to play innocent! You just tried to have us caught by the Pope!"

"No, I didn't! He came to see the sculpture. I couldn't

get him out here if I wanted to. I don't tell the Pope what to do."

"But you knew! You could have warned us he was coming!"

"I've been calling Gigi since I found out this afternoon." Vincenzo held out his phone. "She's got nearly twenty texts from me."

"We have been busy."

"*I know.* Scortini's spy reported that he watched you two having sex. I was an idiot to think you could be trusted to be discrete!"

"Do not try to change the subject. You are lying to me," Markus countered. "You brought the Pope here to frighten her away from me!"

"That isn't what happened at all. He really only came to see the sculpture."

Markus paused, and then seemed to accept his explanation. "Now that you and I are alone again, we are not leaving this room until you tell me what lie you and Giselle are living." The icy blonde inched forward menacingly. "Why did you not take her virginity? Do you not desire her?"

"No! What? She's very desirable, but I've never done *that* with her."

"Done *that?* You say it with distaste. You think sex is something bad?"

"I'm not going to answer to you...you...*gigolò!*"

In a flash, Markus grabbed him and bent him painfully backward over a table.

"What did you just call me? Why do you not fulfill her needs?"

"Get off me!" He tried to pull the iron hands off his neck and kick out, but this powerful artist was becoming enraged.

"You think sex is something sinful?" he snarled.

"No, I have sex all the time!" He could barely choke out an answer. Markus' grip was so tight he could barely breathe. He was seeing spots, and had to get this man off him *now.* "*With Leonardo!*" he blurted.

"*Leonardo?*" Markus rocked back on his heels and released him, letting him drop onto the table. Gasping for breath, Vincenzo rolled off the table onto the floor. Markus stood over him with his hands on his head.

"Who is Leonardo? You are homosexual? How long has he been your lover?"

"None of your business." It came out as a squeak.

"Stop this pretending!" Markus put his hands on his knees and leaned over him.

After a fit of shallow coughs, he said, "He's always been my lover." He gingerly touched his windpipe.

Markus appeared relieved as he bent down and helped him off the floor. "I am sorry if I hurt you. You know I have been desperate here. This secret life you have been leading with Giselle has been plaguing my mind."

"I can only imagine. You really hurt my throat." He twisted his back gingerly. "And I think you hurt my back..."

"You must toughen up. You may have to defend yourself against this man, Scortini. Have you ever been in a fight before?"

"No, and I'm not about to fight Scortini."

"I could tell. You are more like a dancer than a tough guy."

"I'm a banker, I don't need my fists."

Markus went to the window seat and sat down, and Vincenzo sat next to him.

"I feel so guilty. Gigi's my best friend, and she knows that my family has a special relationship with the Church. It would be complete heartbreak for my family—a disgrace for the Vatican—if they discovered that I'm homosexual. My family has never even suspected it. I've always surrounded myself with girls." Warming to his argument he continued, "And Gigi and I have a wonderful life together…"

"That is no marriage," Markus said. "How can you take her love from her? You have her living the life of a nun while you enjoy a lover!"

Vincenzo shook his head, trying to convince himself. "She's the one who proposed it."

"Not fair! A schoolgirl idea…a heart-broken orphan…in mourning when she walked to the altar."

"She's my wife. I can't lose her." He dropped his head into his hands. "We love each other."

"You have *friendship*." Markus stood up, getting agitated again. "That is not the same. *So selfish!* She is trapped by your secret. She has had no one to talk to about your lie."

Vincenzo began feeling defensive, and a bit angry. "And yet you've gotten her to do so much more than *talk* to you." He looked up at this stranger standing over him. "We don't know you. And I'm not going to let you put your hands on me ever again. I only need to give Petro the word, and he'll put you off this property."

Markus headed for the door. "Do not try a power play

with me Vincenzo. You will lose. Come now. We will go to *her* and plan what to do next."

The two returned to the greenhouse, stalking side-by-side in silence. His father, the Pope, and Giselle were wrapping up their conversation over her blueprints as his mother looked on.

The Pope declared, "I propose that you create a housing design based on this…" He tapped his fingers on the blueprints, "and submit it to the consortium. I believe this is God's answer to the housing dilemma that we face. I see Verdu Mer becoming a special place that the world will look to for inspiration."

His father gave Giselle a stern look. "I must insist that you stop working with your irrodium spindles immediately."

She ducked her head, looking ashamed.

He reached out and pulled her to him in a hug. "Dearest Gigi, who could have known that your family legacy would afford you such comfort with deadly things?"

"What can be done to keep this lethal artwork safe?" Juliette gestured to the triumphant sculpture arching outside. "What if a bird flies into it?"

"Close it off." Vincenzo looked from Giselle to Markus. "Will the two of you get an enclosure for *Star Fall* right away? Bernard's farm supplies in Aiglemont sells those enormous prefab barns that his men can set up quickly."

Looking chagrinned, they both nodded.

Juliette clapped her hands together. "Then let us eat before we rush back to Italy."

Giselle hung behind with Markus and Vincenzo as Papa and her in-laws returned to the château. She looked up at Markus.

"Have you heard that Salvio had a spy here today? He saw us together and alerted Salvio, who called Papa."

"So that is why he came into the stable house? He thought you were inside with me?" Markus ran his hand over his bristly hair, looking frustrated. "He almost scared Carolette to death."

"What did I miss? How did Carolette get mixed up in this?" Vincenzo asked.

Markus shrugged. "I came out of the shower, and Carolette had gotten naked on my bed. The Pope walked in as I found her. He must think that Salvio's spy mistook her for Giselle."

"That was too lucky." Vincenzo shook his head. "But now the Vatican will have to reprimand Scortini, and that's going to make him more desperate."

Markus shoved his hands into his pockets. "And he knows about us."

Giselle moved to Vincenzo, wrapped an arm around his waist, and smiled up at him reassuringly. "So, we'll just have to outsmart him, and make everything we do look normal."

"You're going to have to be more discrete than you've been so far." She could see he was disappointed, and trying not to scold her. "Gigi, I told Markus about Leonardo."

"Oh." She was surprised and then felt relieved. "I'm glad you were honest. And please don't worry. Your secret is safe with him."

Markus seemed puzzled. "I do not understand. There have been homosexuals since the beginning of time. Why must you keep your sexual preference a secret? Even the Catholic Church knows that homosexuality is natural, do they not?"

Vincenzo answered, "No, the Church does not consider homosexuality natural. In fact it's considered a sin, and right now I'm concerned about Salvio finding out about Leo. If he does, he'll twist our transgression into something political. Papa would have no choice but to condemn us as deviants." He lowered his voice and sounded pained. "Gigi, are you absolutely sure you want to be with Markus? If you're just having some fun, I understand that. But what we have..."

"Listen, you selfish..." Markus was glaring at Vincenzo.

Giselle held up a hand up for silence. "Enough, Markus. V, I've never felt this way before. I don't know why. How can I make you understand? I love you—as a brother. You've been my favorite person on earth since my family died, and having you as my husband has been enough for me."

Markus gave Vincenzo a brooding look. "You are not telling me everything. It is time for you to tell me what the price could be if your homosexuality is discovered, and why the two of you guard it so."

Gigi could see Vincenzo begin to retreat behind a mental wall. "Please, V. It's pointless to try to keep hiding this from Markus. We all have to work together..."

Vincenzo walked even more slowly to delay their return to the others. "My family...we are the oldest guardians of

Catholicism on earth. We serve as the glue that holds the
Vatican together, and we work through ancient channels to
bring man's 'quality of life' needs before the Church. We
orchestrate compromises that are the foundation of charity
in the infrastructure of today's global world. We help when
the Church cannot be directly involved in a matter for
political or religious reasons."

"You are kidding."

"No, it's true." Giselle nodded solemnly.

"So your family is personally responsible for making
sure that the Catholic Church treats people humanely, and
that they help the poor regardless of their religion?"
Markus looked incredulous.

"*Sì.* But our responsibility is so much more. Each Verona male is born to support the papacy, because one man
alone cannot bear the weight of that responsibility. We
pray and listen for direction to bring God's blessings to
those who need it most...always to serve the highest good
of mankind. We are our planet's foremost philanthropic
force. Above all, our duty is to unite all of the Vatican's
power players. Without our family's ancient alliances and
constant efforts, the Church would turn against itself."

Markus raised his brows. "Then I...thank you and your
family for this service. But..." He stopped with a sharp
intake of breath. "Ah! You believe that the Catholic Church
and the whole world would suffer if you were cast away by
the Pope?"

"Mankind would suffer. Without a Verona in place to
support him, a pope would be torn apart by fragmenting
forces even within the Vatican. You have no idea the

corruption within the Holy State. Although I don't believe that Sua Santità would 'cast me away' per se, there would be serious worldwide repercussions."

Giselle tried to make Markus understand. "The Pope is truly a father to Vincenzo, and it would break his heart if he had to declare anything against his godson. Papa prays continually for us to give him a grandchild..." Clearing her throat, she continued lamely, "Which neither of us were prepared to face."

"I am sorry for you, Vincenzo." Markus shook his head. "It is not fair for your private love to be a potential weapon to jeopardize your family's work."

"V, I can't give Markus up." Giselle spoke tenderly. "I never understood the love I saw between you and Leonardo, I'd never been in love myself." Her tone lightened and she smiled. "And you've been a wonderful husband, V."

He smiled back at her, but she could see how conflicted he was.

Markus cleared his throat. "Vincenzo, you should have no fear of me. I will guard your secret. I will keep what Giselle and I have secret, too. We will be more careful to appear platonic."

"Thank you." Vincenzo looked relieved.

"That is, until you find a way to release Giselle from this false marriage." He tucked his chin and gave Vincenzo a serious look from beneath his brows. "You need to tell me more about this Scortini. I will help you as I can."

As they arrived at the house, Giselle walked alone to the kitchen to find Carolette and Fauve. Caterers were moving briskly about, carrying bottles of champagne and Pellegrino, and setting up staging areas for chafing dishes, plates, platters, and all manner of crystal glassware. The florist and her team were putting the finishing touches on arrangements and carrying them to the dining room.

Carolette and Fauve rushed up to her and pulled her into the Moroccan room where they could have some privacy. Pushing Giselle onto a sofa in the corner, Carolette dramatically dropped her head into Giselle's lap and yelped, "I was about to seduce Markus, and I got caught by the Pope!"

Fauve fanned Carolette's head with her hand. "Could she be right? I thought it was just V and his parents coming. Is it true? Is Pope Leopold here? So many people have arrived to set up for the party, I couldn't have walked past the Pope could I?"

Carolette huffed her indignance and twisted her head sideways to glare at Fauve. "I may not be the best Catholic, but I know *the Pope!* My mother has a picture of him above our dinner table."

"He's here." Giselle patted her prostrate friend's back. "He came to see my sculpture. We were just out back going over my blueprints, and now he's conducting some business in the library."

"Do we get to meet him?" Fauve lit up with excitement, and then looked down. "Oh, well, apparently Coco's already met him."

Carolette moaned. "Of all the horrible embarrassments in a person's life, nothing can top this shame!"

Fauve blurted, "Giselle, she was completely naked, and...you know...putting herself out there for Markus..."

"Right. You know, I was hoping he'd pounce on me, and I've been dieting, and I tell you, my body is looking really good." Giselle could tell her friend was working herself up for one of her long rambles, but Fauve was really keyed up, too.

"It's all that spinning. You do look really good." Fauve patted her friend's leg.

Carolette brightened for a moment. "So I was doing a Playboy pose on the bed, and Markus came into the room, and his body is completely unbelievable, and—"

"Does he have good abs?" Fauve demanded.

Carolette made moaning sounds and looked a bit gaga. "Oh, just incredible! He looks like sex on two legs! He has muscles that are totally different than a six pack, more like a twelve pack, and these muscles that run down across the top of his hips—"

"And, Gigi!" Fauve cut in and then clamped her hand over her mouth, giggling. "She actually asked Markus to have sex with her before dinner!"

Giselle felt a pang of jealousy. "You did?" She flushed with pride that her lover's body caused such a reaction. She couldn't agree more.

"*Boh ouais*, I propositioned him. But he looked right past me over to the door, and so I looked over too, and *ohmonDieu!* the holiest man of God and his guards were standing right there behind my naked butt! I'm emotionally scarred! Oh, please let me wake up. Who does this happen to? No one in history, I'm certain. How could this happen to me?"

Giselle was petting her friend's frizzy blonde hair, trying to smooth it back into her hairpins. "Don't you worry,

Coco. Papa is confronted by big sins constantly. Seeing your body is not the worst that could happen."

Fauve agreed. "That's right. He's preoccupied with genocide and things. Don't give it another thought. Your body is nothing to be ashamed of."

"Oh, *mon Dieu!*" Carolette moaned. "My behavior most certainly *is* something to be ashamed of! I'll never be able to eat at my mother's table again without seeing the Pope staring at me while I was doing a Playboy pose on Markus' bed!"

"Well, you certainly went for it, Coco." Giselle coughed out a laugh.

"Yeah. I really thought he'd go for me," she sighed.

Fauve asked, "Well, what did Markus do *exactly?*"

"Other than stand there looking like my perfect sculpted fantasy lover?" Carolette pushed herself upright, forgetting about her humiliation for a moment. "Nothing. He must have walked into the bedroom at exactly the same time as the Pope. But he was naked. Markus—not His Holiness. Oh, my no! Anyway, Markus was naked and well, wow! I've never seen a body like his. It's perfect! And not bulky with muscles. He's slim without his clothes on, but well, he's just perfection and his skin is flawless and his dick is good sized even though it was soft! And it was straight. It didn't bend to the side like some do..."

"I'm so sorry you had to be embarrassed like that," Giselle soothed.

"*Oui*, the least that one of those guards could have done is whistled or something to make you feel appreciated," Fauve interjected.

"I agree! I would have felt appreciated and good about myself if someone had had the decency to whistle...though not the Pope, of course..."

"*Oui*, a whistle would have made it better." Fauve was warming to her bizarre attempt to make Carolette feel better. "Or a compliment. They were just thoughtless."

Giselle looked up as Juliette walked into the room with Selma and Ippy. "Come ladies, let us have dinner. Our honored guest must depart, and I am afraid we will return to Italy, as well." She looked from Carolette to Fauve. "Both of you know how to curtsey?"

"Sure do, we did them in *A Midsummer Night's Dream* for the school play."

"Ah, *sì*. I remember now. *Bene*, then come."

While they followed the contessa into the dining room, Carolette whispered to Giselle, "Laetitia, Solange, and the boys will die when they realize what they've missed."

"Well, it's their fault for being in Paris with Pierre today."

In the library, the men stood at attention over by an enormous flower arrangement, and as the ladies entered, Henri winked at Fauve who gave him a proud smile. Giselle stood nearby as Juliette presented Selma, Fauve, and Carolette to the Pope. Each of them curtsied, kissed his ring, and received a blessing. When it was Carolette's turn, after the blessing he leaned forward and murmured, "I hope that you have recovered from your fright."

"Can you ever forgive me, Eminence?"

He looked at her with a mixture of gravity and kindness. "Carolette, I am not called 'Eminence.' I ask you to reflect on your life, and make a full confession to your priest. You are in my prayers."

"I will. *Merci*, Holy Father." She seemed on the verge of grateful tears.

When Markus was presented, the Pope whispered, "I believe you will be getting married soon, Markus?"

"That is my hope."

⚬

Markus sat at the dinner table, relieved to finally understand Giselle and Vincenzo's relationship. Count Gabrieli Verona brought him out of his reverie.

"So Markus, I'm pleased to meet you. But I'm disappointed you'd allow my daughter-in-law to handle dangerous chemicals." Markus was considering a reply when he continued, "That being said, I don't know anyone who can resist a request made by Giselle."

The Pope spoke slowly while looking squarely at his goddaughter. "You follow your own convictions. And if Markus had refused to touch those vials, you would have gone around him to do exactly as you had planned, without his help." He looked at Markus. "That is the nature of Giselle with her art." He paused and turned to admire her. "She is all art, all of the time."

Giselle bowed her head in acknowledgement.

"Thank you for understanding," Markus said. "I have tried to keep her safe."

Vincenzo spoke up. "I'm going to ask that you take special care to assure her safety now, and move your things into the château so you can stay close at hand."

Markus nodded in unspoken acknowledgement of the favor Vincenzo was doing them.

"*Oh, sì!*" Juliette was clearly relieved. "Markus, please stay close to our girl." Turning to Selma, she asked, "Did Tiberius ask you to set the dogs out to roam the property for as long as Giselle is here?"

Selma nodded. "*Oui*, they're out patrolling now."

Satisfied, Juliette turned back to Giselle, "And once you have secured the sculpture, you plan to return to Paris?"

"*Sì.*" Vincenzo pressed. "Now that you're not going to finish the sculpture, you should come back home, darling."

"Tomorrow we'll go to town and buy a shed enclosure. But there's still so much we can do on the sculpture that doesn't involve the spindles. We could stay away from the chemicals, but I—*we* have come so far to simply stop..."

The Pope raised his hands in supplication to heaven. "Oh Giselle, please—for my heart's peace—promise me that you will not continue with the sculpture. I am against you working anywhere near those vials."

She ducked her head and answered, "Of course, Papa. How selfish of me. I promise."

The count added, "I have no idea how those vials should be disposed of, but for now please keep them locked away."

"I will. I promise." She sounded glum.

"Is there more irrodium in your father's laboratory?"

"A few containers." It was a whisper.

Count Verona ran his fingers through his hair and made a gesture to his wife that said, "Kids!"

Turning to Markus, the Pope asked quietly in Polish, "Do you understand Polish?"

"*Da.*"

The rest of the table knew they were not invited to the private conversation, and went on eating and talking.

The Pope continued, "Your accent is not Russian. You sound Western Slavic to me."

"*Pravda,* I am not Russian. I am Western Ukrainian," he replied in Ukrainian.

The Pope raised both eyebrows and continued in his native tongue. "Ah, then you must find it difficult when people mistake you for Russian."

Markus gave him a look that only another Eastern European would understand. "It is because they do not know better. Russia has made my people invisible."

The Pope smiled. "You are a tolerant man." Quietly, almost to himself, "I know there are Ukrainians who would kill for being called a Russian."

Markus blew a gush of air between his lips. "*Da.*"

D on Giancarlo Petrosino looked out over the Tyrrhenian Sea. He was sitting in the office of the cliff-side
building that served as his Palermo headquarters. His son,
Primo, was giving a business update and his consigliere,
Paolo Bianchi, was taking notes. As the richest and most
feared Mafia boss in Sicily, Gio kept his finger on the pulse
of his empire. It was as natural to him as breathing.

His pocket vibrated, and he pulled out his cell phone.
Glancing down, he was surprised to see the name that
appeared on his screen. *So, the aloof Venetian is calling me.
This should be interesting.*

"Hold on a minute. It's Salvio Scortini."

"That kid's a bum." Paolo looked disgusted.

"*Sì*, but he's richer than Midas, and he's got a few things
that I want."

"Tell him we know he stole those patents." His attorney
twirled his pen.

Gio held up a finger and smiled a bad-boy smile. Paolo and Primo fell silent as he answered his phone.

"*Pronto.*"

"Petrosino? Scortini here."

"Ah, Salvio. Let me offer my condolences. Your father was a great man."

"What?"

"I enjoyed our time together. I admired Sal's honesty. And while we never worked together, we would have made great partners."

"My father met with you?" He sounded doubtful.

"You sound surprised. We met, and it was always a pleasure."

"This isn't a social call, Petrosino. I'm about to give you the opportunity of a lifetime."

"Oh?" *Rude little prick.*

"I have a proposition that would bring you into Verdu Mer. If you're interested, you'll get on a plane and be at my home before I change my mind." The call disconnected.

Gio stood, reached for his suit jacket, and turned to Paolo. "Make those changes to the contracts, and send them off." Turning to Primo he said, "Get the plane ready. We're flying to Venice. Scortini is gonna invite us to the Verdu Mer buffet."

"That's a very big buffet." Paolo smiled, then he pulled a face. "But that kid has no class."

Primo was already out the door, signaling for their driver to pull up, and dialing their pilot. Gio climbed into the back seat of the car and thought about his past attempts at getting a foothold in Venice's building infrastructure. He'd always failed to close a deal there because of the iron grip Salvatore Scortini had on construction. Sal was a gentleman and took his calls. Sal had even had dinner with him in public on occasion as Gio tried to explore ways they could work together. But while Sal was respectful and even nice to him, he made it clear that the Mafia wouldn't be given an inch in Venice. Gio had made a few small moves in Venice on his own to see what the Brotherhood of Iron Workers would do, and unfortunately they did exactly what Sal had predicted—they clung to the Scortini coattails and froze Gio out. He came very close to getting his hands on some lucrative patents that would have given him some real bargaining leverage, but the Brotherhood signed them away to Sal and put an end to his plans. Gio had ended up in court, but he'd been acquitted.

When Sal died, Gio called Salvio to offer his condolences, but the little prick refused to speak to him. Now this phone call piqued his curiosity. Salvio had no business reputation at all, and as far as Gio knew, he wasn't running any projects. But offering a piece of Verdu Mer would get Gio to drop everything and fly to Venice. His jet was fast, so it was only a ninety-minute flight from Palermo to Marco Polo Airport, and Gio wasn't about to give Scortini time to change his mind.

During the flight, he called Drea, his favorite pilot, to meet him with her boat. The flight was uneventful, and after landing, Drea zipped them through the canals to the Scortini Palazzo. As he and Primo climbed the steps to the palace door, their eyes scanned for guards, cameras, or infrared sensors, but there was a bizarre lack of security. They shared a look of disbelief, but said nothing. Primo examined the ancient stone-and-brass horse-and-boat shaped doorbell before he reached up and gave the key a turn. Nothing could be heard from their side of the solid door, but an elderly butler let them in, and then showed them to Salvio's office.

While Primo stood on guard just outside the office door, Gio waited in a chair in front of Salvio's desk. Scortini popped up unexpectedly at his elbow, and Gio jerked out of his chair in surprise. He didn't like the eerie look of pleasure Scortini attempted to suppress. Gio returned to his seat as watched Salvio swagger behind his desk and take a seat. He decided right then, Salvio would pay for that childish prank. He was lucky Gio didn't have an itchy trigger finger. Was Salvio so stupid that he didn't know not to surprise a Mafioso?

Scortini raised his chin and looked down his nose at him. Staring back, Gio got to the point.

"So what's your involvement in Verdu Mer?" He looked at Salvio with no emotion. "My sources tell me that Count Verona's the one in charge."

"I was working with Verona on the project. But I've discovered that he's a deviant, and his entire family is corrupt. The Pope has to distance the Vatican from the Veronas. They are a cancer we have to cut out. So if you're interested, I'll take *you* as my partner."

Gio nodded. "You won't regret bringing me in."

"Your first responsibility as my partner is to kill Gabrieli Verona and make his body disappear forever."

He watched Salvio pick up a gold drapery tie and wind it around his hand. *Hmmm, so he kills his business partners?*

"This I can do."

"No farming this out to goons. Take care of it personally."

"I don't work with goons."

Salvio fondled the golden cord. "Every night at sunset he takes a walk along the Rio de la Verona near his home."

"I assume he still has protection?"

"*Sì*, one bodyguard."

"Not a problem."

"Tomorrow night after you've completed this task, you'll be my full partner at the helm of the biggest project in the history of Italy."

Gio regarded Scortini levelly. "I have your word and you have mine. We only have trust between us. I like it that way. It makes the best partnership." He extended his hand across the desk, and Salvio gave it a perfunctory pump.

"If you do exactly as I say," Scortini stood up abruptly, "you'll have the treasury of the Vatican at your disposal."

"You don't need to repeat yourself. I've given you my word." Gio got up and left the office, Primo trailing silently behind him as they walked out of the gloomy palace.

———⬥———

At that moment, Raphielli released the switch on the listening control panel. She moved silently down the secret passage to her bedroom. Moments later Rosa arrived to prepare her body for the impending torture of her matrimonial duties. Raphielli arrived at a decision and set her mind at last. Odd, she thought, that she could endure her own suffering at the hands of her husband, but she would die before she'd allow him to harm another person. A feeling of calm settled over her as she resolved to save the Veronas. But, how could she send them a message without Salvio finding out? He'd be notified if she asked one of their staff to send a note. She didn't have a cell phone, he'd locked up the house phones, and she wasn't allowed to go out alone. She'd have to think of something before tomorrow night.

Thirty minutes later as Salvio performed his husbandly duties, he almost choked her to death when he yanked a golden drapery cord around her neck and throttled her as he climaxed. She lost consciousness before he shoved her off the table.

———◈———

Early the next morning, Raphielli wore Marilynn's scarf to cover the wound that encircled her neck. She was ready to save Count Verona's life when the Dour Doublet accompanied her to Sunday Mass. All three of them were dressed in similar black crepe dresses with ballerina-length hems and sensible black shoes. Salvio insisted they escort her to and from church, and it was the only time she ever saw them. He'd made it clear that he didn't want them in his home, and they'd been rebuked for being pushy, so they stopped inventing reasons to ask for invitations.

As she followed them into the Basilica di San Giovanni e Paolo, Raphielli paused to scan the crowd. It was critical that she accomplish this part of her plan without drawing any attention from her chaperones. They were always on

Salvio's side, and constantly nagged her to be a better wife. If she did anything out of the ordinary, they'd see it as an opportunity to ingratiate themselves to Salvio and rush to tell him. And that would be the pathetic ending to the story of her life.

She spotted Contessa Verona looking incredibly chic, wearing high-heeled shoes that Raphielli couldn't imagine walking in. The contessa was seated on the aisle and chatting with people sitting around her. Raphielli announced to her mother that she needed to use the toilet, and before her mother could object, she dove into the crowded aisle where worshipers were bunching up at the ends of the pews attempting to find seats. Making her way along the aisle that would get her within earshot of the contessa, Raphielli began loudly clearing her throat to get her attention. When the contessa looked up, Raphielli mouthed, "*Aiutami!*" As the contessa stood up, Raphielli moved past her and whispered, "Follow me, I have an urgent message!" then slipped down the hall and into the bathroom.

Hovering in the busy vestibule near the sinks and mirrors, she fairly jumped when the contessa walked in. She pressed a piece of paper into the noble woman's hand.

"Raphielli!" She spun around to see her mother looking irritated, and then glanced back to see that the contessa was reading her note. Trying to look innocent, Raphielli answered, "Coming, Mama," and followed dutifully as her mother marched back out of the lavatory.

Raphielli made her way to a pew while listening to her mother's tirade about lack of planning and bladder control.

They were rejoined by her grandmother, who wore an expression of sour disappointment and grumbled, as usual, about Raphielli's childless womb. As they took their seats, she watched the contessa walk back through the church, heading toward the door. She was holding her cell phone. Good.

Immediately after Mass, Raphielli and her chaperones moved forward with the crowd toward the confessionals. The moment she reached the head of the line, Contessa Verona stepped out of the last confessional and held the door for her saying quietly, "God be with you." Once inside, she could see through the privacy screen that Cardinal Negrali was holding her note.

"Raphielli, tell me everything you know about your husband's plan to kill Count Verona."

"Oh, Father!" Trying to keep her voice low despite the urgency of the situation, the words gushed out. "Salvio hired a man named Petrosino. He's a Mafioso from Sicily, and he agreed to Salvio's plan to kill Count Gabrieli tonight. In return, Petrosino believes he'll be made full partner with Salvio in the Verdu Mer project."

"How do you know about this?" He asked.

"He's been saying the most terrible things about Count Verona."

"I know, he did so in front of the College of Cardinals."

"Well, now he's way beyond just talking."

"*Sì!* But, I must know how you know about Salvio's plan."

"I've been listening in on my husband's private conversations."

Negrali squinted through the screen at her. "May I ask how?"

"He's bugged some rooms in our palazzo, and I found his listening booth." Raphielli plunged on, "Also Salvio has private detectives working to find anything that could make the Pope prefer Salvio over the Veronas. He's been trying to ruin them."

"This I already know." Negrali shook his head. "The Pope has called an inquest in Rome to make Salvio answer for his spying."

"I'm so relieved that you believe me!" Raphielli let out a relieved breath she hadn't realized she'd been holding. "He met with Petrosino last night, and the don plans to kill the count *tonight*. Father, if you can keep Salvio away from our palazzo this afternoon, I'll call Petrosino and tell him everything. Will you vouch for me if the don doesn't believe me?"

"You mean expose Salvio as delusional?" Negrali hesitated. "You plan to tell this Mafioso that there is no chance Salvio will be given any part in Verdu Mer?"

"*Sì*, I'll tell him the truth. Tell him Salvio's promise of access to the Vatican treasury was a lie."

"The audacity! I will ask the College of Cardinals to call Salvio to our chambers as soon as I leave here. We will try to keep him in questioning until we adjourn at five o'clock tonight. Will that be enough time for you?"

"If I can reach don Petrosino, it'll be enough time. If I can't find him, I'll have to think of something else. At least the contessa will make sure the count doesn't take his usual walk tonight."

"You have extraordinary courage for such a young girl, Raphielli. But be careful." Negrali's voice was grave. "If Petrosino needs corroboration of your story, send him to the Little Church. The priests there can always find me, day or night."

Raphielli tried to appear natural as she left the confessional, but she needn't have worried about the Dour Doublet's watchful eyes. They were too busy complaining about something to the woman who sold the prayer candles. They accompanied Raphielli home, and then walked off together when her butler, Dante, answered the door. Raphielli asked him where her husband was.

"Ah, *signora*, the College of Cardinals sent for him, and he left just moments ago."

Wanting to keep her staff busy, she thought fast.

"Dante, where is Rosa?"

"Over on the Lido, it's her day visiting her mother. Do you require anything?"

"Nothing from her that can't wait. But I would like for you and Guiseppe to set up all of our patio furniture on the roof top." The old wrought-iron patio furniture was an over-sized seating for twenty, including chairs, lounges, sofas, tables, and umbrellas. It would take them hours to get them out of storage, remove the tarps, move them into place, clean them properly, and set the cushions.

"*Naturalmente, signora.*"

It wasn't a normal duty for either of them, but she knew it wasn't in their nature to refuse her.

"Have it all set up on the west side of the rooftop patio, situated to provide a vantage for watching the setting sun."

"It is unfortunate that we no longer have that beautiful rented furniture up there."

"*Sì, sì,*" she agreed. "I know you'll do your best to make it nice."

Dante headed down the hall in the direction of the service elevator.

She hurried to the back hall and ducked behind the heavy tapestry that covered the secret passageway. Once inside, she moved in the direction of Salvio's office, and then peeked from behind a tapestry panel. Relieved to find it empty, she rushed inside and straight over to Salvio's desk. Flipping through his personal diary and telephone directory, she found nothing. Then, seeing her late father-in-law's address book, she grabbed it from the corner of the desk and found the number she needed. With shaking fingers, she dialed the Mafia don.

A man answered in a smooth tone, "*Pronto.*"

Squeezing her eyes closed she stammered, "S-s-ignor Petrosino?"

"*Sì.*" The voice on the other end hesitated. "Who's this calling from Scortini's phone?"

Raphielli looked down at the bracelet she'd worn since she was a girl. It read: *The truth shall set you free.* "I'm Raphielli Scortini, Salvio's wife, and I have to speak with you right away."

"Oh?" The interest was apparent.

"*Sì, per favore,* but Salvio can't know. I'm at home alone. Please come right away to the old water entrance under Il Ponte Diamanti. I'll wait for you there."

"I'm on the water not far away. I can be there in a few minutes."

"*Grazie, signore.*"

"*Prego, signora,*" the voice answered pleasantly.

——— ⦿ ———

As soon as Gio hung, up he turned to Primo. "Something's up. Scortini's wife wants me to sneak back to his house to meet her alone."

"His wife?"

"Yeah." He got up and walked over to his favorite blonde badass who was piloting them through the canals. "Drea, change of plans. Take us to Palazzo Scortini right away."

When he was in Venice, he always hired Drea as his driver. She was the best driver he knew, loyal, and had an intimate knowledge of the canals. And while her boat wasn't showy, it was incredibly powerful. Gio settled back in his seat and tried to set aside his natural distaste for a wife going behind her husband's back. He'd listen to what she had to say and keep an open mind. He thought back to the Scortini wedding photo that had been in all the papers. He didn't remember the bride at all.

When Drea brought the boat up to Scortini's water garage, Gio pointed toward the shadowy bridge off to the side. "Is that Il Ponte Diamanti?"

She nodded.

"Get me over there."

The boat eased forward, bobbing in the chop from the passing boat traffic.

"Stay out of sight, and wait for me over by that moss-covered bridge farther up." He climbed out of the boat and down the crumbling old ramp. Gio moved carefully down the broken steps that led under the decrepit bridge, and then along the slick walkway access tunnel under part of the palazzo. It was several degrees cooler down at the water's edge, where the air smelled green and faintly of petroleum. He began inching into the blackness, wondering if this could be a trap. He reached inside his jacket pocket, took out his phone, and was about to dial Primo to come join him on this creepy mission when a frightened-sounding girl's voice called out tremulously, "Don Petrosino?"

He flicked his finger across his phone, activating the flashlight.

She gave a startled cry and clamped her hand over her mouth to stifle the sound. Tears slipped down her cheeks, and she brushed them away, blinking into the bright light.

He scanned the light over her from head to toe, then turned the glare away and pointed it at the stone ceiling above them, illuminating the oozing stalactites hanging from the cut stone.

Standing before him at a partially open door was a petite teenager who looked ready to burst into tears. She whispered, "I'm Raphielli Scortini."

"Sorry I scared you. I was being quiet because you'd been so secretive on the phone. I'm Giancarlo Petrosino, you can call me Gio."

"Your sudden bright light scared me almost to death, kind of like Salvio's entrances."

"He likes to play the *fantasma*. Very childish of him."

Raphielli had the appearance of a lush gypsy girl. She was pale, with big dark eyes, dramatic brows, and a full mouth. Her raven hair was coiled tightly at her neck in a large bun, but it looked ready to tumble down into a riot of curls. She was wearing a cheap sack-of-a-dress that couldn't hide her spectacular breasts and curvaceous hips. Around her neck was a green silk scarf that looked expensive and out of place with her cheap dress and clunky shoes. He offered his hand to steady her.

"One more step and you're liable to fall into the water. We can't stay under here. Where is Salvio?"

"He's not home," She whispered.

"Let's go back the way you came. Through that door, I take it?"

"I think I've gotten rid of the house staff..." She sounded uncertain.

"I'm not afraid of your house staff. Take me inside."

She took his hand, and they went into the house. She whispered, "You're right, Gio, Salvio likes to scare everybody."

"Someone is gonna teach him a lesson."

She gave him a doubtful look, and then said, "Please pull that door closed behind us. You have to pull hard, it sticks."

She wasn't kidding. The old frame must have settled, and he had to heave on it to get it to close. They were in total darkness now, apart from the beam from his phone. As they walked down the corridor, he placed one hand on her shoulder so he wouldn't walk on her heels, and to help keep her calm. When they came to an interior door, Raphielli opened it, and light poured through the gap. She poked her head in, looked both ways, and then drew him into a hallway inside the palazzo.

"Stay close to me." Now moving quickly, she scooted down a hall, and he stayed right behind her. They ducked into an abandoned corner room and closed the door behind them. Not bothering to offer him a seat, Raphielli whirled to face him and whispered in a rush, "Gio, we don't have much time. I've called you here to tell you that Salvio can't make you a partner in Verdu Mer."

"Oh?"

"No, he's not even part of that project. He's been trying to distance Count Verona from the Vatican, he even hired private detectives to discredit him. But now he's finally so desperate to gain control of Verdu Mer that he..." She clamped her lips together and put a hand over her mouth.

"It's okay, Raphielli, tell me everything."

"Well, I overheard him asking you to kill the count."

He didn't want to frighten her, so he kept his face calm. "How is that?"

"Please don't kill me. He has bugs around the house, and I found his listening booth."

"Listening booth?"

She turned and pointed along the wall. "His office is in that direction, and just out there in the hall is a tapestry. Behind that tapestry is the entrance to a secret passage that leads to the listening booth, his office—"

"That's how he sneaked up on me in his office."

She nodded enthusiastically. "It's the same secret passage he uses to come to my room."

Her scarf slipped, and he tried not to stare at the horrific damage to her neck.

"You listen to your husband's meetings?"

"Please don't ever tell him. I...I..."

"I understand, Raphielli. Knowledge is power, and it looks like you were just trying to keep yourself safe. Am I right?"

"*Sì, sì!* I don't want to be married to a man I have to eavesdrop on, but it's really helpful to know his state of mind! I promise you!" She summed up her plea, "Cardinal Negrali is willing to meet with you and verify that Salvio will never get Verdu Mer. Personally, I believe Salvio is more likely to end up in a mental institution."

"Mental institution?" He was confused.

"*Sì*. Nobody knows it, but Salvio believes he is the actual Son of God."

"I don't need to meet with the cardinal. I've spent some time learning more about Salvio today. Word here in Venice is that your husband is a big talker, but he no longer has the clout his family enjoyed. And I have some bad news for you. Instead of an institution, he may be going to prison."

"Prison?"

He put his hand on her shoulder. "I've been making some inquiries since my meeting with your husband, and I believe he killed a young man named Reynaldo Falconetti."

"Oh, no!" she choked. "*No!*" She began wringing her hands as tears spilled down her cheeks again. "Poor Reynaldo! I know his parents! Poor Marco and Agata! Salvio's temper is pure evil!" She absentmindedly touched the scarf at her throat, and he eased it down with one finger and took in the full extent of the gashes and bruises marring her tender young skin.

"*Sì*, it is." He adjusted the scarf to cover her neck again. "I'm glad you came to me. You were smart to listen in and learn what you could to save yourself...and now Count Verona. I'm not going to do what your husband asked of me, but he's gonna have to pay for trying to use me."

Raphielli opened her hands to him. "Please, promise not me you won't kill him."

"Is that your request?" Gio was perplexed.

"*Sì*," she replied with touching conviction.

He took both her hands in his and gave them a gentle squeeze. He wanted her to understand the significance of his next words, so he turned one hand over and placed a formal kiss in her palm. "Raphielli, I promise that I won't kill your husband. There are fates worse than death for someone like him."

The moment was broken by the sound of loud footsteps approaching in the hallway, and then running past the door. Then an old man's voice, "*Signore*, Guiseppe is up on the roof. Will you need him to bring you dinner in your office?" It sounded like the butler he'd met last night.

"Nothing!" It was Scortini's voice. "Now leave me! I have to speak to the Pope! Get away from me!"

He heard Scortini's nearby office door open, and then slam shut. The hall was silent again.

Gio looked at Raphielli and said quietly, "Take me to that listening booth."

With Raphielli leading the way, they moved into the deserted hall and hurried along the wall. She lifted the edge of a tapestry, and they slipped behind it into the secret passage. She motioned for him to stop when they'd reached the insulated listening booth, where she turned on a tiny red light and then flipped one of the switches. They heard Salvio pleading, loud and clear.

"No! I must speak to the Pope! *Sì!* I've just left the College of Cardinals, and I must personally tell Sua Santità about some urgent news I've just uncovered!"

There was silence. After a pause, Salvio blurted, "Holy Father, it's me, Salvio Scortini. Please forgive my mistake with Giselle Verona."

After another long pause, he wheedled, "*Sì,* Holy Father, the College informed me that I was mistaken. But Father, you must see that I have only ever had the Church in my heart, and the poor residents of Verdu Mer. I did it because in my soul I could feel there was something very wrong in that family. I'm loyal to the Veronas. Gabrieli and I have always been closer than brothers..."

Another pause and then, "Well, okay, that's true, but I can honestly say that I love Verona like a brother, and I would like to spend more time with him. But it was the feeling that something was wrong with his family that was making me sick, Father."

Another pause. "Father, I beg you to allow me to continue what I have to say. Through my investigations, I've uncovered a plot to kill Verona, and I'm the only one who can save his life now. I've discovered that an odious Sicilian *dog* named Petrosino is going to try to kill Verona *tonight.*"

Raphielli gasped and clutched Gio's arm, fingers digging in. She looked up at him with a mixture of terror and disbelief. Gio put his hand up in a calming gesture as Salvio continued.

"He's come up from Palermo to try take over Verdu Mer for the Mafia! Only minutes ago I informed the police that the Mafia dog is lying in wait to murder Gabrieli. Father, you must see that you and the College have taken my fidelity and interest the wrong way. I'm your faithful servant. Now that I have saved Verona's life, he and I can manage the project together."

Petrosino's rage was building, but he kept his cool. He and Raphielli listened to the rest of the conversation, and Scortini's assurances that he alone had saved Gabrieli from the dog Petrosino. Gio took hold of her elbow; in the dim shadows he could see she was on the verge of fainting from sheer stress. He mouthed into her ear, "It's okay. So this passage comes out in his office?"

She nodded and pointed.

"What's in the other direction?"

"Back past the spot where we entered is my bedroom."

He made an excusing motion with his hands, and she retreated down the secret corridor to her room. When he heard Salvio hang up the phone, he felt his way down the passage and sprang out behind Salvio, who uttered a strangled cry just as Gio's crushing hands clamped around his throat. Gio yanked him backward and savaged one of his kidneys with a knee. Holding Salvio in a one-armed chokehold, he reached into his pocket, took out a metal cylinder, and tapped the little hypodermic needle out. He slammed the drug into Scortini's neck, and then let him drop to the floor. Minutes later, he and Primo carried Scortini to Drea's waiting boat. When the body stowed, Gio went back alone in search of the girl.

He went through the secret entrance, back down the hall, into the secret passage, and headed in the direction she'd fled. He peeked out from behind a heavy curtain into a cold, dark room that smelled of an old woman's perfume. He almost turned back to keep looking, when he spotted her. She was attempting to brush her thick hair with shaky strokes, in the most depressing bedroom he'd ever seen.

"Psst. You alone?" he whispered.

She startled, dropped the brush, and ran to him. "Gio! What happened?"

Stepping into her room, he said, "You won't see or hear from him again. You should make up a story about him going away. I have a feeling nobody likes him, so no one should give you a hard time about seeing him in person." He thought about her vicious neck injury, and then patted her shoulder. "Practice signing his name, and you'll be fine financially."

Raphielli burst forward and hugged him hard. "If he comes back, he'll kill me."

He pulled back so he could see her, and smoothed the black curls from her face. "I understand that, Raphielli." He gave her a smile. "I'll keep him securely locked up for you." Then he pulled her to him and hugged her. He stood rocking her in a paternal way for a moment, and kept his voice soft. "My son and I will take Salvio away, and you'll be free."

"*Grazie*, Gio." He could feel her shuddering breaths as she began crying tears of relief from her prolonged state of anxiety. "Will you send me updates?"

"There's no need for updates," he murmured, while thinking of all the possibilities. "But if I ever need to give you news about Salvio, I'll send you a note inside a box of tea. No one would think to look in a tea box, right?"

She nodded.

Gio gently pulled her away from his chest and looked into her eyes. "Find a good man, Raphielli. You deserve better than him. He's trash." He wiped her tears with his thumbs, turned back behind the curtain, and left her staring after him.

⟢ ⬤ ⟣

Giselle and Markus had spent most of the day packing away the unused sculpture materials while barn-building contractors erected a pre-fab enclosure around *Star Fall* with brisk efficiency. Her most captivating work was being exiled, sentenced to glow inside a dark shed...until she could figure out a way to complete it. It left her feeling depressed, an emotional state she hadn't felt in years.

"I'd thought of several scenarios for this sculpture, but I never considered the possibility of *incompletion*. I feel *miserable*."

Markus closed the greenhouse door and fell into step beside her. "This I can imagine. You could not have foreseen the men in your life bringing the Pope for an intervention."

Giselle laughed in spite of herself. "Aww, don't try to make me laugh, Markus."

"Maybe you will feel better after a shower."

They walked in silence with the guard dogs trailing

them, and as they climbed the steps of the château, the dogs trotted off across the driveway on their patrol.

Once inside Markus said, "I researched irrodium online. There is a good reason it was banned." He enunciated carefully as he recited, "Blood exposure causes death almost instantly." He shook his head. "Which must be a relief since it is apparently a very painful toxin. You do see that your sculpture is a beautiful death trap, no?"

Walking with her head down, she offered a weak justification. "We were careful to avoid blood exposure and...its impact on the art world is worth the risk...oh, I'm so...I don't know what to do with this frustration." She stopped as inspiration struck. "Hey! Can I go hit your broken sculpture?"

Markus looked surprised. "It is already in the trash bin."

Genuinely interested, she asked, "Did taking a cane to your sculpture make *you* feel better?"

"Let me consider your question." Markus ran his hands over his ultra-short hair. "Breaking glass *can* be a release. But no, what made me feel better was you coming into my room and giving me your virginity."

A laugh escaped her. "Oh! Right. That would do it."

"Mm-hmm." He headed for the grand staircase. "There are ways to relieve frustration that are much more enjoyable than smashing things."

His sexy tone was all it took to divert her attention—she really was becoming obsessed with him. But she feigned innocence as she climbed the stairs, overtaking him.

"Oh, I don't know. I have a lot of frustration. My artistic dream has been stifled. I may need an entire team of therapists."

Markus was unbuttoning his shirt as they paused on the second-story landing.

"Sadly, I have no virginity to sacrifice to your problem. Maybe you will settle for a bit of distraction?" Shivers ran down her back as she followed him to her bedroom.

Sometime later, they lay tangled in the sheets as the sun dipped low over the forest, casting the room in a dusky glow.

"Ah, that was magnificent, Giselle."

"I wish I could tell the girls what you do to me, *mon amour*."

Markus bit her inner thigh. "Your friends would attack me, I think."

"Oh, it's true." Giselle looked down at him with all seriousness. "If they knew what you can do, they'd kidnap you and make you pleasure them."

He pretended to look frightened. "You are right. You must not ever tell them."

"Unless what you do is what every man does. Is it? Are all men the same in bed?"

"I do not know." He shrugged as he got out of bed and pulled her to her feet. "Maybe it is so."

He picked her up and swung her over his shoulder, then headed toward the bathroom to shower. "I understand why Vincenzo carries you like this. It is wonderful." He bit her hip playfully, and his fingers wandered to her exposed sex.

Giggling, she shrieked in surprise. "Aei! He never did that!"

"No. Friends do not do that. Do they?"

In the shower, Markus massaged soap along her back. "Giselle, you are like nothing I ever imagined."

"Hmm, now you sound like Yvania."

"*Da*, imagine the Czerney's excitement when they find out that we will be married."

"You want to marry me?" They stepped out of the shower and began toweling off.

"Can you doubt that I want you to be my wife? Now that I have found you, I want to be with you forever. Will you marry me?"

"*Oui!* You'll love being married to me! I'm a good wife, and now I'm learning to do the one thing that I didn't do before!"

"Make love?" He arched an eyebrow.

"*Oui.*"

After a relaxing dinner, Giselle let her creativity come alive on paper as she transformed her *Star Fall* design into an architectural blueprint for a home. She studied a photo of the Pope's sketch that Vincenzo had sent her. What had appeared to him in his dream was indeed the same graceful, arching shape. The creation of a practical floor plan flowed quickly, and Giselle was quite pleased with the resulting design.

Markus traced his finger along the spans between where she'd placed the front door and the back of the arch. "Kitchen and bathroom in back with the two bedrooms above? The house will feel big inside because of the height of the arch."

Her phone rang. "It's Vincenzo," she said as she tapped the speaker button.

"*Alo.*"

"Are you all right, my dear?" The voice was her father-in-law's.

"*Oui*, Gabrieli, everything is good. I'm sitting here with Markus working on the house design."

Vincenzo cut in, "Gigi, we've just learned that Salvio hired someone to kill my father."

"*He what?*" She felt adrenaline surge through her body, and her heart began to pound.

"We found out hours before any attempt was made, and are taking extra precautions." Gabrieli sounded calm.

"Okay. Good." She took a deep, calming breath. "Can you have Salvio arrested for his plot to kill you?"

"The police just went to his house, and apparently no one knows where he is."

"But they will find him and put an end to this now, right?" Markus asked.

"That's our hope," Gabrieli said. "Oh, I do have more news. We just met with the consortium about your light-emitting stars."

"Good news, I hope."

"Not what I would call good news. While there was initial excitement about your chemical light source, it was hard for them to see it as more than just a parlor trick, and even harder for them to consider it worth their time to investigate."

"My light source is hardly a parlor trick," Giselle grumbled.

"*Sì*, my dear, we know that. The team was doubtful they could recreate a safe chemical light source, but they assured me they would consult scientists to do just that...within safety standards, of course."

"I understand."

Vincenzo cut in, "Gigi, you know we're clearing away the hazardous conditions the residents have been living in. We would never want to make them a beautiful new neighborhood where they could be harmed by the lights we'd installed."

"No, I know my stars are dangerous," she conceded with a sigh.

"Deadly, Gigi. Not dangerous, they're deadly." Vincenzo was firm.

"I know," she said.

"*Sì,* I know you see it as we do." Gabrieli's voice was soothing, like he was talking to a child. "And while it's unlikely your stars will become part of Verdu Mer, the building planners are eager to see your house design."

"I have to say that even *I'm* impressed with how beautifully *Star Fall* lends itself to a living space." She said.

"When will we see your sketches?" Gabrieli's excitement was audible.

"I'll send you drawings of initial concepts and room layouts soon."

"Good. Now my dear, I must go speak with a police detective who has just arrived. We'll talk soon, eh?"

Once his father was gone, Vincenzo cleared his throat. "Markus, may I speak with Giselle alone?"

"You are asking me?" Markus looked surprised. "Of course."

"Gigi, can you take me off speaker?"

She took him off speaker and walked toward the kitchen for privacy. "What's up?"

"I've been a wreck." His voice sounded faint, hurt. "I want to make up with you."

"Make up with me? We haven't been fighting, silly."

"I love you so much, and I've been doing a lot of soul searching. I've been so unfair to you. I'm a complete shit."

"What? No, no. I married you and it was great." She sighed. "But now I need more."

"I need you to forgive me, but what I did is unforgivable."

"There's no need for me to forgive you, V."

"Leo said you'd say that. Thank you. How are you Gigi? You sound happy."

"I am happy." She thought about Markus and grinned. "I'm really great."

"This thing with Scortini trying to kill my father, and the pressure for me to figure out a way to free you...it's just been so stressful...and I'm used to having you at my side to discuss everything with." He sounded so sad.

She made her way back to Markus and sat down. "You know that Leo has always been there for you, even before we met. I think he's been more of a rock for you than you realize. You should trust him to help and support you now. Stay safe, and don't make yourself crazy. You sound like you need some sleep."

"I do."

"So go get some sleep, and we'll talk soon."

"I love you, Gigi."

"I love you too, V. Give my love to Leo."

"Okay. *Ciao.*"

Markus helped roll up her drawings and put them away, and then they headed for the bedroom. Walking through the great hall together, he wrapped his arm around her waist and let his fingers play over her stomach.

"You know that we will make a baby soon."

"Mm-hmm..." Giselle nodded very slowly and gave him a sidelong look. "I hear that can happen when two people have sex."

"Odds of a baby go up when two people have sex *frequently*." Markus smiled darkly, his blue eyes shining from beneath his lashes.

She spun playfully into his arms and wrapped hers around his neck. "I want to have babies with you."

"And I want babies with you, too. But first we should find a way to get married."

She stroked the back of his neck with her fingertips. "And I want to be your wife." She tried the name. "Giselle Shevchenko." She spun away from his grasp to lead him upstairs. "But right now, I have no idea how we can free me to walk down the aisle with you."

"You have been passive for too long, Giselle." Markus followed her down the long hall.

"I don't think of myself as passive."

"It is strange. You are not passive by nature, but your destiny must frighten you, because you have given the reins of your life over to Vincenzo."

"You see a lot, don't you?" They entered the bathroom to brush their teeth.

"*Da*, and while I can understand a girl who just lost her family being frightened and hiding with her best friend, I cannot believe that you stayed frozen at his side this long."

"I was never interested in anyone before you."

He smiled at her reflection in the mirror. "I am so happy to be part of your destiny."

"What should I do after I take the reins back from Vincenzo? Give them to you?"

"No! You should ride in the direction that is true for you, and I will ride by your side...most of the time."

"Most of the time?"

"You would not want me to give up my own destiny."

"True."

"And I do not think anyone can keep up with you." She heard resignation in his voice.

"They can if I keep starting sculptures that I never finish," she pouted.

"Let us have a party to cheer you up."

"Great idea!" Giselle's mood lightened instantly. "That's what I need!"

"Your silly Killing Kings card game and your friends will do you good."

They brushed their teeth and headed for bed.

13

Raphielli felt that she was standing at the metaphorical crossroads spoken of so often in poems and plays. She had a strong urge to change directions. She was done being a helpless bystander as everyone else made plans, voiced their opinions, and pursued their own dreams. She was going to take charge of her life. And while she was at it, she was through being intimidated by the Dour Doublet. She was going to return to her true self—energetic and practical in equal parts.

Gio had given her a piece of shrewd advice, and she was going to take it. He was right; nobody wanted to see Salvio face-to-face. She'd just carry on as if her husband had gone away. Salvio didn't have a single friend, and she had enough nerve to keep up the ruse. When Cardinal Negrali called to check on her last night, she'd told him that Petrosino had taken Salvio, and she could have sworn she heard relief in his voice when he'd recommended they never tell a soul what really happened to Salvio, and that she take charge of the house. She knew she was up to the task. How hard could it be to run this household? She felt certain she could do a better job than Salvio had. She would figure out how to access some of the estate funds and hire a proper staff. Just not too soon, or the ruse of expecting her husband to return would be blown.

Without the constant threat of Salvio's disproval hanging over her, she felt confident to deal with this situation. When the police came late last night to question Salvio about his report of a plot to kill Count Verona, she had remained calm and told the officers that he'd left the house with no word of when he'd return.

It was the beginning of a new day, and Raphielli called Rosa, Guiseppe, and Dante to the dining room. She told them that Salvio had left on a religious retreat and had not disclosed the location or duration. She asked them to carry on as usual so the household would be in good order whenever Salvio returned. It had been easy. Guiseppe, who fit squarely in the category of people who did *not* wish to actually see Salvio, looked relieved as he left to sew some shirt buttons. Dante and Rosa were unfazed, and went on about their business as usual.

Raphielli entered Salvio's office, sat at his desk, and spent an hour practicing his handwriting and signature. She'd been quite good at copying sacred script when she was at the abbey, and it wasn't long before there was no difference between her work and Salvio's writing. She penned a neat little note in his script, which she placed in his top desk drawer.

"I long to hear God. I have left on a religious journey and will return in God's time."

She carefully gathered up every sheet of her practice paper, took them to the big office fireplace, tossed them into the flickering flames and watched them burn. Then, going through his desk she found financial ledgers, as well as a list of accounts and passwords poorly hidden in the bottom drawer. She reviewed the ledgers, then accessed the accounts online, and was surprised to find that Salvio had what appeared to be limitless hordes of cash and real estate holdings all over the world. He owned at least twelve islands around Europe, and one off the coast of Castine, Maine in America.

While Raphielli was sitting at Salvio's desk, the phone rang. She was fairly certain who was on the other end as she answered, "*Pronto.*" Smiling broadly, she thought she sounded like a good secretary.

There was a moment of hesitation. "May I speak to Signor Scortini?"

Raphielli recognized the voice from listening to Salvio's meetings with the private detective. "He's left Venice. May I ask who's calling?"

"Alphonso Vitali. Can you tell me when he'll return?"

"He'll be away indefinitely, signor Vitali. But of course, you need to be paid your fee. Is it convenient for you to come over and collect it now?"

"Yeah, sure. I'll come right away."

"Good. Please wait in the alcove outside the front door. Don't ring the bell. I'll open the door for you."

"Okay."

Setting the phone down, she decided to terminate his association with Salvio, and satisfy the payment to him and his associate. Pleased with what seemed to be a simple plan, she went to the reception rooms in the front of the house and found her butler.

"Dante, is the woman who cooks our household meals still in the kitchen?"

"*Sì, signora,* she is still preparing lunch and dinner."

"While Salvio is away I'd like to eat the sort of food they serve in restaurants. Please go and tell her that I want to be excited by the food on my plate...oh and drinks, you know, teas, coffee, juices. You know, wow me."

"*Sì, signora.* It is good to enjoy one's food." The side of the butler's mouth lifted in the tiniest smile as he moved off in the direction of the kitchen. There was no one around when she opened the front door.

When she opened the front door, the private detective was standing in the shadows of the marble alcove. He was nothing like what she'd imagined. Salvio had called his head colossal, but the detective was tall and handsome like Samson in the Bible, with creamy olive skin, kind brown eyes, full lips, and dark hair falling almost to his shoulders. He was wearing non-descript clothes in muted browns and blacks that blended in with the shadows of the alcove. He straightened up when she stepped out.

"I'm Alphonso Vitali."

They shook hands as she smiled up at him. "Signor Vitali."

"Alphonso, please."

"Alphonso, I'm Raphielli. Please come this way."

She ushered him inside, closed the front door, and led him quickly through the halls unseen to Salvio's office. Choosing not to sit behind the big desk, Raphielli settled the two of them in the visitors' chairs. Alphonso nervously craned his neck to peer behind him, before turning his attention back to her with an inquiring expression.

"I'm glad you called, Alphonso. Salvio's gone away, and he left instructions for me to terminate the project you've been working on. " She nodded.

"He took off, eh?"

"Right, he went on a spiritual retreat." She nodded again.

"Really? When?"

"Well, it was sudden. He went away last night." She continued nodding.

"And?"

"And he said that I should pay you and your associate."

"Excuse me, Raphielli, but why are you lying to me?"

"What?" She refused to get nervous. She had felt safe and comfortable with him. But then, she had felt safe with Gio, too. Was she too trusting? Pushing that thought aside, she studied Alphonso's face and remained silent.

"I'm a detective, Raphielli. I can tell that you're lying, and I'd like to know why."

"I don't mean to lie to you."

"Now, that I believe."

"And I want to pay you."

"*Sì*, that's the truth, too."

"I think that's all you need to know."

"Raphielli, do you like Signor Scortini?"

"Why do you ask?"

"Ah." He smiled and nodded.

"What? I didn't say anything."

"You didn't have to. Your face answered for you."

"It did?" She felt herself blush. "My face?"

"*Sì.* You showed a flash of revulsion before your expression changed to confusion. You don't like him, so I'd guess you aren't in allegiance with him."

"No, I'm not. You're very good, Alphonso."

He gave her a lazy smile. "*Grazie.* Now I'm going to have to trust you by telling you that I'm trying to get as far away from my obligation to Scortini as possible. And in order to do that, I'd like to know where he is and when he's coming back."

She could feel him reading her. She was conflicted, and didn't like making decisions in front of him.

He pressed. "Please, Raphielli."

She considered whether she could trust him. But figured that this talented detective would snoop around and find out the truth.

"Salvio's been taken away by the Mafia. He won't be allowed to return to Venice."

"Do you know where?"

"No."

"If you had to guess?"

"Perhaps Sicily."

Craning his neck to look around again, Alphonso whispered, "Just the same, it's hard to shake the feeling that he'll pounce out of nowhere." He turned back to her. "Mafia, huh?"

"*Sì*. Salvio's a very bad man. He tried to come between the Pope and members of the Verona family. He failed. Then he hired and double-crossed a killer. That man took Salvio away as punishment."

Alphonso leaned forward, and she now knew his eyes were scrutinizing her body language and expression, so she kept very still. He settled his elbows on his knees, his interest piqued.

"Punishment?"

"Sort of a purgatory. He made a mortal enemy of this killer."

"So if Scortini's not dead, he will be soon?"

"No, the Mafia don is a man of his word, and he's promised me that he won't kill Salvio. I believe him."

"Made you a promise, eh? You personally spoke to this Mafioso?"

"*Sì*. However, I don't believe you'll be surprised to hear that I also hope Salvio never returns."

"I'm with you Raphielli. I hope Salvio never comes back. But you may have taken too high a road in keeping him alive. He's a maniac."

"I know," she whispered.

"I don't even want to hear his name again." He leaned back in the chair and rubbed his palms on his knees. "You said he left my payment?"

"Well, that was not entirely the truth."

"Oh, ho. You'd like to take care of his financial obligations, even though he didn't leave instructions to do so."

"*Sì*. I've been listening in on some of Salvio's meetings, which is how I know about you and your cousin. So here's what I'm proposing. I want you two to stop spying on the Veronas, and I need you to agree that you'll never divulge anything that you learned during this invasion of their privacy. I'd like to pay you and terminate your association with Salvio so we can put an end to this whole endeavor."

"Nothing would make us happier." Alphonso's relief showed. "We'd like to forget any of this ever happened."

"Okay. I'll need your help getting into Salvio's safe."

"It makes sense he'd never tell you the combination to his safe. You're his personal assistant, I take it?"

"No." Raphielli replied. "I'm his wife."

Alphonso's mouth dropped open. "Wife?" He whispered, "What a lucky guy."

She ran her hands over her exuberant black curls self-consciously.

Alphonso suddenly looked shocked and sucked in a gasp, "Oh my God!" Her scarf must have slipped, because he was staring at her throat. "You poor girl! I hope nobody ever has to see him again—least of all you."

She smoothed the scarf back into place and nodded. "Right now, let's get your payment out of that old safe, shall we?"

They looked at the ancient safe standing nearby, and Alphonso approached it. "Sure. I've seen Salvio open the door without bothering to dial the combination, so maybe it's unlocked."

"I don't think so. I've already tried...unless I'm doing something wrong with that big lever."

After they took turns with the handle, Alphonso shrugged and reached for his cell phone. "I'll call Zelph.

He's a whiz when it comes to locks. This'll be no problem for him." He pressed an icon on his cell phone. "Hmm. I'm not getting any signal in here." Raphielli walked over to the window and beckoned him to join her.

"This big stone house is so bad for reception. I've never seen anyone place a cell call without going to the window. Come over here."

He got Zelph on the phone. Hovering at his elbow, she held her hand out to speak to him.

"Can I ask him to come in through a secret passageway? I can't have people seeing you two coming and going with Salvio away."

He handed her the phone and she gave specific directions to Zelph, and after the call she led Alphonso through the secret passage to the access under Il Ponte Diamanti. Shortly, the cousins and Raphielli were breaking into Salvio's safe. She was happy for their company, even though she knew they were only here to collect their payment. But she liked them both on sight. They looked so alike, they could be brothers instead of cousins.

Sitting next to the desk she watched the safe cracking progress. "I can tell you're both good men. How did you come to work for Salvio?"

Alphonso raked his fingers through his long hair and shrugged. "I'm a private investigator, and Salvio told me he'd heard of some of my cases. I needed money to pay off a gambling debt..." He jerked a thumb between himself and Zelph. "We both do. We don't gamble anymore, but our last debts need to be paid off soon."

Raphielli pursed her lips, and then she smiled at a happy

thought. "However large they are, let's pay off all of your debts with Salvio's money."

Incredulous, the cousins smiled too. Alphonso said, "I don't know what to say. I'm speechless by your generosity but...at the same time I feel a twinge of uneasiness taking Salvio's money this way."

"You shouldn't, I'm certain there's plenty."

Zelph kept his eyes on his safe-cracking efforts, but blurted, "You're too good to be true, woman!"

Raphielli gave them both pious looks like a disapproving schoolteacher. "Now that you no longer gamble, will you have to keep spying on people for money? Or is there something you can do to make a more honest living?"

As Zelph concentrated on slowly turning the safe dial, he mused, "Well, my cousin wants to open a restaurant."

Alphonso rolled his eyes. "Don't talk nonsense."

Standing, up Zelph announced, "Here we go!" He tensed as if he thought Salvio might pop out of the safe, and then pulled the heavy door open.

The three of them peered inside. It was packed with stacks of money, neat cubbyholes of official-looking papers, and trays of very old jewelry. They quickly got down to business. The Vitalis sat in front of the desk as Raphielli withdrew two trays of euros, and then went to sit in Salvio's chair.

"Tell me how much Salvio owes you, and how much you owe on your gambling debts."

"After our last advance, Salvio owes us sixty thousand. That'll cover our debts."

Her abbey upbringing taught her to reject gambling as

sinful, and these two men shocked her. "*Maria, madre di misericordiosa!*"

The cousins ducked their chins and looked embarrassed.

"Well, you must be very bad card players. It's a good thing you stopped, or I think maybe the two of you would also disappear."

Zelph twisted his mouth to avoid smiling, and then he relaxed his full lips. "We're actually both excellent card players." His expression darkened. "But Pim is a dirty cheat."

"Although we can't prove it," Alphonso added.

"Well then, you have bad judgment in whom you choose to play cards with."

"We can't argue with that." Alphonso appeared charmed by her.

She pushed stacks of money over to them. "Now help me count out a hundred thousand for your payment, plus a bonus."

The three began counting, and when Raphielli was done with her bills, she got up to search for a large envelope. "Your past poor judgment with this man Pim worries me. I need to know that I can count on your discretion and good instincts—one hundred percent."

The cousins returned their neatly stacked money to the center of the desk and gave her their full attention.

"Salvio'll kill me if he ever finds out what I've done here. I need you both to make me two promises. First, that you'll never admit to anyone that you've had any contact with me, whatsoever."

"So if he ever resurfaces, we act as if he still owes us our payment?"

"*Sì.*" She nodded. "And second, you never, under any circumstances, tell anyone anything that you've learned while spying on the Veronas. You'll protect their privacy."

"We're happy to make both promises. We're indebted to you—literally—and we'd never want to hurt the Veronas. They're good people."

"Raphielli, we can't thank you enough for trusting us and telling us the situation with Salvio...and for being so generous."

Zelph cut in, "Yeah, you've changed our lives here. After paying Pim, I'm gonna go into business for myself. Start fresh."

"That's what great wealth is for, I think." She gathered her curls into a twist at the nape of her neck and slid a pencil in to secure it. It was a very schoolgirl thing to do, but she felt comfortable with these two men. They seemed like teenagers themselves.

"Before you go, we should plan what the three of us should do if Salvio ever comes back."

She shared Gio's plan to secretly send her a message in a box of tea, and the cousins nodded appreciatively at the Mafioso's foresight.

"Okay, as a contingency plan, let's trade phone numbers. If we hear that Salvio's back in Venice, we call each other."

"I don't have a cell phone," she said.

"We'll buy you one, and deliver it here with our numbers programmed into it."

"*Grazie!*" She clapped her hands lightly.

"Are you kidding? We're happy to do it. You'll have it tomorrow morning."

"What if I'm not able to answer your call?"

"Good thinking. If one of us doesn't answer, we'll leave a text message."

She felt nervous about this plan. "It must be a message he won't understand if he ever gets my phone."

Zelph offered, "Yeah we can say something like 'weather report.'"

"Okay. If we get that 'weather report' message, we should meet somewhere safe. Will you meet me at the Little Church? It's Cardinal Negrali's church, and he'll help us coordinate communication...or keep us safe if it comes to that."

She saw them look at each other when she said the Cardinal's name, and noticed they didn't look surprised.

"Uh, you know Cardinal Negrali?" Zelph asked.

"*Sì*. He's been helping me with this Salvio problem. Do you?"

Again the cousins looked at each other.

She narrowed her eyes. "Well, now *I* can tell that you don't want to tell *me*."

"You trust the cardinal?" Zelph asked.

"Implicitly," she answered firmly.

"I've been tailing the count, and I know there's a connection between Negrali and the Veronas. That's all. Really."

Satisfied, she said, "Then we have a plan. If any of us hears anything about Salvio, we alert the others and stay out of his way until we can get together at the Little Church. I think you boys had better go pay that man, Pim, now."

"Yeah." Alphonso got up and she stood as well. "We can never thank you enough. You're the best, Raphielli." He took both of her hands and kissed her knuckles. "I wish—"

Zelph stepped over and pushed his cousin out of the way. Apparently he was a physical kind of guy because he hugged her warmly. "*Sì molte grazie,* from the bottom of my heart, Raphielli, truly, *grazie mille.*" He pulled back from her and looked into her eyes. "You keep yourself safe, you hear?"

"Oh, I will." Flustered, she nodded and felt a blush burning her cheeks.

"You'll soon have a phone, so you need us, you call us." Alphonso gave her shoulders a squeeze. "Oh, and you're not a good liar. So when it comes to your story about Salvio going away, say as little as possible."

She nodded.

"And that's one of your tells." He pointed to her head.

"My what?"

"People who don't believe what's coming out of their own mouths nod. It's a subconscious thing they do to try to convince themselves that their lie is plausible. Stop nodding when you lie." He winked at her, and then the Vitalis ducked behind the tapestry and left the house via the secret tunnel.

Raphielli looked around Salvio's silent office. She felt a sense of accomplishment now that she had put an end to the Vitalis spying on the Veronas. Thinking of the few conversations she'd overheard, she considered what else she could rectify. Now that the safe was open, she decided to look through it for anything resembling the Brotherhood of Ironworkers patents she'd heard Salvio yelling about. She began pulling out random drawers and discovered thousands of documents. Some of them appeared to be on parchment and looked like they'd crumble to dust if she lifted them.

Hours later, she set the Brotherhood of Ironworker's patents aside, leaned back in the big desk chair, and closed her eyes to think. A very powerful person came to mind, someone who could help her return these patents, and without nodding her head or getting caught telling a lie, she would find a way to put this right. She sat up, grabbed her late father-in-law's desk directory, and dialed Mayor Buonocore's private number.

Thirty minutes later, the mayor sat across from Raphielli, looking over the Ironworker's patents. He pulled at his lower lip as his eyes scanned the pages.

"You surprise me, my dear. But I can do what you ask with no problem. I'll work with the necessary players to challenge Salvio's claim to these patents and get a court order."

"*Grazie.*" Raphielli was exhausted. She moved to the sofa, let out a long exhale, and lay her head back until she was looking up at the ceiling. Her mind was tired, it was hard for her to think clearly. "So no one would know I initiated this? I was obeying a court order to return these documents."

"Exactly."

"I knew I could count on you to think of something."

He glanced down at the note on the desk before him. "So Salvio has had an all-consuming desire to hear God, and went off for some spiritual isolation...indefinitely?" He flipped Salvio's note back into the drawer where he'd found it, and pushed it closed.

Being careful not to nod, Raphielli let her tired eyes slide over to meet the mayor's. "*Sì.*"

He returned the patents to the safe. "When you're served with the warrant for these patents, just hand them over."

"Perfect."

"I'll meet with Tosca of the Brotherhood tomorrow and tell him the good news. I won't mention you by name."

She smiled. "*Grazie.*"

"I admire what you're doing here. Call me or Elene if you need help while Salvio is away." Then he walked over to her and took her hand. "Come on, I'll start helping right now by getting you to bed."

He reached for the servant's bell and gave it a pull. She heard Guiseppe racing down the hallway as if he'd been shot out of a canon. He looked terrified when he arrived, looking around the office, and then drew himself up when he saw the mayor of Venice standing in the middle of the room.

The mayor addressed him. "Please arrange for *signora's* maid to prepare her a steamed milk, and put her to bed."

"*Sì, onore.*" Guiseppe nodded animatedly.

The mayor continued, "I understand that Signor Scortini is away on a religious journey. Being left alone is a strain for one person to run a household of this size."

Guiseppe wrung his hands. "Oh, *sì!* I agree."

The mayor moved toward the door. "I've offered to serve this household in any way that I'm needed so Signor Scortini's important work is not disrupted by his spiritual quest." And then he left.

14

The morning after meeting with the Vitalis and the mayor, Raphielli lay in bed mentally preparing herself for another long day of studying Salvio's financial affairs. The bank statements she'd ordered for Salvio's Southern Hemisphere accounts would be delivered soon. Mercifully, he had no accountants that she needed to lie to about his disappearance, so by entering the correct security codes, Raphielli had access to more money than she knew what to do with.

Her thoughts were interrupted as her door opened, and she sat up excitedly when she saw that Rosa was carrying the most divine breakfast tray.

"What is this?"

"Breakfast in bed, *signora.*"

"Breakfast in my *bed?*"

"The cook insisted that the important women who have employed her in the past have all enjoyed their breakfasts in bed."

"I've never heard of such a thing."

"She assures me that it is entirely proper."

"How lovely!"

Rosa set the tray before her on a stand that straddled her thighs. *Oh my! Look at this!* Before her was a bowl of ripe fruit, a chocolate muffin that was wafting cocoa-scented tendrils of steam, a pot of tea that smelled of cinnamon spice, a pitcher of hot cream, and a stem of hibiscus in a bud vase. *This is living!* She picked up the menu that informed her the spices she smelled were called "chai," and she felt a pang of hunger at the sight the food. No more seed cracker and water for breakfast!

As Rosa went to tend the fireplace, Raphielli wrapped her shawl around her shoulders to stave off the chill in her gloomy room. Looking more closely at the tray, she noticed an envelope with her name on it.

"Rosa, what is this envelope?"

"I do not know. Dante found the message with the flower and vase outside in the alcove next to the front door."

"When did it come?"

"No idea. It was there when Dante went to turn out the entrance lights this morning." She shrugged. "You know, that is how messages used to be delivered before phones, though not with crystal vases. That looks very expensive."

Raphielli opened the envelope, read the note, and for the first time since leaving the abbey, she was excited about the day's prospects. Contessa Juliette wanted to meet her at the Little Church at eight thirty this morning. She slipped the note back into the envelope and began to eat. Everything tasted so good, she let her eyes roll back in ecstasy. *Here and now, I'm going to make myself a promise: I'll never eat another seed cracker as long as I live.*

She lingered over her breakfast, relishing every bite. The fruit was the sweetest she'd ever put in her mouth, and according to the menu, it had been dressed with honey syrup. Incredible! She lifted the hibiscus bloom from its vase and smelled it—such a nice gesture. When her tray was empty, she hopped out of bed and headed to her bathroom to get ready. She was looking forward to seeing Cardinal Negrali. He felt like so much more than just a father confessor now. And thinking of Juliette, Raphielli felt like she was going off to meet a friend. A silly thought, because until recently she'd only greeted Juliette twice, and both times Salvio had yanked her away, telling her to stop fawning.

Dressed in one of her church dresses, Raphielli wrapped Marilynn Bergoni's green silk scarf around her neck to hide the devastation there. The silk was so refined, she felt beautiful wearing it. *It's incredible how the people I meet are so generous to me, while my own husband was so brutal.* When she told Rosa that she was going out, her maid simply nodded and went about her routine of keeping the fireplaces going in the few rooms they still used. As Raphielli walked down the hall she passed Guiseppe, and it occurred to her that Salvio's absence would probably add years to his life. She'd need to find something worthwhile for that sweet man to do.

It was a beautiful fall morning, and she enjoyed walking by herself as the boat traffic churned and bobbed its way up and down the canals. She breathed in crisp air and diesel fumes punctuated by strong whiffs of espresso as she passed cafes. Arriving at the Little Church, she stepped into the cool silence, dipped her fingers in the marble font of holy water, and blessed herself by making the sign of the cross. The flickering of votive candles and the ubiquitous aroma of hot wax brought her comfort on a deep level. She recognized Monsignor Treme as he approached her.

"Ah, Signora Scortini, you are looking well."

She dropped into a brief curtsey and bowed her head. "*Grazie*, Padre."

He came close and lowered his voice to a whisper. "Let me take you to our safe place."

She followed him to the back of the church and through a series of hallways and doors before they stopped at a smallish door of solid wood. The Monsignor unlocked it, opened it, and standing aside, he nodded for her to enter. Inside the ancient stone chamber were Contessa Juliette and Cardinal Negrali. The room was well lit with electric candelabras, and on the table was a bunch of cheerful red and white hibiscus. She heard the door close and lock behind her. They were certainly being secretive. The contessa rushed over and scooped Raphielli into her arms, cradling her.

"Raphielli! Oh, you poor, brave, sweet girl!"

Cardinal Negrali rose from his seat at the table, came over and patted Raphielli's back.

"This is a secure place, my child. Come, let us sit."

Contessa Juliette said, "My dear we thought it would be best to meet here so I can thank you in private. My family and I admire your strength and courage."

"Oh my goodness, Contessa, of course. I'm sorry, I didn't know that I'd married a monster. But when I overheard what he was trying to do to your family, I *had* to stop him."

"Hi! You must never call me by my title, my dear. *Never...*" She leaned back and brushed her hands in little sweeping motions through the air. "Pfft! Pfft!" Then leaning forward, she took up Raphielli's hands. "Between us there will never be formality. Never. We are equals. Okay?"

Flattered, she felt a lump in her throat. "Okay *Juliette.*"

"Good." She laughed and patted Raphielli's hand playfully.

Father Negrali said, "Now, let us fill each other in on what has happened."

She told them most of what she knew about Salvio's plot, and then Father Negrali told how Salvio had tried to enlist the College of Cardinals. But neither Raphielli nor Negrali used the Mafia don's name. She didn't think it was a good idea to speak for a man like that—better safe than sorry—and clearly Negrali felt the same way. Raphielli also neglected to mention that she knew the names of Salvio's spies. She felt protective of Alphonso and Zelph—even from her father confessor and Juliette—and at the moment saw no need to involve the Vitalis further. When Juliette divulged what had occurred in France with the Pope, Raphielli was mortified thinking of what Alphonso could have witnessed.

"So, uh, Salvio's detective mistook this Carolette for Giselle?"

They nodded.

She'd never met Giselle, but the idea that a family member of Juliette's could be unfaithful to her marital vows was beyond comprehension. "Well, of course Giselle would *never* do such a thing!"

"Of course not. But it is an easy mistake to make." Juliette tipped her head side-to-side. "Carolette is a blonde woman of the same age, at the same house. Our friend Fauve tells me Carolette has been in love with Markus since they were introduced. Of course, they should be married right away. And the Holy Father told me that Markus confirmed his intentions to marry her."

Negrali took a deep breath and looked relieved. "Salvio's plotting came to nothing."

"Well, he's gone, and I hope he stays gone forever." Raphielli didn't know what else to say on the matter, but then she got an idea. "Will the two of you advise me on what I should do with my life?"

"Most assuredly!" Negrali slapped his thighs. "I believe you should be of service to your fellow man. It will do your spirit good."

Juliette broke into a radiant smile and placed her hands flat on the table, her ancient rings sparkling in the lights. "Why not open a shelter for abused women?" A shadow passed over her face. "I believe you can relate to the plight of women who must escape the men in their lives."

"That's a perfect idea! I can get the money from Salvio's hoard."

Negrali seemed to momentarily lose his enthusiasm. "But this may be too ambitious. What if Salvio somehow comes back?"

"I believe our best protection is each other. I plan to tell him that I found his note and acted in the best way I could think of to uphold his reputation while he was gone."

Juliette bit her lip. "Would he think it was the Mafioso who left you the note?"

"I would hope so."

"Come. I know of just the place for your shelter. It is a charming building practically adjoining my homeless shelter. It has a cozy feel, but it is quite big when you add up all the rooms. And you will need all the space you can get to offer beds to the women, and cribs for their children, and day care, and therapy, and medical services."

"It is for sale?" Raphielli reached into her purse for a paper and pen.

"Oh, *sì*," Juliette replied breezily. "It has been on the market for almost a year. It needs some work."

Raphielli practically hugged herself with excitement as she thought about signor Tosca. "Maybe I know some builders who would help me with renovations."

Juliette took the paper and pen from Raphielli, jotted the information, and handed them over.

"I will call my realtor and arrange for you to see the building. Can you make it today, say three o'clock?"

"*Sì*, that'd be great."

"Consider it arranged, then."

"Now that Salvio is away, everything should return to normal." Father Negrali rose, went to the door, and unlocked it. Turning to the women, he spoke in a cautious tone. "But I still do not recommend you two ladies be seen together in public."

"I agree, Americo." Juliette stood up and took Raphielli's hand again. "If Salvio hates my family the way I believe he does, there is no telling what his reaction would be if he found out his wife was associating with me."

Raphielli nodded, and then followed them through the halls back to the Little Church's narthex. Taking his leave of them, the cardinal retreated into a small office and closed the door.

Juliette planted a quick kiss on each of Raphielli's cheeks. "I would like for you and I to become better friends. Can we make a plan to meet on Saturday afternoons? I will find us safe places where we can spend time together."

"I'd like that." She gave the contessa's cheek a quick peck. "I'm so glad your husband's safe now."

"Thanks to you."

Juliette left the church first, and as Raphielli waited in the narthex, a children's choir began practicing *Gloria Deo* in the loft just over her head. A few minutes later, Raphielli stepped out of the Little Church into the bright sunlight, and strolled through the most beautiful city on earth. She had time to kill before meeting the realtor, but she couldn't bear to go back home just yet. So she did something she'd never done before. She took a seat at an outdoor café, ordered a decadent cappuccino. She loosened the crocheted tie on her purse and peeked at the roll of euros inside. Now she had money and could go anywhere she liked. Sipping the rich milk and espresso, she began to feel the effects of the caffeine. And although she'd never tasted espresso before, she'd smelled it so many times that the taste was familiar to her. It tasted like liberation, and she reached a hand up to hide the smile on her face. *I'd better try to look less happy. People will think I'm a crazy person, sitting here grinning like a clown.* She turned down the wattage of her smile and took another sip of heaven from the heavy ceramic cup, thinking that if she were back at the abbey, she would be in ecumenical studies right now. After her treat, she left the waiter a generous tip and then walked home to study the Scortini estate financials. She had two hours before meeting the realtor.

At three o'clock Raphielli was standing in front of an old building that had seen better days. It had steps to the front that ascended like a tiered wedding cake, approachable from three directions. Next to the front door, was a small caged enclosure that looked a like a magazine stall or tobacconist. Behind that was a cute little private bridge that spanned a narrow canal and probably accessed a rear entrance. The building was four stories tall, and years ago someone had painted it a shade of pumpkin beginning at the top floor and made it most of the way down, but gave up at different levels of the first floor which remained a non-color mélange of greys. So the upper part of the building had a warm sunny hue, and the bottom was as drab as a prison. There were heavy bars on the windows that looked like they'd survived the middle ages. They would protect the women she'd shelter here. Raphielli liked the cheerful turquoise color of the window shutters. She agreed with Juliette, this place had potential, but right now it smelled of rotting wood and stagnant water. This purchase should have felt impetuous, but Cardinal Negrali and Juliette were right—her soul positively *hungered* for the chance to help people. And her first-hand experience of isolation and abuse provoked a powerful urge to help women who'd suffered similarly.

Just then, a jovial-looking man with a round potbelly came striding over a bridge. As he approached her, he raised his hand in greeting, and swung a big set of keys in the air with his other hand.

"Raphielli? I'm Joccomo. Juliette will join us soon, but told me not to wait for her." He looked like a professor in his blazer, soft pleated pants, and penny loafers. But then, she'd never met a real estate agent before.

"How nice of you to come so quickly, Joccomo."

"I never turn down a chance to do Juliette a favor." He accompanied her to the front door. "I bet you're eager to get inside."

"I am."

As he worked the keys in the locks, he said, "She tells me you plan to open a shelter for women."

"*Sì.*"

"She also tells me you're a Scortini."

"*Sì.*"

"Well then, any favor I can do for you will be my pleasure as well."

"You're very kind."

"I do what I can, but I haven't opened up any shelters like you two ladies. I'll have to rely on you and Juliette to throw a rope over the pearly gate so I can get into heaven." He let out a chortling laugh that was so surprising and funny that Raphielli laughed too.

"You're laughing at my laugh." More chuckles burst out of him. "Everyone does." He sounded as if he took it as a compliment and laughed some more.

She put her hand over her mouth to try to contain her giggles. "It's wonderful."

"So I hear." And he let out a final chortle.

They stepped inside, and she felt instantly that this was where she'd do the work of her lifetime. Halfway through the tour, they were joined by Juliette, who did some gentle haggling with Joccomo and struck a good deal on the purchase price. He gave Raphielli the keys to the building and left to draw up the necessary documents. Raphielli had access to enough of Salvio's liquid assets that she could wire the necessary funds with no problem. Walking out through the kitchen's back door of the future women's shelter, the two women figured out how to lock the old door, and then Juliette hooked her arm through Raphielli's.

"Come with me, I want to show you my Rifugia della Dignità." They walked through a little zigzag courtyard, then Juliette unlocked a side door to a big building and drew Raphielli into her own lively kitchen—it was much larger than the one they'd just left.

"It breaks my heart that Venice has so many people with no place to live. But in here, my family can give them a place to call home and regain their dignity while they learn skills to help them make a better life. We can spend time together making dinner for them." Juliette looked energized. "Do you like to cook?"

Raphielli's heart fell. "I've never been allowed in a kitchen."

"Well, you enjoy eating, right?"

"Oh, *sì!*"

"Then you must learn to cook the foods you crave."

"I like the sound of that."

"Step into my kitchen for your first lesson." Juliette led the way to a big commercial kitchen where volunteers were busy assembling ingredients and supplies.

Raising her voice, Juliette called out, "*Ciao,* my dear ones!" Her team all offered hearty greetings, but didn't stop their activities. Everywhere Raphielli looked, people were scrubbing vegetables, filling pots, and sharpening knives with care.

A familiar voice called out, "Good to see you, Juliette!"

Raphielli scanned the space looking for the owner of the voice, and her heart skipped a beat when she saw Alphonso weighing out flour next to trays of eggs. *What's he doing in Juliette's kitchen? Oh my lord! Could he still be spying?*

Raphielli stood frozen as Juliette went over to him. "Ah! I have missed you, my romantic friend! Today we practice the gentle touch." She reached out and took hold of both Alphonso's wrists. Giving his hands a shake to limber them up, she teased, "*Non li strangolare,* Romeo. Today we are tucking the baby into bed."

Alphonso's brows shot up when he saw Raphielli staring at him from around Juliette's shoulder. But before either of them could react, Juliette took hold of Raphielli's arm, and positioned her right next to Alphonso.

"Romeo, please help my friend, Raphielli, with an apron." Then Juliette strode to the center of the kitchen and called out the day's instructions with the precision of a drill sergeant and the enthusiasm of a cheerleader.

Raphielli felt her scalp tingling with nervous tension, as if someone had just up-ended a bottle of San Pellegrino over her head. Alphonso took an apron from a shelf, and when he came back he placed the strap over her head.

"I'm glad to see you." He smiled and his brown eyes searched her face. "But you don't look glad to see me."

She glanced around, not knowing what she was looking for. Some sort of proof? Perhaps Zelph lurking about? Alphonso moved around behind her, gently lifted her curls from under the apron strap, and then she felt his fingers graze the nape of her neck as he adjusted her scarf. He crossed the ties around her waist. His arms encircled her, and he said into her ear, "Take these." She took the apron strings, and he came back around in front of her and tied the apron at her waist. "Did Zelph give you your phone yet?"

Keeping her voice low and trying not move her lips, she hissed, "You had better not be spying anymore! What possible justification do you have for being in Juliette's kitchen right now?"

"No! I'm not spying. I'm a great admirer of Juliette and her cooking. You have no idea the treat you're in for!" He sighed and kissed his fingertips, and his face lit up.

"Oh, thank heavens." Raphielli was flooded with relief. "And no, Zelph hasn't given me my phone yet. I've been out most of the day."

"You didn't tell Juliette about me, did you?"

"No, of course not. I wouldn't do that. Your secret's safe with me."

Juliette came up behind her, produced a hair band, gathered Raphielli's ponytail into a bun, and then swooped in between her and Alphonso. "Okay, my two pasta assistants. Let us first wash our hands, and then we will make my *letto del bambino pasta al forno.*"

For the next two hours Raphielli gave herself over to learning the new skill of making pasta sheets. She loved feeling the soft dough come together in her fingers, and the texture change as they fed the dough through the rollers of the pasta machine. She also got to know a bit more about this big, tall man with the perceptive eyes, like that he had a kind heart. Under Juliette's tutelage, they learned to make *involtini melanzana,* tucking each little bundle of *melanzana* between supple sheets of fresh pasta, and finally under a blanket of fresh mozzarella. When the dish came out of the oven, the little mounds did indeed look like babies in their beds. That is, if you tucked a child under a bed of golden bubbly cheese! *Delizioso!*

The police had heard nothing from Salvio for more than a week, and Detective Luigi Lampani had been on the lookout for him. He'd been sitting across from the Scortini palazzo when he spotted Scortini's young wife walking home. She was certainly more beautiful in person than the wedding photos he'd seen online of her looking miserable. The wedding dress she'd worn was so huge, she'd looked twice the size of the curvaceous woman in the faded black dress who was walking toward him.

As he stepped into her path, she stopped and scanned his face, apparently trying to place him.

"*Mi scusi*, may I speak to you, Signora Scortini?"

"*Sì*, okay." She smiled tentatively but was looking him directly in the eye in a frankly open way.

He reached into his pocket, took out his identification, and handed it to her. "Detective Luigi Lampani, I came to your home looking for your husband recently." He smiled, but his smile faltered as his sharp eyes zeroed in on the bit of her neck visible where her scarf had slipped—someone had throttled her. As he winced at the cruel damage, she noticed his reaction and her hands flew up to readjust her scarf. He suddenly felt protective of her.

"I've come to ask you a question, signora."

"Please call me Raphielli." She handed his ID back.

"Raphielli, do you know where your husband is?"

She didn't hesitate. "No. But if I find out, I'll be happy to tell you, detective."

"*Grazie*." He stepped closer, studying her expression. "It's very important."

"Is this about Marco Falconetti's son?"

"*Sì*, Reynaldo. I believe your husband killed him."

"I don't know anything about the crime, but I believe you're right."

"And why is that? What did Salvio have against Reynaldo?"

"Nothing that I know of. But Salvio has a terrible temper. If Reynaldo upset him, he could have snapped."

From the looks of her neck, he trusted that she knew what she was talking about. He felt a headache threatening just behind his eyes, and pinched the bridge of his nose to stave it off.

"Did he ever mention problems with the Falconetti family?"

"No. I know Salvio has hopes of continuing to work with them the way his family always has."

"So he hopes to preserve a long-standing business relationship between his building empire and their marble business?"

"*Sì.* He wants Marco Falconetti to trust him."

"Killing Marco's son would hardly help his cause."

"No."

"All right." He offered her his business card, which she studied carefully but declined to take.

"When Salvio comes home, he'll find that card and be...*displeased.*"

"Okay then. *Grazie* for your time and honesty Raphielli." He put the card back in his pocket, turned to go, and then turned back to face her. "I don't think I need to mention that when Salvio comes back, I should be the first call you make."

"Absolutely. I'll call you right away."

"*Grazie.*" He nodded and walked off down the *calle.*

———◦(◉)◦———

As Raphielli climbed the steps to her palazzo, she repeated Detective Luigi Lampani's name and number to herself...just in case. Then she went to Salvio's office, picked up the phone, and called Alphonso.

"*Ciao,* Raphielli. Long time no see." He sounded so

happy to hear from her that her mood automatically perked back up.

"*Sì*, it's been almost half an hour." She laughed, and then became serious. "I just called to tell you that a police detective named Lampani is investigating Salvio for the murder of Reynaldo Falconetti."

"Oh?"

She told him about the brief encounter.

"Yeah, well Zelph and I wondered if the police'd be interested in Salvio for that. They'll probably get a warrant for his phone records, and find out about us. We have no problem telling them that Salvio hired us, but that it had nothing to do with Falconetti, and we can't alibi him for the time of the murder."

"Will you say what Salvio hired you to do?"

"If this Lampani asks, I see no reason not to cooperate. Anyone who can build a case against Salvio deserves as much accurate information as they can get, in my opinion. I don't mind saying that we were looking into the lives of the Veronas...and found them to be really good people."

"*Sì*, okay then. That sounds fine." She didn't know what else to say. "Well, that's all I called about."

"Thanks for giving us the heads-up. Now that you're home, I'll tell Zelph he can drop off your new phone."

"Ooh, I can't wait!" She felt giddy at the prospect of learning to use technology.

"He's loading it up with apps and books and special ring tones for you."

"I'm so excited, Alphonso! Now I'll be like everyone else and have a phone."

"Zelph'll teach you how to use everything."

"Good. Otherwise I don't think it would be of much use to me."

"All right then, call me with it some time."

"I will. Well...*ciao,* Alphonso.

"*Ciao,* Raphielli."

⸺◦◉◦⸺

With Primo at his side, Giancarlo Petrosino walked down the stairs below the basement of his cliffside building in Palermo, descending to the entrance of the cistern. The old watertight room under his consigliere's office was the perfect place for Scortini to spend the rest of his life. Air circulated through the open gutter slits near the room's ceiling, and there was a natural opening in the floor that allowed water to drain through a jagged fissure down to the Tyrrhenian Sea. At one time a big iron plate covered the four-foot-square grate in the floor to make the room watertight, but currently the iron plate leaned against the wall. Scortini could squat over the grate to relieve himself over the rocky gash below. Even if Scortini grew tired of using the natural drain as a toilet and found a way to pull up the metal grid, the fissure below offered no chance of escape. At its narrowest, the drain wasn't even large enough for a rat to navigate. So if Scortini lowered himself down, he'd fall thirty feet below and get caught in the rocks, trapped within the teeth of the mountain. No one would hear him scream for rescue. Gio wouldn't mind that at all. If Scortini pursued that feeble attempt to leave his prison, and was swallowed up by the cliff, the world would be rid of a madman, and Gio would still have kept his promise to Raphielli.

Gio unlocked the door, and below him lay the scion of the Scortini family, face down and limp on the gritty cement floor. Scortini's suit was a mess from the waist down, because at some point on the trip from up north he'd soiled himself. Gio raised a hand for Primo to stay on guard in the hallway, and then descended the wrought iron steps into the cistern. He walked over and looked down at the man who lay contorted at his feet.

"Don't bother to get up, Scortini. I'm only able to stay a minute—but then you probably won't recover any concept of time for another day or so. You've demonstrated to me that you're a man who enjoys surprises, so I surprised you with this getaway...some solitary isolation for your spiritual growth. In order to facilitate your travels, I gave you a sedative." Gio adjusted the legs of his tailored pants and crouched down to get a better look at the inert psychopath on the floor. "I'm going pay you the compliment of speaking to you frankly, Scortini. You have some character defects. It was one of those defects that caused you to kill Marco Falconetti's son."

He leaned in close. "And your call to the police so that they could catch me just after I'd killed Count Verona wasn't a good way to begin our partnership. You see, my son, Primo, was going to handle that hit." Gio was caught off guard at the emotion those words stirred within him, and his voice became tight. "And I won't forgive that call. Nobody endangers my son. Your plan to have me get

Verona out of the way so you could take over Verdu Mer was a bad strategy overall. But, don't bother yourself about it now. You'll have plenty of time to think of a way to explain yourself to me."

Wrapping up his visit, Gio stood. "The sedative I gave you is called veleno, and it's usually refined before its administered to minimize some really unpleasant side-effects. But the doses I gave you today were crude...unrefined, so you're gonna be in pain for a while yet. Nothing you can do about it, they're just temporary after-effects...albeit really fucking horrible ones. I don't envy you."

He looked down at the mess around Scortini's hips. "I've never seen it loosen anyone's bowels before. It was probably the fourth dose that caused such a thorough evacuation." Gio turned away, climbed back up the stairs, walked out the door, and locked it securely behind him with a satisfied smile. There were fates worse than death for a megalomaniac.

15

The sun peeked over the Ardennes forest and through the bedroom curtains onto Giselle's face. She blinked her eyes open and looked around for Markus. He was still fast asleep beside her, his skin glowing honey-gold against the pale sheets. Snuggling naked beneath the bedding, she felt more than excited, more than content, more than happy. Sometimes it felt like he was a dream, she would awaken from, and V would come walking barefoot into her room with coffee and his usual morning chatter. But that had been her old life, everything was different now. She felt reborn, but at times overwhelmed by her feelings for Markus. He was always on her mind, and she constantly craved his touch. So this was love?

Usually Markus woke up before her, so she took this rare opportunity to admire him the way her friends did. When he was awake, he had no patience when he caught her staring. She lifted the sheet to peek at his naked body.

It was sleek, muscular perfection, very different from the way she and V were built. He had a light trail of soft blondish-brown hair down his lower stomach that drove her wild. God, if V looked like this, she would have gone out of her mind!

Recalling her first encounter with Markus in the Metro station, she remembered the way her stomach dropped when he put his arm around her. Inexplicably she wanted to kiss him right then as he was handcuffed to the railing. When he'd looked into her eyes, it felt like she'd been pushed over a waterfall. She wanted to have him look at her now. She snuggled close to him and bent low over his chest. Watching his peaceful face, she circled her tongue around one of his nipples. His long brown eyelashes fluttered, and a smile played at the corners of his mouth. Making an inquiring moan, he reached for her and they reveled in each other until it was time to start their day.

By the time Selma arrived at the house with the maids to prepare for Giselle's departure, Markus was back in the stable house workshop packing up the last of his tools. Her friends arrived mid-morning, and now that *Star Fall* was safely enclosed in the new shed, she was able to enjoy the day eating, playing cards, and whacking croquet balls. As twilight approached, the last of her friends had departed, Selma went off to release the dogs, and Veronique arrived to take up residence in the château. She spoke with Veronique, then went up to change into a blue sheath dress and cream-and-gold peep-toe pumps. She locked the big front door and walked down the steps. Markus had pulled the Tank around, so she climbed behind the wheel, and he hopped in beside her asking, "Does Selma also stay in the château while you are away?"

"No, she stays at their house down the lane."

"Veronique can handle this place by herself?"

"Absolutely, she's completely capable and loves the routine. I'm sure right now she's in the kitchen making a cup of tea, then she'll go back to her little apartment behind the Moroccan room."

"She must be a solitary woman."

"That's a good way to describe her. She loves living in the château by herself for extended periods of time. She even knows how to repair the old gas boiler if needed."

On the train back to Paris, Vincenzo called to check in.

"*Alo,* Gigi. I wanted to let you know that everything's fine here in Venice. But we don't know where Salvio is."

Giselle was careful not to say anything specific about Salvio in case his spy was sitting near them on the train. "Oh? Could he be in Paris?"

"We don't know. But we heard from Cardinal Negrali that Salvio's been kidnapped."

Giselle's mouth dropped open, and Markus leaned forward. Their eyes swept the train as she tried to sound casual. "Oh, really? Hmmm. Well, that's unexpected if it's true."

"*Sì,* Gigi. And I believe it's true. It's just that we have no proof."

"Mmm, *oui.*" Giselle tried to look bored, so she made a show of studying her nails. "Hard for us to prove, wouldn't you say?"

"Right. No one who abducts a person provides the public with proof of their captive."

"From what you say, it's hard to imagine anyone wanting him."

"You've never met him, but you're right, it's hard for me to imagine anyone wanting Salvio Scortini."

Giselle smiled, and Markus relaxed visibly.

"Gigi, since we still don't know what's going on, I'd feel better if you didn't go back to our house in Paris tonight. Is there somewhere else you can stay? Someplace no one would think to look for you? Maybe we can arrange for you to stay with Efran?"

Giselle's mouth dropped open. "The Louvre curator? Why?"

He sounded pained. "I don't know. He's our dear friend, and he keeps the Louvre's paintings safe. Maybe he can safeguard you until we can be sure no one is following you."

"You're crazy!" Giselle laughed. "I'm not a painting."

"Well, Gigi, I just want you safe." He sounded tired. "We hope to learn more about Salvio's whereabouts, but until we do, try to stay out of sight."

Giselle had an idea, and she whispered into the phone. "I've just thought of the perfect place. I'll stay with Markus and his friends. Their building is a small fortress, and I don't imagine I've ever been followed there."

"Okay. That makes sense...all right."

Markus looked pleased at the prospect, and he gave her a sexy smile.

She glanced around the train car again. "I'll call you when we're settled."

"Okay. And don't forget, father hopes to get your housing designs soon."

"I'll have them ready tomorrow."

"We'll send a courier for them. Just text me the address."

"Will do."

"I miss you..." Vincenzo's voice became small. "...very much...I wish you'd come to Venice so we could talk about...everything...but I know I've taken too much of you already...and you want time with...to..."

"Oh, V, I miss you too. But, *ouais*, I want time with him. Everyone will understand us being apart for a while. You have work to do, and you can tell them I'm planning a new sculpture. I'll call you later tonight."

She disconnected the call and looked up at Markus, who was smiling a lazy smile of contentment. "Happy?"

"I am. I was picturing you in some of my clothes tomorrow morning. I think I will like seeing you wear one of my shirts."

"Oh, right. I don't have any clothes."

"Mmm, I like this plan."

"Well, I'm not wandering around Ivar and Yvania's home in one of your shirts."

He shrugged his shoulders. "I can dream."

"If Salvio's spy is watching my home in Paris, I don't want Marcella to bring me anything from there. She could be followed." She called her favorite personal shopper and, as always, Henriette answered breathlessly. "*Alo,* Giselle, what can I get you?"

"*Alo,* Hen. I'm going to be staying with friends for a bit, and I need you to get me a week's worth of clothes and toiletries."

"Cool! When do you need 'em?"

"First thing tomorrow morning, please."

"I'm on it. I'm staring at three racks of the new Cacharel collection, and about ten pieces in particular that are simply *made* for you! I'll swing by Au Printemps to get you everything else. I'm working on a window display there tonight, and I'll ask the manager to put everything on your account. Just text me where to have everything delivered."

"You're a doll."

"No, you're the doll that I love to dress. Kisses to Vincenzo."

Giselle popped up a message window and handed her phone to Markus, who entered the Czerney's address and hit send. "Do not think I will forget my dream." He handed the phone back to her.

"When we have our own place, I'll be happy to wear your shirts."

"Mmm, will you do that dance I saw you doing, the one with your arms up over your head?"

"Of course."

He started to get that dangerously sexy look in his eye and then glanced self-consciously around the crowded train car. "We should change the subject or I will need a cold shower, and I do not think this train has one." For the rest of the journey, they made sure they kept alert for Salvio's spy.

When they arrived in Paris, Giselle followed Markus' lead and slipped off the train in the middle of a stream of passengers. They made a quick stop at the porter's station to claim his wooden box, and then continued on with the crowd. Nearing the taxi area, Markus tucked her behind a crepe stand and asked her to wait there in the shadows while he signaled for a taxi. The first car in line at the curb zipped up to him and stopped. He motioned for the driver pop the trunk, quickly stowed his things, opened the back door, and then signaled her to join him. She hustled over and dove into the cab with Markus right behind her. She tried not to act paranoid, but couldn't help scanning the nearby cars as he gave the address and the taxi merged into traffic. She felt the driver's eyes studying her face in the rear view mirror every chance he could safely ignore the road ahead. Finally he got to his question.

"You're Giselle, aren't you?"

"*Oui,*" she answered politely. *Ah, here we go...*

"*L'artiste dangereuse!*" His face lit up.

"*Ah, oui. C'est moi.*"

"My brother has a little gallerie off Place des Vosages. This man is not the Italian count. Not your husband." He tipped his head to indicate Markus, with a completely undeserved look of disapproval on his face.

"No, he's an artist I'm working with." In an effort to end the exchange, she picked up her phone and pretended to check messages. She could feel Markus watching her.

He said quietly, "I can see you putting on your mental coat of armor."

She whispered, almost to herself, "Paris is very different from Gernelle."

"So you change with the geography?"

"I don't know. I guess I change with the expectations."

"You may not want to do that forever. It could make you forget who you really are."

It was an uneventful ride. No one appeared to be following them, and none of the nearby cars slowed as their taxi turned down the Czerney's quiet street. When they arrived at the little brick building, Markus paid the driver, got out first, and took his things from the trunk over to the door of the building. Then he looked around the empty street, and came back to take her hand. The driver pulled away with a wave that left Giselle feeling uncertain.

"Markus, what are the odds that Salvio's spy would contact the taxi companies in Paris?"

"The odds of him finding that taxi driver is very small."

As they approached the door he said, "Gigi, I will not lie to Ivar and Yvania. They are family, and we can trust them with our secrets. I will not share what Vincenzo has asked me to protect with anyone except these two people."

"You're right, I know we can trust them. I don't want to lie either. Oh boy, this will be quite a surprise. They don't have heart trouble do they?"

"No, they are both as healthy as horses." Markus unlocked the factory door and followed her inside with his luggage. "But I will be ready to grab Ivar's walker." As he closed and locked the door, Markus called out, "Ivar, Yvania! I am home! Giselle is here too. I am sorry it is late."

"Ah, Markus! We are coming. Is everything okay?" Ivar's voice answered from upstairs.

"*Da*, everything is good."

The couple came down the stairs, bundled in robes and cozy slippers. Without her clogs, Yvania was the size of a child. Ivar let go of the handrail and brushed past the walker that stood waiting for him at the bottom of the stairs. He beamed when he caught sight of Giselle, and tipped his head to her in a silent question.

Oh, he knows something's up. She gave him a smile.

Yvania fanned her face as if she was having a hot flash. "Oh! Giselle! Look! Here I must be frightening you with how I am looking!" She passed her hand over her hairnet and headed straight for Markus, who bent over to receive her motherly hug. Then pulling back from giving him a squeeze, she gave him a stern look. "Ach! What? You cannot call for me to making the readiness?" She reached around and pinched him on the back of his upper arm.

"Ow!" He moved away and rubbed the spot vigorously. "Ow! I *am* sorry Yvania. We just decided to come here at the last minute."

Ivar opened his arms to Giselle. "I am happy to see you, my dear."

Yvania pulled her robe tighter about her midsection and came forward to hug Giselle. "*Da*, we are happy to see you."

Giselle was glad to be back with the Czerneys again, especially now that they were going to be her family. "We're sorry for coming so late. We should have called, but we've been a bit preoccupied."

"Come." Ivar gestured toward the kitchen and took hold of his walker. "Tell us of your work in the country. How is the big sculpture coming?"

Yvania bustled ahead of them, flicked on the overhead light, and headed for the refrigerator. "I have just made some *kompot* today, of fresh apples and cherries. Now we drink a leetle bit of sipping." She retrieved a pitcher of pink juice and picked up a small tray already set with old-fashioned cordial glasses.

As they settled around the table, Markus began. "We have a lot to tell you, and it is not all about the sculpture."

"*Da.*" Ivar raised his brows and looked from Giselle to Markus. "I can see that it is both good and bad."

"I see this, too." Yvania poured juice into the dainty glasses and sat down. "Always start with good news."

"Okay, good news first." Markus cleared his throat. "Please swallow your drink, Ivar."

Ivar had just taken a sip of his juice, so he swallowed it and set his glass on the table. "You do not want to get the spray of *kompot* in the face, eh?"

Giselle found herself tense. What if they didn't approve of her? What if they liked her fine as a friend, but felt she wasn't good enough for him?

Markus took a breath and let it out. "I have found the woman I am going to marry."

"Congratulations!" Yvania clasped her hands to her bosom.

"That *is* good news." Ivar smiled and searched Giselle's face. "When are we meeting her?"

"It is Giselle." Markus put his arm around her.

Ivar gave her a knowing look, and then his brows knit in worry.

Giselle's breath caught. *Oh no, he doesn't approve! Well, that's just because he doesn't know the whole story. He thinks I'm cuckolding Vincenzo…or that Markus is a home wrecker.*

"What has fall on your head?" Yvania jerked upright and her arms flew about gesturing dramatically. "She *has* the beautiful husband!"

"I think I can see the bad news." Ivar looked from her to Markus and back again. "I will go get the *horilka,* and you tell us the whole story over proper Ukrainian vodka."

"What is the joke?" Yvania slapped both her own cheeks as if she might faint. "I do not understand this joke."

It took forty minutes to fill them in on what had transpired, and to Giselle's relief she saw acceptance in their expressions.

Yvania had been leaning forward on her elbows with rapt attention, hanging on every word of Markus' explanation. When he was done, she sat up and smoothed her hands over her robe coquettishly. "I am so happy for you both, but this poor Carolette! Her embarrassment has helped you so much."

Ivar looked at them with a thoughtful expression. "I could see the attraction between you from your first afternoon together, and so I am not surprised that you have come together in this way."

"It sounds like there's a 'however' you're about to add, Ivar," Giselle said quietly.

"It is late. Let us continue this talk in the morning." Ivar patted his wife's hand.

———※◉※———

Yvania was in a daze as she took their glasses over to the sink. She was struggling to process Markus' encounter with the Pope, Vincenzo being a homosexual, and Markus' plan to marry the famous and daring artist whose photo was everywhere! A million thoughts whirled in her head as Ivar appeared beside her and placed the rinsed glasses over the draining board.

Giselle stood up and said, "It's late. I should call Vincenzo to let him know we've settled in. I don't want him to worry."

Yvania didn't know why that sounded so bizarre to her. The idea of the lovers wanting to call the husband felt crazy, even though he was not…well…it took some getting used to! She turned to comment, but Ivar employed her pinching technique and she bit her lip instead.

As Markus led Giselle down the hall, he called over his shoulder, "Good night. It is good to be back with you again."

Yvania rubbed her arm as she followed Ivar down the hall to the stairs. "Our Markus finds himself mixed up with an angel, the Pope, and a Venetian devil. The world has gone sideways! But at least he has found a wife."

"Come, my dear…" He set his walker aside, took hold of the handrail and climbed the stairs. "I do not think Markus has found his wife."

"You think she is only playing with him?"

"No, I can see that she loves him, but I think chances are very good that she will continue protecting her husband, and break Markus' heart."

"I hope you are wrong."

"Come, that vodka has made us both drowsy."

Arriving at their bedroom door she lamented, "That poor Carolette!"

Ivar yawned, "I am very interested to get a look at Vincenzo's lover, Leonardo."

She gasped dramatically, "Ach! Can you imagine what *he* is looking like?"

———※◎※———

Giselle got up early the next morning, received two suitcases packed with new personal items, and put the finishing touches on her housing design. They were ready for Gabrieli's courier when he arrived to pick them up. With that accomplished, she sat down to enjoy breakfast with Markus, Yvania, and Ivar.

"What will you do if your design is chosen for Verdu Mer?" Ivar asked.

"Hmm?" She blinked. "I...what do you mean *do?*"

"Have you not given any thought to working with the project team in Venice?"

Accepting eggs from Yvania, Markus looked at Giselle. "He is right. No one knows your design or..." he searched for the word, "its *nature* but you."

Giselle pooched out her lower lip in dismissal. "Oh, well, I assumed the building experts wouldn't want *me* around. They'd accept the design and take it from there."

Ivar buttered a muffin and shook his head. "I would not think so. Each house will need slight modifications. You know making a neighborhood is not like putting uniform toy blocks together."

Markus asked, "Giselle if you are needed in Venice for Verdu Mer, would you go?"

"I'd love to, but I'm not an architect."

Ivar patted his lips with a napkin and shook his head. "You would work *with* the architect team, y*ou* are their designer."

"Perhaps not." Giselle pointed thoughtfully at the ceiling. "Papa believes it's God's design that came through me."

"What?" Yvania had started clearing dishes. Over her shoulder she asked, "Who said this?"

"She calls the Pope 'Papa.'" Markus answered.

"He's like a father to me, Yvania. May I have another muffin?"

"It is very nice to have the Pope as a father to you."

"I can't get over how good these are." Giselle accepted a muffin, pulled it apart and took a bite while examining it.

Yvania laughed, "It is crushed apples inside, makes them..."

"Moist," Ivar helped her find the word.

"They're incredible." Giselle looked between the men. "You know, to make the houses really special, they should have your windows."

Ivar nodded agreement, but Markus gave her a quizzical look. "An entire new neighborhood will require many, many, many windows."

"You can teach your craft to the Venetian artisans, can't you?"

The Czerneys and Markus shared a brief conversation in Ukrainian, and when they had reached an agreement Ivar looked pleased. "Da. We can teach them, and the windows will be beautiful."

Giselle thought of the possibilities and got excited. "Ooh! And skylights!"

"*Da*, we can make those too." Markus sounded proud.

Ivar pointed a fork directly at his wife. "If we go to Venice, you will not make any mistakes. You will keep the secret for Giselle and Markus and the boys."

Yvania nodded vigorously. "*Da*! I will button my mouth now." She motioned as if locking her lips and tossing an invisible key over her shoulder. "I know back in Chechnya when I was a girl, this homosexuality could be a death sentence. I know this."

Giselle looked to Markus and Ivar for reassurance and then nodded tentatively. "Okay, I'm open to all of us spending some time in Venice. Let's see what the building experts say after their meeting this morning."

Giselle was happy to be able to spend time in the workshop with Markus, particularly since Vincenzo had asked her to stay out of sight. When her phone rang, she saw that it was Gabrieli.

"*Alo,* Giselle?" His voice sounded upbeat.

"Gabrieli. Did you get my drawings?" She felt a sudden pang of insecurity about them.

"*Sì!* We're excited about your home design. It's very graceful. The consortium particularly admires your room layout and storage space."

"Oh, good!" She felt relief wash through her.

"But what everyone was most impressed by were your notes on window placement. How each unit can be modified to capture every ray of natural solar energy for light and heat efficiency."

"Well, I made solar panels in science class years ago, and it really made an impact on me. I won a regional science prize for them."

"Your gifts never fail to impress me. But, let me get to the point, Giselle. I think you have a God-given talent for home design. What you've created is revolutionary. Everyone is so impressed, that our reference to it as "The Divine Concept" is no longer uttered as a joke."

"*Grazie, grazie.*" She grinned and Markus came over raising his hand. She high-fived him as she listened to her father-in-law.

"It's dual natured, both very old-fashioned and very fresh and modern. The team feels that with these homes, the neighborhood will become a worldwide destination for architects and city planners wanting to see these houses firsthand. The consortium's vote on housing design is scheduled for two days from now. Our senior planner is certain your design will win, and he'd like to meet with you in preparation for the project. Will you come here to meet with us?"

"Sure, and the windows I have in mind are very special. They look modern, but it's actually a very old process. Markus and his teacher, Ivar, can bring some samples of their work and teach it to your builders. I'll bring Markus, Ivar, and his wife, Yvania. We can be there tomorrow."

Gabrieli sounded relieved. "*Ottimo!* Send Vincenzo your schedule. We'll have rooms ready for our guests. We'll all be so glad to have you home safe."

"Okay, *a presto. Ciao.*"

Giselle hung up and called Vincenzo, who insisted on acting as her assistant to schedule her meetings and travel.

Then she and Markus went to the kitchen to share the news.

Yvania made happy little gestures with her hands. "Hokay, we go to Venice!" and she bounced in place on the wooden bench. "Do we stay in the palazzo?"

"My in-laws insist. Here in Paris, Vincenzo and I have our own home. But when we're in Venice, it's family time, so we live in the palazzo."

"Does Leonardo have a room in the palazzo, too?"

"No, V and Leo have an apartment, but everyone thinks it is just Leonardo's. Leo's office is there, too, so they do a lot of long accounting sessions as far as everyone knows."

Yvania raised her eyebrows but then appeared embarrassed. "Sorry, this is none of my business, I know."

"We will keep our curiosity to ourselves," Ivar said, and then asked Markus, "Will you help get our suitcases out of the storage room?"

"*Da.*"

———◦(◦)◦———

Salvio sat in his prison and tried to piece together the events of the past several days. He barely functioned between bouts of excruciating pain, and while he wasn't sure how long he'd been there, he was trying to settle into a routine of eating and drinking to regain his strength. If his mind wasn't playing tricks on him, he'd been abducted from his home office. He'd heard that the Mafia liked to use veleno to subdue victims, and he could only surmise that Petrosino had found a way into his office and poisoned him. How had Petrosino figured out he'd double-crossed him? Surely he had no contacts in the Vatican. Perhaps he had people inside the Venice police department?

Salvio couldn't imagine a punishment more cruel than what he was experiencing. The malignant after-effects of the veleno were taking forever to wear off. He loathed the way filth clung to human bodies, so having to endure his personal temple in this disgusting state was a constant source of anger and shame. God was testing his resourcefulness, but Salvio would not disappoint Him.

A dimwitted Mafia soldier brought his food twice a day while ignoring him completely. He opened the iron door with a key that made a screeching sound in the lock, and then ordered Salvio to stand against the far wall. After Salvio complied, he'd come down the stairs, set a tray of food and a large plastic bottle of water on the floor. Then he'd pick up the previous tray and bottle and leave. He ignored Salvio's sign of blessing from across the room, and Salvio made a show of appearing crippled to lure this Sicilian grunt into a false sense of physical superiority. The idiot failed to notice that each time he entered, he was forced to take a half step farther into the room because Salvio kept placing the tray slightly farther from the door. Sicilians were all so smug, and that sin of conceit was precisely the weapon he would use against the soldier. It wouldn't take long to outsmart this idiot and be free again.

The food was disgusting—the young grunt must be getting it from a vending machine. But Salvio ate every last crumb to keep his temple strong, and while he drank almost all of the bottled water, he'd use a small amount each day to wash his body and try to launder his soiled suit. The dampness and poor nutrition were wreaking havoc on his gout, and his ankles were obscenely swollen. Around the tops of his feet, the skin was stretched tight like glossy purple stockings. When he was alone, he tried to renew his regimen of deep knee bends, and exercised as best he could to stay nimble. He knew that regaining his catlike reflexes was his ticket to freedom. But he made sure to keep his pant legs rolled up, so the servant could see this ugly infirmity and misjudge him as frail.

Salvio pretended to be unaware of his surroundings, and never asked questions, except once when he tried to impress the soldier with his pedigree. He'd heard the key screech in the lock, stopped exercising, and fell to his knees in prayer. The soldier set the food and water down, and stepped into the room to claim the previous tray. From his vantage point on the floor, Salvio saw the servant's ankle holster and gun. Salvio addressed him in a weak voice, "I'm grateful for your kindness, *signore*. I am Salvio Scortini, and I'm going to ask the Pope to remember you in his blessings."

"Sure, you do that," the servant called over his shoulder.

"*Sì*, my friend. We can call him now, do you have a phone?"

The door slammed and the lock screeched in reply. Unperturbed, Salvio got up and went back to his deep knee bends. After a rigorous exercise session, he ate the soggy *panino* and, after brushing as much salt as he could off the potato crisps, he ate those too. *Perhaps Petrosino's plan is to torture me with this velano, and then kill me via sodium poisoning?* Then he went back to work prying the grate out of the floor with the edge of his metal tray.

16

The private jet carrying Giselle, Markus, and the Czerneys landed at Venice's Marco Polo Airport and taxied to the Verona's private hanger where Vincenzo and Petro were waiting. Looking out the plane window, Yvania asked, "That is Leonardo who is there with Vincenzo?"

Giselle shook her head. "No, that's Petro, Vincenzo's bodyguard."

Ivar reached over the supple leather armrest and put his hand on his wife's shoulder. "Best you do not talk much."

"*Da.* I know nothing. What can I say but I do not for knowing. Right?" Her grammar suffered when she was excited. She pantomimed buttoning her lip again, and turned to Giselle. "Not for worrying. As a girl I was in the war in my homeland of Chechnya. I know how to protect the secret."

Giselle raised her eyebrows, and felt oddly reassured by her little friend. "I'll introduce you to everyone, don't worry."

As she stepped off the plane, Vincenzo rushed over to hug her. He murmured in her ear, "This is awkward for me. I normally scoop you up." She wrapped her arms around him and squeezed.

"Oh, V! I've missed the hell out of you!"

"Out of respect for Markus, I'll control my exuberance." He planted a chaste kiss on her cheek before turning to clap Markus on the arms. "We're glad to have you as our guests."

"It is a great opportunity for her." Markus stepped in closer. "Any word of Salvio?"

"Nothing. No one has seen or heard anything of him since he contacted the police and the Pope."

Giselle brought Ivar and Yvania forward. "Vincenzo, this is Ivar Czerney, who is a great window artist."

Vincenzo smiled in greeting, "I'm pleased to meet you, Ivar." He looked down at the walker. "I hope the travel wasn't too much. How can I be of assistance?"

Ivar shook Vincenzo's hand and then lifted the walker easily with his other hand. "Ah, do not let *this* fool you. A habit from an old operation. Now it is mostly for show," he kidded. He put the walker back down, but didn't lean on it.

"And this is Yvania." Giselle sensed Yvania's intense interest in Vincenzo—and how hard she was trying to hide her curiosity—so Giselle held her breath at what might come out of her mouth.

"*Ciao,* Count Verona." The little babushka stepped forward. "So nice you are flying us, and letting us help for Giselle's working."

"We're happy to have you, Yvania. Now, I'll take you to our home."

"*Da!*" Her face lit up. "I will begin the knocking out of your mother!" She patted her hands together lightly and nudged Giselle.

When Vincenzo glanced at Giselle for clarification, she kissed her fingertips. "Wait till Juliette tastes Yvania's cooking, it really will knock her out."

"Well then, Yvania," Vincenzo smiled down at her, "you won't find a more grateful household than ours."

Drawing herself up to her full five feet four inches, including the three inches of old-world clogs, she proudly sashayed toward Petro, who escorted them to the family's boat. A porter followed with their luggage.

Fall was settling in, and it was decidedly chilly as the group cruised to the majestic Verona palazzo. Giselle zipped her coat and raised her collar as the wind came across the water. Pulling up to the Verona's water garage, they saw Juliette, who was flanked by her staff at the door. Her mother-in-law was wrapped in a heavy shawl and waved excitedly when she saw them. As they disembarked and came up from the private pier, Juliette swept down the marble palace steps, heading straight for Giselle.

"I am so relieved to have you home." She hugged Giselle tightly. "Now I can sleep soundly, and you can realize your sacred vision at Verdu Mer."

Juliette turned to the rest of the group. "Ah, Markus, *grazie*. You have kept our girl safe, and now you bring us new friends." Giselle introduced the Czerneys and they entered the palazzo where Juliette addressed them. "Come now, we will get you settled in your rooms. You would like some time to rest after your trip, I would guess."

"I will help with the cooking." Yvania walked over and took Juliette's hand. "No need for bedroom now, please take me to your kitchen."

Juliette's face lit up. "As you wish. If we do not have the ingredients you desire, you and I can go shopping together. Have you ever been to the open air market here in Venezia?"

As they disappeared toward the kitchen, Vincenzo trailed behind with Giselle and the others.

"Gigi, you have a meeting with Verdu Mer's head of building in the morning, but today I'll take you over to the site. The demolition team has a temporary construction office where you can see the project plans. Markus, we can talk about your and Ivar's glass making on the way."

"If you can use the old-world Crimean tradition of window craft, we can teach it," Ivar said.

"We have brought some glass samples, and can show you photos of our work on the Internet," Markus added. "Your Venetian team may want to learn the artistry that he taught my father. It will give this new neighborhood a look that is both old and new."

"The consortium really liked the idea of special windows."

Giselle looked around. "Where are your father and Papa?"

"In Rome, but they'll be back for dinner. Gentlemen, let me show you where your rooms are, and then we can head to Verdu Mer."

"Is it far from here?" Ivar asked.

"No, it's an easy walk, but we'll take the boat."

Ivar nodded. "That will be good."

"Let me go change clothes and put on some different shoes." Giselle clicked off down the hall in her pumps.

When they stepped ashore at the project site, Vincenzo gave them a brief tour of the vacant slum and an overview of the reconstruction plan.

Markus commented, "There are not as many workers here as I expected."

"No, not above ground there aren't. At the moment the work is mostly underwater at the bottom of the canals." Vincenzo pointed to scuba tanks here and there on the broken paving stones as they walked past. "You'll see members of the sub-aquatic surveying team pop up and swap their tanks for fresh ones before heading back down to continue working. They want to get most of their work done before winter arrives."

When they came to the door of an old apartment, Vincenzo stepped around orange caution cones and moved a sawhorse out of the way. He selected hard hats for each of them from a shelf next to the door, Vincenzo distributed the hats and then led the way into the makeshift construction office. He cautioned them, "You can't be too careful in here." He gestured to the ceilings that were held in place by scaffolding and sagging braces. "The whole place is crumbling."

He flipped a switch on a yellow electric cord suspended just inside the door, and an overhead light came on, illuminating the bare room. "In addition to serving as our little office, this is where most of the sub-aquatic surveyors enter the canal to work." He pointed to a big hole broken out of the cement floor. The group skirted the hole and walked over to a makeshift surveyor's desk, where blue-prints for the project were tacked onto the wooden surface and surrounding walls. Together they reviewed the sketch-es and visual overviews to see the improvements planned from the canals below their feet, to the new houses, school, and cathedral to come. The dusty space was cold, and the humidity made the room feel frigid. Both Vincenzo and Markus reached out protectively every time Giselle took a step. When they'd seen all the plans, they stepped back outside, and Vincenzo locked the office door and pocketed the key.

"Now, let's go home and relax."

⸺◈⸺

Casimir and Gabrieli had just concluded their meeting with the Apostolic Camera, Vatican financial officers, and the president of the Banca d'Italia to review invoices for Verdu Mer. Funding for the resident relocation and first phase of underwater construction was going smoothly, and Casimir was pleased with their progress. The two friends left the Hall of Ligorio deep inside Vatican City, and headed for the helipad where the helicopter was waiting to shuttle them back to Venice for a relaxing evening.

"So, Casimir, Giselle has brought Markus and his friends to stay with us. Apparently she feels strongly about using Markus' window artistry for The Divine Concept house."

"Well then, I am eager to see the windows. Are these friends also Ukrainian?"

"*Sì*, I believe so."

Casimir nodded.

When they arrived at the palazzo, they learned they had just missed Vincenzo and the group. Gabrieli went to his room to change, but Casimir was diverted on his way to his suite by a glorious aroma coming from down the hall. He let his nose lead the way to the kitchen and found Juliette and a little dumpling-of-a-woman performing an energetic culinary pantomime, punctuated by superfluous bursts of Italian and Ukrainian. The women were engrossed in an earnest game of monkey-see-monkey-do, with Juliette doing her best to imitate techniques the sturdy little Ukrainian cook was demonstrating. She had just picked a steaming red pepper up by its stem when she noticed Casimir approaching. She cried out, "*Svyata korova!*" and dropped the pepper onto the tiled floor with a wet *plop*.

Casimir inhaled deeply, puffed his chest out, and his eyes drift closed. In Polish he declared, "God has certainly saved you a place in heaven, woman! I am home at your side!" He then wrapped the little cook in a warm embrace. Gently rocking her, he murmured, "My dearest lady, please let me join you in cooking, and stay by your side as long as you are here with us."

As he released the little lady, the heels of her wooden shoes clacked sturdily back onto the floor. He hurried to a drawer for an apron as a maid cleaned up the fallen pepper.

Juliette laughed and said, "Casimir, allow me to introduce Yvania Czerney. She came with her husband, Ivar, and Markus. They are our guests. Yvania, may I present Pope Leopold XIV."

Yvania stood in awed silence.

Juliette grinned at him. "Oh! Casimir, you must taste the cabbage masterpiece that is in the oven!"

He donned hot mittens and was pulling a big casserole out of the oven as Yvania admonished in Ukrainian, "Holy Father, it will be ready for tasting in one hour. Save the surprise, please."

Feeling like a stubborn little boy, he shook his head and answered in Polish. "No, sorry, I cannot wait. You have a different accent than Markus. Are you from the Caucasus Mountains?"

Taking the big pan from him, she dished him a serving of her cabbage rolls. "Ah, of course. You must be hungry. Sorry, Holy Father. Yes, I am originally from the Caucasus Mountains. You have a good ear."

The rest of the afternoon was a dream come true for the three of them, who bonded instantly over Yvania's food.

———※———

As usual, Leonardo arrived at the palazzo in time to join the conversation in the lounge before dinner. He greeted the Pope first, "*Santo Padre,*" and bowed with quiet reverence. As always, he savored the feeling of grace emanating from the Pope. Gabrieli came over to make introductions.

"Leonardo, we have the good fortune to welcome Ivar Czerney and his wife, Yvania, as our guests. Ivar is responsible for some of the most remarkable windows in Eastern Europe, and the sublime aromas from the kitchen are Yvania's generous gifts."

Leonardo nodded to the older couple and smiled as Gabrieli introduced him. "Leonardo is part of our family, like a second son to us. He's not only Vincenzo's best friend, but his accountant—like a business partner."

"I'm happy to meet you," Leonardo greeted the Czerneys.

He noticed that when Yvania opened her mouth, Ivar deftly pulled her into a sideways hug as if to silence her. Ivar covered the maneuver by saying, "We are happy to meet you as well, Leonardo."

Yvania looked ready to burst. "I am happy also!" She seemed pleased with herself as she retreated over to where a deadly handsome man with honey colored skin and a shorn head was leaning on a credenza. She whispered something up to him.

Gabrieli continued, "And Leonardo, this is Markus Shevchenko. He's the artist who was working with Giselle on her *Star Fall* sculpture. He's a world-class window artisan as well."

Leonardo squared his shoulders and planted his feet in front of Giselle's lover. "*Buonasera*, Markus."

Markus straightened up and extended his hand. "It is good to meet you."

When Gabrieli moved off to get them drinks, Leonardo moved in to give Markus' shoulder a squeeze. Under his breath he said, "What I've heard is true—you're handsome, I'll give you that. But if you hurt her, I'm not sure what I'm capable of."

"I respect that." Markus nodded and whispered back, "I see she has two brothers."

"He is good man, I promise." Yvania pushed close to join in the whispering. "And you are so handsome, too!"

Disarmed by the little woman, Leonardo laughed and let her reach up to pinch his cheeks.

Giselle came to him and took his arm, leading him over to the window for some privacy. "I promise you, you don't have to worry about me. It's V who needs your attention."

He agreed, "*Sì*, he's convinced himself that he's used you cruelly. He's really torn up over it."

"Oh, that's such rubbish."

"So, you're staying here at the family palazzo. Not much chance of you getting alone time with Markus."

"I know. I figured that out on my arrival when Nigella helped me change clothes. She's so excited to have me back, she keeps following me every time I leave a room."

"Give your maid a break, she's trying to anticipate anything you need. She's finally got her mistress back under the roof."

"Leo, I'm surprised how quickly I got used to being sexual. I don't know how you and V kept from losing your minds for so long."

"We were both born patient. And when patience wore thin, we got creative." He gave her a devilish grin and a little punch on the arm.

They walked back to the rest of the group and joined the conversation about the highly anticipated dinner menu.

Salvio was doing his best to preserve the condition of his clothes. God would free him from this prison any time now, and he didn't want his suit to attract unwanted attention during his escape. He couldn't tell if it was day or night outside, but that didn't bother him. Now that his bouts of veleno-induced agony had subsided, his schedule of cleaning his clothes and his body, plus eating and exercise, kept him busy. He felt calm and purposeful. When God was ready to free him, he'd rely on his instincts, which he knew wouldn't fail him.

Once he'd pried the iron grate loose from its fastenings, his inspection of the fissure below hadn't taken long. He'd been prepared to lower himself into the blackness to investigate it as an escape route, but after throwing some food down, he could tell by the sounds that they were only falling about thirty feet before becoming wedged in the rock. It was likely he was being held near Petrosino's main Mafia operations, so he was probably in Sicily. And if he was very near where that dog operated, he was probably in Palermo.

He was thinking about escape options, when the screeching lock interrupted his reverie. He dropped the grate back into place and threw himself to the floor, quickly yanking up his pant cuffs to put his bulging ankles on display. When the jailor entered, he would illustrate how painful it was to sit up. But when Petrosino stepped through the door, Salvio's instincts told him to stay down. *Ah! So it isn't that stupid servant. I need to be careful, here.*

Petrosino leaned against the wall looking at him, and someone Salvio didn't recognize stood guard in the hallway. The young man had a pitiless expression and features that resembled Petrosino's. *So this is his son.* Salvio's anger flared. Was he the only man on earth without a son? Why was God testing him to such extremes? Petrosino's son was holding a gun pointed straight at him. Salvio put on an expression of stupid confusion and let his eyelids slide to half-mast.

"Oh, come now," Petrosino coughed out a laugh. "You can drop the helpless moth-on-a-pin act. I know what kind of cunning maniac you are, Scortini. And the truth is, I admire the first trait in a business partner. But the second one makes you useless to me."

Salvio squinted and kept looking dumb, hoping this profane criminal would divulge some information—specifically where his plan had gone wrong. And how had he gotten into Salvio's office?

Petrosino ran his tongue across his upper lip, and he relaxed against the wall a bit more. "I'd have come sooner, but...I'm gonna be blunt here...I think you're a piece of shit...and I don't like being around shit."

Salvio's pulse roared in his head and he felt his eyes bulge. No one had ever spoken to him like this. Unable to simply lie down and take it, he rolled onto his side, transitioned to his feet, and began pacing the far side of the cell. But he stayed silent, and the gun stayed trained on his head as he moved.

The Mafioso went on. "Seeing as how with our handshake we're partners, I want to make absolutely sure that you see where I'm coming from...where *you* are concerned."

Instead of being tricked into lashing out and getting shot for his trouble, Salvio didn't respond. He clenched his lower belly and his sphincter, and had to press the root of his tongue into the back of his throat to get a hold of himself from the inside.

"Back when your father died, I came up to Venice to pay my respects, and to inquire whether you were open-minded about a partnership. You refused to show me the basic courtesy of meeting with me. Your father and your grandfather had been respectful to me and to my family over the years. True, they were never interested in working with us, but they were gentlemen and treated us as such. So when you suddenly entered into a partnership with me, I made some inquiries in the building fraternities of Venice. And, well, they can't stand you either. Without exception, the consensus in the Venetian building community is that you are obnoxious, sanctimonious, a poor businessman, and a patent thief who has anger issues. Now, after your boorish demands, attempt to manipulate me, and engineer a possible life-sentence for my son, I have to say that I agree with the Venetian building brotherhoods."

Despite the fact that this scumbag criminal was trying to inflame him, Salvio had the strangest sense that he was finally hearing a truthful account of opinions he'd suspected since he was a child. This sensation was immediately followed by the certainty that he would make everyone in the Venetian building community pay for their ill-formed opinions of him. But then again, how could he expect anything else from the jealous mewing of common workers?

Gio straightened up and brushed off his jacket sleeves. "So, I don't know when I'll pay you another visit." He turned to leave, and tipped his head toward the grate in the floor. "But feel free to attempt spelunking your way to freedom." And then with the clank of the door and screech of the lock, the Mafia dog and his gun-toting son were gone.

17

The morning Raphielli became the legal owner of her building, she went to the Brotherhood of Ironworkers headquarters to meet Signor Tosca, who had invited her for a visit. She settled into a chair in front of his desk, and liked the look of him immediately. He reminded her of the nice priest who'd been her Catechism instructor when she was little.

"Signora Scortini, I haven't seen you since your wedding."

"Please call me Raphielli," she smiled.

"*Grazie.* And I'd like you to call me Genero."

"Genero it is, then."

"My dear Raphielli, I believe the Brotherhood owes you a secret debt of gratitude, one that we can never repay."

"Well, I know I can't apologize for another person, but I am so sorry for what... well...for what..."

"*Sì*, you cannot apologize for him, but you reversed his efforts effectively enough. We have our patents back where they belong." He returned her smile and continued. "I understand that you are a property owner now, and have plans to turn your new building into a shelter for women."

"You know a lot."

"Don't let that surprise you, Raphielli. There's nothing to do with real estate in Venice that we don't know. I've asked you here to offer our services to make your building not only a thing of beauty, but also a secure place for women."

"I'd hoped that was why you asked me here." She was relieved and excited. "How much will it cost? What do you need from me? When can the work begin?"

"We don't need a thing from you. Your master contractor is already on board, and every one of our members is making your job their top priority. We'll move heaven and earth to get you up and running before you know it."

"I have the keys here in my purse." She fished inside her little crocheted bag.

He chuckled. "We don't need keys, my dear." He glanced down at his watch. "Your front and back doors have already been removed to make way for the necessary interior demolition, and the old plumbing is being removed as we speak."

"That's incredible!"

"We take our debt seriously and don't even try to pay us, we won't accept any money from you. It's our honor to take care of everything including your permits, and we're offering generous gifts to your neighbors to calm them during the mess."

"*Grazie.*" Then she couldn't help but ask, "Genero, since you know what happens in Venice, may I ask why the

Brotherhood allowed Salvio to go on bragging about Verdu Mer when he didn't have a thing to do with the project?"

"Ah, that's a very perceptive question, Raphielli. Well, while we know everything there is to know about building in Venice, we have only a general understanding of the relationship between the House of Scortini and the Pope."

"*Sì*, Salvio's father, Salvatore, had been very close to the Pope."

"God rest his soul." He crossed himself. "And Salvio's grandfather, Savadore, was an intimate of the Pope as well. We have benefitted from the House of Scortini's relationship with the Vatican, and it was a puzzle to us how Salvio was included, if at all."

"So you couldn't discount that Salvio may have been given a special role in Verdu Mer..."

"We didn't want to alienate him in case he ended up with some authority in the project."

"I know I shouldn't be, but I'm embarrassed for him."

"Oh my lord, don't be." He waved his hand in alarm.

Then he looked her over, and from his expression, she could tell he was censuring himself, and his change in demeanor tempted her to fidget.

"Is there something else?" she asked.

"Well, if you'll forgive me, may I say something that is well-intentioned?"

"Um, of course." She smoothed her scarf with nervous fingers.

"May I recommend that you go shopping and buy some new clothes?" His eyes moved to her bag. "And a proper purse."

"Oh, all right." Her face was suddenly hot with embarrassment.

"There's certainly nothing wrong with what you're wearing, but you're a business woman now, and should wear clothes that communicate that."

"I hadn't thought about that."

"If you just go see Evelyn," he was jotting information down on a slip of stationary, "at Coin Excelsior department store...she's in the women's department and will help you pick out some business apparel. She selects all of my wife's clothing."

"That would be great." She took the paper, but couldn't imagine actually going to find this Evelyn.

"Would you like to come with me and see what we're doing at your building now? You can meet your contractor."

"Oh, *sì!*" She followed him out of his office and into the chilly morning sunshine.

＝＝◉＝＝

Autumn advanced and Venice grew chillier by the day as the little orange building first disappeared behind scaffolding and then reappeared. From the first day at the new building, it was apparent the workers enjoyed working for Raphielli. They repaid her secret patronage by working around the clock with the utmost efficiency, swiftly remodeling the old palazzo into a modern women's shelter. Plumbing was replaced in record speed, and within a week a good-sized portion of the shelter was habitable for employees, women, and children.

Mayor Buonocore introduced Raphielli to Kate, the local Women's Health Bureau Chief, who enjoyed a reputation of equal parts dedicated public servant and brilliant politician. Kate was extremely capable, and used to being deluged with the need for public assistance on a shoestring budget. So having a major patroness appear in the form of the rich and beloved Scortini family, Kate struck while the iron was hot—or the philanthropic endowment was hot, as it were. The busy Bureau Chief cleared her schedule to assist Raphielli with staffing and appointments for a board of physicians, and worked alongside the mayor to fast track the necessary government approvals for the shelter.

Raphielli, the mayor, and Kate all agreed that the need for this live-in resource was so urgent, they would begin staffing and housing women and their children in batches as sections of the building became ready. Women in the most critical situations were able to move in and get assistance as the paint on the first section was drying.

Raphielli named her shelter *Porto delle Donne*—Women's Safe Harbor—and worked alongside Kate fourteen to eighteen hours every day. They had no problem ignoring the noise and dust of ongoing construction, and Kate quit her bureau position to accept Raphielli's generous offer to head the shelter. They had taken in their first residents, some of whom brought children with them, and their first resident staffers had moved in as well. Raphielli often had to be pushed out the door after working all night. She'd go home for a few hours, and after freshening up, return to the energetic haven that the women's shelter had become.

Raphielli had never been so tired in her life, nor so deeply fulfilled. Now that she was a regular dinner guest of the mayor and his wife, and spending Saturdays with Juliette, her life felt full. It was as if she'd discovered family she'd never known, and she thought of the Vitalis as brothers whom she worried about. They sent flowers congratulating her on her endeavor with a card signed, "Your admirers." She was also playing word games with them on her phone.

⟢ ⬦ ⟣

Giselle and her Ukrainian contingent had been busy during their stay with the Veronas. Giselle's house design had been approved, and every day she'd been called upon to generate new modifications to her plan for every contingency the construction team threw at her. The designers fell in love with the windows that Markus and Ivar showed them, and approved the two as master teachers to train the Venetian craftsman to make skylights and windows for the new homes.

Most mornings Gabrieli, Giselle, Markus, and Ivar left the Verona household as one big happy group for their work at Verdu Mer before heading off to separate locations. Most mornings Gabrieli met with Chizzoli's team for an update on their underwater foundation work, and then met the demolition manager for his progress report. Markus and Ivar would open a workshop on the edge of the construction site and hold classes for the glass craftsman. Giselle usually photographed the specific locale of her requested design modification, and then began work on a new blueprint. She looked like the chicest architect in the construction zone, with her Keen Atlanta work shoes and her Nike action clothing.

Yvania and Juliette went into cooking overdrive, and started to co-write a cookbook. The family declined all outside invitations so they could eat exquisite home-style feasts together every night. Even the Pope spent time in the kitchen with his two cooking instructors, who never struck his hand; not only because he was arguably the most powerful man in the world, but he was also an exemplary student.

———— ◈ ————

Giselle sat with the family around the grand dining room table absently picking at the edge of her biscotti with a fingernail. It had been too long since she'd had a chance to be intimate with Markus or begin a new sculpture, and she was feeling out of sorts. Everyone else at the table was enjoying their breakfasts and chatting about plans for their day, when she glanced up to see Vincenzo looking at her. He raised his brows in an old secret signal. She lowered her brows in response. Markus eyed the two of them and gave her a questioning look, which she pretended not to notice.

Vincenzo rose from the table. "Well, I'm off to close the venture for the co-op building."

"Oh good, dear." Juliette nodded. "How soon will that property be ready to start holding classes?"

Vincenzo went over to kiss his mother's cheek. "I'll let you know as soon as I find out." He looked at Giselle. "Darling, come walk me to the door."

She rose and went to his side, and they walked away arm in arm. She whispered, "What's up?"

He threw his arm around her and whispered flirtatiously next to her ear, "Well, Leonardo and I know it must be killing you and Markus not to be able to be...you know...*together* here in at home."

Giselle rolled her eyes and whispered, "Ugh! This palace has more bodies scurrying around than a performance of Swan Lake. And then there's Papa under the same roof. We just don't dare."

"You haven't found any way to get together?"

"It's not like we can just check into a hotel for a few hours. I'd be recognized. We started something we almost couldn't stop the other evening in the library. Your mother would have walked in on us if Yvania hadn't caught her right outside the door and herded her off to the kitchen while we got a hold of ourselves."

"You can't take chances like that." He stopped walking and his expression went from stern to lusty. "Ah! Look at the sexpot! Little Gigi wants it!"

Giselle dug her nails into her husband's jacket. "Oh, I do, V! I really, *really* do!"

The Pope walked serenely past. "Ah, true love. It is a thing of beauty."

"Good morning, Papa," they greeted him in unison.

As the Pope disappeared into the dining room, Vincenzo handed her a key. "Leo and I understand what you're going through, so we're offering you the guest room in our apartment for a little fun this afternoon."

"Oh, V!" she squealed. "Wait till I tell Markus!"

Salvio's body felt pain free and he was ready to make his move. God had visited him in a dream, and his vision was clear; the time had come to escape his cistern prison. Upon waking, he felt perfectly ready to be of use to the Almighty. He dressed quickly, went over and pulled up the iron grate from the floor, set it against the far wall, and then climbed down onto a scant ledge about five feet below the opening of the drain. He sat down to wait, his feet dangling over the sharp rocks that jutted from the sides of the fissure. When he heard the screeching of the lock, he hopped lightly onto the balls of his feet and crouched, pressing his back against the jagged stone.

He heard the servant open the door and mutter, "Ah, so you pulled the drain cover up, eh?"

Impatient footsteps descended the iron stairs. "Yuck. Listen you cripple, I'm not pulling you out of that sewer if you're stuck. You'll have to wait until I'm done with my rounds and I can get someone else down here to help."

The second Salvio saw the servant's face appear upside-down above him, peering into the hole, Salvio popped up, grabbed a handful of the man's hair and his collar, and yanked him down with all of his strength, hurling him headfirst deep into the yawning darkness of the crevasse. Salvio watched the servant drop more than twenty feet straight down. His head and upper body crashed into the narrowing shaft between sharp rocks, cracking his skull and breaking his neck. He was left suspended upside down, limp and silent. Salvio jumped out of the hole like a jack-in-the-box, trotted up the steps and out the door, pulling it closed behind him. Now was the time to move without hesitation! *The Veronas are about to pay the wages of their sins!*

He didn't encounter anyone as he climbed two nondescript flights of stairs. Listening carefully and moving silently, he found his way to a door and stepped into the shadowy street. Dawn was just breaking in the east, so he judged it to be about five in the morning. Salvio watched a plane climbing into the sky, and ran downhill in the direction of the airport. About a block along his jog, he spotted a truck driver closing his tailgate, and ran over to him.

Salvio gasped, "Please! Help me get to the airport. Family emergency!"

"I'm heading that way. Get in."

When Salvio arrived at the sleepy airport, he skirted the main terminal building and speed-walked back toward the cargo area. Spotting a young worker taking a cigarette break, Salvio sized him up as the criminal type who could be of use. "I need to get on a private plane to Venice, no questions asked. I'll make it worth your while."

The smoker looked him up and down. "Are you drunk?"

"No, I'm very rich, and in a very big hurry."

"Follow me." The runway worker pushed away from the wall, glanced around, and then strolled off in the direction of some private hangars.

Fighting to control his impatience, Salvio pushed him from behind. "Move faster! This is a matter of life and death!"

The worker tossed his cigarette and started to run with Salvio on his heels until they burst through the door of a hanger that looked like a warehouse of bocce memorabilia, except for the beautiful Cessna that took up half the space.

"Hey, Bocce Bill, this guy needs a ride."

A skinny, bald man of about fifty, dressed in khaki slacks and a bocce shirt, looked up from his computer screen. "Uh-huh. Run along, Moochie."

Moochie closed the door behind him, and Salvio charged up to the bald man.

"Listen Bocce Bill, I'm very rich, and I urgently need to be in Venice. If you can take me in your plane, I'll use your computer to transfer a substantial sum of money into any account you wish. I also want you to give me all the cash you have on hand."

Bill leaned back in his chair. "Well, I'm about to fly to Venice, and I can always use a substantial sum of money. Got any ID?"

Salvio didn't have time to haggle so he made a shooing motion with his hand, and took hold of Bill's mouse.

"No, I don't have ID. But I have one million euros that I'm about to transfer to you." After a minute of brisk keystrokes, he was signed into his bank account. He noted that there was approximately four million euros missing, and then initiated the transfer of a million euros. "You just need to enter an account number here." He pushed the mouse back at Bill, who reached into his desk drawer and retrieved a bankcard.

"I like a simple man with a million euros to spend and places to go." Bill entered his account number before relinquishing the mouse to Salvio, who completed the transfer.

"How much cash do you have on hand, Bill?"

"Grab that bocce bag over there. It's my traveling money. There's just short of a hundred thousand euros inside."

"Get me to Venice in ninety minutes, starting now." He reached inside the bag, pushed a rose gold Rolex aside, pulled out two hundred euros, and slapped them on Bill's desk. "This is for Moochie."

Bill scraped the money into his desk drawer. "I'll get it to him. Okay, my flight plan has a scheduled departure thirty minutes from now, but let's get started. I can make a donation to a friend in the tower to let me take off early."

Eleven minutes later, the plane was in the air and headed for Venice. Bill was a criminal who knew when not to ask questions, and Salvio was a man with a mission, a bocce bag full of euros, and a Rolex that was probably stolen. He clutched his colorful sports bag in front of him with both hands like an old lady protecting her purse.

"Bill! How fast can this plane go?" He shouted through the open cockpit door.

"It's got an engine comparable to the Citation X. It can do over a thousand kilometers per hour."

"Good! Pour on the speed!" Salvio kicked the boxes stacked next to him in frustration.

"Not a chance. But we'll go as fast as we can without attracting attention from the authorities."

"Take the chance!"

"You didn't think I was flying bocce balls did you? Now shut up and don't kick my heroin."

Gio was roused from sleep by the phone. In his line of business, sleep was the only luxury he often did without. "What?"

"Your guest is not in the cistern." It was the voice of his consigliere, Paolo Bianchi. "Roberto didn't show up for his five o'clock route stop, and they called me."

Gio looked at his watch. It was 5:20 a.m. "What time does Roberto deliver the breakfast?"

"Usually at four forty-five."

"Get my driver here now. Wake up Primo. Wake the pilot. We have to beat Scortini to Venice." Gio hung up while pulling on pants, then called a contact in Venice.

"Orologio, this is Petrosino. I need you to save an innocent woman's life."

The clockmaker he'd awakened snapped to attention. "*Sì!*"

"Deliver this message inside a box of tea to Raphielli Scortini at the Scortini palazzo: *He has escaped.*"

"*Capisco.* Immediately."

"When you deliver the box, ask if she's home. If she is, demand to see her, and try to take her to your shop. Keep her safe until I get to Venice."

"Okay, I'm doing it now."

Gio slammed out his front door, yanked open the back door of his car, and directed his driver, "Get over to Primo's and then get us to the jet." He got Paolo back on the phone and gave orders for everyone they knew in Sicily to be on the lookout for Salvio, but in his heart he knew that maniac would race straight back to Venice—his seat of power. Then he called Drea.

"Did I wake you?"

"Gio? Everything okay?"

"*Sì.* I need you to meet me at Marco Polo airport in two hours."

"I'll be waiting."

<hr />

Bocce Bill taxied his plane over to the cargo buildings at Marco Polo airport and brought it to a stop. Salvio was off the plane in a flash, jogging along with his bag of cash, and dodging the occasional morning worker. When he reached the docks on the lagoon, he waved to the driver of the first boat he saw.

"Hey! I have an emergency! Get me to the Verona office building!" He pulled out a fat packet of euros and waved it as if he was going to throw the whole bankroll at the man. That did the trick; the guy throttled his engine and came over to where Salvio was coming down the gangplank.

Salvio arrived at the Verona's building just in time to see the buggering son exit the main office door flanked by his smug-looking bodyguard. He trailed them as they made their way along a *fondamenta* and then disappeared into an old co-op building. Salvio sidled toward the doorway they'd entered, and then peeked around the area to get a feel for what was going on. It was deserted, and seemed to be just another one of the Verona's projects, probably a building they were going to rehab. There was a thick wooden door standing ajar that the faggot and his bodyguard had disappeared through, and it was a reasonable assumption that they'd come back through it to leave the building. The walkway was strewn with piles of construction junk. Salvio paused next to a small opening, looked over the side, and saw a ladder down to the canal and a little pier. Leaning over, he saw a banged up old motorboat tied below, empty except for some filthy tarps piled in the back.

Salvio went back over to the pile of trash and selected a heavy pipe from the heap. He hefted it in his hand; it felt good and solid. Returning to the entrance, he hid behind the open door and waited. Within moments he heard two sets of footfalls approaching. Just as the steps got to the other side of the door, he stepped out and swung as hard as he could. The bodyguard's head took the full blow of the whickering arc, spraying an impressive blast of blood onto the wall. The man's body fell backward behind the door. Vincenzo turned as if he was going to try to protect his guard, and then seeing Salvio he tried to dodge to the side. He moved fast, but not fast enough to miss Salvio's pipe coming in a backhand swing at the side of his head. Vincenzo went down like a bag of laundry. As Salvio tossed the pipe aside, he felt revulsion; sodomites were such easy prey.

He bent down, dragged Vincenzo to the canal opening, and shoved him over the edge into the boat below. The body landed on its left arm with a loud snap. Salvio scrambled down the ladder into the boat and hauled the tarps over the sissy boy. A colony of wormy bugs scattered to find their way back into the dark, and into Verona's expensive suit. Salvio climbed over to the motor, and after a few stabs at the electric starter, the engine wheezed into life. The universal law of never touching another man's boat in Venice didn't apply to him. This was God's will. He sat down and steered the boat along the canal toward his home. There was a groan from under the tarp. Salvio kicked out at the disgusting buggerer, and hissed, "After I am done with your father, you'll have time to confess all of your deviant sins to me, you obscene faggot. Then I'll take them to the Pope! But first, I have some business to attend to with that cow I married." There was no response, only the burping and coughing of the engine as they glided through the dawn.

Arriving home, Salvio cut the engine and piloted the boat past Il ponte Diamanti, into the ghostly Emerald Cove. It was completely sheltered and the perfect place to store his prisoner until he was ready to return for their interview. Sailing into the moss-green darkness, there was nothing but the sloshing of the canal water and a deep trickling sound from somewhere within the labyrinth of old tunnels.

Salvio climbed out of the little boat, abandoning the body, and made his way along the ancient stone footpath under Il ponte Diamanti. He felt incredible as he moved through the secret passage into his house.

Vincenzo lay under filthy tarps in the algae-encrusted cove. He didn't hear the irregular waves lapping against the sides of the little boat, nor the metallic sounds the hull made as those waves repeatedly bumped it into the stone walkway. The blood that had been seeping from his head began to clot and bleed back into his skull.

———⫸•⊙•⫷———

During the flight, Gio kept in touch with his team. He learned that Roberto had been thrown down the cistern drain, and that Orologio had been told that Raphielli wasn't home when he delivered the message, so Gio set his hopes on getting to the Scortini palazzo before she did.

His Gulfstream touched down after an eighty-five-minute flight, and rolled top speed to the edge of the runway. The jet's stairs extended, and Gio bolted down them so fast he barely touched the steps, with Primo close behind him. Racing toward the Drea's boat, they jumped in and grabbed hold as she swung around in an illegal maneuver, spraying a wall of water across the lane of early traffic. The drivers and their passengers yelled invectives and waved their fists at being soaked to the skin. Pulling himself up next to Drea as they roared forward, Gio shouted over the big engine, "Il ponte Diamanti. *Now!*" He swore under his breath and hoped he'd arrive in time to save Raphielli. Gio had no doubts whatsoever that the lunatic was headed straight home to his seat of power.

———⫸•⊙•⫷———

Raphielli stepped out the front door of Portò delle Donne. Beyond exhaustion, she put a hand out to steady herself as she pulled the cheerful yellow door closed behind her.

Their new security guard watched her from inside the locked watchman's cage in the entry alcove. He offered a sad smile and shook his head.

"Another all night shift? You'll make yourself old before you're twenty-one."

"Too late. I feel like I'm old already." She patted the cage and stifled a yawn. "I'll be back soon, Alexi."

She wasn't the only person who had worked all night. Kate had worked straight through on legislative paperwork they would be filing this morning, while Raphielli helped their nurse log in and lock away all of the medicine that had been delivered late yesterday. Then she'd checked in the supplies and put them away in the storeroom before sitting down to review the new residents' case files. Kate didn't seem to need sleep the way Raphielli did, and powered through hour after hour on ginger tea and Mentos. Sometime in the early morning, Raphielli lay down on the office couch and fell asleep for an hour. Now she needed to make herself presentable for their meeting at city hall.

Pushing herself to shake off the remnants of her nap, she headed home for a hot shower and fresh clothes. Plodding over the bridges and along the canals to her house, she made gentle circles with her shoulders and tentatively rolled her neck as her cramped muscles protested. She was going to have to get a bigger couch for the office she shared with Kate. She would have slept in one of the beds, but every last one of them was already in use by women in need. All of the new cribs were occupied too, which made her heart flame with compassion and pride.

Stepping through her front door, Raphielli's eyes fell on a box of tea sitting on the old-fashioned receiving table. There was only a beat of confusion, and then Gio's words came back to her. She snatched up the box and raced for her bedroom as her fingers fumbled with the lid. She plucked the note out with hands shaking so badly she left tea scattered in a trail behind her running feet. *What? No specifics? Just "He has escaped"?* She skidded into her bedroom, raced to the window, and threw open the sash. She leaned out a bit to get some cell reception. Trying to steady her shaking hands so she wouldn't drop the phone out the window, she called the Little Church.

A voice answered, "*Buongiorno*, how can I help?"

"Find Cardinal Negrali immediately. Tell him Salvio has escaped!"

She ended the call, but couldn't remember the detective's name and number, so she dialed 112 Emergency. After three rings a flat voice came on the line, "*Uno uno due*, what is your emergency?"

"Please! A killer is loose in Venice!" Then his name came to her. "Tell Detective Luigi Lampani that this is Raphielli Scortini, and Salvio has returned!"

Ending the call, Raphielli was a trembling wreck as her fingers kept accidentally scrolling past Alphonso's contact. She couldn't recall how Zelph had taught her to send a text, and she started to cry. *This plan is no good! I'm going to get someone killed! Stupid! Stupid! What a fool I was not to have a better plan!*

Finally dialing Alphonso, she eyed the water below as his voice message picked up. Hopping foot to foot in frustration, she waited for the beep and then blurted, "It's me—!"

That was all she got out before she was hit from behind and her ribs were crushed painfully into the windowsill. The phone tumbled to the water below, the air rushed from her lungs, and she felt something tighten around her neck.

"Getting an early start to your day?" Salvio's voice was eerily solicitous in her ear.

She was dragged backward to a corner of the room. She couldn't see him, but he seemed to have climbed onto the cedar chest and was hauling her backward by whatever was around her neck. She reached up and clawed at his hands, but he thrashed her side to side until she fell against the wooden chest painfully. As the rope was pulling tighter, he said in a helpful tone, "You should climb up if you don't want your spine to come apart, you cow."

Raphielli blindly grabbed at the cord above her head as she felt herself being lifted off her feet. She swung away from the big chest and hung onto the cord with her right hand for dear life. She reached out her other hand as he swung her toward a small, delicate table. *He's not strong enough to lift me like this. He must have thrown the cord over the wrought iron chandelier and is hanging me with his own body weight!* Exhausted, she pulled herself up, supporting herself on the table until her feet were teetering on it. The noose pulled her even higher until she pirouetted on the toes of her left foot. She got hold of the cord overhead with both hands now and tried to lift herself a bit to draw in more air.

She heard Salvio hop down to the floor and walk around in front of her. She couldn't look down to see him;

her head was thrown up and back, and the noose was so tight.

"That's not a very sturdy little table you've chosen to hold you, but then I don't suppose you could have reached the dresser with your stubby legs. I have to leave you now to take care of some business, but I'll come back. And if God chooses to spare you a hanging death, you're going to tell me what you've been doing since I've been away. It seems that I've been robbed. Maybe you can shed some light on that crime for me."

She heard only a few footsteps before she was alone. Her impromptu gallows were unbelievably solid. It held her dangling while her toes cramped in their sockets and her shoulders and forearms burned. She couldn't draw in more than a sip of air at a time, and her lungs were screaming to be filled. She tried to clear her mind and not think of what it would be like to lose her balance, tip from this table, and choke to death swinging in her late mother-in-law's bedroom. Then Rosa screamed and Raphielli lost her balance, kicking over the little table.

———◈———

Gio and Primo were at the front door of the Scortini palazzo pushing their way past the butler when a piercing scream echoed down the empty hallway and then it became a shrieking wail. Gio raced toward the sound and burst into Raphielli's bedroom where he found an old woman trying to support her mistress, who was kicking and spinning at the end of a noose.

"She was standing on the table!" the maid screamed. "She was about to hang herself!"

"She's alive!" Gio rushed forward.

He got under Raphielli and supported her on his shoulder as Primo jumped onto a cedar chest, whipped out a knife, and slashed at the cord, releasing the semi-conscious girl. Gio lowered her to the floor. Primo's fingers gently unwound the cord from her throat while Gio grabbed hold of the maid. "Where is Salvio?"

"He isn't home." She looked confused. "He's been away for weeks now."

The don looked down at the sweet girl lying on the floor, and felt his rage building. She looked like a raven-haired doll that had been badly misused by a disturbed child. Unable to leave her on the floor, he knelt down, gathered her in his arms, and lifted her onto her bed. Primo covered her with a blanket as she dragged in deep hiccupping breaths only to let out ragged coughs.

Starting toward the bedroom door Gio barked to the maid, "Lock yourself in here with her. Don't open the door for anyone but the police, *or me*. And keep an eye on that secret passageway!" Gio pointed to the curtain.

"I don't know you!" She glanced suspiciously at the curtain and turned to argue. "I won't let you back in here!"

Gio yelled over his shoulder, "Her husband did this to her! Just don't let *him* back in!" He ran out the door with Primo at his heels, and together they stormed into Salvio's office. It was empty, but the bocce bag sitting on top of the desk told Gio precisely how Salvio had gotten to Venice so quickly.

Primo spotted it too. "Fuck me! Scortini hitched a ride on the heroin express!"

"Hey!" A little servant came skidding into the office. "You don't belong here!"

"We're here to save Raphielli!" Gio shouted. "Have you seen Scortini?"

"No, he's away on a religious pilgrimage." The man tried to set his quivering jaw. "I can take a message for you. Then you need to leave, you can't be here without an invitation."

Gio ignored the valet. "Primo, if no one saw him, he used his secret passage. Let's go." He pushed the tapestry aside and they hurried down the dark path, pushed out the door, and found themselves under Il ponte Diamanti. Arriving at the water's edge, he looked around uncertainly. He heard the strange, repeated sounds of hollow metal banging into stone echoing from off to the left.

Following the sound, Gio and Primo made their way along a footpath and through a short tunnel that went back under the property, and came out past another bridge inside a moss-covered cove. A little boat was being bounced into the stone jetty by a series of wakes coming down the canal. As Gio approached the boat, he saw expensive shoes peeking out from under the edge of a tarp. He jumped down into the boat and lifted the covering. There lay the body of a well-dressed young man, face down. Carefully turning him over, Gio recognized Vincenzo Verona. His injuries were obvious; there was damage to the left side of his head, and his left arm was at an odd angle. But he was still alive.

"Primo, get out of this tunnel and call 112! Get an ambulance here now. It's Vincenzo!"

"Okay. I'll make sure they don't see me. But, where do you think Scortini went?"

"He's gotten Vincenzo and Raphielli. Now I bet he's going after the count." Gio took off running to get his monster back.

———◦◉◦———

Salvio was jogging across a quiet piazza, he felt robust and righteous. He didn't know where Gabrieli Verona was, but he knew how to find out. He made a beeline for a youngster on a cell phone and grabbed it from him.

"I need to make an emergency call. I'll pay you." He realized he'd forgotten the bocce bag in his house, but from the looks of it, this boy didn't need any money. He hung up on whoever was on the call, and then stared the kid down as he dialed directory assistance. "Connect me to Verona Enterprises."

The wimpy kid grumbled loudly and walked over to his friends who were standing nearby, and they all started to make angry taunts and gestures.

When a Verona operator answered, he barked, "Connect me to Gabrieli's office." He waited a beat, and when the assistant answered Salvio yelled, "Where is Gabrieli? He's late!"

"*Mi scusi?*" Startled, the cool voice quickly recovered. "Who am I speaking to?"

"This is Salvio Scortini! I will not stand for incompetence! He's supposed to be a man of his word!"

"I'm sorry Signor Scortini, I didn't see you on the meeting agenda, but they are all at Verdu Mer."

"I know where he's *supposed* to be! We *are* at Verdu Mer, but he's not here, and we find his unprofessional behavior shocking!"

"Not there? Did you go to the temporary construction office at number six eighty-seven for the—"

Elated, Salvio threw the phone at the youngster, who deftly caught it and flipped him the finger. Salvio took off running at top speed, feeling younger than he had in years. Vitality coursed through his muscles, and he felt loose and happy. He was going to avenge the House of Scortini. Gabrieli was going to be so surprised! Somewhere Salvio registered that he should be tired, but he was bursting with adrenaline as he ran up to the construction gate. He tipped an invisible hat to the guard in the security shack as he raced past.

"I'm late, I know. Number six eighty-seven."

The guard tossed a construction hat to Salvio, who caught it and clamped it on his head. He slowed to a trot as he headed down a deserted *calle*. The old access walks to the crumbling houses in this *sestiere* were tiny. Everything was deserted and boarded up, but ahead on the right he could see sawhorses and orange cones around some expensive-looking equipment. He clutched the hat to his head, and picked up his pace again.

He skidded to a stop outside the door to a makeshift office and peeked into the little space. There was no meeting inside this dim hovel, just some more saw horses, a couple of worktables, and a tin lamp hanging from an extension cord. He inched inside, feeling disappointment begin to curdle his stomach. Then he heard an old man's voice in the dark.

"Giselle, Gabrieli wanted to go over these notes when they return from the canal survey."

A smile began on Salvio's face and then unfurled until it felt like it extended all the way to his ears. He tingled with excitement at the name, and then bent down to pick up a length of rusted rebar. As he moved into the dark room he called, "Giselle Verona?"

"*Sì?*" a distracted voice answered.

She was in the far corner of the room, standing next to a table that was nothing more than a big board propped on top of a couple of wooden crates. *So considerate of her to have her hard hat lying on the table beside her—so much easier to smash her evil, sluttish head in! And that old man leaning on the walker will get to watch!*

Directly in front of the corner where the blonde whore and the geezer were now trapped was a big, irregular hole in the broken cement floor. Salvio would have to get her to come to him, or he'd have to get around the hole to her. It made no difference, he could manage it either way.

The old man startled when he saw Salvio. "You look sick, friend."

"*I am not the one who is sick!* It's that piece of *degenerate rot* you're standing next to who is *sick!*"

The slut grabbed hold of the old man.

Salvio snarled, "Keep your filthy hands to yourself, *whore!*"

The old man raised his walker, extending it in front of them in a feeble show of protection.

"Careful you don't drop your crutches," Salvio taunted. "So, are you putting your dick into her putrid place too? Is that it, old man?"

"Giselle, do not worry, he is not going to kill me," the man said, keeping his eyes on Salvio. "Go get security. *Now!*"

The force of the old man's command surprised Salvio, and Giselle obeyed as if slapped. Salvio paused at the edge of the hole, unable to believe his eyes. In a blink, she'd jumped onto the makeshift table and climbed up the broken wall. She seemed to be some sort of a rock-climbing acrobat.

"Oh, but I *will* kill you, old man, after you watch me ram this rod up her and ream out the ungodliness inside her. You'll watch me nail her to the floor for her whoring sins!"

He extended the walker a bit farther over the water. "Giselle, go! Now!"

—————— ◦(◦)◦ ——————

Giselle neatly lifted a panel of corrugated tin out of the ceiling and pulled herself up through it. She'd just crouched on the roof when she heard a gibbering laugh of insanity from below.

"The diseased sow thinks she can escape the hand of the Almighty?"

Next she heard a hollow crack followed by a splash. Giselle dropped to her knees and poked her head back down into the office. There was Yvania, standing proudly on a crate and putting her clogs back on. The little fireplug looked up at Giselle and waved.

"Never have your back to a Chechen in a fight!" she grinned. "You can come back down now."

Ivar shuffled carefully around the hole toward his wife. "Ah, my girl! You can never take the rebel out of the Chechen!"

Yvania hugged her husband. "This crazy who would murder Giselle is Salvio?"

Giselle called down, "Did you knock him into the canal?"

The Czerneys nodded. "*Da*, but we do not see him now."

18

V*incenzo sat at the low table, the sounds of his classmates nearby, the scent of tempura paints and crayons heavy in his nostrils. Leo was tracing a sun in orange with his brush as Vincenzo added the finishing touches to the blue water on their shared painting, bare knees pressed against one another's under the table.*

Vincenzo ran with all his speed, Leo stride-for-stride by his side, catapulting himself off the cliff, and they both flew, for just moments, before plummeting down and into the sea below. Head bobbing to the surface, gasping for breath, he looked for and found Leonardo, just a few feet away, laughing in the water, eyes shining. His body felt impossibly strong and alive.

Twelve years old, Vincenzo lay in Leonardo's bed in his child-hood home, buried under the warm covers. Inseparable, whispering secrets, their noses touching. Sharing dreams, making plans, holding each other.

Fourteen years old, sculling across the water, seated behind Leonardo, watching the muscles of his back and shoulders work, flexing and stretching. He felt that mixture of calm and excitement spread through his limbs like it always did when he was with Leo. They slid their oars into the water in unison, pulling as a team. Not just when rowing, they were always stronger together.

In the shower, hot water pounding, breathing in the heavy steam, soap lathering and sliding over their skin, Vincenzo looked into his best friend's eyes and saw his own hunger and readiness reflected back at him. Slowly and tentatively leaning in until his lips reached Leo's, they fell into each other, kissing with a passion that fed on itself until the hunger was too much. He was enraptured at the things Leonardo was doing to his mouth, and he grasped his best friend to him, plastering their wet bodies together. The last barriers fell away, and he experienced for the first time complete union with another human being.

Seventeen years old, walking into that hospital room, Leo lying in the bed looking so pale and frightened, drains snaking from down in his groin, drips of antibiotic disappearing into the tube in his arm, orange antiseptic stains across his stomach and down both legs, Vincenzo's heart seized in his chest and then galloped. Sitting by the bed, holding Leo's hand, not daring to cover him with comforting kisses as he yearned to. He cried when Leo told him, "Impaled on some metal rebar under the water at Verdu Mer, in agony and certain I was going to die, I called for you. Only you. I only wanted you."

Each day, bringing a bright red balloon, a private token of his love easily dismissed as a boy's cheerful gift to his friend. One red balloon every day, until the room was so full of red balloons the nurses began threatening to pop them if he didn't stop. But the boys just held hands and whispered to one another when no one else was around. And Vincenzo kept bringing red balloons.

Visiting Leo at his family home during his long and painful recovery. The red balloons had been banished, but he came every day and always brought something red, if even just a slip of paper. Talking together quietly, worried and wondering what this horrible injury would mean to their passionate physical love for one another. The day they discovered he was as good as new, they recklessly achieved a record number of orgasms by the next morning. Lying in bed together, they laughed at the improbable chance this injury had given them. Everyone assumed Leo would be impotent for life, the perfect cover for their secret relationship. They had always been so lucky. It was as though their union was blessed.

There had never been anyone for Vincenzo but Leonardo, and they loved one another completely. He loved to do little things to make Leo smile. He was warmed by everything Leo did to make their secret apartment a sacred place of sharing. When they had a day alone together, sculling or playing football, having long discussions about books they'd read, cooking, and listening to music—it made life complete. Leonardo was all the goods things in life: laughter, kindness, nurturing, encouragement, strength, excitement, and the strong morals that made him good through and through. Vincenzo wanted to stay enfolded in Leonardo's scent, wrapped in his strong arms, listening to his laugh, forever.

But right now he needed to rest, because this headache was so very bad...

Gio made his way out from under the labyrinthine bridges, jogged up the steps to the *calle*, and turned the corner in front of Scortini Palazzo, almost knocking over a cardinal dressed in formal vestments who was rushing toward the palazzo steps. It had to be Raphielli's cardinal; she must have called him before Salvio hung her. Gio called out, "Excellence Negrali?"

"*Sì?*" Negrali skidded to a halt, nearly losing his balance. "Who are you?"

Gio clasped the cardinal's shoulder. "I'm a friend of Raphielli's. Salvio returned to Venice and attacked her."

Negrali took a harsh intake of breath, and made the sign of the cross.

"She's alive, but that poor neck of hers has really paid the price."

"*Santo Madre!*"

"But, she fared better than Vincenzo Verona."

"What? *What?*" The cardinal became frantic.

"He's under the far side of the palazzo in a little boat." Gio turned and pointed to the path under the private bridges. "Scortini smashed his head in. I've called an ambulance. You should go give him his last rites."

"Oh, no!" Tears began coursing down Negrali's face, and he choked back sobs.

"*Aspetta!*" Gio grabbed Negrali by his vestments to prevent him from racing off. "I've got to stop Scortini. Where is Gabrieli? Do you know?"

Getting himself under control, the cardinal choked, "Every morning now he is with his team at Verdu Mer." Negrali pointed. "It is just past the market *calle*." Openly crying now, he turned away from Gio. "I must go to Vincenzo now." And he rushed off in the direction of the decrepit green cove.

Gio ran in the direction the cardinal had pointed, and when he arrived at the construction site he stopped at the guard shack.

"Has a strange man wearing a dirty suit just come through—someone you didn't recognize?"

"*Sì*, five minutes ago. A man in a rumpled suit. He was late for the meeting."

"I have to stop that man." Gio grabbed a hard hat off a shelf next to the guard. "Where's the meeting?"

"First lane on the left, and then all the way down, where the orange cones are. Can't miss it."

"Where is Count Verona?"

"Not here. He left with Chizzoli."

Gio ran off, trying to get his rage in check but also chomping at the bit to get medieval on Scortini, the twisted little fucker. When he arrived at the door beyond the cones and sawhorses, he pressed against the outside wall, un-holstered his gun, and peered inside. It was quiet and Scortini wasn't there. Just an old man and woman talking to a blonde head that was hanging upside down from the broken ceiling. Holding his gun down by his leg, Gio stepped inside and asked, "Where's Salvio?"

The three people tensed and asked in unison, "Who are you?"

The old man said, "Stay there at the door. Do not come closer."

"My name is Gio, and I've come to stop Salvio Scortini. It's very important. I believe he's here to kill Count Verona." The old woman pointed to a hole in the floor, as the most beautiful woman he'd ever seen swung elegantly from the ceiling, climbed down the broken wall, skirted the hole in the floor and shimmied under a sawhorse to stand next to him. The goddess joined him in peering down through the hole into the canal.

"Yvania cracked his head with her clog." She gestured to the stout little woman.

Yvania shrugged and held up a finger as if counting. "First, I say to you that Salvio was trying to kill her! Second, I say he is too stupid to be a good killer. Who is not looking around everywhere and just walks into a room?"

The old man nodded. "She was behind Salvio the whole time."

Gio's eyes swept the dark surface of the water below, looking for a sign of Scortini in the canal. "He's my responsibility, so I'll find him and take him away for good."

The old man sucked his teeth and then made a "good riddance" motion with his hands. "It is okay if drowning is his end. Okay with me."

Gio stood up and offered his hand to the stunner standing next to him. "I'm Giancarlo Petrosino. At your service."

"Giselle Verona."

Gio reflexively grabbed both of her hands and pulled her over to the door. "Giselle, get over to the hospital. Your husband was just attacked by Salvio. Vincenzo has a head injury and should be on his way there right now."

Without a word of response, Giselle was out the door like a shot and sprinted out of sight.

The old man hurried to the door yelling, "Markus! Markus! We have to go tell Gabrieli!" Yvania rushed after him.

Standing alone in the little office space, Gio whipped out his phone and called Primo. "Did the ambulance come?"

"Yeah, they're taking Vincenzo to the hospital."

"Where's the cardinal?"

"He went inside the palazzo to check on Raphielli. Did you find Scortini?"

"He got knocked into the canal in the Verdu Mer construction area. Get over here right away. Come down past the market *calle* and avoid the guard shack. Slip in without being seen."

"On my way."

"Stake out the tidal outlets and pull him out of the water, dead or alive."

"Got it." He heard Primo mutter, "Hope the fucker's dead."

"I'm calling Drea to come get me. I need to get in to see Raphielli."

When Drea dropped him off in front of the Scortini palazzo, he avoided the butler and anyone else who might be milling about inside by ducking unseen under Il ponte Diamanti. Following the secret entrance again, he silently bypassed the police team under Il ponte di Smeraldi. Feeling his way, he found Raphielli's room, and lifting the heavy velvet drape he called out, "Raphielli? It's Gio. I've come to say goodbye."

The maid jumped. "Don't you come near her!"

Gio ignored her and came forward. "Where's the cardinal?"

"He went to the hospital." She glared at him.

Raphielli made a tiny dismissive move with her hand

toward her maid, who reluctantly left the room. Gio was glad to see Raphielli resting in bed. Her neck was wrapped with cold compresses. He went over to her side and was relieved to see her smile up at him.

"Ah, a smile." He smiled too. "Good." He choked up with emotion and swallowed hard. "Raphielli, I can't tell you how sorry I am that he escaped. I came the *instant* I heard, and...well...I underestimated his resourcefulness and his speed."

With eyes wide, she mouthed, "*E'incredibile*, I know," as if trying to communicate just how well she knew her husband's speed and viciousness.

"Don't try to move your neck or shoulders for a while. I'm impressed you were able to hold onto that cord."

A hint of pride showed in her expression.

"Primo is looking for him now." Gio rubbed her hand. "We'll get him, and I'll never, ever let him escape again."

He could see her relief.

"I assume Cardinal Negrali told you about Vincenzo." She squeezed her eyes shut.

Gio bent over her. "If you go to the hospital you'll have the police crawling all over the palazzo and asking stupid questions. You and I both know this was Salvio and how he got in here. So I'm sending the best doctor I know to come take care of you. He'll have you singing in no time. I promise."

She made a face at the mention of singing, and waved her finger back and forth in a singsong motion. He kissed her forehead, and for a moment he was tempted to kiss her lovely lips.

"The police are working the crime scene where Vincenzo

was found, but it'll take them a while to figure out that it's actually part of your house. It doesn't even look like it's connected to the palazzo."

She blinked her eyes.

"Stay out of it. Nothing good can come of you talking to the police about this, and you don't need the stress."

Looking exhausted she blinked again.

He headed to the door of her bedroom and then turned back. "None of my business, but this should *not* be your bedroom. Find a sunny room in this big old palace, and have it decorated to suit your taste. I can't stand to think of you sleeping in this dismal old room."

Raphielli mouthed, "*Grazie.*"

"And it has the smell of old lady."

She made a face and waved him off with a flick of her fingertips.

Gio made his way back to Drea, and she found an ingenious route back to Verdu Mer. She deftly cruised the patchwork of canals until they caught sight of Primo down a deserted inlet, where Gio joined him in the search for Salvio. In almost no time they spotted him dragging himself hand-over-hand along the waterway. Gio motioned for Drea to bring the boat closer, and Primo reached into his jacket pocket for a syringe. Together they dropped flat onto the ground and pulled Scortini from the water by grabbing hold of his hair, shirt and jacket. Salvio's reflexes seemed a bit off, and he hissed and flailed ineffectively until he saw the syringe. Then he erupted in an all-out, blood-curdling scream, and went berserk trying to scratch and bite. Primo slammed the needle in deep, injecting the veleno. Salvio shivered and went limp as they hauled him up the algae-clotted embankment and rolled him onto the pavement. The screams would bring police, so they went into high gear. Drea pulled the boat over, they dumped Salvio onto the deck, and she threw a canvas over him as Gio and Primo hopped onboard. Construction workers were gathering along the lanes trying to identify where the screams had come from, as Drea expertly piloted them from the scene in a casual manner.

"Let's get this animal back in his cage." Gio turned his back on the inert monster and looked toward the open water as they headed out into the lagoon.

Giselle looked expectantly at Vincenzo over the top of the card and felt her patience fizzle. "I know you know this one V, and if you would stop letting yourself be distracted, we could get through this deck."

"Well, give me a moment." Vincenzo gave her a quizzical look and tried to readjust himself on the enormous sofa they were sharing. "It looks like either a Rorschach inkblot test, or you've inverted an outline of Switzerland."

She sneaked a quick glance at the front of the card and then turned it right side up. "Correct. It's Switzerland." She flipped up another brain teaser card and stared at him. "Come on now, the sooner we get through these cards the faster we can get to your French and Latin review."

Leonardo came over to help, and while avoiding Vincenzo's cast, he scooped his lover under the arms and gently lifted him into a sitting position. Leo was looking at Giselle like he wanted to help *her* as he busily plumped pillows and then stuffed them under the small of Vincenzo's back.

She uncrossed and then re-crossed her Cerruti boots on the back of the sofa and narrowed her eyes at him. "I feel as if you're about to make a speech."

Leo held up his hands and sighed. "Not a speech, Gigi, but you're pushing too hard. It's not just you. We were *all* affected by the attack on V, but he's healing just fine. His brain is *fine*."

"Pushing too hard? The doctor said that doing brain teasers and language review would be beneficial. *Beneficial*. I'm *helping*."

"I know you too well to buy any of your rationalizations. You're coping, but you're stressed to the max, girl."

"We could finish this work if you weren't distracting him."

Vincenzo spoke up. "You're the one who's distracted, Gigi."

She gathered up the cards and handed them to him, then swung her legs down and got off the couch. Pacing back and forth in front of them, she ran her fingers through her hair gathering it into a ponytail, and then began winding it around and around until she'd made a knot on the top of her head.

"Arrgh! When you're right, you're right...and I know you're right!"

Vincenzo sighed. "You couldn't be with two people who understand more how you feel."

"Of course *you guys* understand—*you're* the ones who're responsible for making me feel this way."

Leonardo glanced around. "Where's Markus? Haven't you two found any way to be together?"

She stomped to a halt and did her best to show her incredulity. "Hmmm, let's see... Any time Markus and I are here in the palazzo we're in the vicinity of any number of servants, my in-laws, Ivar or Yvania—although they told Markus and me they're ready to find some ruse to put the two of us into a closet together so that our moods improve. I don't think I have to mention what it's like to have the Pope and his security team here. Then of course there's Nigella who's about the most attentive lady's maid on record. Every time I turn around, I nearly trip over her."

She turned at the sound of approaching footsteps for fear it was her maid, but it was Markus carrying a platter of sandwiches.

"Juliette and Yvania have sent their latest creation for our opinions." He set the snacks down and started to move toward her, but paused and moved over to a chair instead. He looked between the three of them and asked, "What is happening in here?"

Leonardo retrieved one of the little bites, took it over to Vincenzo, and before taking a bite of one himself, he answered, "We were just commiserating with Giselle about your current lack of privacy."

"Right. About that." Markus stared from Vincenzo to Leonardo. "What are we going to do now?"

"What do you mean?" Leonardo narrowed his eyes at Markus. Giselle could tell he knew exactly what Markus meant.

"Do you not agree with me that now would be a good time for you and Vincenzo to tell his parents about your relationship?"

"No." Leonardo's jaw tightened.

"Why not?" Markus asked. "It is the perfect time. They are so relieved he is not dead, they will accept his sexuality."

"I can't believe I'm hearing this." Leonardo rubbed his face with his hands, and Giselle could see he was flushing an angry red.

Markus pushed, "Do not try to put me off with your temper. When are you two planning to set Giselle free?"

"This isn't anything that can be rushed. We will, when we can figure out how to handle the ripple effect of the disclosure."

Giselle felt hopeless. "Oh, God! Just tell us what your plan is, guys. That's fair isn't it?"

Vincenzo shook his head at her. "Well, we're just going to need a bit more time. Can't you reel in your hormones? You never showed a trace of sexual interest in your entire life until you found Markus, and now all of a sudden you're a wanton woman?"

"I've tried!" She tried to keep her voice down. "But when I see him my whole body reacts. And it's not just that. I love him. We want to start our life together."

Markus grumbled, "I am ready to rip a wall down out of frustration."

Leo focused on her and offered her a plate. "Gigi, can't you lose yourself in your art?"

She shook her head at the plate of offered food and went to stand in front of the huge fireplace with its crackling fire.

She ran her fingers through her hair, bringing it cascading down from the makeshift bun.

"Actually, no. You know I'm flattered to be designing the houses for Verdu Mer, but making all these adjustments to blueprints isn't art, and it isn't what I'd call *fulfilling*."

Around a mouthful of food Vincenzo said, "But your housing design is an artistic legacy that will live on for generations. People will be living in the spaces you're creating."

Markus interrupted, "You are changing the subject. We are not discussing art. I am staying on the subject of making Giselle my wife."

"Just a minute here, we're not going to be bullied into—" Leonardo was getting angrier.

"Your strategy of jumping in to protect Vincenzo and going on the offensive by calling me a bully is not going to work. The woman I love has just asked her friend to do her the courtesy of telling her what he is planning, and he owes her that."

Just then Juliette swept into the library along with Yvania. "What do you think? Honest opinions now." Oblivious to the argument she had just interrupted, she plucked a napkin off the tray as she passed and draped it across Vincenzo's chest. "I must say this is possibly one of the most successful experiments Yvania and I have had in weeks!"

Giselle saw Yvania's perceptive eyes scanning between her and Markus, and her lips became a thin line as she regarded Vincenzo, who seemed to wither momentarily beneath her displeased gaze.

Leonardo, who looked relieved to have the women's unintentional interference, stuffed the canapé into his mouth, nodded enthusiastically, and gave them a thumbs up.

"This is unbelievable! Is this fried shrimp?" Vincenzo said. "May I have another?"

Yvania selected another canapé and brought it to him. "We found at the Rialto Market today the most beautiful shrimp, and we make a special batter to cling to them *just so!*"

Juliette added, "It is like a *fritti,* but with corn flour, and Yvania made a sauce of mustard and cream and…"

"Cardamom! And we put on leetle slices of my bread I make from back home."

Giselle took a bite of the miniscule open-faced sandwich, and of course it was heavenly. When she'd swallowed she asked, "What are the vegetables under the shrimp?"

"The thinnest slices of beetroot and fennel that we gave the quick poach in a bath of lemon and garlic." Yvania gave a little pantomime with her hands to illustrate her description.

"So?" Juliette looked around the room. "How is the brain stimulation proceeding?"

Vincenzo gave his mother a winning smile. "*Bene, bene.* But Giselle was just telling us that her work on the Verdu Mer project isn't as fulfilling as her art."

Juliette turned to stare at Giselle. "But the homes you are designing *are* works of art, my dear." The concern in her voice was evident. "They are a beautiful vision from God."

Giselle gave V a quick peeved glance to let him know she wouldn't forget him throwing her under the bus. "It's complicated. I need my art to have an element of danger, I need to be thrilled. It's my way of expressing..." Her voice faltered when she saw the look on Juliette's face.

"My dear, we cannot all have everything we desire, and your time to create dangerous art must come to an end. You should settle down and get pregnant."

Yvania's eyes narrowed and she gave Leonardo and Vincenzo a quick look of reproach. Giselle watched their guilt-filled eyes drift away. Poor Juliette, she was the only one in the room who didn't know the score. No one wanted to break her devoted heart, but her perfect Catholic son was going to have to come out of the closet.

Dear Reader,

I hope you enjoyed this book—the first in my Venice trilogy. I'd love it if you could post a review about it on Amazon. Getting reviews helps other people to consider reading stories by indie authors like me. If you're not used to leaving reviews, it can be as simple as mentioning what character was your favorite or what parts you liked best.

If you would like to be on the mailing list for the next book in the Venice Trilogy, please sign up for notification at AnnaBendewald.com. I promise never to sell your information, share it, or spam you.

Sincerely,
Anna

I would like to thank the following for their inspiration:

Venice, Italy
Paris, France
Palermo, Sicily
Zalishchyky, Ukraine
Gernelle, France
Aiglemont, France
Musée Maillol
Nyakio Beauty Products
Père Lachaise Cemetery
Passero's Coffee
Caapiranga Brazil
Africa Outreach Project
Izod
Gucci
Riva Iseo
Cessna
Queen
George Harrison and the Beatles
Armani
Cacharel
Au Printemps
Versace
Google
Spanx
Armani
Bruno Magli
Osteria Da Fiore
École des Beaux-Arts

Le Louvre's Pavillon de Flore
Exagon Furtive-eGT
Jeep
Bobcat
Jaguar
Università Ca' Foscari
la Biblioteca Nazionale Marciana
Abbaye d'Orval
Cerruti
La Meurice
Too Faced Bunny Balm
Nike
Keen Atlanta
Renault
Prada
Dustin Hoffman
Bill Murray
Jessica Lange
Debbie "Blondie" Harry
France Gall
Fiat
Lexus
Range Rover

Anna Erikssön Bendewald is the author of Meet Me At Père Lachaise, Stealing Venice, and Storming Venice.

She is married to Mason, and they live in Los Angeles and New York with their daughters Jem and Julia.

Anna is a bookworm, a foodie, and a passionate champion for animal issues.

Made in the USA
Middletown, DE
18 July 2019